In the Shadowlands, strangers wear familiar faces, myths are reality, and lies hide behind the most beautiful stories.

FIRST LIGHT

Lachlan Murray disappeared without a trace. As his girlfriend, twenty-nine-year-old Carys Morgan refuses to accept the police's explanation —that he simply left her. She travels to Scotland to seek help from Lachlan's twin brother Duncan, and learns she was right—Lachlan didn't leave *her*, he left her world to return to his own.

The Shadowlands are a mirror of the world Carys knows. Every human in her world also exists in this one with one key difference— *magic.*

Humans aren't supposed to be able to wield the magic of the Shadowlands, but when Carys learns she can talk to dragons, she's drawn deeper into a complicated world that would as soon kill her as keep her. And if magic and murder weren't enough to overcome, she must navigate complicated feelings for two identical men from vastly different worlds.

USA Today Bestselling Author Elizabeth Hunter weaves an enchanting adventure, full of mythology and romance, in the first installment of a brand new romantic portal fantasy!

PRAISE FOR FIRST LIGHT

Magic, mythology and dragons oh my! I have read so many books that have some the elements that *First Light* has, but never have I read them so uniquely and beautifully combined into one brilliant story.

— THIS LITERARY LIFE

This book took my breath away, made me laugh and cry, it was wonderful! An epic adventure with so many fairy tale characters come to life. The story is magical and takes you right in.

— LINNETTE P., GOODREADS REVIEWER

The story had me from the first pages. I am desperate for the second book! World building and epic storytelling is a talent for this author. I LOVED this book!

— NICOLE R., GOODREADS REVIEWER

Cleverly woven storylines with descriptions so vivid you can hear the strange noises in the fairy murder forest. All wrapped up in my favorite way for her to end a book. An epic battle and the promise of more of the story to come.

— SHELLY K., GOODREADS REVIEWER

Once I picked this book up I never wanted it to end, and when it did end my jaw may have dropped and had me searching for the date of the second in the series. Add *First Light* to your list of reads and then ask yourself this... Do you believe in fairy tales?

— JAIME, GOODREADS REVIEWER

FIRST LIGHT

SHADOWLANDS BOOK 1

ELIZABETH HUNTER

FIRST LIGHT

SHADOWLANDS
BOOK ONE

ELIZABETH HUNTER

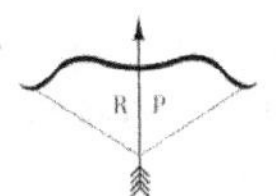

Fɪʀsᴛ Lɪɢʜᴛ
Copyright © 2023 by Elizabeth Hunter
All rights reserved.
ISBN: 978-1-959590-49-1

Content editor: Amy Cissell
Line editor: Anne Victory
Proofreader: Linda, Victory Editing
Cover: Damonza.com
Interior illustrations: ArtCreationsDesign
Printed Edge Design: Painted Wings Publishing

For everyone who ever dreamed of dragons

PROLOGUE

She dreamed of flying when she slept. The cold wind cut through the leather armor that shielded her body, creeping down her neck like icy water over rocks. She soared over mountains draped in fog where the dark tips of pine trees jabbed the shadowed sky.

There was no moon. No stars. The only light that touched her face came from the glow of fire coming from the belly of the beast that carried her.

She dreamed of flying, cradled in a smooth, curved claw that wrapped around her body and held her in its grip.

Nêrys.

When she closed her eyes, she heard the thundering voice in her mind and the fire burned her eyelids like a fever dream.

It *was* a fever dream.

"Take this." A potion touched her lips. "Take it. It will heal…"

The words died away in a rush of pain that twisted her belly and speared into her chest, wrapping iron fingers around her heart as it raced, raced, raced to escape the thread of fire.

She heard it thundering in her ears.
His voice.
Her heart.
She felt the cold licking down her throat.
Then everything went silent, and her heartbeat stopped.

CHAPTER ONE

Carys Morgan felt like she was going to shave off the left side of her car. "This was such a bad idea."

"Going to Scotland to look for your missing boyfriend?" Kiersten asked over the speakerphone. "Or deciding to drive?"

"The driving part!" A dark hedgerow seemed to rise up in front of her. Carys jammed on the brakes, and the car came to a stop.

A thin man emerged from the hedgerow, cocked his head at her, and pulled his cap down lower over his face. Then he loped across the field, stepping over a low stone wall that bordered a green pasture before he disappeared into a copse of leafless hawthorn trees dotted with bright red berries.

She blinked and the thin man was gone.

What was she doing? She slowly guided her car back into the lane. This was the worst idea in her twenty-nine years of life on this planet. This was such a bad idea.

And she couldn't stop now.

"I don't think we should be talking to her while she's trying to navigate the wrong side of the road." Her best friend Laura was also on the call. "Mostly I'm feeling guilty that neither of us went with you."

"Don't be ridiculous." The road after the curve widened, and Carys's heartbeat slowed to a nonfatal rate. "Both of you have lives and jobs and aren't insane. I am a mentally unbalanced mythology professor whose boyfriend disappeared."

"You're not mentally unbalanced. And you've been a lot better in the past few months."

Ever since she'd met Lachlan, which was why she had to figure out what the hell was going on. She'd taken a leave of absence from work when her depression dragged her down, but she was slowly crawling back from it. And then...

And then.

"I'm doing the right thing, right?"

"Yes." Both her friends spoke at once.

"We know Lachlan," Laura said. "Something very weird is going on. He would not just leave you without a word. He didn't call. Didn't text."

"He didn't even take his car," Kiersten added. "Something is obviously wrong."

"Right." Carys nodded. *Right.* She knew that.

Even though the police in her small town on the Northern California coast seemed to think she was a jilted girlfriend with too much time on her hands, she knew something horrible had happened to her boyfriend, and she wasn't going to ignore it.

"Did you ever get Lachlan's brother on the phone?" Kiersten asked. "Maybe if he saw a UK number, he'd pick up."

"She still has her American phone," Laura said.

"Oh right."

"His brother is avoiding my calls," Carys said. "I got through one time, asked for Lachlan, and the man hung up on me. I called back and no answer."

No matter how many times she told the Baywood police that something strange had happened to Lachlan, they said there was nothing to investigate. Some of her boyfriend's clothes were missing, and she and Lachlan had only been together for four months. That was proof enough for the police that her boyfriend had taken off and just hadn't bothered breaking up with Carys before he left.

"He might be as worried as you are," Kiersten said.

"I don't think they're very close," Carys said. "But I mean... Yeah. He'd have to be worried, right?"

She swerved and nearly hit a tractor that was coming up the road. "These roads are insanely narrow."

Along with his car, Lachlan had left his passport, his guitar, his papers from the lawyer who was trying to get him a visa extension. He'd left an unfinished book on the bedside table and a massive hole in her life.

Carys was going to find out what happened.

Even if it did look like she was the unhinged ex-girlfriend.

"Murray Smithworks is on this road." Carys looked for numbers when she passed houses on the country lane, but nothing seemed to be marked. "How are you supposed to find anything in this country?"

"Lachlan's brother is a blacksmith? I didn't know they had those anymore."

"It's some kind of family business that Lachlan used to work at. I have a feeling that's part of why he left home."

I'm a disgustingly wealthy prince who's run away from home for a bit to enjoy being unemployed. It was what he told her the first time they met.

He had struck up a conversation about George MacDonald fairy tales at Redwood Pages while she was shopping. He was charming and handsome, and she fell for all of it. There were hints of family money, but he didn't mention it more than the joke about being a prince. He was smart and curious and kind.

He was almost too good to be true except that he wasn't. Lachlan had become Carys's lifeline during her recovery from depression. He was bright and caring, and he loved her friends.

"Lachlan is a musician," Laura said. "Not a blacksmith. They should respect that."

"They should respect numbering houses," Carys muttered.

"What do you see?" Kiersten asked.

Carys kept her speed low and looked around the grey-and-green Scottish landscape. "Trees with no leaves. Green hills. And cows."

"Fuzzy cows?"

"Oh my God, Kiersten, enough with the fuzzy cows."

"They're so adorable though."

"Wait." Carys spotted a crooked red sign in the distance. "I see something that has Murray on it. I think."

She pulled closer and saw that it wasn't Murray Smithworks but Murray Garden Center. "Maybe it belongs to a cousin or something. It's a garden center, but the name is the same. I think I'm on the right track."

"Okay, do you want to keep us on the call with you?"

"I think I'm okay now."

"Remember," Laura said, "you're not insane. You know Lachlan, and something happened to him. He would not have left without talking to you."

The road curved again, a sinuous *S* that rose over a hill, then dropped down into a picturesque valley blanketed by bare trees and green hills. On the slope of the hill in the distance, Carys could just make out something that looked like a stone circle.

It was a real-life version of one of her mother's fantasy watercolors, and Carys wished more than anything that she was visiting Scotland for the first time with Lachlan. They could take their time, explore his childhood haunts, and she could see in person some of the mythology she'd spent her life studying in books.

And Lachlan could do the driving.

A car horn dragged her attention from the stone circle in the distance and back to the road where a small delivery truck—a lorry— was pulling out into the lane and right into Carys's way.

She swerved to the left and raised a hand in apology, but as soon as she passed the truck, she realized where the truck was coming from.

Murray Smithworks.

The sign was in faded paint on a large stone barn behind the wall where the truck had come from.

Carys found a place to turn around, then slowly drove back to the business that the Murray family owned. She turned left into the yard surrounded by a carved grey stone, then directed her small rental car toward a low building that appeared to be an office.

She parked and took a deep breath before sending a quick text to Laura and Kiersten.

Found it. Wish me luck.

Good luck.

Don't let him brush you off.

Carys opened her car door and stepped out into the cool Scottish morning. The sky was overcast, but it didn't look like it was going to rain, and the temperature was a chilly forty degrees, fairly close to what Baywood had been when she left home.

Experiencing the weather in Lachlan's childhood home made Carys realize why he'd taken the weather on the North Coast in stride. It wasn't as foggy as Baywood, but the climate was remarkably similar.

She walked to an old wooden door with peeling paint and a small plaque that read OFFICE. She knocked, then cracked the door open. "Hello?"

"Just a moment, dear!" a friendly voice called from the back. "Just a wee moment."

A "wee moment" later, a round woman with curly hair and a rosy face walked from the hall at the back of the office. "These boys." She sighed. "Can't fill out a sales order to save their life." She settled at a large desk with a computer and two different phones. "How can I help you, dear? If you're looking for the garden store, it's just down the lane and all the metalworks are there. We don't sell any directly here at the smithworks; this area is for restoration projects, construction, and the like."

Carys raised a hand. "Oh, I'm not here for garden... things. I'm looking for Duncan Murray."

The woman cocked her head. "American? And you're looking for Duncan, are you?"

"Yes, Duncan Murray. He's the owner here, right?"

"He surely is, but he doesn't receive guests at work most days." She smiled and rose, and then her smile fell. "You're not a reporter or anything like that, are you?"

"No." She found herself reluctant to volunteer information. "Just a friend of a friend."

"Of course, dear." The woman's smile returned. "And your name?"

Oh shit. She supposed she had to give the woman something. "Carys."

"Lovely name." The woman beamed. "I'll see if I can find the man."

Moments after the woman walked back into what Carys assumed was the workshop, a burly man came storming down the hallway. He froze for a moment, staring at Carys, and his mouth dropped open.

So did hers. "Lachlan?"

He wasn't Lachlan. She knew he wasn't, but this man was her boyfriend's mirror image. He was rougher around the edges, his hair was shorter, and he had a beard you couldn't grow in less than a month. His hair was the same reddish brown as Lachlan's and his eyes were just as green, but his shoulders were thick with muscle and his arms were massive.

Duncan Murray wasn't only Lachlan's brother—he was his identical twin.

"You." The man's voice was low and rough. "How—"

"I'm Carys Morgan." She boldly stuck out her hand. "I'm Lachlan's girlfriend from California, and I need you to tell me where the hell your brother is."

CHAPTER TWO

His blank expression quickly turned to a glare. "Out."

Nice to meet you too, Duncan Asshole Murray.

Carys glared at him. "Excuse me?"

"Not excused." He pointed to the door again. "Out."

"Not until you tell me what happened to—"

"Outside," the man practically bellowed. He stalked toward Carys, herding her toward the door. "Out. Now."

The sweet office manager followed Duncan, clearly distressed. "Duncan, I didn't mean to—"

"Fiona, you're fine. Carys, I will talk to you. *Outside.*"

He held the door until Carys walked through it. She left the warmth of the cozy office and strode toward her car.

She had to fight the urge to hug him. He looked like Lachlan. Sounded like Lachlan. The only problem was that he was glaring at her like she'd just kicked his dog.

She fought the tears that welled in her eyes. "I'm sorry for just showing up like this, but you wouldn't return my calls. Lachlan's phone went dead and—"

"For good reason."

She gaped at him. "What?"

"You've no right to come here." Duncan crossed massive arms over his chest. "Especially not to my place of business." His scathing eyes looked her up and down, from the top of her head to her sturdy walking shoes. "You are... not right for him, and that was obvious to everyone but Lachlan."

Carys blinked. "Wh-what?"

Was this a joke? Was she misunderstanding his measuring look?

Sure, Lachlan and his brother both looked like advertisements for Scottish tourism, but did he have to be so rude?

Carys was an assistant professor. She owned her own home. And while she wasn't a supermodel, she was perfectly nice-looking. She had long brown hair that couldn't decide if it wanted to be curly or wavy. But she *liked* her hair. She had her father's blue eyes and, sadly, his nose too, but she wasn't an ogre or a piece of trash.

Duncan lifted his chin. "Lachlan left you. It's a shit situation, but relationships end every day."

How could he be so cold? She had lectured herself on remaining calm, but she found her anger rising. "I don't believe you."

"I don't know why not. You weren't together very long."

"Are you telling me your brother has a habit of traveling the world, making women fall in love with him, and leaving them with his car in their driveway and not a single word of explanation?"

Duncan opened his mouth, then closed it. From his guilty expression, she knew that wasn't what had happened.

"Do you know where Lachlan is?" she asked. "Is he okay?"

"Yes," Duncan forced out. "And... yes. I believe he is fine."

Carys squared her shoulders. She wasn't leaving without answers. "I want to talk to him."

"You can't."

"Is he here?" She looked around. There was no one in the yard, probably because the air was frosty and the sun was completely covered by dense clouds, but maybe someone was coming out for a smoke break. Maybe there was someone she could ask.

"Carys." Duncan's expression softened. A tiny bit. "Lachlan did tell me about you. He should have... He has responsibilities here." The man would barely look at her. "You shouldn't have come."

"He left all his things in California. Not just his car. His passport. His bank card."

"I'll take those and give them back to him if you want."

"No! He left his books and... things his wife gave him before she died. He wouldn't have left those things behind, Duncan. No one would."

The big man said nothing.

"Did your family..." It seemed almost impossible to think. "Did your family *kidnap* him?"

"My family has nothing to do with it!" Duncan's tenuous patience broke, and he shouted at her. "Listen, there was a lot that my brother didn't tell you about himself. And I do understand why you're confused. I didn't know how to explain things to you, so I didn't call you back. I figured you'd move on. My God." He let out a harsh breath. "Lachlan told me about you, Carys. You're a bright woman and a college professor. It sounds like you have a wonderful life in California. You're going to be fine."

Carys was momentarily stunned by the compliments coming out of the antagonistic man's mouth. "I... Thank you?" She shook her head. "That's not the point. I *love* Lachlan."

Duncan stepped closer and stared at her. "Do you now?"

"Yes." She'd had weeks to think about it, to examine every moment of their relationship. "Lachlan made me feel alive after a really horrible time in my life. He was kind and generous and he *saw* me. I love him, and I'm not leaving here until I know what happened to him because I know you're not telling me the truth."

Duncan moved closer still, and the heat from his body cut through the chill of the cool Scottish morning. "He wasn't honest with you, Carys."

Her stomach dropped. "Is... is he married? Did his wife not really die?"

Oh my God, oh my God, oh my God. Was she the other woman? Was she in love with a married man?

"No." Duncan's answer was emphatic. "That wasn't a lie. Lachlan was widowed about two years ago. Seren was…" He paused and stared at Carys. "It was very hard for all of us to lose her, but Lachlan was wrecked."

"It's been two years." She knew it was, because Lachlan had lost his wife right around the time Carys had been diagnosed with depression. It was one of the things that had bonded them so quickly. "Is it so wrong that he doesn't want to be alone anymore? Is that the problem? Your family doesn't want him to—"

"Carys." Duncan's voice was harsh. "Lachlan has responsibilities here. He was supposed to be on holiday, and he took things a bit too far."

"A bit too far? We were together for four months. He was working on getting a visa. We were going to—"

"It was never going to happen," Duncan said. "It's not possible."

"No." She shook her head. "I want to talk to Lachlan. If he's here, I want to talk to him." She looked around the yard. "Where is he?"

Duncan stepped toward her. "He's here, but he's not *right* here."

"So how do you know he's okay?"

Duncan shook his head. "I know *where* he is, but I can't take you—"

"Why the fuck not?" Carys was starting to feel crazy again. Duncan was acting like this was all a bad breakup, but nothing about Lachlan's disappearance was normal. "I'm not leaving Scotland without talking to Lachlan."

"Well, good luck." Duncan offered her a tight smile. "You can ask around, but no one is going to help you."

"What does that mean?"

The door to the office popped open. "Can I get you a cup of tea, dear?"

Duncan's head swung to the open door. "She's not staying, Fiona."

Fiona's eyes went wide. "Sorry," she mouthed.

"Don't be a bully." Carys had come to the smithworks feeling timid, but now she was furious. "Why are you being a bully?"

"I don't know what you mean." Duncan crossed his arms again.

"You order me around. You bark at your secretary. You imply that Lachlan is a... a liar. You're acting like everything about this is normal. It's not! I know Lachlan, and he wouldn't just—"

"You knew a part of Lachlan," Duncan said quietly. "And that's all any of us knows in this world." He stepped away from her car. "Go home, Carys Morgan. Live your life. Leave my brother in your memories because that's all he'll ever be."

"I'm not done with this." She opened her car door, spitting mad. "Do not think for a second that I am leaving this country without talking to your brother."

Duncan didn't say anything else. He walked back into the office and shut the door behind him, leaving Carys alone by her car.

She looked up, over the top of the barn where a hill rose sharply behind the building, dotted with dark grey crags. A bright red fox perched on a boulder, watching her from a distance, but when Carys stood up straight and walked toward it, the animal darted away.

CHAPTER THREE

Carys was drunk, and she was rarely drunk. But the Four Crowns public house was right next to her hotel, and it had seemed like a good idea when she arrived back in town at three in the afternoon to start drinking to calm down.

Now she was calm.

Very, very calm.

"Can I get you another, dove?" The bartender was an intriguing dark-haired man with an angular face, a fine jaw, and brilliant blue eyes that looked at her like he could see into her soul. He had a line of fine gold rings climbing up his left ear, and his hair fell over the right side of his face like a golden-brown waterfall.

God, she was really drunk.

Carys squinted. "Is everyone in this country attractive?"

The bartender flashed her a wicked smile. "I guarantee you no."

As if to prove his point, a group of three old men with overgrown beards walked into the bar, laughing raucously and shouting at the woman behind the bar to get them three pints.

"See?" The man's eyebrows went up.

She smiled and raised her empty glass. "Point made."

"You're visiting from America." He narrowed his eyes and looked at her, then leaned down and stared into her eyes, his mouth falling open a little.

"What?" She looked down at her shirt. Had she spilled something? It was highly possible. "What are you—"

"You *aren't* American, are you?"

Carys frowned. "I think I know where I'm from." What a strange man. The gorgeous cheekbones were not making up for the intrusive questions and the staring.

"But you were born on this side of the ocean, weren't you?" The man kept his eyes on hers. "In Cymru."

"Wales." She blinked. "I was born in Wales. How did you know—"

"Oh yes. *Wales.*" The man's shock melted away, and a glorious smile spread over his face. "So you're visiting this side of the waters. Isn't this delicious?"

"Visiting?" Carys sighed. "Kind of. It's not exactly a vacation."

The long-legged man slid into the booth across from her. "Do you mind? I love a good story." He leaned forward. "In fact, I *live* for them."

His cheekbones were high, and his jaw was dusted with black stubble. Blue eyes shone out from arching black eyebrows that reminded Carys of blackbird wings. His lips were full and red, as if he'd been eating blackberries in the summer. She tasted the sweetness just looking at his lips. The tart burst of blackberry juice—

Carys blinked. "I should probably get a coffee and not another whiskey."

"Should you?" The dark man pulled a whiskey bottle seemingly out of nowhere and refilled her glass, then the glass that was suddenly in front of him. "Why did you come to Scone?"

That's right. She was in Scone, Scotland. Lachlan's hometown. The town where he'd run through the dense pine forest and hunted deer with his father. The town where he'd learned to ride horses and all the other idyllic things he'd told her about.

She stared at the glass in front of her. It hadn't been there before, had it? Or had there been a glass sitting on the table the whole time?

The room around her began to spin.

"My dove?" The man leaned in and spoke softly. "Why did you come to Scone?"

"I... I'm looking for someone."

"Who?" The man took a drink and watched her.

She hadn't seen the forests or deer that Lachlan had talked about. The trees she'd seen had been sparse and leafless from the cold. There were more sheep and cows than deer.

Maybe she was in the wrong place after all. The childhood Lachlan had described seemed like it had come from one of the fairy tales she taught in her Intro to World Mythology class, not a rural village an hour outside the Scottish capital.

"Who are you looking for?" he asked again.

"Lachlan Murray." Carys blinked, looking up into the man's blue eyes. "Do you know him?"

His mouth formed a small *o*, but he quickly hid his surprised expression behind a cocky grin. "Lachlan of Moray? Oh aye, I know that name. Tell me more."

"It's Murray, not..." She blinked when she heard his accent. "You're not Scottish."

His smile curved slowly. "No, I'm not. In your way of thinking, I'd be called Irish, I suppose."

"So is this an Irish pub or a Scottish pub if the bartender is Irish?"

His smile got bigger. "It's my pub. Do you want to know my name?"

She looked around the pub, but it was strangely quiet. She saw people on the other side of the room, but their voices were distant and muddled. The only one she could hear clearly was the man across the table from her.

She blinked, trying to clear her head. "Are you hitting on me?"

"Hitting you?" He sat back, his eyebrow rising in shock. "What are you talking about?"

"Not hitting me. Hitting *on* me." She racked her brain for the Scottish term Lachlan had used once. "Chatting me up. Are you chatting me up?"

"Am I?" The man's red lips curved into a smile again. "Do you want me to?"

"No." She shook her head. "I'm looking for Lachlan. I *love* him. And he loves me. That's why none of this makes sense."

He let out a soft sigh. "Oh, it makes too much sense, doesn't it?"

"What makes sense?"

His glittering eyes softened. "The distances we travel for love."

"Yes." She reached for the glass and realized it was empty. Where had the whiskey gone? Had she drunk it already? She didn't remember drinking it. "You understand then. I came here because I love him. And I need to know what happened."

Do you? A teasing voice that sounded like her mother's whispered in her mind. *Curiosity, my Carys. You will follow the rabbit into the forest, never seeing the wolf that follows at your back.*

She opened her eyes and saw the man more clearly. "How do you know Lachlan?"

He leaned back in the wooden booth and lifted the whiskey bottle. "How about another drink?"

She heard the door to the pub open again, and a gust of cold wind dusted her shoulder, making her shiver and pull her sweater up her neck. "I don't want any more whiskey."

"It warms the blood." The man looked amused. "But I suppose it depends on what kind of blood you have."

His dark hair fell past his shoulders in curling waves that reminded Carys of the whorls of grain in polished maple her father had loved.

"He made my mother a drawing table from that wood." Carys's head was spinning.

The man narrowed his eyes. "What wood? Who made a table?"

She was really drunk.

Her father had been a shop teacher at the local high school and a carpenter in his spare time. He'd loved the redwood forests of California and had built a small house with his own hands after moving his wife and infant daughter from rural Wales to the American West Coast.

When she closed her eyes, she was back in Baywood, standing behind that house on the edge of the forest, looking into the trees and peering through the shadowed trunks where the light jumped and danced as branches moved in the breeze.

Her parents weren't dead in this memory. They hadn't perished on a hillside in the dead of night, lost to a car crash in the wilderness. Her mother was still painting in her studio, and her father was still polishing wood in the barn.

She watched the faint lights in the forest, dancing like fireflies at twilight. *Don't be curious, my Carys,* her mother's voice whispered in her mind. *Leave the rabbit to the wolf. Never follow the lights. They want to lead you away from me.*

"Duncan Murray. Here to collect your American friend?"

The bartender's voice roused her, and Carys opened her eyes.

Duncan was standing over the booth, his arms crossed over his chest. He nodded at the bartender. "Dru."

Carys looked up at him and squinted. "You."

The bartender looked up and smiled. "I was just about to ask your friend her name. Perhaps you can tell me."

"Out of the booth, Dru." Duncan's voice was gruff. "You don't need her name."

"But I'm fairly sure I know one of them." The strange man's eyes were twinkling. "Don't you want to tell me the other, my dove?"

Carys looked at the man and tasted the sweet burst of berry juice on her tongue. "Nothing you say makes any sense."

"Not now, but wait." Dru winked at her. "Very well then." He slid out of the booth. "Your seat, Duncan?"

"And a glass," the brutish man said. "Leave the bottle unless it's one of yours."

Dru flipped the neck of the bottle with his fingertips, and it seemed to disappear. "I'll bring you another."

Duncan slid into the booth across from Carys as Dru walked away. "Of all the pubs you go to, it had to be this one."

She pointed over her shoulder. "It's right next to my hotel."

"Of course it is." He was folding his hands, then unfolding them. "Listen, I'm sorry I was rude today, but you surprised me and—"

"You shouldn't have been surprised. I called you, like, a dozen times after Lachlan went missing." She was far too drunk to be polite. "What did you think was going to happen when your brother up and left my house and five hours later, his phone was pinging in Scotland?" She leaned forward. "Five hours, Duncan. That's not possible. At one thirty his phone was at Mad Creek Bridge, and four hours later it was in Edinburgh."

Duncan stared at her. "You didn't tell me that part."

"You didn't really give me a chance."

"Fine. Tell me what happened."

Carys sighed, trying not to think of how many times she'd told this story in the past month. To Laura and Kiersten. To the police. To her dean. "He went for a hike in the forest behind my house."

Duncan scratched his beard. "You two liked to hike. He told me that."

"Yeah, and we know how to be safe in the woods. We don't hike after dark. We take water and protein bars with us. We take a compass because cell phone service is shit back in the hills."

"What's in the woods?"

She frowned. "What do you mean, 'what's in the woods'? Trees. Bears. Too much poison oak. He knew all that stuff. He'd been around long enough."

"Four months." He stared at the table. "When he was in Baywood, did anyone come around looking for him? Did he mention anything strange?"

"No. I would have told the police. Search and Rescue went out to Mad Creek looking for him and they looked for like four hours, but by then I'd come back to the house and some of his stuff was gone, so then I checked where his phone was and… poof! Scotland. Which…" Her head was swimming. "How? But there were his boots, so…"

Duncan frowned. "What about his boots?"

How was he so dense? "Someone took some of his clothes and his *boots*. Then they left his old muddy ones by my back door. So the police think he took off."

"But you don't."

"Of course I don't." She waited for him to say more, but he didn't. "He left his passport, his stuff. He left his car, Duncan. That is not a normal 'hey, this isn't working out.'"

"No," Duncan muttered. "I can see why you were confused."

"You've talked to him, right? You said you've talked to him since he's been back."

"Uh…" He frowned. "Not exactly."

"So how do you know he's okay?"

"Because I know." Duncan sighed. "What can I do to convince you to leave this alone and go back to your life?"

"Nothing. The man I love is *missing*." She finished the whiskey Dru had poured for her. "I shouldn't drink any more, but this is better than any whiskey I've ever tasted."

"Oh, I bet it is." He snatched the glass from her hand. "Don't drink that. If you insist on more, wait for the next bottle."

"Why not?" She tried to grab it, but his hand moved too fast.

His hands were pocked with small scars and burns, callused from work, though his nails were neatly trimmed. While the rest of Duncan looked just like Lachlan, his hands were very different.

Carys blinked at him through bleary eyes. "Maybe I should just go to the police. I can give them all the information I have from the police in Baywood." Her voice rose a little bit. "I got a copy of the report there. I can give them *your* name. Lachlan's passport. The screenshots of his phone pinging in Edinburgh. All his paperwork and the name of his lawyer in California and—"

"Stop." Duncan put his hand over Carys's and lowered his voice. "Carys Morgan, you need to stop. Leave this be. Leave Lachlan be."

Don't follow the rabbit into the woods.

Carys was going to disappoint her mother so much. She probably already had. "I don't believe you that he's fine." She glared at Duncan. "I think someone forced him to come back here, so until you let me see him, I am going to stay here and raise so much noise that nothing about your life is going to be peaceful. Ever again."

The first hint of panic touched his brilliant green eyes. "Please."

"I'm persistent and I'm pissed off. At you. At Lachlan. At... the stupid police back home. I'll call the police here. I'll call the newspapers. I'll call—"

"Okay, stop." He swallowed. "Carys, stop."

"Take me to see Lachlan."

Dru walked over and thunked a bottle of whiskey on the table before he walked away again.

Duncan watched him until he was back behind the bar, then turned to Carys. "You want to see Lachlan?" He cracked the bottle open and poured two fingers of scotch in his glass and then in hers. "You *really* want me to take you to Lachlan?"

"Yes. I do." Wait, was he really going to do it?

He downed the whiskey with one gulp. "Fine."

"Fine? Does fine mean yes?" Was he really going to take her to see Lachlan?

"Yes. I'll take you. And if anyone complains about it, I'm blaming my fucking brother."

<hr>

THE NEXT MORNING Carys woke up with a massive hangover and a note on the bedside table. Carys rolled over, squinting in the grey morning light, and saw a message written in surprisingly graceful writing.

Check out of your hotel and come to my house. Bring all your things. This may take some time.

Below that was an address, or at least what passed for one in Scotland. She'd have to ask the woman at the front desk how to get there, because after her roundabout drive the day before looking for Duncan's factory, she didn't have any confidence in her navigation skills.

She rolled back into bed and closed her eyes, pressing her fingers to her temples.

She'd been rude to Duncan the night before, but she'd been so angry. She could feel the shadows of depression threatening her mind, like coastal fog waiting to roll onto shore. She kept pushing it back with action. With anger. With determination.

She wasn't leaving this country without Lachlan. At least not without an explanation.

Carys reached for her phone and called Kiersten. The phone rang a few times before she realized it was probably really late in California.

Luckily, Kiersten was a night owl and picked up. "Hey! How did today go? Or... yesterday? I'm not sure."

"Complicated. How's home?"

"Good. No sign of Lachlan yet?"

"No, but I did meet Duncan."

"The brother! How was that?"

"They're twins. Like identical twins. So that was weird."

"Whoa. I bet. Did Lachlan ever tell you his brother was his twin?"

"No. And Duncan was rude as hell, but he said he'd take me to see Lachlan today."

"I knew it." Kiersten watched too much true-crime television. "There's family drama there. I bet Lachlan got roped back into some toxic family dynamic he was trying to get away from here. He's kind-hearted. Dysfunctional people will prey on that."

Carys could always depend on Kiersten for a positive take. She was notoriously forgiving.

"All I know is that on top of being worried, I'm pissed off. I understand needing to go back to sort out family stuff, but there's no excuse for not calling me."

"If they took his phone though."

"There are other phones in Scotland, Kiersten."

"Okay yes. But tell me this: Do you know anyone's phone number anymore?"

Carys fell silent. *Shit*. That was a good point.

"See? I probably can't even remember Laura's, and she's had the same number for fifteen years."

Carys suddenly felt foolish. Or was she still pissed off?

Yeah, still a little pissed off. "You know what? I'll decide how I feel about Lachlan when I see Lachlan. Right now I just need to *find* him." She grabbed the paper on the bedside table. "And figure out how to find... Murrayshall House."

"That sounds fancy."

"I hardly think it's going to be that fancy. His brother is a blacksmith."

"Being a blacksmith sounds like a cool job." Kiersten's voice perked up. "Your dad would have loved that."

"My dad was the kindest and most considerate man in the world," Carys said. "I don't think he'd have loved someone who tried to brush me off when all I'm doing is trying to find out what the hell happened to Lachlan."

"Still. Blacksmith or finance bro, Lachlan's family drama reeks of OMP."

"What the hell is OMP?"

"Old money problems. Trust me, I've dated enough trust fund boys to know. All this shit? The disapproving siblings, the mysterious 'responsibilities' back home. The extended travel. All of it sounds like old money problems to me. Besides, who can actually make enough money with a blacksmithing business to randomly fly across the world for months at a time?"

I'm a disgustingly wealthy prince who's run away from home for a bit to enjoy being unemployed.

"Oh my God, I think you're right." Carys closed her eyes, and her temples pounded. She groaned and fell back into bed. "Kiersten, I should just leave now."

"Absolutely not! Lachlan was happy with you. They were paying him to sing at the pub, you know. He even asked me about how to get work at the mill a couple of weeks before he disappeared."

"You didn't tell me that."

"He told me not to say anything." She took a deep breath. "He was making a new life in California, and if his family took him away from that with... lies or guilt or some shit like that, he needs you."

Carys took a deep breath and sat up again. "You're right. He needs me." *And I need him.* "Okay, I'm taking a shower, getting some aspirin, and checking out of the hotel. I'll try to call you later, but reception around here is hit or miss."

"Sounds good. Love you, Carys."

"Love you too." She turned off her phone and set it on the bedside table. Then she rubbed her face, reached for the bottle of aspirin on the table next to her, and tried to calm her wobbly morning belly.

Whiskey was dangerous.

CHAPTER FOUR

The road to Murrayshall House was even more twisted than the one to Murray Smithworks. It led out of the town and up into the hills of Perthshire where the track dipped and rose over hills, crossing small creeks and winding through forested creases in the landscape.

The lady at the front desk had been disappointed that Carys was checking out early but was happy to give directions to "the auld house" when Carys mentioned Duncan's address.

She got a cup of coffee from the café down the street, then struck out in her rental car, her belly fluttering from the idea of possibly seeing Lachlan after a month of silence.

If he was really okay, what would she say to him?

What would he say to her?

Was she angry? Confused? Hurt?

She was all those things, but mostly she was worried.

If Lachlan had really decided to just call it quits, why hadn't he given her a reason? Why had he turned off his phone? He wasn't on social media, but he could have contacted her. He was a grown man, and she wasn't in hiding.

Messages could be sent.

The road widened on a turn, then narrowed again over a bridge. The trees grew taller and the shade deeper. The sun had broken through the clouds, so the light under the trees flashed like light on water, the dappled tapestry of green, grey, and black punctuated by occasional flashes of a red roof or a yellow bunch of wildflowers struggling to life.

She came to a large wrought iron gate that was cracked open with a sign hanging off it.

Murrayshall House.

"Okay, this is it."

The gates and the stone wall on either side of them framed a large cobbled driveway that led into dense woods on either side of the road.

She navigated her rental car through the gate and wound through the trees as the driveway twisted through a forest.

The farther she drove, the more Kiersten seemed right. If this was all part of Lachlan's family home, the Murrays were sitting on a lot of land in a very small country.

There was a stone archway with another wrought iron gate on either side; then the road widened into a large courtyard with a giant house sitting at one end. It was a massive edifice framed by two round towers that rose on each corner, complete with a steep roof covered in moss-flecked tile. The manor house was built of light brown stone that shone with a pale pink wash in the morning light.

Behind the house in the middle of a lush meadow, a grey stone castle rose in the distance, its narrow towers framing the hill in the distance where another ruin was barely visible through the trees.

Carys stopped the car. "Holy shit."

Castle. Lachlan's family had a castle. Apparently.

She pulled in where she saw other cars parked. A red compact sedan, two beat-up Range Rovers, and a pickup truck with a tarp over the bed.

Carys grabbed her purse, leaving her suitcase in the car. She was not making any assumptions about staying in this place. It wasn't that far from town, and she could afford the gas—petrol—to make the half-hour drive back to her very nice, non-manor-like hotel next to the Four Crowns.

She walked across the courtyard, gravel crunching beneath her feet, toward the nearest door that looked like someone might answer. There were multiple doors to the house, but she went to the smallest one on the side and knocked.

A few moments later she heard laughter, and then the door was yanked open and a cheerful-faced woman answered the door. "Can I help you?" She narrowed her eyes. "Are ye looking for a tour or something?"

The woman was in her late forties or early fifties if Carys had to guess, and her accent was thick. She had a headband holding back a mass of brown curly hair, an apron around her waist.

"Hi. Maybe I'm at the wrong place." She looked around, but she didn't know what kind of car Duncan drove. "I'm looking for Duncan Murray. Or Lachlan Murray if he's here?"

She cocked her head. "Okayyyy. Yer looking for Lachlan?" Were her eyes a little bit afraid? What was that about?

"Or Duncan, yes." She stuck out her hand. "Sorry. Hi. I'm Carys Morgan."

"Why are you coming to the kitchen door, love?" She smiled a little. "If you're here to visit the laird, ye should be going to the front." She leaned forward and pointed to the left. "Is he expecting you?"

"Duncan?"

"Aye, the laird."

"I think so." Her fingers closed around the note. "He left me a note and—"

"No worries, my girl. I don't need to know the details." She nudged Carys toward the path. "Go on then. Mary will meet you at the front. Just ring the bell."

Carys pointed to her right. "At... the front door?"

"Aye, the front." The woman seemed amused. "I'll go ahead and put the tea on though, so thanks for giving me the heads-up." She winked at Carys, then closed the door in her face.

Carys stepped back and then started down the stone pathway that ran along the front of the house. She passed immaculately kept formal garden beds and some stone statuary before she came to a set of grand stone steps that led to a pair of massive carved wooden doors.

She saw a bell to the right of the door and pulled the chain hanging from it, which produced an echoing, clanging sound inside the house. A few moments later, a younger woman opened the door.

"Miss Morgan?" She held out her hand. "I'm Mary Burris. My husband is the groundskeeper here, and I run the house. Duncan told me to expect you this morning, and Samantha already shouted from the kitchen." She opened the door wider. "Please come in. Welcome to Murrayshall House."

"Thank you." Carys had never been on a Scottish estate, but she'd watched movies, and Duncan's house looked like a movie set. There was a wood-paneled sitting room to the right and a large dining room to the left with a collection of armory hanging on the walls.

"Please have a seat in the front room," Mary said. "I've already started a fire. This house is magnificent, but it's an ice box this time of year."

"Right." She had never been more grateful for her cozy cabin in the woods, because Duncan's housekeeper was correct. She could nearly see her breath in the air. "I think I'll keep my coat for now if that's all right."

"Perfectly." Mary smiled and pointed to her wool sweater. "But we do have plenty of good wool jumpers if you'd like to borrow one."

"I'll let you know."

"Duncan was out with Andy this morning," Mary said. "That's my husband. He should be in shortly. Would you like me to keep you company while you wait for him? Or would you like a tour of the house? We usually only do them in the summer months for the tourists, but I'd be happy to give you the brief version if you want to keep moving."

"Uh…" She looked around the big empty sitting room. It had large windows and comfortable-looking couches, but Carys didn't like the idea of waiting for Duncan by herself. "Sure. That would be great."

"Excellent." Mary smiled. "Let's start in the dining room. How much do you know about swords?"

———

HOWEVER MUCH CARYS had known about historic arms, she knew more after Mary's tour, which covered the building of the four-hundred-year-old house by the ancestral owner of the land—the Laird of Murrayshall—of whom Duncan was the current iteration.

It wasn't a royal title, according to Mary, but a traditional Scottish one that had passed from Duncan's father to him on the old laird's death a few years ago.

There was not a single mention of Lachlan, and Carys didn't bring him up, but she was silently judging a family that had numerous family portraits with one son and not the other. Was Lachlan illegitimate?

How did you have an illegitimate twin brother? That wasn't possible. What the hell was going on with this family?

Then again, Lachlan had failed to mention a lot. He hadn't told her his brother was a laird. He hadn't said much about his family, but she'd definitely gotten the impression they were closer than they appeared.

"Mary!"

They were in the library when Carys heard Duncan's voice.

"Mary!"

Mary rolled her eyes. "The way he bellows, you'd think I was deaf." She motioned toward the door. "I'm sure the tea is ready, and the man is clearly ready for company. Don't yell at me, old man!" She gave Carys a cheeky smile. "He never had a sister, so I try to needle him as much as I can."

"I think he needs it," Carys murmured.

Mary smiled. "I like you. You don't come from a grand family, do you?"

Carys almost laughed. "My dad was a high school woodworking teacher, and my mom was a somewhat successful artist. No blue blood in these veins."

"Right." Mary nodded. "Like you even more."

Carys followed the housekeeper back into the large central corridor that ran down the center of the house and back toward the entryway.

Duncan was glowering in the entry, his pants caked with mud up to the knees. "Your damn husband had me pushing his tractor out of the back meadow when he knew I had company coming today."

Mary laughed. "He told you about that days ago. Not his fault you were too busy with your hammers and your fire."

"Will you..." His eyes found Carys. "Miss Morgan, good morning." His voice held more propriety than it had the day before. "Excuse my appearance. My groundskeeper is an ogre who enjoys tormenting me." He turned back to Mary. "Pour Carys a cup of tea while I change. She and I need to speak privately." He lowered his voice. "Lachlan."

"Of course."

So Mary did know about Lachlan.

Carys followed Mary into the front room, which had warmed up considerably since she'd arrived. A carafe of tea was waiting, which Mary poured from before she left the room.

Carys sat by the fire, trying to digest the revelations that morning.

Duncan was a laird, which basically meant he was rich, which likely meant that Lachlan was also rich. The "disgustingly wealthy prince" line hadn't really been a joke.

Still, there was something odd about all this. Mary knew about Lachlan, but none of the family portraits in the house, covered with blue, green, and red tartan, showed two boys' faces. There were plenty of pictures of a younger boy who could have been either Lachlan or Duncan, but none of the boys together.

The door open and Duncan walked in. "Carys Morgan."

Duncan had clearly taken a shower because he smelled like spice and leather. His beard was freshly trimmed, and he was dressed in clean khaki pants and a worn olive-green sweater that brought out the color of his eyes. Somehow his massive shoulders didn't look out of place in a room like this one with rich wood, armor in the corner, and swaths of tartan decorating the throw pillows.

He didn't look like a brute—he looked like an ancient warrior come home.

She rose. "Duncan, thank you for agreeing to take me to Lachlan."

"You're the lady." He walked over and stood across from her. "I rise when you enter the room, not the other way round."

Carys sat down. "I'm not a lady, but I feel like you're... some kind of lord or something," she said. "Is Lachlan one too?"

Duncan sat. "We're not lords in the English way, thank God. I'm a laird, which means my family owns the estate here and we have for... many years. And Lachlan..." He huffed out a breath and leaned forward. "Can I convince you that Lachlan is fine? He's healthy and he's fine. And it would be far better for you to leave him to his life and continue with yours?"

"Can I convince you that my next stop is going to be the police station if I don't see him today?"

He closed his eyes. "Fill the fetters," he muttered. "I'll take you to Lachlan, but this isn't a simple thing."

"So he's not here?"

"No, he's not here." Duncan sat back and his shoulders dropped. "You're going to hate me," he said softly. "You don't think that now, but you will."

She raised her chin. "What do you care if I hate you or not?"

"Just remember that I tried to talk you out of this" —he kept his voice low and steady— "when you start to hate me."

"Enough. Fine, I'll remember." She gripped her hands together. "Where is Lachlan?"

He looked into her eyes. "Do you believe in fairy tales?"

*C*ARYS LOOKED *up from the book she'd been reading into the eyes of a man she'd never seen before. "Excuse me?"*

"Do you believe in fairy tales?" He had an accent. Scottish? The man nodded at the book in Carys's hand. "You're looking at George MacDonald's work. Fairy tales, yes or no?"

"Do you believe in the sun?" It was the strangest encounter she'd ever had at Redwood Pages, the outdoor bookshop where she usually shopped. Most book browsers kept to themselves.

Probably too many years in the library.

"Do I believe in the sun?" The man's brow furrowed. "What kind of question is that in this place?"

Carys cocked her head. The man had an odd way of phrasing things. "Fairy tales are as real as the sun. They exist. Folk stories and myths and legends are told all over the world." She put the used volume of MacDonald in her basket. She liked the marbled endpapers and the faint scent of cherry tobacco in the pages. "Asking if I believe in fairy tales is like asking if I believe math is real or if trees grow." She motioned to the towering redwoods that soared overhead. "Fairy tales just... are."

The man said nothing for a moment, then smiled.

And Carys realized if she hadn't believed in the sun before—a fair doubt when endless winter fog had set in on the Northern California coast—then she'd believe in it after seeing this man's smile.

"Y*OUR BROTHER ASKED* me the same thing the first time we met," Carys said softly. "I was shopping for books and found an old copy of George MacDonald. He saw it and asked me...."

Duncan kept his eyes on her. "What did you tell him?"

"I asked him if he believed in the sun."

Duncan snorted out a laugh. "And what did he say to that? I'm actually dying to know."

"Nothing, he just smiled."

Duncan looked at her with an expression she couldn't read. It was… intent. Then he stood and walked to the fire, bending down to add wood to the flames.

"I'm a mythology professor," Carys explained. "My father told me stories from the Mabinogion before I could speak. I learned to read from *The Hobbit*, and I was obsessed with Greek myths when other kids were playing soccer."

"So that's a yes," Duncan muttered.

"I'm saying I study myth the way that other people study history. So yes, of course I believe in them." She looked out the window at the forests surrounding the house, thick with pine trees and dense shrubs. "Fairy tales tell us about ourselves in ways that might make us uncomfortable, but that doesn't mean they're not their own version of truth."

Duncan stared at the fire, and the silence seemed to stretch across an ocean. "Maybe this will be easier than I thought."

"Tell me."

He turned and leaned his back against the mantel, crossing his arms over his chest. "I was seven years old when a boy with my own face walked out of the forest."

Carys felt her heart skip a beat, but she remained silent.

Duncan's voice stayed low and steady, his gaze fixed on the ground near his feet. "My nanny was the superstitious kind. I didn't follow the lights into the woods. I didn't speak to strangers in the wild. And I never gave my name to anyone I didn't know."

Carys frowned. "Do you mean—"

"I need you to let me finish." He looked up and met her eyes. "And if you want to leave after it and write me off as cracked, that's good. That would be better."

That stiffened her spine. "I'm not leaving until you take me to Lachlan."

Duncan stared at her for a moment, then shook his head. "I saw him, but I couldn't believe what I was seeing. I ran away and the boy chased me, speaking in an accent I didn't recognize. Using words that didn't make sense." Duncan shrugged. "Eventually I stopped running and I let him catch up. I was tired and… curious. But I wasn't scared."

He looked at her. "There was something about him that was so warm. He wanted to know me, and if you knew my father—or any of the rest of my family—you'd know that was a rare thing."

Carys had to assume that Duncan's family wasn't affectionate, but she kept her mouth shut and kept her eyes steady. So Lachlan and Duncan hadn't grown up together like Lachlan had told her, but the men were clearly the same age and looked identical. Half brothers? It would hardly be uncommon for a rich man to have an illegitimate child or two.

"The boy ran up to me, and he said his name was Lachlan and he only wanted to play. He said he'd never been in the forest before, and he didn't want to get lost." Duncan turned and leaned against the mantel, his back to the fire. "I was confused that he looked like me, but I was a lonely seven-year-old boy. Presented with a playmate in the forest behind my house, I didn't question it. We started to talk and then explore the forest, the ruins, the streams and gullies around the place. I ran back to the house and got food for us, and at the end of the day when the sun was starting to set, he left. Went back into the forest with a wave."

Duncan walked over and sat across from Carys again. "And I missed him. The moment he was out of sight, I felt like half my own self had gone."

"You'd only known him one day."

"Have you ever met someone and the connection is so immediate that you'd swear you'd known them your whole life? Maybe in another life even?"

"Yes. Lachlan."

Duncan nodded. "Aye, he has that way, doesn't he?" The corner of his mouth turned up. "Lachlan came back over and over, and eventually he told me that he lived on the other side of the forest. That was all he'd tell me, and I didn't question it. The village was on the other side of the forest, so that made sense."

A slight frown marred Duncan's forehead. "Over time, I thought of Lachlan like a brother, but he never came to the house. If I had friends over, he would come visit and play with us, but he was never around the grown-ups. Not my parents. Not the staff. He wore clothes that didn't match our own. He spoke Gaelic along with English, which none of my other friends did, but he taught me." Duncan folded his hands together. "I was ten when I asked Lachlan if we could go to his house for a visit."

A knot twisted in Carys's belly, and she didn't know why.

"He told me that we could, but that his home was different than mine. That we would have to go in the nighttime and that I couldn't bring any of my usual kit." He swallowed. "My grandfather had given me an old compass that we played with and a pocketknife. He said I couldn't bring them, and I said that was fine."

"You trusted him."

"Didn't you?"

"Yes." She'd always trusted Lachlan.

Carys felt the room cool, and a log broke in the fireplace, falling to the stone hearth with a crack. Duncan rose, walked over, and added two more pieces of wood.

"I snuck out that night—it wasn't the first time—and I met him on the edge of the forest. There was a tall man with Lachlan. A man with dark hair and gold eyes. Pale skin—pale even for a Scot—and no expression. None at all. I was afraid of him, but Lachlan took my hand and told me he was a friend. Told me he was our guide and we'd follow him so we didn't get lost."

"Duncan, why would you—"

"I was with Lachlan, wasn't I? I didn't question it. He's so... confident." Duncan shrugged his massive shoulders. "So reassuring. You do things for Lachlan that you'd never do for anyone else because he makes you feel special, Carys. And he means it. He *does*. He's completely sincere in his affection for people, and I'd never tell you different because I know you've felt it. I know you know it."

She didn't say another word.

"We walked into the forest, and I didn't blink when we followed the lights no matter what my nanny had said. I had forgotten all her lessons. The wisps—"

"Wisps?" Carys filled in the blanks. "Will-o'-the-wisps? The little glowing lights?"

Like the lights in the forest behind her house. Ghost lights, they called them in America.

"They seemed to move in front of us as we walked, and I followed Lachlan, who followed the man. We walked into the forest, and I knew where I was, but it got darker. It grew... stranger. I heard things. I saw shadows I couldn't explain. But I kept going because I was with Lachlan, and he wasn't scared at all. Eventually I didn't recognize where we were. Nothing was familiar, but I saw a light, like the sun rising on the horizon on a winter morning."

"You'd walked all night?"

"No, Carys Morgan. We'd walked into the Shadowlands. That was Lachlan's home. That's where he came from, and that's where he is now." Duncan sat back. "If you believe in fairy tales, you'll come with me tonight and I'll take you to Lachlan. And if you don't, then you can walk out the door right now, dismiss me as the crazy blacksmith spinning tales to excuse his brother's bad behavior, and fly back to America."

Carys felt the fire grow, warming the room, but she was frozen inside, automatic disbelief battling with what she knew of gruff, practical Duncan Murray who ran a business, owned a huge estate, and pulled tractors from the mud on a Thursday morning.

This was nonsense.

And Duncan believed it. She could see it in his eyes.

"The second choice is what I'd prefer," Duncan said quietly. "But if you insist on finding Lachlan, I will take you."

CHAPTER FIVE

Carys and Duncan were back at the Four Crowns pub in town, sitting in a corner booth and waiting for someone.

"You said you'd take me, and the minute I agree, you drag me back into town." Carys was annoyed and starting to feel like Duncan was leading her on a wild-goose chase to try to run her off. Maybe he'd been right and she should have laughed in his face and driven back to Edinburgh.

What are you doing, Carys? She was unhinged. This was stupid. This was an absolute ridiculous situation, and when she finally found Lachlan, she was going to give him hell about making her trot off into Duncan's delusions to find him.

She looked around the dark pub, which smelled like beer and... oddly, moss. "Why are we back here?"

"We need a favor." Duncan grimaced. "From Dru."

"The bartender?"

"He's that as well," Duncan muttered. "He can take us, but we'll need to bargain with him. Don't say anything, and don't tell him your name."

Wow. So Duncan was... *really* into the fairy tale thing. "What are you—"

"Duncan Murray."

Carys turned and saw the lithe figure of Dru walking through the growing crowd at the bar. It was Thursday afternoon, but they were far from alone in the afternoon rush.

"Dru."

The tall man slid gracefully into the booth across from them and smiled. "And Carys Morgan."

"You know my name." The man's beauty was startling all over again, his lips full and pink like berries she wanted to bite. The dark stubble on his jaw begged for her touch.

"Not from her, you don't," Duncan said. "So don't be getting ideas."

Dru smiled. "I asked about the American visiting and asking questions about Lachlan. People here are so friendly and forthcoming."

"So you might guess why we're paying you a visit." Duncan's voice was a borderline hostile growl.

Dru pulled another bottle of whiskey from seemingly nowhere, and three glasses were on the table in a blink. "Do you need my help, Duncan Murray?"

"You know I have leverage."

Dru's eyes narrowed. "Are you saying that you want to trade one of your favors? For her?"

"Don't make this complicated, Dru." Duncan lowered his voice even more and switched to Gaelic, which Dru apparently understood and Carys didn't.

The two men went back and forth for several agonizing minutes while Carys grew increasingly impatient. She hated not knowing what was going on, and all of this reeked of insiders keeping secrets.

She hated that.

Carys hated cliques and secrets. She abhorred gatekeepers and insiders. Her father used to tease her about it, calling her his "very American daughter."

"Enough." Carys broke into their hushed conversation. "Either tell me what you're talking about or I'm leaving."

Dru's eyes lit up. "And who are you to dictate the terms of this negotiation, Carys Morgan, stranger to two worlds?"

Duncan blinked. "What are you talking about?"

"She'll know when she knows." Dru turned to Carys and poured a finger of whiskey in her glass. "Drink with me and I'll know you. See that you don't get lost in the shadows tonight."

She eyed the glass with suspicion, then turned to Duncan. He gave her a slight nod. Dru poured another finger of whiskey in Duncan's glass, then in his own.

"We have an agreement then."

Carys didn't know what made her do it, but just before Dru was about to pick up his glass, she reached over and switched her glass with the strange man's.

He looked at her with amusement, picked up the glass he'd poured for Carys, and drank.

Duncan sighed, then downed the whiskey. "Done."

Carys picked up the cold glass holding the golden liquid, tipped it up, and drank it in one gulp. "Done."

Dru's eyes came alive, and the vivid blue seemed to get darker as she watched him. "I'll see you on the edge of the forest, Duncan Murray. Be there at sunset."

"Leave it." Duncan took her phone and tossed it on the bed. "We don't have much time. The days are short this time of year."

"I'm not leaving my phone—"

"If you don't leave it, they'll take it."

"*Who* will take it?" She shook her head. "You keep telling me all these mysterious rules, and I know a lot of them are based in old European superstitions, but—"

"Ha!" He snorted. "Old European... Yes, it's all superstition. Listen, woman, I traded something quite valuable for this passage, so you'll listen to the rules I give you. Don't take your phone. It'll be safe here at the house with Mary and Andrew, and if you bring it to the forest tonight, you'll lose it. Trust me, I've tried. No cameras. No film of any kind. No metal that's not fine—"

"What does that mean?"

"No iron or iron alloys." He looked at her necklace. "Is that gold?"

Carys wore a necklace that had been her mother's, a gold chain with two Welsh dragons on it, one in gold and the other in silver. "It's gold and silver, yeah."

"That should be fine," he muttered. "Basically, anything modern, just leave it. I can't even take a pocketknife to this place."

She pointed to the knife hanging on his belt. "What's that then?"

He drew the blade from the leather-wrapped sheath. "It's bone with a flint blade, and I'll be hiding it before we meet Dru."

Carys was starting to feel like she was entering someone's delusion. "Is this going to be *dangerous?*"

Was Duncan Murray really a serial killer who was going to dispose of her in the forest tonight?

After meeting you at a pub in a small town and introducing you to his housekeeper?

She listened to too many podcasts.

"Dangerous?" He shrugged. "Could be. Could be fine. You wanted to see Lachlan, so we're going."

"You said you went to this place when you were a kid, so I assumed that this was..."

"What?"

Some kind of elaborate prank to be honest. Carys was going along with all of Duncan's plans, but in her heart, she didn't really believe in any kind of alternate dimensions, shadow worlds, or different timelines no matter how many times her levelheaded engineer friend Laura told her that the science behind dimensional shifts were entirely possible in theory.

In theory. Not in practice.

"Text your friends," Duncan told her. "Tell them you're going camping with Lachlan for a few days and that you're fine. Leave your phone here and give them Mary's number. The last thing we need is more Americans showing up to harass my staff."

Carys knew leaving her phone was good advice, but it also made her feel naked. But practically speaking, she knew that even if wherever they were going was just a remote area of Scotland, the signal probably wouldn't work.

"Fine."

"Good."

Duncan was annoying her the longer he lingered in the room where Mary had put her luggage.

"Can you give me some privacy please?" She looked at him from the corner of her eye as she texted Laura and Kiersten her location.

"Fine, but be ready in an hour and dress warm."

Carys told Laura and Kiersten she was going camping like Duncan had said and that if they were worried to call Mary Burris at Murrayshall House. She also told them that Lachlan and Duncan were some kind of minor Scottish royalty, that everything was fine, and she'd explain later.

She was going to come back to two hundred messages, she just knew it.

Duncan left the room, and Carys walked to the window to stare at the forest where they would meet Dru later that night.

Though the town was only a short drive away, the forest behind Murrayshall House and the old castle felt primeval. The dense forest reached up the giant hill—not quite a mountain—surrounding the ruined castle and an even older-looking fort on the hill above it. Grey stones butted up from the top of the ridge where the old fort had been built, like jagged teeth from the jawbone of a monster.

There was a stream running down the hill and into the meadow around the house, curling and bounding over moss-covered rocks and twisting between the curves of the earth. A waterfall was barely visible between the trees.

And somewhere in that forest was Lachlan, at least according to his brother.

She changed her mind. *This* was the worst idea in her twenty-nine years of life on this planet. Going into a dark forest with her missing boyfriend's not-twin brother.

She was following that bunny all the way into the woods, and the wolf was probably the one guiding her.

Carys changed her trousers to the heaviest khaki canvas she owned, pulled on wool socks and a microfiber undershirt, layering a wool sweater over her shirt before she donned a wool coat that Mary had loaned her.

Apparently her bright red puffer coat was a little too conspicuous.

She finished her trekking outfit with sturdy boots, then walked down the stairs to meet Duncan, who was waiting at the door in similar sturdy hiking clothes.

"Ready?" he asked.

No.

He cocked his head. "Last chance to leave it."

Carys lifted her chin, walked past him, and opened the front door.

THE FOREST WAS dark but hardly silent. As they approached the edge of the woods, she saw Dru waiting on a fallen log. His pale skin shone in the gathering darkness, and he almost seemed to glow.

They said not a word when Dru rose, but Duncan took her hand and closed it within his own as they followed the strange man into the woods.

"Don't let go of me," Duncan said quietly. "Keep your eyes on Dru as we walk. Keep your wits about you, and whatever you hear, don't react."

"What am I going to hear?"

"Things that aren't real." He glanced at her over his shoulder. "And some that seem too real. I'll explain when we're through the gate."

Gate? Carys bit her tongue and went with it. Whatever this was, Duncan was taking it seriously, and as long as he took her to Lachlan, she'd go along with it.

Dru walked along the path through the woods, over stones and through the trees. The farther they got into the deepening darkness, the harder it was to keep her eyes on him. He seemed to blend into the trees, disappearing and reappearing as the forest grew darker and deeper.

They walked over a small bridge and down a set of carved stone steps into what looked like a grotto covered in moss where faded ribbons were tied around branches and copper pennies were pushed into tree trunks.

"Duncan?"

"Shh." He squeezed her hand. "Don't speak. Whatever you hear or see from now on, don't speak to them."

Them?

The three travelers passed through the grotto and under a narrow cut in the rocks where a fallen log had created an archway. The forest grew darker as the sun set, and the sky—which she could barely make out through the tree canopy—deepened from a faded grey to a velvety midnight blue.

There was a chittering, crawling sound in the dense brush beside her, and a branch snagged her pant leg. Duncan hissed something in Gaelic, and the noise scattered. An owl hooted, then another, the birds calling to each other over their heads while a crow squawked somewhere in the distance.

Carys heard more clicking in the forest and the sound of something small scurrying behind them.

She started to turn, and Duncan squeezed her hand and tugged her closer.

"Don't turn. Eyes on Dru. Just Dru."

Cold creeped under her collar and down the back of her sweater, raising goose bumps on her skin. Her feet tripped over another branch that she hadn't seen Duncan step over, and something else grabbed her pants.

She felt fingers, and her heart jumped into her throat.

"Duncan!"

"Shh!" He linked their hands and drew her nearly into his body.

Carys's senses went on high alert, and she tried not to panic. The tapping sound was all around them now, like branches snapping underfoot or pebbles falling onto dry leaves. The ground beneath her was soft, and she saw blue lights in her peripheral vision. In the distance, there was a rush of sound like waves from an ocean she couldn't see.

Don't follow the lights. It was her mother's voice in her head as they walked in the forest behind their house in the late afternoon. *Don't ever follow the lights, my Carys. They want to lead you away from me.*

Through the winding narrow path, Dru walked with a careless gait, tossing his hair and whistling a low tune that caught in Carys's mind. She focused on it, especially when Dru began to sing.

> Sing me a place where sea becomes sky
> Where stone swallows mountain
> Where this world goes to die

Duncan kept her hand in an iron grip as the forest around them turned into a cacophony of sound and winking blue lights tempted her from the corners of her eyes. She heard a baby crying and another laughing. More crying. Wailing.

Something in her heart broke to pieces and fell on the forest floor, trampled under her own stumbling feet. Tears pooled in her eyes, her feet grew heavy and her legs stiff as Dru continued to sing his odd, haunting melody.

> Write me a poem of heather and firth
> Where forest touches night and night becomes earth

She didn't know where night ended and forest began. The darkness was everywhere. The shadows moved like figures in a dream, appearing on one side, then another. The sound of wings overhead, and the whoosh of feathers before a tiny screech and silence.

"Don't listen. Don't speak," Duncan whispered.

Carys wanted to close her eyes, but she kept them on Dru, determined not to lose herself in the disorienting rush of sensation. Their strange guide continued to sing as if he was taking a pleasant walk in the woods, though his words grew increasingly dark.

> The shadows, they call you when life becomes still
> They call you to taste them
> They tempt you to thrill

More laughter. More crying. A baby wailed in the night, and Carys's heart turned toward the pitiful sound, but she couldn't move. She was nearly plastered to Duncan's back as she trudged along the dark path, ignoring the catch of fingers on her clothes and the brush of feathers along her neck.

> The darkness it holds you
> Don't try to turn back
> Its wild weathered places
> Are all that you lack...

Dru's song trailed off as they walked through another narrow stone passage with arching branches overhead. Carys heard water in the distance, not the disorienting rush of waves that sounded like a distant ocean but the grounded, gritty slap of water on stone.

There was one last burst of laughter in the trees behind her before a kiss of light broke through gloom, illuminating something that nearly seemed like dawn.

It wasn't dawn though, but the dim light of a midwinter day in the northern latitude. She looked up but couldn't see the sun anywhere.

Duncan's hand released its pressure, and she saw his shoulders start to relax. "They wanted you," he murmured. "That was strange."

"Strange?" Carys's mind was racing. "Duncan, what the hell was that?"

"Shhhh."

The path widened, and Duncan pulled her to stand beside them. The trees were thinning, and Dru stopped just before another fallen log. He turned and faced them, and Carys gasped.

He had scratches on his neck and jaw, welling with something that looked like glycerin. The wounds marred the unearthly beauty he'd worn when he entered the forest. Even more, there were dark marks on his forehead and his neck, swirling blue sigils that matched the color of his eyes.

He caught Carys's expression and smiled. "Not what you remember, Carys Morgan?"

Dru walked past them, brushing against Carys's shoulder on the path before he walked back toward the forest. "Duncan Murray, our bargain is complete."

"This portion of it anyway."

Dru halted, turned, and his eyes landed on Carys. "Are you sure there isn't anything you need from me, Carys Morgan?"

With the shadows behind him and the light coming from over her shoulder, the swirling sigils on his forehead were even clearer, as was the heavy water dripping from his wounds.

No. Not water. She narrowed her eyes, examining the scratches. In the dim near-dawn light that shone on Dru's face, she saw the truth. The wounds were weeping with a silvery liquid the consistency of blood.

Because it was blood.

Dru had silver blood.

"What are—"

"No." Duncan squeezed her hand. "Don't ask him."

The strange man's eyes pulled her in. "Finish the question, Carys Morgan."

She shook her head, her rational mind battling with the reality she saw in front of her. "Thank—"

"No." Duncan spun her around to face him. "Remember what you know. Remember what you've read. You're not in your books anymore, Carys. Never thank them. Never *ever* thank someone here." He turned to Dru. "We are grateful that our passage through the gate was safe."

She looked over her shoulder at the rolling hills below the precipice where they were standing. The forest was behind them, and beyond the trees was a gently undulating land threaded with hedgerows, streams, and rocky outcrops. It was a patchwork of deep green, blue, and a grey so dark it was nearly black. It looked like the landscape she'd seen around Duncan's house, but there were no power lines. No signs of human habitation.

There was no sign of civilization anywhere.

She turned her head to Dru, who was waiting for her to speak, and she thought about every fairy tale she'd ever read, every superstition her father had ever thrown her way, and every warning from her mother that had never made sense before this moment.

She nodded slightly and thought carefully about her words. "It was good to meet you, Dru."

Dru smiled wider, and his blue eyes danced again. "It was my pleasure, Carys Morgan. Welcome to the Shadowlands."

CHAPTER SIX

They walked along a narrow path down the hill and over a few streams that rippled along with the land. The dark forest fell back in the distance behind them, and when Carys looked over her shoulder, the grabbing hands and noisy chaos of their passage felt farther and farther away. The dreamlike melancholy that had pressed down on her as they walked through the darkness lifted, and she felt more like herself again.

"You said that was a gate." She looked at Duncan's back. "A gate between what?"

"The Brightlands and the Shadowlands," he said. "Between our home and Lachlan's. Quiet now."

Carys held on to the million questions that were jumping in her mind as she focused on the path they were hiking.

The hills evened out as they walked down the slope from the dark forest and through a thinner stand of trees. The path switched back and forth, and the undergrowth grew thinner. Hawthorn, ash, and oak mingled together, their discarded foliage leaving a golden-brown carpet between the trees while moss dripped from bare branches overhead. Verdant green blanketed tangled tree roots that reached up from the forest floor.

The moody grey skies covered them, and Carys could see no hint of sunlight. In the deep shadows of the hardwood forest around them, she caught glimpses of movement, thin figures darting among the trees, but she heard no birds.

There was a scattering rush of leaves as the wind picked up the fallen detritus and whirled it across the path.

"And you've been here before," she said. "You walked through that when you were young?"

"Yes."

"What is this place?" Carys was looking around, and she knew in her gut that this wasn't Scotland. Or at least no version of Scotland she knew. The landscape looked familiar, but there were no roads and no people in sight. She didn't see cows or sheep. There were no electrical lines or signs telling her where they were. The light felt flat somehow, as if the sky was painted a wash of grey blue that never changed.

"It should be night," Carys said.

"No, because it's night in the Brightlands, which means it's day here."

An alternate dimension? The thing that Laura had always told her was possible but she hadn't really believed. How on earth had they gotten here? By walking through a forest?

"Duncan, please." She stopped walking. "I need a real explanation. Where are we?"

He turned and glared at her. "I asked you if you believed in fairy tales and you said you did."

"I believe in fairy tales as a metaphor for life and the human experience. They're a learning tool to teach culture and..." She looked around at the strangely familiar but wholly foreign place. She pinched her hand. Hard. "This isn't a *metaphor*."

"Oh really?" He scowled. "I warned you to go back. Now we're here, so unless you've finally given up on this ludicrous quest—"

"No." She wanted to find Lachlan. She had to, but she needed answers now. "I want to keep going, but can you…"

There was a distant cry overhead, and it was not a bird. Or it wasn't any bird that Carys had ever known.

"I'll answer your questions, Carys Morgan." Duncan's voice was low and urgent. "But right now we're in the Borderlands. This is dark fae country."

Dark fae. This could not be real. She was losing her mind.

"And they do not like humans trespassing," he continued. "Especially not Brightkin like us. It's very wild here, so we need to keep going."

She looked back at the forest. "But he brought us."

"They can't stop us from entering because we came with Dru, but they don't like us—he's not very popular either—and we need to keep walking." He glanced around. "We'll be safer in the lowlands."

"Okay." Carys nodded and started to walk again. "Okay."

Duncan reached back and took her hand, squeezing it as they walked.

Dark fae. Duncan had said dark fae like they were real.

And whatever Dru had been bleeding back there, it was not human blood, which meant that Dru… wasn't human, or at least he wasn't human like she and Duncan were.

Wait, was Duncan human?

The movement in her peripheral vision was subtle and quick, but anytime she turned her head to look, the forest was a still landscape, like a painting hanging on a wall, save for flashes of red hawthorn berries breaking the monotonous canvas of brown, green, and black.

"Stop looking," he whispered. "They've noticed you."

"The dark fae?"

"Please, for the love of all things holy, be quiet and let me explain when we're not *here*."

She sucked in the torrent of far more important questions and muttered, "Really glad I'm not wearing that red coat."

He grunted something that might have been a laugh.

Long minutes later, the land evened out and the forest grew thinner. The occasional bird fluttered overhead, and insects began to chirp and saw through the bushes. Dark pines gave way to lighter hardwoods, and the occasional evergreen dotted the landscape along with hedgerows and widening paths.

Duncan's shoulders slowly relaxed as the land around them turned from brown, black, and grey to green and blue. "I keep a cottage that's not far from here. We can rest there, and you can change."

"Change?"

He paused, turned, and looked her up and down. "Yes."

They paused when a tall woman crossed their path. She came walking through the trees, stopped, and stared at them for a moment.

Carys couldn't speak. The woman was thin as a willow branch and nearly as tall. Her golden-brown hair was straight and fell down her back, threaded with leaves and a few bright, berry-laden twigs. Her skin was golden brown, her ears were pointed, and gold rings pierced the tips.

Duncan paused and gave the silent woman a deep nod, but he didn't speak.

She stared at Carys with obvious curiosity, and Carys stared back. The woman cocked her head and blinked thick-lashed brown eyes. Like Dru, she wore sigils on her face, but they were delicately drawn, fine lines curling like tendrils from the arches of her cheeks up to her temples and into her hairline.

The woman stared for a few silent moments, and then Carys blinked and she was gone.

After a long moment, Duncan kept walking, gripping Carys's hand in his.

"What was she?" Carys couldn't stop the question, but she kept her voice low. "Was that an elf?"

"Light fae. You'll see them out and about more than the dark."

Duncan helped her over a stone wall and across a rolling meadow with lights dancing just over waving heads of ripe wheat. The horizon was growing lighter but never truly bright. It was as if a thick fog covered the sun, making the sky glow but with no clear radiance.

As they walked, the land grew warmer and the colors brighter. It was awash in hues that reminded Carys of a watercolor painting. Purple and deep green trees, blue-green meadows, and soft-gold fields. She saw the first sheep when they climbed over the next stone wall, this one cut with steps from whatever shepherd trod the path they were walking.

Carys sighed with relief. "Sheep and stone walls. Things are getting more familiar."

"Wouldn't be any kind of Scotland without sheep," he muttered. "Even an alternate one."

There was smoke in the distance, a curling grey puff of human habitation that tickled her nose with its familiar smell. They passed into a lane that was rutted with narrow wheel tracks and turned right, following the well-worn mud path.

"My cottage is just over this next hill."

She wasn't winded, but she felt tired. Still, the thrill of the unknown pulled her to waking and her body responded. The hills rose beside them, blanketed in colors that became more familiar the longer Carys looked at them.

The colors, the light, the clouds in the sky. She remembered where she'd seen them before.

"My mother painted landscapes like this." She smiled a little bit, a wave of inexplicable calm touching her soul. "This place looks just like one of her paintings."

"She was an artist?"

"Yes. I can't draw anything though."

"You're a teacher." He nodded. "Like your father."

Carys frowned. So few people associated her mythology studies with her father's humble high school wood shop, and she was surprised Duncan had made the connection.

"Yes. My father loved to teach."

"Your mother wouldn't have been here." Duncan looked around.

"Maybe… in a dream. People dream of this place. Maybe some kind of memory through the eyes of her Shadowkin." He glanced over his shoulder. "But people from the Brightlands don't come to this place. Not on purpose."

"We're here."

"Yes, we are." He didn't sound happy about it. "And I'm going to hear about it."

When they reached the top of the hill, she saw it in the distance, just as she knew she would. A stone castle with four round towers, flags flying from the turrets and a high ridge with an old stone tower backing up to the castle. On the hills beyond, a dark forest stretched on for miles and miles. The only things missing were dragons flying overhead.

"I've seen this before," she murmured. "I know it."

"Come this way," he said quietly. "Quickly. They're used to seeing me, but you'll attract attention."

Duncan hustled her down a wider path, past an old oak tree hung with ribbons and bright coins. She could see what looked like a farm in the distance and more stone houses with smoke coming from them.

After the ribboned oak, they turned right and walked through a gate leading to a narrow path bordered by thick hedges. There was something in the underbrush that sounded like laughter, and a small animal scurried away.

"Mischief," Duncan muttered. "She better have been keeping the house if she's causing mischief."

"Who?"

"Auld Mags." He glanced over his shoulder. "I'll explain later."

"Yeah, you say that a lot."

The hedges opened, and in the middle of a bright meadow filled with long grasses, ferns, and coneflowers sat a round stone cottage with a thatched roof. There was a stacked chimney, and the garden around the house was filled with herbs and some overgrown vegetables.

"This is your house?" Behind the cottage was a neat shed with firewood stacked on the side, and beyond the shed, more trees. The forest was everywhere in this place. Lights winked from between the trees, and birds sang in a riot from the canopy. "It's beautiful."

Duncan grunted as they walked the winding path through the wild garden. "Lachlan keeps a room at Murrayshall House," he said. "He gave me this cottage for when I'm here." He walked to the arched wooden door, pushing it open and ushering Carys inside with one last guarded look over his shoulder.

"You don't keep it locked."

"I don't need to—it's protected." He immediately walked to the fireplace and threw some wood into the hearth, lifting an empty bowl that was sitting on the stones. "Let's get warm; then we'll find you some clothes and answer the million questions I see flying around your head."

She looked down at her sturdy hiking pants and shoes. "What's wrong with my clothes? I'm warm."

"You'll stand out." He looked her up and down. "That's going to be unavoidable, but we'll do what we can."

What Duncan could do was offer Carys a thick pair of overlong trousers made of a heavy woven fabric and a tunic that fell past her hips. He gave her a long tartan scarf to use as a belt and wrapped it around her shoulders for added warmth.

She walked out of the small bedroom at the back of the cottage to see Duncan already changed into a heavy kilt, a thick coat, and woolen clothes wrapped around his legs for warmth.

Carys looked down at herself—there wasn't a mirror in the place. Duncan looked like a highland warrior in a movie, and she looked like a child dressing in her older brother's clothes for a renaissance festival.

He nodded. "That'll do. Plenty of the women here don't wear dresses. The trousers won't stand out."

"As long as I don't trip on them."

"You can stuff the legs in your boots." He frowned. "Boots might be a problem. None of mine will fit you, and the cobbler will take time." He glanced up. "No department stores in this place."

"Why can't I wear my own?"

"I already told you you're going to stand out enough already."

Carys walked over and sat on the wooden bench across from Duncan. They were next to the fire, and the warmth was more than welcome in the stone house. The bowl was back on the hearth, this time full of what looked like milk.

Carys frowned at it. "Okay, question-and-answer time."

Duncan rose. "I should get you some food. Are you hungry?"

"Food later, answers now."

He wanted to say something else, but instead he sat back down.

"Fine." He crossed his arms over his chest. "What do you want to know?"

"Where are we?"

"Dru already told you. The Shadowlands. Scotland of the Shadowlands to be precise. They call it Alba."

"Alba." That was an old name. "And Lachlan was born here?"

Duncan frowned. "In a way. This is where he grew up."

"So this is an alternate dimension of some kind?" She felt like a fool just asking it, but was there another explanation?

"I asked you if you believed in fairy tales, Carys. *This* is the fairy tale. Or this is where they come from." He leaned forward and put his elbows on his knees. "All over the world, people used to believe in magic, in monsters, and in gods. You think they were stupid? They were as intelligent as you or I. Maybe more."

"So you're saying that this world used to be our world? That they... split somehow?"

"I don't know. Maybe things were more fluid once. There are gates between the Shadowlands and the Brightlands. The forest behind my house only has one of them. Things get through sometimes. Not often, but sometimes. That's why there are still fairy sightings in Scone. That's why there are still Bigfoot sightings in your home."

"Bigfoot isn't real," she murmured.

"Isn't he?"

A creeping fear slid along her skin. "If fairy tales are real. I mean *really* real—"

"You know they are." He stared into her eyes. "You're here. You saw the forest. That fae woman passed us on the road. Did you imagine that?"

"No, but—"

"But what?" He sat back and put his feet near the fire. "You've probably passed these gates before, but you won't want to go near them. Something about them would make you uneasy. Make you want to move away. And your modern, technology-trained mind probably dismissed strange lights in the forest or a shadow that seemed to move when it shouldn't." Duncan leaned forward. "A feeling in the pit of your stomach that doesn't make sense."

Carys looked into the fire. "That... flicker in the corner of your eye."

"Exactly."

Or the forest behind her house where her mother spoke to the trees.

Carys looked back at Duncan. "So you're saying that this place... the Shadowlands... have always been here?"

"I don't know." He shrugged. "I'm no expert on these things. You probably know more than I do based on what you teach. Whatever it is, wherever it came from, we're here now. This is the magic place, the otherworld—*not* the underworld—that's something else entirely according to Lachlan."

"The *other* world?" The annwn of Welsh mythology was the first thing that popped into her mind. Valhalla was another one. Worlds beside worlds, otherworlds where the gods dwelled and the brave survived even after death. She frowned. "Can people die here?"

"Oh yes." Duncan nodded. "People die. Fae can die too. I told you this isn't the underworld."

Carys's mind spun with the possibilities. A magic world living next to the real, grounded world. A world where magical creatures and magic existed. A world where Lachlan had grown up.

Duncan closed his eyes and sighed. "I've thought about this for years, and I still don't understand all of it. I suspect that over time, as our world became more and more steeped in science and technology, the gates became narrower, maybe some disappeared." He sat up and leaned toward the fire, holding his callused hands out to warm them. "The magic withdrew, but it didn't disappear. This place remained, populated by the wildness we'd left behind."

"So the humans here are...? Is Lachlan magic?"

"He's human." Duncan stood and started to pace a little bit. "But Shadowkin can learn to use magic. And some of them are a bit... They call it fae-touched here. Some humans have some natural magic. Lachlan is a bit fae-touched when it comes to music."

"So he was born here. If he has magic—"

"Nothing is born here but by magic," Duncan said softly. "Every person you meet here is the twin of another person in our world. A Shadowkin. Our wild twins. A mirror self we've lost in the mundane world." Duncan's voice grew quiet. "They're born when we are, souls taken by magic and brought here."

Carys blinked. "By who?"

"By the old gods? The fae, spirits, goblins." He shrugged. "Any of them? All of them?" Duncan turned his back to the fire but didn't sit down. "I don't know, but you've seen Lachlan. He's my mirror image, and according to my mother, she only had one baby on my birthday. I've seen others too, people here wearing the faces of men and women I know in my world, people I grew up with. Neighbors I pass in the street. The same faces but not the same people."

"Lachlan and you *are* identical," Carys mused. "Except in personality."

"Aye, that's the truth. He's the uninhibited me. The charming one. The artist and the dreamer." A brief smile twisted Duncan's mouth as he sat across from her again. "Not practical, pragmatic Duncan

Murray, the laird of Murrayshall." There was a sadness behind Duncan's eyes. "Everyone here is like that."

"You're saying everyone has a twin here." She frowned. "Everyone? Even me?"

Duncan turned his face to the fire. "Where were you born?"

"Wales. In a place called Caernarfon."

He nodded slowly. "Then your twin would have been taken there."

Carys tried to wrap her mind around that. "Shadowkin." Another her, walking around in this place steeped in magic. A sister in a sense, like Duncan and Lachlan were brothers. "So everyone we know in our world has a twin here?" She'd always wanted a sibling. A wild thrill fluttered in her chest. Maybe....

"No." Duncan's voice was harsh. "I said everyone in our world had a twin when they were born. Not all children..." He lowered his voice even though they were alone. "You heard the voices crying in the forest."

Carys felt a twisting in her stomach. "You mean..."

He nodded.

Duncan had said the dark fae lived here. And far from being bright, happy creatures of modern movies, real fae—those in the old stories— were tricky and conniving, immune to human morality, and they also hunted children. Sometimes for sport, sometimes to steal them for amusement, and sometimes to consume them as food.

Those stories didn't usually make it into the animated kids' movies.

But so much of this world... It felt familiar. Fae stealing children. Fairies granting gifts. Magic and the mundane living side by side. She'd read about this. She'd studied this.

She just never imagined she'd be living it.

"There are children who never make it out of the forest." Carys had seen the blue lights. She'd heard the cries. The broken part of her heart knew what it had been hearing.

Duncan stared at the fire. "My nanny told me that will-o'-the-wisps are the souls of lost children who weren't baptized. Maybe there's some truth in that."

It was a terrifying thought. "So Dru is fae?"

"Yes, but he left this place. He chooses to remain in the Brightlands."

"Fairies can do that?"

Duncan shrugged. "They can if they can find passage, but they rarely do. What's a fae without their magic? To live in the Brightlands, they have to be willing to give up most of their power and live surrounded by iron." He shook his head. "Hardly any are willing to do that."

"But you needed a fae to bring me here?"

"A fae. A wolf. A unicorn. Anything magic that's not human. The first time you go through the gate, you need a guide. Something native from the land. Things that live here can't enter our world unless they're guided, and mundane humans like us can't come here unless something from the Shadowlands brings them in. Once a gate knows you, it will usually let you pass—not always, they tend to have their own minds—but if you have no introduction, it will turn you out and turn you around."

"What else is here?" She stood and walked to the window, wondering about the creatures in the forest and the ones in the garden outside. What had that sound been? The bird that wasn't a bird.

"Dark and light fae obviously." Duncan sighed. "I haven't explored out of this area, but there are stories... You've seen the wisps. Nymphs in the water and sprites in the trees. Brownies take care of the houses." He motioned to the bowl of milk on the hearth. "They're quite easy to get along with as long as you respect them."

"What else?" A flash of realization hit her. "Other creatures? Magical creatures?"

He frowned. "Selkies in the ocean. Be careful for kelpies in the rivers and lochs, of course. Then there's—"

"Dragons?" The images from her mother's paintings filled her mind. "Are there dragons?"

"Aye." Duncan slowly nodded. "In some places there are dragons."

"Where?" Her heart began to race.

The corner of his mouth turned up. He knew exactly what she was asking. "There are dragons all over the world according to what I've heard." Duncan rose and walked toward her. "But in this land—Briton as they call it here—the dragons live where you were born, Carys Morgan. The dragons live in Wales."

CHAPTER SEVEN

"Dragons." She stared out the window as she munched on an apple Duncan picked from the small orchard behind the house. "I might see a dragon."

"As I said, the dragons live in Cymru. They don't call it Wales here —it's Cymru." He stuffed food into a pack, adding apples and wrapped wedges of cheese. "Are you ready?"

Carys wore a pair of boots stuffed with wool, an oversized coat, and a heavy hood that covered her head. "As ready as I can be. How far is the walk?"

"Not far. Half an hour maybe."

She wore her hair down at Duncan's instruction. The long dark waves falling around her shoulders not only helped to conceal her face but also kept her neck warm.

As they walked, they passed through a small village and met a few people, all of them greeting Duncan in Gaelic. He waved back but didn't introduce her, and they didn't ask. Children ran around the village, climbing on wagons and running from house to house.

"Do you know these people?" she asked quietly. "Or know them in the other world?"

"Some but not all." He nodded at a couple who was standing outside what looked like a butcher shop. "She's a teacher at the village school. I think he's a salesman of some kind."

"But the same couple?" she asked. "Married here and there?"

"It's fairly common," Duncan said. "People seem to be drawn to each other. Families even. Humans in the Shadowlands can't birth children, but the fae usually give children to their mother's twin or another close relation." He kept his voice low as they walked. "It's not a rule. Remember, twins are different people."

"That's evident."

Duncan was harsh and grumpy and borderline rude most of the time while Lachlan had never met a stranger and made you feel special just by smiling at you.

Still, she couldn't deny that Duncan was protective, and in that moment, it was comforting.

"So Lachlan came back here," she said. "On his own?"

"No." He glanced at her. "At least I doubt it. I saw fae in the woods behind my house the day you say he disappeared," Duncan said.

"You think the fae are the ones who took him?"

"They can travel from gate to gate differently than humans can. That's why he could be in California one moment and Scotland the next." Duncan nodded at a passing man with a handcart. "So I imagine it was the fae."

"Why would they care if he was in the Brightlands?"

"They wouldn't, but they'd be doing a favor for Lachlan's father." Duncan scowled. "Our fathers were the same on both sides. Arrogant, imperious, and commanding. But while mine was an aloof business mogul who is dead, his father is the living king of Alba."

Carys whispered, "Shit."

Lachlan really was a rich prince running away from responsibilities.

"King... Chieftain." Duncan waved a hand. "They don't have government the way we do. It's not that organized. Things are much more fluid here. Robb is more like a chief of chiefs than a king, but because this area is closest to the other kingdoms in Briton, he's the figurehead. It's not like that in Anglia or Cymru. They're more formal in the hierarchy."

Carys nodded. "Right. Wales is Cymru here."

"Yes. They use the old names for—"

"And Wales is independent?"

Duncan scoffed. "Independent? They have *dragons*, Carys. No one fights a king who commands dragons."

She felt a well of pride and satisfaction and could only imagine how her father would have felt. To the day he died, Gareth Morgan had been a staunch believer in Welsh independence.

"We have dragons," she whispered to herself. And her mother had seen them. Maybe, as Duncan had told her, only in dreams. But maybe not. Maybe she'd also wandered through a gate without knowing. Just because Duncan didn't think it was possible didn't mean it didn't happen.

A shout from a little boy had Carys looking up, and she saw that they'd turned on a road that led up to the great stone castle she'd seen from the hill. Standing below it, it seemed far more imposing and grittier than it had looked from a distance.

The road leading up to the castle quickly grew crowded with tradespeople, horses, and carts, and everything seemed to be made of wood. She glanced at Duncan. "Not much work for you here."

"What's that?"

She pointed to the wooden carts. "No metal?"

"Ah." He shook his head. "No *iron*. Some copper. More bronze."

"Definitely no cars."

"No buildings over three stories either." He looked around. "This place is backward, and it's mostly because of the iron. Iron and magic."

"So the iron thing is true." It had been ages since she'd actively studied Celtic mythology and British fairy tales. Most of her current classes were far more academic than practical.

In fairy lore, the fae hated iron and were burned by its touch. It made sense that in a realm they controlled, the metal would be forbidden. "That makes sense."

Duncan shot her a look.

"I mean it makes sense for fae," she muttered. "It's their biggest weakness. Right?"

"Yes. The fae control all the resources here. There's very little mining. There is nothing electric. That's why I said to leave your phone." He patted his waist. "Even blades are very limited."

"Why do they have so much power?" She looked around. "There are so many people here."

"There are people because the fae allow it."

"How—" She sucked in a breath and whispered, "The gates. Population control."

Duncan nodded grimly. "They hate anything modern that humans have made, and since they control the children, they make the rules." Duncan grumbled. "Human rulers pay tribute or their population declines swiftly."

Barbaric.

And effective. No human population was going to rebel when their hope for a future was held like a blade to their throat.

"Are there more fae than humans?"

"No," he said. "But they're more powerful."

Duncan and Carys got in the line that formed at the gate of the castle, and she saw guards checking all the people going inside. The guards were wearing thick armor of layered leather over heavy woolen clothes and carrying swords at their waists that looked like they were made of bronze.

There were archers stationed on a lower wall above them, but they seemed at ease, and Carys could hear joking and laughing as they strolled along the parapet.

"Just go along with it but keep your cloak up," Duncan said in a low voice. "Some of them will speak English." They slowly moved forward in the line. "They're used to foreigners at the castle. All the traders come through here."

They reached the front of the line, and a male guard checked Duncan for weapons, exchanging a few words with him in Gaelic that sounded routine. A woman in lighter leathers with a bow on her back walked over to check Carys, patting her down with indifferent efficiency.

The guards tied a bright red knot around Duncan's small blade and waved them through.

"Did the guard look at your face?" Duncan's voice was soft.

"Not really. She was checking my clothes."

"Good."

"Why?"

Duncan growled under his breath, "That's for Lachlan to explain."

Through the gates of the castle there were markets and trading going on in earnest, voices going back and forth between English and Gaelic. Women and men wearing white aprons were negotiating with farmers for vegetables and livestock. Tradesmen smoked pipes and shouted out their wares as they sat on the back of wooden carts. Men and women wearing leather armor strolled through the melee, seemingly at ease with the security of the castle yard.

The people around her looked familiar despite the clothes. Faces were as diverse as those in any major city in Europe.

Carys smiled. "Doesn't look like any fantasy movie we've seen on-screen, does it?"

Duncan frowned until he noticed her watching a family of traders with light brown skin and brightly colored clothes that appeared to be Middle Eastern.

He smiled. "Well, not everyone in Scotland these days looks like me, do they?"

Carys smiled. "True."

"I think they're from the south." He nodded at the wagon selling beautifully worked copper pots lined with tin. "Many traders from Anglia will make their way north to sell their goods, and most things from the continent go into London first."

"Makes sense, I guess."

Carys was startled to see a grubby-faced boy run past with a cartoon character on his shirt, which he quickly covered up when he saw Carys looking. His cheeky grin had her eyes going wide.

"Did he have a—"

"Superhero shirt?" Duncan nodded. "Aye. Everyone here knows the Brightlands exist. They're not ignorant. There's a bit of a black market for anything that comes from there. I could make a fortune in millet if I wanted to import designer denim jeans I bet." He smirked. "But I have quite enough millet."

He led them through the bustling yard and toward a stone edifice with red-painted double doors and spoke to the guards in English.

"Duncan, Laird of Murrayshall, for Lachlan, son of Robb."

The guard smiled. "Laird Duncan, welcome back to Sgàin Castle. Lachlan is hearing audience in the North Hall with his father today. Would you like to be announced?"

Duncan cleared his throat. "I'd prefer to speak to him privately if that can be arranged."

The guard turned to Carys. "And your compan— Gods alive." The man's face went pale when he looked at Carys. "My lady." His face flashed through a dozen expressions in the space of a moment. Shock. Fear. Happiness. Confusion. "My lady?"

Duncan jumped in. "Sir, we need to speak to Lachlan."

Carys looked between the men, trying to keep her head down, but it was impossible to miss the look of shock on the guard's face. Was it so unusual to see someone from the regular world here? They hadn't reacted to Duncan that way.

"We need to speak to Lachlan," Duncan repeated.

"Of course." The man looked at Carys again with wide eyes, then turned and opened the door. "You know the way, Laird Duncan. If you could..." He trailed off, looking at Carys again, then back to Duncan. "They're in the North Hall."

"We'll find him." Duncan put his hand on the man's shoulder. "I appreciate it, and please be discreet."

The guard nodded. "Of course." With one last look at Carys, the man closed the door, leaving Carys and Duncan in a round stone chamber that branched into two corridors lit by glowing blue lamps.

"What is going on?"

Duncan took Carys by the hand and turned left. "We're going to find Lachlan, that's what's going on."

Her heart was racing, and despite the strangeness of the journey to get there, despite the unearthly world they were in, the castle, the guards who looked like they were a historic reenactment, all she could think about was seeing Lachlan again.

She looked at Duncan and felt grateful. Despite everything, she was grateful. "Listen, Duncan—"

"This is the part where you start to hate me." His voice was brusque. "Just so you know."

A twisting knot of dread landed in her belly and quelled her excitement. Hate? Why would she hate him?

They walked swiftly down the corridor, Duncan dragging Carys behind him. As they walked, voices speaking in English grew louder, the sound echoing from various directions. Carys was completely turned around until Duncan abruptly turned right, walking straight through an archway guarded by four more guards who shouted at them.

"Lord Duncan—"

"Not a fucking lord here or anywhere," Duncan growled. "I'm here to see my brother."

"Lord Robb is entertaining emissaries from the Northern Islands today and—"

"Don't care."

The crest at the end of the hall was a giant gold shield with two brilliant unicorns rearing, their horns touching as a purple thistle grew between them.

A throne sat under the shield where a dour man sat with a simple gold circlet banded around his forehead, and to his right...

Carys couldn't stop her smile. "Lachlan."

She felt her heart leap in her chest.

He was wearing a gold circlet the same as his father's, his long hair flowing over his shoulders, longer than it had been when he left her. Their eyes met and he stood, his jaw falling open though no words came from his mouth.

Carys's heart raced, and she let out something between a laugh and a cry.

He was alive.

She blinked back tears. Carys had almost been afraid she'd imagined him, that he'd been a dream she had conjured from loneliness and grief. But he was there, the same beautiful green eyes. The same soft smile. He was staring at her, and his eyes were full of love.

Whispered voices grew in the hall, dozens of voices whispering in Gaelic as more and more people turned to her and Duncan.

A young woman with long braided hair sitting beside Lachlan turned, looked at Carys, and cried out, a hand going to her mouth to cover the sound. Her dark eyes went wide, and she shook her head back and forth.

An older woman with silver-blond braids sat on the king's left side, wearing a crown set with purple and green stones. She rose to her feet, and her head cocked to the side as she stared at Carys. She was the first person who spoke, and it was in a gentle English accent.

"Seren? Gods alive, is it really you?"

CHAPTER EIGHT

The hall behind them erupted in voices speaking English and Gaelic as Lachlan rushed toward them, grabbing Carys by the arm and shoving Duncan through the archway and toward a passage to the right.

"Lord Lachlan!" the guards shouted at them. "Sir!"

"No!" He threw up a hand and kept his face on the corridor in front of them. "Leave us."

Moments later, they were in a long corridor with heavy purple curtains covering the archways, a rich brown carpet under their feet worked with silver thread, and gold-framed portraits lining the walls.

Carys's heart was racing when Lachlan finally turned to her and threw his arms around her.

"You're here." His arms were like a vise. "Oh gods, you're here." He took her face between his hands and planted a desperate kiss on Carys's lips.

She soaked it up like a tree dying for water. Her arms came around him, her breasts pressed to his chest, and their lips met in a desperate reunion. Lachlan kissed her over and over, like a man starving, his arms binding Carys to his body as she melted into his chest.

Duncan cleared his throat. "I'll just…"

"No!" Lachlan pulled away, still keeping Carys locked in his arms. "You stay." He turned back to Carys and swallowed hard. "You're here. How are you here?" He couldn't stop looking at her. "Gods alive, Carys, how are you here?"

"What are you talking about?" She started to cry. "You disappeared. I wasn't even sure you were alive until I saw you a minute ago. You disappeared without a word or a note or anything, and I knew that wasn't like you. I knew something was wrong."

"I didn't want to go. Trust me." He kissed her forehead, her cheeks, her eyes. "I never wanted to leave you. I was walking in the forest, and I strayed too close to a fae gate. They took me and—"

"Again…" Duncan tried to speak. "This is private and I'll just—"

"What were you thinking?" Lachlan wheeled on his brother. "You know the danger of bringing her here!"

"You didn't leave me much choice, did you?" Duncan stalked toward Lachlan. "The way you romanced her, ye daft idiot. What was I supposed to do when she comes knocking on my door and threatening to go to the police with a passport that you know was forged with *my* likeness on it?"

Lachlan shoved Carys behind his back and stood between her and Duncan. "Don't blame this on Carys. Don't you dare blame her."

Duncan jabbed a finger in Lachlan's chest. "I'm not blaming her, I'm blaming *you*."

The brothers fell into yelling at each other in a confusing mix of Gaelic and English, Lachlan speaking more in the Scottish tongue and Duncan speaking more words that Carys recognized but made no sense nonetheless.

"Lachlan, please." Carys tried to break in. "Can we not argue? Duncan's right—this is my fault. I forced his hand."

"He knew better." Lachlan kept his voice low but urgent. "You being here is so dangerous I don't even want to—"

"What did you expect her to do, Brother? She's nae an idiot. You had to know she was going to have questions."

"And you couldn't think of a better way to explain all this?"

"Are you joking?"

Carys stepped to the side and raised a hand. "Still here."

Duncan shoved Lachlan toward her. "Look! She's here. Your ladylove, Brother. Go. You might have a few things to explain now, don't you think? She's not an idea or a dream, she—"

"She was never that and you know it. I never intended to—"

"Oh, but you did, didn't you? You never *intended* to stay so long. You never *intended* to make her fall in love with you. You never *intended*—"

"I love her!" Lachlan shouted at Duncan, the words ripping across the argument, leaving silence in their wake.

Duncan stepped back, and his face was a stoic mask.

"She..." Lachlan looked at Carys, and she saw tears in the corners of his eyes. "She made me want to live again." He started to shake his head. "I never meant to fall in love. I know we come from different worlds."

Duncan swallowed hard. "What you've done..." He let out a ragged breath.

Lachlan shook his head. "I'll not apologize. I refuse to apologize for loving her."

"I love you too." Carys swallowed the tears that welled up in her throat and tried to get Lachlan to turn to her. "It's okay, Lachlan."

"No." Duncan's mouth was a thin, angry line. "It's really not."

Lachlan broke into Gaelic again and walked away from Carys, shoving Duncan against the wall. Duncan pushed back, responding in the same language while the argument escalated.

Carys tried to follow what they were speaking about, but none of it made sense and most of it was in a language she didn't even understand. She was worried the two men might come to blows, but she knew there was no way she could stop them, so she got out of the way.

Even with all the shouting, Carys felt like she could breathe for the first time in a month. Lachlan was here. In front of her. He was alive, and even though the circumstances were... confusing to say the least, she felt the familiar swell of warmth and comfort as soon as she was in Lachlan's presence.

He was here. He was safe. And he loved her. They could figure out the rest.

She looked around her at a corridor that reminded her of Duncan's home in Scotland. There were family portraits as old as the ones in Duncan's house and some that looked considerably older.

The tartan in the pictures was different, and while many of the faces were familiar from Duncan's family home, most of the faces were new. As Lachlan and Duncan continued to fight, she found herself drawn to the canvases that decorated the walls.

Green eyes, dark hair. Red hair, blue eyes. Lachlan's parents appeared to be the same as Duncan's, at least in their appearance. She glanced over her shoulder to see the two men, so alike in appearance but so different in personality.

Lachlan had turned on his charming voice, as if he was trying to reason with Duncan, and Carys scoffed, knowing that was unlikely to do anything but enrage the ornery man.

Duncan's voice dropped to a low growl as Carys continued walking down the hall, until her eyes fell on what appeared to be a wedding portrait and she froze.

Lachlan's face.

Her face.

Her face.

The woman in the portrait was her mirror image save for the dark brown braids draped over her shoulders, threaded with ribbon and falling past her waist. Her chin was lifted in pride, and a bright gold dragon crest was pinned to her red velvet dress. She wore a crown fixed with rubies, and the frame at the bottom of the portrait read:

Lachlan, Lord Moray, son of Robb, wedded to Seren, Nêrys Ddraig, princess of Cymru.

It was Lachlan and her.

Not her.

Not Carys but Seren, the name that the woman in the hall had called her.

The name of Lachlan's late wife.

"Tell me about your wife."

"We grew up together. I can't remember a time I didn't love Seren. Then she got sick and I lost her. I thought I'd die too, but I didn't."

Her fingers touched the surface of the portrait, touched the cheek of the woman who could only be her twin in this world, and Carys halfway expected to feel her fingertips touch her own skin.

Seren. Her twin.

She turned to Lachlan and Duncan, who had stopped arguing and were staring at her.

Lachlan walked toward her, his hands raised. "Carys, I can explain."

"What is this?" She pointed to the portrait.

Lachlan spoke slowly. "It's my wedding portrait."

To a wife who wore Carys's face.

She felt her stomach drop. "Oh God."

The room around her started to spin, and she pressed her hand to the wall near the portrait, her fingers digging into the cold stone.

"Carys, I can explain."

"Can you?" She forced out the words, forced her eyes to focus on Lachlan. "Who am I?"

"You're you," Duncan said through gritted teeth. "And don't forget it."

"Of course you're you, Carys." Lachlan's voice was low and soothing, a voice she loved coming from the man she loved. "And I love *you*."

"Who is... *she*?" She was trembling with rage. Fear. Confusion. She felt the tears welling in her eyes because she knew.

She knew.

"Seren," Lachlan whispered, looking into her eyes.

Carys's hands were shaking, and she gripped them to keep herself from shattering to pieces. "She's me, isn't she? She's *my* twin. And your wife. The one who died."

"Her name was Seren," Duncan said. "She died two years ago."

Two years ago, the same time that Carys had been laid low with a bout of depression that had never made sense. A grueling blackness that had left her feeling like half her soul was missing.

Because it had been.

"Oh God." She gasped. "Oh *God*!"

Lachlan ran to her. "You have to understand. I was drowning in grief." He grabbed her wrists, trying to look at her. "All I wanted was to find you and see your face and know that part of her was alive somewhere in the world and then..."

Don't say it. Don't say it. She squeezed her eyes shut to try to block out the betrayal.

"I love you." Lachlan pressed his cheek to hers and whispered desperate words. "You have to believe—"

"It wasn't me." Her heart shattered. "You didn't love *me*."

"I did. I *do*."

She shook her head over and over again, wrenching her arms away from him. "You never loved me. It was her. You loved her so much that you... *Oh God*."

She wanted to fall. She wanted to curl up in a ball and fade into nothing, but that would leave her at the mercy of Lachlan and Duncan, the two people in the world who knew what a fool she'd been.

"No!" Lachlan shouted. "Carys, that's what I'm telling you." His beautiful eyes pleaded with her. "Please, you have to believe me. I love you. My love for Seren—"

"Best not bring up that name at the moment, Brother," Duncan muttered.

"Shut up!" Lachlan's face turned red and he rounded on his brother. "This is your fault!"

"My fault?"

He's not real. He's not real. None of this is real.

Carys saw a half-open curtain at the end of the corridor and she ran.

SHE THREW up the hood that had covered her face—to hide her resemblance to her twin, she understood that now—and searched for the first door she could find. The castle was a labyrinth, the blue-lit sconces flickering eerie shadows as she ran down one hall and then another.

Carys was searching for anything that looked like daylight or whatever version of it existed in this place. She had no identification, no escort, but she was hoping the guards would be less concerned about those leaving the castle than those entering.

She had to get away. If she could find her way back to the main road, she might be able to find Duncan's cottage. She wanted her own clothes. She wanted to get back to the creepy forest— Okay, she didn't want to go back to the fairy murder forest, but she wanted to get home more than anything. Or at least back to Scotland.

Duncan was right. She'd been stupid to come here, foolish to want to see Lachlan. She should have walked away the moment the grumpy Scotsman asked if she believed in fairy tales.

None of the magic of this place could soothe the pain that was tearing at her chest and making her eyes well with angry, heartbroken tears.

She turned right, then left, trying to find a way out of the castle maze.

"Carys!" She heard Lachlan's voice echoing somewhere in the castle. Or maybe it was Duncan's. Impossible to tell; even their voices sounded the same. She took another right.

"Carys?"

None of it was real.

What were you thinking? Every nasty doubt she'd pushed away and tried to overcome at the beginning of her relationship with Lachlan reared its head and whispered in her mind.

He's too good for you.

Who would love a depressed academic with boring taste in books?

You're a burden, with your sad orphan eyes.

She ducked to the side as what looked like a group of cooks walked down a hallway. Carys darted past them, desperately searching for a door, turning down a narrow corridor when she heard voices that sounded like those in the courtyard earlier.

Handsome princes don't want damaged goods.

Behind her, she heard voices starting to rise, and someone shouted her name in a voice she didn't recognize.

"Carys!"

"Seren?"

Seren.

Lachlan's wife. The sister she would never know, the sister who had loved Lachlan best, the proud princess dressed in red velvet with a dragon on her shoulder. How could she compete with *that*?

"Carys!" It was Duncan's voice. Something in the rough timbre told her it was him, and he was getting closer.

She hated him. Hated him for bringing her here, hated him for forcing her to see the truth.

You were right, Duncan. I really do hate you.

She pushed open a wooden door and nearly fell into a cobblestone courtyard teeming with traders, workmen, and soldiers. She looked over their heads and saw the large arched castle gate in the distance. She picked up a broken basket someone had discarded on the ground and pulled her hood forward, hoping to blend in with the market customers.

In the short time she'd been inside, the castle yard had become a riot of energy. Voices of every type, women pushing apples into her face. Children darting around her legs, and somewhere above it all, a group of men were singing.

Carys pressed into the crowd and walked toward the great wooden gate she and Duncan had walked through, gasping a little when she nearly ran into a giant wearing green corded leggings. She looked up to see a man with dark curling hair, arched cheekbones, and rich reddish-brown skin looking down at her with a curious expression. She blinked when she saw his pointed ears pierced with a dozen gold rings.

"Sorry," she muttered at the tall fae before she tried to move around him.

"Nêrys ddraig?"

Carys blinked. "No, my name is—" She caught herself before she gave her name to a fae. "Not Nêrys."

Had she misheard? How could the fae man know her name?

She pressed on, turning away from the fae but still heading toward the gate. A dog barked at her ankles, and a short figure pulled it by the collar. It looked up, and Carys realized it wasn't a child as she'd thought but some kind of shorter creature with large eyes, a stubby nose, and a wispy beard.

It shouted something in a language she couldn't understand.

Not real. Not real.

Except it was so very, very real.

Her feet were raw and blistered in Duncan's oversized boots, but Carys blocked the pain and kept going. She might not be a star athlete —might have failed on every school team she tried out for—but one thing she was really good at was walking.

She walked over rough cobblestones and muddy puddles. Around wagons and through the overwhelming barnyard smell of cows, horses, and pigs that were herded through the castle yard.

The massive wooden gate loomed in the distance, and she hunched her shoulders and walked in that direction, hoping that whoever had been calling her name was still searching the twisting hallways of the stone edifice behind her.

Get out. Get away. Back to the cottage. Back to the forest.

Soldiers stood on either side of the gate, but as she'd expected, they were watching who was coming in far more than who was leaving.

She scooted closer to a group of brightly dressed traders who were speaking in English, laughing about a deal they'd just made on fabric. Keeping close to their group, she slipped past the castle guards, under the massive wooden portico, and crossed the drawbridge.

She was out.

CHAPTER NINE

Once the castle was behind her, Carys let out a sigh and slowed her steps a little, moving out of the way before she was run over by a market cart. She stood on the side of the road to survey the lane before her and the dark rise of the hills beyond.

The main road bisected the town that surrounded the castle. To the left, lanes led off toward taller wood-and-plaster buildings that climbed up the hill leading toward the ridge where an old stone tower stood guard. There were carts and horses walking through the lanes. Signs hung from shop windows, and men and women swept off the wooden stoops in front of the tall buildings.

To the right, sloping downhill, were squat houses and patched gardens. Dogs trotted through cobbled streets, and cats lazed on thatch roofs. There was an eye-catching mix of homespun garments and brightly dyed T-shirts hanging from clotheslines. The garish mix of modern and ancient arrested her eyes as she took everything in.

Outside one house, a line of plastic flags flapped along the top of a woven wattle fence. There was a broken mirror hanging prominently on the wall of a whitewashed house, and a plastic cartoon mouse topped a scarecrow in a back garden.

This was a human world, but it wasn't hers. There was no metal, no hum of electricity in the air. There were no phone or electrical lines crossing overhead, but the atmosphere was anything but silent. The town clamored as she walked through it, bursting with the magical and the mundane.

To her right, a rotund shopkeeper conversed with a squat creature that looked like a dwarf or a goblin of some kind. Their postures reminded her of the old farmers back home—both the man and the creature stood with their hands on their hips, heads nodding as they chatted.

A willowy fae woman was bent over in a garden plot to her right, examining something next to a housewife with long grey braids. They chatted in Gaelic, the human woman gesticulating passionately as the fae woman nodded along.

Carys saw birds she didn't recognize flying overhead and the occasional flutter of something that might have been a sprite or a nymph that flashed brightly in the flat morning light, then disappeared before she could make out anything concrete.

She was walking through a fairy tale but not like any she could have imagined. Nothing like the stories she'd been told. This was gritty and familiar, but walking through it instead of reading in the safe pages of a book meant that Carys was becoming overwhelmed, and it wasn't only because of the emotional turmoil of seeing Lachlan again.

She needed to get back to Duncan's cottage. Even if she had to find her way back to the fae gate by herself, she needed to get away.

Beyond the houses sloped a huge meadow that looked almost like an athletic field. The town commons maybe? She saw some animals grazing and a group of children flying kites. There was a small lake at the bottom of the hill, and birds flew low over the water.

Past the town the hills rose up, covered with trees. One side seemed much darker than the other, so she decided to head that way.

The Borderlands, Duncan had called it.

She needed to find Duncan's cottage, get her stuff, and get back to the Borderlands. From there, the giant creepy fairy forest that stole tiny human souls should probably be easy to find.

Carys started walking again, down the main road and past the shops, the houses, and all the morning traffic, barely looking up until the crowds thinned and the road grew narrow.

When she reached a fork in the road, she finally looked around and saw that the houses were scattered, the town was far behind her, and she had no idea where she was.

Dammit.

She swallowed hard and debated what she should do. Duncan's cottage. If she could find that, she'd have a start. Maybe she could wait a little bit. He'd probably come back, right? If Duncan came back, maybe he could take her back to Scotland.

She hated both Duncan and Lachlan, but that seemed like the best option.

The trees and greenery around the road where the forks branched off looked like the area around Duncan's house. She had no idea how long she'd been walking, but maybe someone would recognize his name.

"Sir?" She pulled her hair forward to hide her face as much as possible and flagged down an old man pushing a cart up the hill toward the castle. "Do you... speak English?"

He held his fingers together. "Little."

The old man was dressed in clothes much like her own, woolen trousers and a long tunic belted around the waist. At his neck, she saw a metal chain of some kind that winked brightly beneath all the brown and tan clothing.

She cocked her head, and the man saw her looking.

He grinned and pulled the necklace from his tunic. It was a charm she'd seen a thousand times at a hundred tourist shops on the California coast, a pair of crossed surfboards with bright orange and yellow enamel, the word CALIFORNIA spelled out in swirling green letters.

"California." She smiled.

"Brightlands," the man said carefully. "From Brightlands."

She smiled. That charm had traveled as far as she had, and she suddenly felt a little more at home. "Duncan Murray?"

"Laird Duncan?" He nodded dramatically and pointed to the castle. "Castle."

She shook her head. "House? Uh... cottage?"

"Ah." He walked toward the left fork of the road and pointed in that direction. "House."

"That way?" She pointed at the left fork.

"Yes." He pointed, then made a gesture that looked like his hands were growing into branches. "Craobh."

Carys asked, "A tree?"

"Yes." The man nodded. "Tree. Craobh-dharaich." He made the gesture for the tree again, then moved his hand in a hard right. "Ri taobh na coille."

"Turn right by the tree." Carys nodded. "Duncan's house?"

"Yes." He nodded again. "Duncan Murray."

"Th—" She quickly caught herself. The old man was human. Probably. Better safe than sorry though. "I appreciate it."

"Tapadh leat." The old man winked at her.

"I don't know what that means." She kept smiling and nodded a little bit.

"Thank you," the man said carefully. "Tapadh leat."

If the old man was saying thank you to her, it was probably safe to respond the same way, and all the manners Carys's father had drilled into her demanded she show gratitude. Taking a chance, Carys mustered up the memory of the rudimentary Welsh her mother had taught her. "Diolch yn fawr."

"Ah!" The man's bushy grew eyebrows went up. "Cymru?"

Carys put her hand over her heart, feeling a swell of warmth. "Yes. I'm... Cymru."

"Good." The old man gave her a thumbs-up. "Good."

Carys waved goodbye, then started down the lane in the direction the old man had indicated. She walked for a few minutes, then saw a large oak tree growing in the middle of the road with ribbons hanging from the lower branches, pennies pushed into the trunk, and offerings of flowers, cakes, and milk left in bowls nestled among the gnarled, mossy roots. Just beyond the tree was a pathway that jumped over a stone wall and led into a stand of trees.

Carys didn't recognize the oak tree from her morning walk with Duncan, but maybe she'd taken a wrong turn. She didn't clearly remember all the paths that Duncan had taken this morning, but she did remember that his house was on the edge of a forest. The old man had seemed very certain that Duncan's house was right by the tree. Maybe this was the back way to his cottage.

She walked into the forest, wary of the dense trees that reminded her too much of the fae forest where she and Duncan had entered the Shadowlands, but there was none of the whispering voices or darkness that she remembered.

Though it was shadowed and dense, the oaks and ashes looked like an ordinary forest. Dotted among the hardwood trees were taller pines, first sparse, then growing thicker the farther she walked down the path. There was no bright sun casting shadows above the canopy, and the forest floor was littered with unfamiliar leaves, but the trees felt peaceful and birdsong filled the air.

The path through the forest was wide and even, indicating to Carys that this was a well-used path. There were occasional signs along the path that she couldn't read with arrows pointing off in some directions.

It felt a little like a city park. Carys reached out and ran her fingers along the trunk of a pine, and immediately a whisper came to her through the trees that made her freeze.

There were words on the wind, songs she couldn't understand that reminded her of some faint childhood memory of sand and sea and her mother singing to the cedar trees.

She lifted her hand from the tree trunk and looked up to see a black crow peering down at her.

"Caw!" The bird looked at her with a shining black eye, then hopped down the branch a little. "Caw!" It looked again, then flew away.

She felt a tug in her chest, urging her to follow the bird. She craned her head around a gnarled oak tree and peered down a narrow, winding path leading toward a darker part of the forest. The trees grew taller there. They were dense and wild, overgrown with moss and dotted with bright red hawthorn berries. She felt it again, a tugging instinct in her belly.

She forgot the pain in her swollen feet, and the taste of ripe berries touched her tongue.

Something was there. Was it the path to Duncan's cottage?

She heard whispers as she stepped onto the path; the crow looked at her, then flew a little farther. From the corner of her eye, light danced in the distance and Carys froze.

Don't follow the lights, my Carys. They want to lead you away from me.

Her mother's voice whispered in her mind, and she stepped back onto the wide forest path. No. This wasn't the time or the place to explore.

As Carys stepped back onto the path, she thought she heard the faint sound of laughter coming through the trees, but she turned her face and started walking again.

Back to the cottage.

Through the fae gate.

Back to the normal world.

Fly home to Baywood as soon as possible.

Try to forget Lachlan Murray ever existed.

The last thought left an ache in her chest.

How was she supposed to forget the man who'd made her feel alive? How was she supposed to stop loving Lachlan when her heart told her it didn't care if he loved Seren first? Did it matter? Maybe she could live with knowing she was second best.

She was immediately disgusted by her own thoughts.

Self-respect, Carys. She heard her father's voice. *Pick your head up, my girl. You're as good as any of them.*

"Better." She continued walking on the path.

She came to a clearing and heard a rustling in the bushes, then a child's cry.

Carys froze, wary of any unfamiliar sounds, but this time there was nothing otherworldly about the small noise. There was a huff, a pained exhalation, and then a whimpering sniffle that turned into a plaintive sob.

She stepped toward the trees, peeking around the yellow-leaved brush to see a little girl around five or six on the ground, her ankle twisted in a hole. She had a grubby face, brown hair, and dark brown eyes that were filled with tears when she looked up at Carys.

"I hurt my foot."

Carys was surprised the girl spoke English, but she immediately bent down to help. "You poor thing. Did you trip?"

The little girl nodded. "I was running after my cousin, and he ran away with his friends and I couldn't catch up. They run much faster than me."

"Don't worry." Carys dug around the girl's ankle, loosening the soil in what looked like a small animal burrow. "You'll catch up when you're bigger. In fact, I bet you'll be the fastest runner of them all." She pulled the girl's narrow ankle from the hole, already seeing where the joint had swelled. "Oh kiddo, that looks like it hurts."

"It does hurt." She sniffed. "But I won't cry. I promise. Do you have a potion?"

Carys's eyebrows went up. "A potion?"

The little girl nodded. "For my ankle. Humans have potions sometimes."

Carys stood quickly and looked down at the little girl. "Humans have... Are you not human?" All of Duncan's warnings about talking to the fae came rushing back, and Carys felt like a fool.

"I am right now, silly." The little girl leaned forward and tried to stand but couldn't. "Can you help me?" She held out her hand.

The child wasn't acting like she was trying to trick or trap Carys, and it was impossible to leave a helpless little girl in the middle of the forest when she was injured. Could fae even get injured?

After a moment of hesitation, Carys squatted down. "Can you ride on my back if I help you up?"

The girl giggled. "Yes."

"Okay, let's try that." She turned, and the little girl put her arms around Carys's shoulder and her legs around her waist. Soon she was carrying the child through the forest like a backpack.

"This is fun!"

Carys was glad the little girl sounded cheerful. Her ankle was swelling to the size of a grapefruit. "Can you point me the way to your house?"

"Oh, we don't live in a house, but I can show you where our meadow is."

"Your... meadow?"

"It's the prettiest meadow!" The little girl started bouncing. "Come on. I'll show you where to go."

Okay. Maybe the girl's family was itinerant. Maybe they lived in wagons or tents. She didn't look hungry, and while she was grubby from playing in the forest, her hair was neatly braided, and from the weight on Carys's back, she was well fed.

The child proceeded to give Carys directions through the forest, taking small paths and jumping over little streams that flowed downhill toward a glimmering blue body of water that peeked through the trees.

"Is that a lake?"

"The loch?"

"Right," Carys whispered. "A *loch*."

The loch stretched out from the forest, calm and smooth and bright as it reflected the pearl-grey sky. Birds sang in the trees, and the only break in the glassy surface of the water was the ducks cutting across the mirrorlike surface with a line of ducklings paddling behind them.

As they reached the edge of the loch, the child pulled on Carys's shoulders. "My mother told me not to go near the water."

Carys smiled. "That's good advice when you're alone, but you're not alone, are you?"

The path they'd been taking through the forest was twisted and uneven. Roots and rough stones threatened to trip Carys in her large boots, and it was hard to watch the path when she was getting directions from her little guide.

She looked at the smooth ground running along the edge of the peaceful loch where birds nested. Just then, a deer broke through the trees in the distance, walked to the edge of the water, and bent his head down to drink.

Carys watched the deer for a moment, holding her breath and waiting for anything sinister to emerge, but after a few moments, the animal lifted its head and loped away.

"Okay, I promise I'm a really good swimmer and I'm not going to drop you." She turned and headed toward the grassy verge on the edge of the loch. Carys knew she'd walk twice as fast if she could hike on even ground, and her feet were a blistered mess. She was far more likely to stumble on the rocky forest path. "Don't worry, okay? This is safer for both of us. I don't want to trip and drop you. That might hurt you worse."

"Okay." The little girl's voice was still cautious, and she hugged Carys's shoulders tightly.

They walked down the green slope to the edge of the water, and Carys enjoyed the crunch of smooth gravel under the soles of her over-large boots. The wind on the water curled ripples along the surface of the lake, tossing small waves onto the shore and singing a haunting tune as it threaded through the trees.

Carys smiled, remembering all the lakes that her mother had painted over the years; Tegan Morgan was fascinated by the play of light and darkness in the depths. She had loved taking her easel to the beach and watched in delight as Carys and her father played in the cold Pacific waves.

"It's just past that log," the little girl said. "Walk over the log and then go back into the trees."

"Sounds good."

"What's your name?" The little girl rested her chin on Carys's head. "I promise I won't steal it."

"Are you fae?"

According to most fae stories, a fairy who had your true name could enchant you, steal your free will, or even hold you captive in their world. The variations on stories were countless, but every tale she'd ever read told her that giving a fae your true name meant handing over power.

The little girl giggled. "Don't be silly. Did you see my ears?"

Carys *had* checked her ears. She'd also looked under the layer of grub to check for any kind of sigil but had seen nothing.

"I'll tell you my name first!" she said. "It's Azar." She pulled on Carys's shoulders. "Now you promise not to steal it."

For a child raised in this world, that had to be a constant threat. "I promise. That's a pretty name. My friends call me Carys."

Azar didn't sound like a Scottish name to Carys. Then again, the Shadowlands reflected the Brightlands, and there was no lack of different faces from what she'd seen so far.

"Just up here." The little girl patted Carys's shoulder. "The path on the right."

"Okay." Carys turned to walk back toward the trees, but her eyes caught on a reflection in the water. She turned and stared at the hypnotic face that slowly appeared in the grey-blue gloom. It was a beautiful man, his pale skin silver beneath the surface.

He looked like he was sleeping.

"Carys?"

She blinked when she heard Azar say her name.

A curl of dread formed in her belly a split second before she realized what she was seeing. "No."

"Run!" the little girl screamed. "Carys, run!"

Carys turned and ran toward the trees but not before a high-pitched shriek came from behind her. She turned, trying to get Azar off her back to shield her from whatever was coming behind them, and saw the terrifying figure of a kelpie bursting out of the lake.

The beautiful man was gone, replaced by the looming figure of a grey-skinned water horse with red eyes and a dripping black mane threaded with weeds and ropes he would use to pull his prey into the water and drag them under.

"Hold on!" Carys pumped her legs and tried to make it up the slope but didn't make it before she felt something snake around her ankle. With all her strength, she flung the little girl toward the safety of the trees before she fell. "Get away!"

The little girl screamed as the rope around Carys's ankle pulled her hard to the ground. Her chest hit the rocky shore with a thud, and she tasted blood in her mouth. The kelpie began to drag her along the gravel at the edge of the lake. She dug her fingers into the ground, trying to hold on, but there was nothing to grab but smooth grey stones that fell away under her hands.

Carys looked up and saw Azar scurry into the bushes. She breathed out a sigh of relief that the child at least had escaped. The kelpie screamed again and dragged Carys toward the water.

She rolled to her back and looked around, searching for anything she could use as a weapon. She reached for a fallen branch that had washed up from the lake, gripped it, and swung the driftwood like a bat as the kelpie reared over her, snorting and spraying her with cold, stinking water.

The water horse's hooves stomped down right next to Carys's head and she wriggled away, but the kelpie's rope was wrapped firm around her ankle, tightening and pulling her ever closer to the loch. She felt her heavy boots slip underwater, and the stuffed wool around her feet grew cold and wet.

No, no, no!

This was *not* how she was going to die.

Carys swung the branch again, making contact with the burning eyes of the creature. She jabbed the branch upward, trying to hurt it enough that she could crawl away, but the kelpie shrieked with rage and bared its pointed teeth. Its black hooves stomped down next to her head again; then it reared up, and Carys realized her hair was caught in the cloven hooves of the devilish creature.

The wheeling hooves threw her forward, and she saw the loch looming in front of her face until the hair caught in the kelpie's hoof ripped free and Carys fell back to the shore, scrambling away until the rope around her ankle pulled her back.

Fuck you!

She was so angry she could scream, but she didn't want to waste her breath. There was a sharp pain on her scalp where her hair had torn away, and blood dripped into her eyes. She gritted her teeth and reached for the driftwood again.

She was *not* going to die like this.

The sound of hooves thundering in the distance reached Carys's ears, and she felt ice curl in her chest.

More hooves. More kelpies. She wouldn't escape if another attacked.

But the kelpie turned his head—his attention caught by something to the left—and whatever was wrapped around Carys's ankle released. She rolled over, keeping the thick branch in her grasp as she wiped the blood and filthy water from her eyes, trying to wrap her mind around what she was seeing.

On the edge of the water, just yards away from her, a golden-brown unicorn reared up, its high whinny drowning out the fearsome shrieks of the kelpie. On its head, a silver-brown horn glowed with a lethal point, and it lowered its head as it charged the kelpie.

The two creatures battled on the edge of the water, the unicorn kicking at the grey water horse and beating it back. The massive animal attacked the kelpie from higher ground, lowering its head to impale the creature's chest as the kelpie let out another rage-filled scream.

Carys was frozen in shock for a moment, and then she realized she was still halfway sitting in the water. She scrambled away from the loch on her hands and knees, into the safety of the long grass and the shelter of the trees. Azar was bouncing with excitement, sitting on a fallen log, smiling and pointing to the glowing creature that battled back the kelpie.

"I called my dad," she said with a smile, patting Carys's shoulder. "Don't worry. You're safe now."

CHAPTER TEN

"You're fortunate." The healer leaned down and spread ointment over the scrapes along her ankles and the palms of her hands.

Carys was sitting on a fallen log in the middle of the forest, and birdsong was a riot around her. Her clothes were still soaked, but the air was shockingly warm, which was a good thing considering the woman who was healing her looked like she was dressed for desert heat and not a northern winter.

"I'm fortunate?"

"The kelpie is angry. He knows to stay away from our foals, but you startled him. And humans have no treaty with the creatures of the loch, even those who have magic." Her long black curls were braided into multiple plaits that fell down her back and over her shoulders. Gold threaded her hair, and while she didn't have the pointed ears of the fae, there was something obviously magic about her. "That could have ended very badly for you."

"Are you a… unicorn?"

She smiled and pressed a woven bandage soaked with something green to Carys's head. "Not at the moment."

Carys felt her skin knit together under the bandage and the pain eased. "Tha—" She bit her tongue. "I mean—"

"It's fine. You are among the blessing." The healer glanced up. "You may thank me without creating a debt."

So unicorns didn't bank favors like the fae did. Good to know.

In the oldest stories, the fae were almost always associated with trickery. They loved to bargain with humans but always seemed to come out with a better deal than the duped person who wanted a favor. Countless human superstitions revolved around not offending the fae and not drawing their attention.

In the folk literature she'd studied, there wasn't nearly as much about unicorns and even less about unicorns who could turn human. Most of what Carys had read told her that these mythical creatures were mysterious, shy, and associated with purity and grace. Not tricks or traps for humans.

Carys felt the tightness in her chest relax a little bit when she realized that these creatures were probably the safest ones she'd meet in this strange world.

"It's nice not to have to watch every word."

"It is, isn't it?" The woman lifted the bandage and removed it. "That's better. Your body accepts magical healing. Another fortunate turn. Not all humans do, but you feel a little fae-touched."

Fae-touched? Was she talking about Dru bringing her through the forest?

It didn't matter that the unicorn spoke in riddles—Carys felt better just being in her presence. "I don't even want to think about what might have happened if you guys hadn't found me."

"You're lucky Azar has such a big voice." The woman's dark brown eyes creased at the corners in maternal mirth. "I suppose I won't be able to chide her for using it so often."

"You're her mother."

She smiled. "I am so honored and burdened."

It was the first time Carys had the urge to laugh all day. "What's your name?"

"Yasmin. And Azar tells me you are called Carys."

"It's nice to meet you, Yasmin."

The woman had light brown skin and lips that reminded Carys of Dru with their berry-red hue, but there was nothing threatening about her. She had a proud forehead and a broad, muscled chest with strong shoulders.

Yasmin bore a gold sigil on her forehead in an intricate, swirling design where Carys imagined her horn would be in unicorn form.

Carys looked around the forest meadow that the little girl called home. "And what is this place?"

"You are a guest of the Blessing of Moray," Yasmin said. "This is our current camp."

The meadow was a wildflower-and-grass-covered island in a forest of pines and cedars. It was filled with bright tents that draped from tree to tree, and the light seemed brighter, as if a glow emanated from the glorious creatures walking among the flowers and trees, a mix of multicolored unicorns and people who were clearly only temporarily in human form.

There were small unicorns and children playing in the grass within the safety of the circle of tents, laughing and jumping in both human and animal form.

"I feel very safe here." Carys hoped that her instincts were right, because if these creatures were evil, maybe she'd just give in to it.

Nothing this beautiful could be evil.

"You *are* safe here," Yasmin said. "The kelpie cannot leave the boundaries of the loch, and Darius will not let anything enter the forest that could bring the children harm."

"Darius?" Carys looked at the golden-brown unicorn who had attacked the kelpie. Azar was draped across his back, braiding his mane and whispering secrets into his ear as another unicorn tended to the wounds on his side.

"Yes, my mate is the one who rescued you." Yasmin's eyes glowed when she looked at the magnificent creature.

"Azar is his daughter."

"Yes. Darius is the chief here, though our blessing grants allegiance to Lord Robb."

"The king?"

The woman smiled. "Unicorns don't recognize kings, but we feel at home here, as have our ancestors for many generations." Yasmin patted the dressing on Carys's ankle. "You'll be healed within an hour or so. Then Darius can return you to the castle."

Carys sat up, shaking her head. "I can't go back to the castle. Can one of you take me to the fae gate so I can go back to the Brightlands?"

Yasmin looked confused. "The fae gate? Why would you want to go there? The Borderlands are dangerous."

"But I'm not from here. I'm trying to get back." At this point damn her clothes. Damn Duncan. Damn Lachlan and all the rest. She had clothes in Scotland and a mobile phone and credit cards that could buy her a ticket home.

Yasmin frowned. "Aren't you of the Shadowlands? You accepted my healing." She stepped back and looked more closely at Carys, turning her head from one side to the other. "You're Brightkin." She blinked. "I know your face now. You're *her* Brightkin."

Nice to have another reminder that Carys didn't have her own identity in this place. She took a deep breath. "I'm from the other side of the gate, and I really just want to go home." Carys glanced at the light overhead, which seemed to be dimming as they spoke. "If it's too late now, maybe I could camp here with you and find the fae gate in the morning."

Yasmin smiled softly. "The blessing will protect you, Carys, as long as you need shelter, but we will not take you to the fae gate. We never go near them." Her eyes grew dark. "That is the place where the innocent are taken."

The innocent?

The twins who never make it to the Shadowlands. Carys pictured the hundreds of tiny lights in the forest, as abundant as fireflies. "You're really *good*, aren't you?"

Maybe that much goodness couldn't bear being around such a twisted place.

The sadness fell from Yasmin's eyes, and she smiled again. "You say that when you have met my daughter." Yasmin wound up a silvery gauze that looked like spiderweb and put it in a woven bag along with the ointment she'd applied to Carys's wounds. "Try standing now."

Carys rose to her feet and found that while her legs were cold and damp, the blisters and scrapes didn't hurt anymore. The burning pain around her ankles from the kelpie's binding didn't even make a twinge.

"Wow." She breathed out in relief. "So much better."

Yasmin stowed her bag in a nearby tent and led Carys toward the open meadow. "Fundamentally, our nature is wholeness. Peace." Yasmin looked at Darius with fierce pride. "But make no mistake, our blessing is lethal in battle when we need to be."

"I believe it." She leaned against a tree. "My scrapes don't even hurt anymore."

"I'm indebted to you for bringing Azar home. Her cousins will get quite a punishment for leaving her alone in the forest." Yasmin shook her head. "I'm glad she wasn't stranded for long; the foals always play too near to the old fae fort."

So there *had* been something magical in the forest. Carys made a mental note to avoid that dark place on the way back.

"Our children are very precious to us," Yasmin continued. "Even if they are rambunctious."

"She's a wonderful little girl." Carys looked at the small child on the unicorn's back. "Someone told me that children aren't born here. That the fae are the only ones who give the people here children. It's not the same for you?"

Yasmin shook her head. "Nothing is born in the Shadowlands except by magic, but a unicorn's fundamental nature is magic." She smiled as she watched the children and the unicorn foals playing. "The old gods bless us with young just like they bless the dragons and the wolves and other magical creatures."

"Wolves?"

Yasmin's expression grew dark. "They live in the south and owe their allegiance to the Anglian rulers." She looked at Carys. "Dread the day you meet a north wolf for they love war."

Carys shivered at the warning in Yasmin's voice until a bright voice distracted her.

"Mama!"

Yasmin's face bloomed into a beatific smile. "Azar." She nudged Carys toward the meadow. "Your new friend is feeling better."

"Did you give her a potion?" The little girl slid off her father's back and held up her ankle. "My foot feels all better from mine."

"I'm glad." Carys bent down to see the ankle the little girl stuck out. "I wanted to thank your father for saving me."

Carys stood up and watched as a golden mirage seemed to overtake the massive form of the unicorn Azar had been riding. Moments later a man appeared, dressed only in a cream-colored wrap that circled his waist. His skin was the color of gold-touched sand, and the first word that popped into her mind when she saw him was *warm*.

The unicorn looked warm even in the winter cold. His hair fell loose and flowing to his waist, and though the cold breeze crept down Carys's neck, the man's skin showed not a single goose bump.

"I am Darius, guardian of the Moray blessing." He was even taller than Yasmin and wore a gold sigil on his forehead where his horn had been. "Welcome, Carys."

His human voice was deep, resonant, and as powerful as she'd expected from the massive unicorn who had battled the kelpie.

"Thank you for saving my life," she said. "I was foolish to walk so close to the loch. I was trying to fight it off, but I'm pretty sure that monster would have dragged me under if it hadn't been for you."

"You saved my daughter's life, and our blessing owes you a favor."

"Honestly, it's my own fault," Carys said. "Azar tried to warn me, but I didn't know about the kelpie, and I've had a bit of a shock today. I wasn't thinking clearly."

"You saved our daughter before protecting yourself," Darius said. "You have our gratitude. Can we see you back to the castle? You are welcome anytime, but we don't have human beds that would make you comfortable this night."

Honestly, the thought of sleeping on the ground with unicorns in the middle of a magical meadow sounded so much better than going anywhere at the moment. The day was starting to catch up with her.

"I don't mind camping here with you, but if you could help me find Duncan Murray's cottage, that's all I need." Carys was sure she could find her way back to the fae gate if she could just get to Duncan's cottage. "I'm not going back to the castle. I don't want to bother you with my problems, but—"

"The problems of a friend are not problems at all." Darius frowned. "Are you in need of protection?"

"Carys?"

A familiar voice calling her name made Carys turn. She saw Duncan on the edge of the clearing with the dark-haired woman from the throne room beside him.

The woman's eyes lit up. "Carys! Thank the gods you're safe."

Too late. Carys sighed. Her problems had found her.

THEY HAD BROUGHT a horse for Carys to ride, but it wasn't something she'd done since she was a kid, so she bounced awkwardly in the saddle, riding between Duncan and a woman he introduced as Aisling.

"Are you comfortable?" The woman was small and fine-boned with clear blue eyes the color of the ocean and dark hair that was braided and bound into a knot at the back of her head. "Seren hated to ride. She complained that it was so slow, but she was used to flying with Cadell, of course."

Aisling chattered in a bright Irish lilt. She wore a flowing green robe over fitted leggings, and her cloak was massive, covering her nearly to her ankles.

"Seren's personal chambers are still at the castle. No one has touched her rooms. I told the maids to clean them while we looked for you. And you're exactly your sister's size, so you can change into some of her clothes." Aisling looked at Carys's boots. "They'll be much more comfortable than Duncan's old things."

Carys appreciated Aisling's thoughtfulness, but she didn't know how to respond. She looked at Duncan with wide eyes. *Help*, she mouthed.

"Aisling." Duncan grunted from his tall perch on a massive brown horse. "She's not staying."

"Of course she has to stay!" Aisling's eyes went wide. "She's Seren's sister! We have to talk, we have to get to know her, and Lachlan—"

"I don't want to see Lachlan tonight." It was the first thing Carys had said since she'd mounted the horse. "If I have to stay at the castle, I want a bedroom with a locked door. I want a warm bath" —she realized that might not be an option— "if that's possible. And I want some food. After that, all I want is sleep."

"Of course you're tired." Aisling's voice was so understanding it made Carys inexplicably irritated. "I will take care of all those things myself. And I only offer Seren's clothes because I know they'll fit you well and be comfortable, but if you'd rather we wash the clothes you have and dry them by the fire, I will take them to the laundry myself."

"No." Carys wasn't a monster. She knew the other woman was trying to be welcoming and she'd clearly had affection for her sister, but her bright cheer still rankled. "Seren's clothes will be fine."

After resigning herself to the fact that she wasn't going to escape Sgàin Castle without another conversation with the son of its king, Carys had fallen into a silent brood.

Fine. She'd go back to the castle.

Fine, she'd listen to what Lachlan had to say.

And then she'd follow Lachlan's surly twin back to Scotland before she flew back to Northern California where she belonged.

She glared at Duncan from the corner of her eye. "Why did you let them look for me?"

"You're Lachlan's... something," he sputtered. "And more importantly, your Seren's Brightkin. Did you think they were going to leave you to fae mercies?"

"The fae aren't so bad really," Aisling added. "Well, the light fae aren't. They brought you to the Shadowlands, didn't they? They wouldn't have let you through the gate unless they wanted you here."

"That's what worries me," Duncan muttered.

"They have so much knowledge, Carys. I'm a healer at the castle, so I regularly meet with fae healers and learn from them." She turned to look back at the forest. "Just as I meet with the unicorns. Magic is not our enemy."

"Is it natural to humans though?" Carys suddenly realized that in this world, Aisling was the professor. Carys had rusty book knowledge, but clearly that wasn't enough. "If you're a healer, you use magic, but the unicorn healer said not all humans accept magical healing."

"That's true." Aisling nodded. "You should come to my workroom sometime and I can give you a tour. The good thing about learning and using magic is that I can make healing potions that all humans can take even if their bodies aren't receptive to magical healing. My own teacher learned from fae potion masters, so the healing recipes are very effective."

"Aisling doesn't mind the fae as we do because she's Irish," Duncan muttered.

"Untrue, you surly beast." Aisling winked at Carys. "He's such a brute, isn't he? I *am* Éiren—not Irish like you say in your world—and it's true we're freer with the Good People at home, but I was raised in Scotland." She let a brogue take over her voice. "So I'm a crotchety, suspicious skeptic too."

It was impossible to remain surly with the woman when she radiated so much good cheer. Even Duncan had to crack a smile.

Carys asked, "Why were you brought up here?"

"The Queens' Pact." Aisling smiled. "Centuries ago, the four queens of Éire, Cymru, Alba, and Anglia grew tired of the fighting and forced their kings to make peace. As a guarantee of that peace and goodwill, they each sent one of their children or a relative like a niece or nephew to the other three courts."

Duncan added, "The idea being if you knew one of your children was in the foreign court, you'd be more hesitant to start a conflict with that country. It happened in our world too."

Carys remembered from her studies of history that hundreds of years ago, childhood fosters were not uncommon among the aristocracy. Odd to think that the practice had continued in this alternate realm, but it was just another confirmation that humans weren't all that different whether they were living with magic or science.

"My mother isn't a queen," Aisling continued, "but my grandmother is, and my mother is married to an Anglian lord." She turned to Carys. "My aunt is related to Seren. *Was.*" Her expression fell a little. "My Aunt Eamer is the queen consort of Cymru. She was Seren's stepmother."

Carys blinked. "Wait, what?"

"It's complicated, isn't it?" Aisling smiled. "There are family trees in the library if that would help."

Duncan quickly added, "Queen Orla was very good at making strategic marriages for her daughters. Aisling's father isn't just a lord—he's a very powerful lord in Northumberland who has the ear of the Anglian king."

"And I'm their third child," Aisling said. "So I'm a humble apprentice mage in the Alban court who still fumbles with my potion ingredients at times." Aisling's dimples softened the sharp angles of her face. "But more importantly, Seren was my best friend, closer than my sisters even." Aisling pushed her mount closer to Carys's. "I know you're not Seren, and this is all so confusing, but I do hope that we can be friends."

Carys was back in the portrait gallery in her mind, staring at the wedding portrait of Seren and Lachlan.

Nêrys Ddraig, princess of Cymru. Aisling said her aunt was the queen of Wales. Cymru. *Seren's stepmother.*

"Nêrys ddraig," Carys whispered.

"It's a title of a dragon lord or lady," Aisling said. "One who can bond and speak with—"

"*Princess* of Cymru."

Aisling nodded. "Yes. Seren was raised here like I was, but when her ability to speak to dragons matured, she went back to Cymru with her father and trained—"

"So Seren's father is the king of Wales." Carys's head whipped around to Duncan. "*Cymru.* Seren's father is the king of Cymru?"

Duncan raised a hand. "Carys, he's not the same man—"

"Is he my father? Is he his twin?" A mad hope surged in Carys's chest. "Is my mother..." She blinked. No. In this place, Seren's father was married to an Irish—Éiren—woman. That couldn't be her mother's twin. But if her father...

"King Dafydd is the Lord of Gwynedd and the high king of Cymru." Aisling's voice grew quiet. "He's a strong man of medium height with dark curly hair and a strong nose. Seren had his eyes. You... have his eyes."

Carys had her father's eyes.

She turned to Duncan. "Duncan, I think in this world my father is alive."

CHAPTER ELEVEN

"Surely you must understand the irony." Duncan's voice boomed on the other side of the heavy wooden door. He was sitting on a bench outside the dressing room where Carys was taking a bath. She didn't know why she wanted the grumpy man close, but she did, and Duncan seemed reluctant to let her wander far even in a castle surrounded by guards.

Guards you managed to elude today before escaping to the forest.

They seemed to be watching a little more closely since she'd returned.

"What irony?" Carys poured the steaming water through her hair. After the fight with the kelpie, the long trek on horseback, and hours of walking in too-big shoes, the warm water brought tears to her eyes.

Even after Yasmin's healing, she was sore everywhere, and the bed in the room outside looked like heaven.

"The irony that you want to stay here now so that you can meet your father's twin—hoping for some kind of connection—when that's exactly why you're angry with Lachlan."

The cup she'd been holding fell in the water.

Dammit.

All I wanted was to find you and see your face and know that part of her was alive somewhere in the world.

She closed her eyes and sank lower into the heavy wooden tub.

Damn, damn, damn.

"You know I'm right," Duncan said.

"Shut up."

"See? That tells me you know." He let out an audible huff. "He's not the same man, Carys. Lachlan said your father was a teacher."

"Yes."

"Who had a quiet life in California and raised a wonderful daughter. Seren's father is the king of a small but very powerful country who can speak and bond with living weapons of mass destruction."

Dragons. She felt a flutter of excitement in her chest. Could she really go back home without seeing a dragon?

She lifted the cup and rinsed her hair. "I know Seren's father and my father are not the same man."

"But you want to meet him anyway?"

"Yes." Her heart softened toward Lachlan because how could it not? She understood his motivation in a fresh way because the idea of even laying her eyes on her father's face one more time filled her heart with aching hope. "I need to see him, Duncan."

"Then I suspect you'll see him. You'll have to get permission from Lachlan's father to stay in the castle, but you know I won't kick you out of the cottage. And the way rumors spread in this place, the king of Cymru might have already heard that his daughter's twin is in the Shadowlands."

"Would it take him a long time to get here? Without cars or trains—"

"Dragons."

"Right." She couldn't stop the grin that spread over her face. "I'm going to see a dragon."

"I can't even see your face, but you sound so Welsh right now."

She couldn't stop smiling. "Are dragons bad?"

"Are dragons *bad*? Are you actually asking that question? They fucking breathe *fire*, Carys."

She didn't want dragons to be bad. She'd been raised with images of them all over her home. The majestic creatures in her mother's paintings. The red dragon of the Welsh flag, the Ddraig Goch. Dragons were a part of her childhood dreams. "You said they can bond with humans though. Doesn't that make them... kind of good?"

"They're not bad if you're their friend." His voice dropped. "Course they're terrible if you're their enemy."

She could be a dragon's friend. She could definitely be a dragon's friend.

"Then again," Duncan continued, "dragons don't really have *friends*. Dragons care for no humans but their lords or ladies. In human or animal form, they are single-minded, fiercely loyal, and absolutely ruthless. *Highly* destructive."

Her sister had been a dragon lord. Dragon lady? How did that work? She was nêrys ddraig according to the portrait in the gallery. "Seren had a dragon."

"Yes."

"What happened to... it? Her?"

"Him. I wasn't here when Seren died." Duncan's voice grew softer again. "And Cadell was gone by the time I returned. He left the castle as soon as Seren was gone."

She narrowed her eyes. "Wait, you said *human* form? Dragons have a human form?" She sat up straight and blinked the water from her eyes. "Like the unicorns?"

"Yes. They'll occasionally speak to humans in that form, but only a dragon lord can speak to them while they're in animal form, and honestly, that's the body they seem to prefer."

She smiled. She didn't care if they were scaly or scary or single-minded or destructive. Her heart raced at the idea of seeing a dragon in the flesh.

"Duncan?"

"Carys."

She wrapped a soapy flannel cloth around her cold neck. "Do you think Lachlan really loves me? Me, not Seren."

There was silence from the other side of the door for a long time, and Carys wondered if he'd left. Duncan wasn't her friend. If anything, he was more loyal to Lachlan than her despite his anger with his twin.

She lifted another cloth to wash her face. "I'm sorry, that's not a fair thing to—"

"How does anyone know another person's heart?" Duncan's voice sounded softer. A little. "We can only see their actions. But I think that when you love someone—*really* love them—you'll cross an ocean to find them again. Maybe even cross a world."

"Like Lachlan went looking for Seren?"

"No," Duncan said. "Like you went looking for him."

CHAPTER TWELVE

Carys woke the next morning to a light knock at the door and a voice saying, "The fire, miss."

She wrapped the heavy wool blanket around herself and walked to the wooden door where she unbolted the bronze lock and cracked the door open.

On the threshold stood the woman from Duncan's office in Scone, wearing a brown dress and a neat apron.

Carys blinked. "Fiona?"

"No, miss." The woman frowned. "My name is Bonnie. Can I start the fire for you?"

"Oh right." She opened the door wider to allow the familiar and not-familiar woman into the room with her bucket of kindling and a lantern. It wasn't Fiona but her Shadowkin.

What were the odds?

"You said your name is Bonnie?"

"Yes, miss." The sturdy maid wasted no time cleaning the ash in the hearth, arranging the embers that were still burning, and adding wood to build the fire. "I'm the upstairs maid for the guest wing. You'll be seeing me every morning if you want a fire."

The room was freezing cold, and the pearl-blue light of the shadow-dawn peeked through the heavy shutters covering the watery glass of the two windows in Carys's room.

After the maid fed the fire, she turned to Carys. "Do you need hot water this morning, miss?"

Carys was trying not to stare. "I took a bath last night, but I appreciate the offer."

The woman cut her eyes to Carys's hair, which was tangled from sleeping. She frowned a little. "I'll brush your hair for you." She motioned Carys to sit at the dressing table. "I'm not a lady's maid, but I don't think they've assigned one of the girls to you yet. Your hair is a fright."

Was she supposed to have someone help her get dressed? Did she *need* someone to help her get dressed?

"Sure, that's... It's kind of you to offer." Carys didn't know anything about how this worked, but she felt immediately comfortable with Fiona—Bonnie. Even though Bonnie didn't have Fiona's sweet smile, she came across as competent and forthright, which was exactly the kind of person she needed.

"Yes." Carys glanced at the large wardrobe in the corner, full of clothing she'd never worn before. She looked at the dressing table with an arrangement of brushes, ribbons, and bottles of gold oil. "I think I would really appreciate your help, but I don't want to hang you up here if you have other work to do." She pointed to the bucket of kindling and the lantern. "Do you have other rooms you need to cover?"

The woman's dark brown eyebrows went up. "That's thoughtful of you, miss, but I left you for last." The woman fisted both hands on her stout hips and looked Carys up and down. "I thought you might need help. I have the time if you need it."

The small act of kindness warmed her more than the fire. "I'm Carys." She held out her hand to shake.

The woman looked at it, and her eyebrows went up again. "Is that the way in the Brightlands?"

"Yes." Carys smiled, still holding her hand out. "We shake hands when we meet someone."

"My hands are dirty." She glanced at the bowl of water and the pitcher in the corner. "I don't suppose—"

"Oh, go ahead."

Bonnie cocked her head and nodded a little bit. "That's fine of you."

Carys waited for the woman to wash her hands in the corner, and then Bonnie quickly opened the shutters, cracked the window open, and tossed the water out.

Carys made a mental note to walk well away from the castle walls in the mornings.

"There, that's better." Bonnie dried her hands on her apron. Then she held out her hand, took Carys's, and pumped it up and down. "I'm Bonnie. A pleasure to meet you, Lady Carys."

"Nice to meet you, Bonnie. I don't think I'm a lady though."

"You're Lady Seren's Brightkin, are you not?" Bonnie bustled over to the wardrobe and threw open the doors. "That would mean you're a lady here too. And you're sleeping in a lady's room, so I'll call you Lady Carys."

"Or just Carys is fine too."

Bonnie turned. "I've been told that there aren't lords and ladies and such in the Brightlands. Is that true?"

"There are in some places, but not where I'm from."

"But you're from Cymru, aren't you?"

Duncan was right. News traveled fast in this place. "It's called Wales in the Brightlands, and it doesn't really have a king either." Okay, that wasn't one hundred percent true. "I guess they do technically, but he's not as powerful as the rulers here."

"Oh." Bonnie nodded. "That's odd. They have a king but not a powerful one?"

"It's... complicated." Carys didn't know if she should be detailing the intricacies of a constitutional monarchy or the current political situation in the United Kingdom, so she turned her attention to the clothes in the wardrobe. "What do you think I should wear today?"

Bonnie scanned the clothing. "These are Lady Seren's old things—she was made a new wardrobe when she was married, but that's still stored in Lord Lachlan's quarters. These should all fit you." The maid opened a lower drawer. "What are your activities today?"

"I know Duncan said I'd have to ask formal permission if I want to stay in the castle, so—"

"Formal clothes if you're going to see Lord Robb." She started pulling things from the wardrobe. "From what I hear, Lord Lachlan is insisting you stay in the castle, so I wouldn't worry." She pulled out a pair of grey wool pants. "Lady Seren preferred trousers to skirts. Are you the same?"

When she was hanging out at home, Carys loved a long, flowing skirt and a comfy tee, but that didn't seem wise within the chilly walls of the old castle.

Carys nodded. "Trousers would be great."

"Excellent." She tugged at a tunic in a bright red color. "She did prefer red and green."

"For Wales." Carys smiled.

"For Cymru." Bonnie nodded. "This is a lovely red color, but maybe *too* formal for today. Why don't we go with the green?"

Bonnie sounded much more knowledgeable about court protocol than Carys was, so she deferred to the older woman. "Sounds good."

She waited for Bonnie to set out the clothing on the bed, and then she yanked off the warm wool wrap, jumped into the tunic before she froze, then the pants—trousers—and watched carefully as Bonnie tied an elaborate knot in the gold-colored sash to give the tunic some shape.

"There you go." She eyed Carys's feet. "Let's get your feet covered so you don't catch a cold. Stockings and boots for you, I expect."

"Please tell me Seren had some spare shoes I can wear instead of Duncan's old boots."

Bonnie's dimples reluctantly peeked out. "Without a doubt. Let's get your stockings on your feet so I can brush and braid that hair."

AN HOUR after she'd woken and dressed, another knock came at the door. Carys opened it, expecting to see Bonnie's face again, but she froze when it was Lachlan.

She knew it was Lachlan from the length of his hair, though he'd grown a light beard in the time he'd been away from her.

"Good morning, Carys."

She stepped back, unsure of everything. The practicalities of the day had been taken care of. She was dressed in warm clothes, her hair was fixed and braided into a bun at the nape of her neck, and she had shoes that fit her.

She should have felt prepared to see him, but she wasn't.

He was still the most beautiful man she'd ever seen, and Carys had the urge to run to his arms, close her eyes, and beg him to tell her this had all been a horrible dream.

But Lachlan wasn't in Baywood anymore. He was standing in a castle, carrying a tray of something with steam coming from the top.

"Can I come in? I brought you tea and fruit," Lachlan said. "Well, apples and herbal tea. We don't have mangoes here. Or tea. Or coffee." He held up the tray and tried for a smile. "Not really grown in this climate. But there are apples."

It was the same thing he'd gotten in the habit of bringing her in the mornings at home. He'd wake early to watch the sunrise, then bring her coffee or tea in bed along with whatever fruit they'd bought at the market. Seeing him at her door like this felt familiar and sweet and... complicated.

She opened the door and allowed him in the room. "Thank you, Lachlan."

He walked over and set the tray on the table near the window, closing the shutters. "There's a draft. I'll have someone come up and seal it so you don't get cold."

She didn't know what to say. He was here, in her room, taking care of her just like he'd done back in California. One of the things she'd fallen in love with was his consideration. Lachlan was the most thoughtful man she'd ever met save for her own father.

He turned to her and stood waiting. "Will you sit with me?"

Dressed in Shadowlands clothes with his long hair flowing, he felt like a familiar stranger, and Carys battled between the urge to run to him and hang on for dear life and the urge to slap his face and scream at him.

She couldn't stop her heart from racing at the sound of his voice. She couldn't stop the bright leap of happiness at the sight of him. But all that was wrapped around hurt and confusion from the revelations the day before.

"Tea." She sat in the chair. "Sure."

Lachlan sat across from her. "How did you sleep? The bed was aired out, but it wasn't new. Do you need a new bed? It's not as comfortable as your bed at home, and I can get something new for—"

"I don't need a new bed." She closed her eyes. Staying mad at him was proving to be difficult. "I slept well. I'm sore from all the riding, but they brought up so much hot water last night. All those stairs," she murmured.

"That's their job, and my father pays them very well, but I know having servants—"

"It's fine." It wasn't fine. "Uh... my feet are feeling better." She stretched out her legs. "Better boots than Duncan's old ones."

"Yes, your clothes fit well."

Of course they do—they belonged to my dead twin sister who was your wife.

Anger.

Then sadness.

Her heart ached, but she picked up the steaming cup of tea and sniffed it. It smelled like honey and spice, not tea at all, but it was warm and delicious when she sipped it. The herbal concoction warmed her belly and settled her stomach. "Lachlan, I know I was angry yesterday, but surely you understand why—"

"I love you, Carys, but I think you should go back home."

She blinked. "What?"

He seemed to force the words out. "Nothing has changed about my feelings," he said. "I love you. I could see myself happily spending the rest of my life with you, but circumstances here are complicated and I don't think it's safe for you. I can't be selfish and keep you here when—"

"You're kicking me out?" She set the tea down. "Are you... Are you joking right now?"

He shook his head. "It's not safe for you here. Duncan is right. It would be better for you to go with him and—"

"So is this Duncan's idea or yours?" Anger flared. "Your brother is the one who wouldn't tell me a damn thing about what happened to you and instead dragged me into a... an alternate dimension. It was all cryptic messages and mysterious motives and then I ended up walking through a fucking *fairy murder forest* to find you. And now I'm inconvenient, so you want me to go home?" Her voice rose on the last question. "Are you kidding right now?"

Lachlan put his "I'm-being-reasonable" face on, and Carys's anger flared again.

"It's the safest option for you," he said evenly. "I'm *trying* not to be selfish."

"Selfish?" She laughed. "You're trying not to be selfish? Now I know you're joking." She stood and started pacing near the fire. "Trying not to be selfish. That is *rich*."

"How?" He scowled. "I never lied to you. I told you I'd lost my wife. I told you about Seren."

"You didn't tell me that your wife had my face!" She stopped and pointed to it. "Do you understand how weird that is, Lachlan? She was my *twin*."

"I have a twin too, and we're completely different people."

"Okay, you didn't tell me that you came from a secret, magical world. How is that not a lie?"

Lachlan stared at her. "Really, Carys? Be honest—you would have thought I was a lunatic."

"Maybe so, but at least I wouldn't have fallen in love with someone who disappeared into thin air." She resumed pacing around the room. "You had to *know*." She blinked back tears. "You're a *prince*. You had to know that your father wouldn't just let you go."

Guilt passed over his face, but he didn't look away. "I didn't know they could find me. I didn't realize there was a gate so close to your house."

"What happened?" She crossed her arms over her chest. "It like... sucked you in or something?"

"No! Getting too close to the gate tripped some kind of... alarm, I suppose. They'd put a spell out to find me, and when I got too close to a gate, they knew where I was. And once my father knew where I was—"

"Are you telling me your dad sent a... a fairy strike force to California to kidnap you?"

He muttered, "Fairy strike force may be the wrong mental picture, but there were around a dozen of them, yes."

"Did they forbid you from leaving me a *note*? Did they forbid you from calling me once you got back to Edinburgh?" She frowned. "You brought your phone through a fae gate? I thought you couldn't do that."

"They *took* it, Carys. Then they smashed it." He took a deep breath. "There's no rule that says technology can't go through gates if fae carry them. They run the portals, not us."

"Thanks for clearing that up. I'll make a note."

"I know you're still angry."

"There had to have been a way to tell me. Something. Anything."

Lachlan stood and walked to her. "There wasn't time. They tracked me. They hunted me. And before I knew what was happening, they took me. They wanted to search your house, but I didn't want them to..." He blinked and clammed up.

She narrowed her eyes. "Didn't want them to what?"

"I didn't want them to know about you. I was worried they might hurt you. The fae who took me, they don't care about humans at all, especially mundane ones."

"Oh *right*." She knew what he was saying, but using the word *mundane* still stung. "I'm not special enough for them to care about."

Of course she wasn't. She wasn't a princess. She wasn't Seren. If she didn't want to see her father's twin so much, she would have agreed with him and just gone home.

"I never said that, and I never would." He huffed out a breath. "Misunderstandings like this are the reason it would be better for you to go."

"I'm not going anywhere. I'm staying until I see Seren's father."

Lachlan blinked. "That's why you want to stay?"

He tried to grab for her arm, but she shoved him to the side and walked out the door, storming down the corridor as she looked for the stairwell she'd walked up the night before.

"Carys, I know you miss your parents, but he's not the same man."

She held up a hand as she walked down the hall, flipping him off before she stomped down the stairs.

"That's very mature. Dafydd is not your father, Carys."

She didn't care about being mature, and she knew he wasn't her father.

Mostly she was furious that Lachlan was trying to act like the reasonable, protective boyfriend when he was a liar. She wanted fresh air and she wanted sunlight, but sunlight wasn't possible here, so she'd at least take the fresh air.

Carys reached the ground floor of the castle and saw the double doors that led out into the courtyard in front of her. Two guards were on either side.

"Lady Ser— Carys. We have instructions to keep you in the castle until Lord Robb—"

"Castle." She nodded. "Fine. I'll stay in the *courtyard*, but if you try to keep me in this stone tower" —she could hear Lachlan's feet coming down the stairs after her— "I will scream bloody murder, do you understand me? I'm pissed off at him" —she pointed over her shoulder — "and I do not want to see him. Make sense?"

One guard looked down at her feet in confusion, but the other nodded. "Please stay in the courtyard, my lady. We can't protect you if you leave the castle walls."

"Fine." She didn't want to make their jobs harder, but she felt a definite punch of satisfaction when she pushed the wooden doors open and walked into the cool morning air.

The castle courtyard was far calmer than it had been the day before. Maybe yesterday had been a market day, but that morning the only people milling around appeared to be workers and a few of the children she'd seen before.

She gulped down the cold air and wrapped her cape around herself. Bonnie had insisted on fastening a cape to her tunic earlier, and Carys had thought it was just for show.

It was not. The air was freezing.

She stalked across the courtyard, heading for a green space where horses were grazing and it looked like there were some small apple trees that still had fruit hanging on them.

Apple trees like the ones behind Duncan's house.

Near the fairy murder forest.

In the magical alternate realm.

Where her father's twin was still living and her boyfriend was a prince.

Carys reached the grass and stopped, breathing in the heady smell of grass and fresh earth that reminded her, just a little, of home. She stood on the bare earth, her feet warm and comfortable in Seren's old boots, and felt the firm ground beneath her when every other thing felt tenuous and strange.

The squat man she'd seen yesterday was sitting on a stone bench under a nearby awning, smoking a thin wooden pipe and staring at her as he idly scratched his fuzzy pointed ears. He narrowed his eyes, staring at Carys until she looked away.

Judging by his ears, he was some type of fae, but Carys didn't know which. There were countless variations on fae mythology across the world, and she had no idea how much of what she'd read in books matched reality in this strange mirror world. There was no listing for the Shadowlands in the *Oxford Companion to World Mythology*.

Maybe Lachlan and Duncan were right. She'd made the impetuous decision the day before that she wanted to stay to see Seren's father, but maybe this was a bad idea. This place was a foreign country on a whole other level. What was she doing here?

She loved Lachlan, but she was mad as hell at him, and the kind, uncomplicated man she'd met in Baywood had ended up being someone entirely different. They'd only been together four months. Did it matter that they'd been four of the happiest months of her life?

Did she even know who he was?

"My lady, can I be of assistance?" A female guard walked over and stood at attention. "The castle guard are at your service."

Carys blinked and looked up. "Uh... no. Th—" God, she had to get out of that habit. The guard was human, but the way she was going, she could accidentally indebt herself to a random fae just by automatic California politeness. "I appreciate your offer, but no."

The guard seemed to hesitate, but then she blurted out, "I served under your sister."

The corner of Carys's mouth pulled up. "Really?"

The guard nodded. "Lady Seren was a magnificent warrior and a dead-accurate archer, my lady. Very admired by the castle guard."

Carys warmed to the stoic woman. "I never knew her. I wish I had."

"She was a great lady, mum." The guard nodded, then broke away, walking back to the group of guards who were gathered by a group of women hanging laundry.

No wonder Lachlan had loved her. Carys's sister had clearly been beloved by everyone in the castle. She was an admired warrior, a princess, a *dragon lord*.

How could Carys compete with that? She was a depressed assistant college professor with no family, a little house in the forest that needed a new roof, and questionable survival skills.

No matter what Lachlan said now, could she ever trust his feelings or her own?

She sat on a small bench under the apple trees and a horse wandered over, nudging her arm with his muzzle.

"Hello, horse." She'd always wanted one as a child, but her mother had always had an odd reaction to them, fascinated by the creatures but always keeping her distance. "Hey, boy." She glanced over. "Girl. Do you want an apple?"

Carys stood to pick an apple from the tree to feed the mare, only to turn when she felt a strange tug in her chest.

It was a warm sensation, not unlike the feeling of a campfire that had just caught. It crackled in her chest, turning her around as she looked to see what was causing it.

She couldn't describe it. It was... living.

"What's happening?" She looked at the horse, but the animal flared its nostrils and swiftly turned away. "Horse?"

She smelled a faint scent of smoke and tensed. Was a forest fire coming? Was the castle protected from a forest fire?

There was a burning in her chest and a churning sense of panic, but her feet felt rooted to the ground. She had the sneaking suspicion that she wouldn't be able to run even if she wanted to.

Carys rolled her shoulders back, but the sensation only grew stronger, the burning more intense. There was a distant sound in the air like the call of a hawk over a canyon.

Carys felt the wind pick up, the smell of smoke grew stronger, and she walked from under the trees, drawn to the distant cry. She looked up, searching for the sun, but it wasn't there. There were only the flat grey clouds that covered everything in this place, the dull morning light that cast the castle and the courtyard in watercolor shades.

Something was coming.

She felt a prickling awareness along her skin, and the hairs on the back of her neck stood up. She felt an instinct, a perception she couldn't explain. She couldn't take her eyes from the sky.

The people milling around the courtyard started to murmur, and then a few shouts rose from the castle walls and the guards began to run.

People were frozen, looking up, but every animal that had been wandering through the courtyard from the horses to the chickens had scattered, fleeing to any awning or covered alcove they could find, huddling against the walls, utterly silent in the human melee.

Carys couldn't understand what the guards were saying, nor did she care. Something pulled her attention back to the sky. Her eyes were drawn to a thin line in the distance, a dark spot on the horizon. Her blood knew what was coming before her mind fixed it.

More shouts from the guards, then a word that was unmistakable.

"Dràgon!"

The beat of distant wings pulled her like a string plunged into her heart. She walked to the center of the courtyard, her eyes lifted to the sky as the worried murmurs of the people around her turned to cries. A woman yelled and a child ran past her, screaming for his father.

The wind grew wilder, whipping around her body, but she couldn't seem to move. Her gaze was fixed on the shape coming closer.

A deep voice whispered in her mind.

Nêrys.

Another hawk's cry, but this one grew from a screech into a thundering roar as the massive creature spread its wings, shadowing the courtyard as it circled overhead.

Shouts from the walls and soldiers yelling as they poured into the keep.

The creature let loose a stream of fire that heated the courtyard even from the clouds.

"No," she whispered. "You're scaring them."

"Hold!" The guard who had spoken to her earlier was shouting at the archers on the walls. "Hold until we receive orders!"

The voice whispered in her mind again, a deep growl, gentle as distant thunder. *Nêrys ddraig.*

Carys shook her head and whispered into the wind. "Not Nêrys. My name is Carys."

With the force of a small hurricane, the dragon winged down in ever-smaller circles and landed in the middle of the courtyard, announcing its arrival with outstretched wings and a thunderous roar that shook the castle walls.

Carys stood motionless, looking up at the magnificent creature with pebbled green flesh that shone with an iridescent light. She could see the column of red fire glowing through the skin at the beast's throat when he raised his head.

Nêrys ddraig. He lowered his head. *Seren.*

"No." The ache was piercing because she could feel the longing from the dragon's burning heart. Tears fell down her cheeks as she looked up and met his eye. "I'm not Seren. I'm her twin. I'm so sorry I'm not her."

The dragon bent his head toward the ground, turning his brilliant gold eye on Carys and blinking slowly. *Nêrys ddraig.*

The whisper held an ache of longing and the shadow of grief.

Carys reached out, fearlessly running a hand over skin warmed by internal fire. "I'm not her, but I'm so sorry she's gone. I can feel how much you miss her."

A pained whisper. *Nêrys.*

"You're her dragon, aren't you?" Carys couldn't believe she was actually touching a dragon. She sniffed and blinked back tears, laughing a little in spite of everything. "You're so beautiful." She let out a shaky breath. "You're the most beautiful thing I've ever seen."

The dragon was bigger than she could have ever imagined in her rational mind, but she knew him. In her soul, she felt the connection snap into place as her racing heart settled and beat in a slow and easy rhythm that matched his own.

There was no fear. No doubt.

She knew this creature like she knew herself.

I feel her in you, Nêrys.

"My name is Carys." She laid her head on the dragon's warm cheek. "But you can call me Nêrys if you want."

CHAPTER THIRTEEN

Robb of Moray, high chieftain of the Scottish lands and lord of Sgàin Castle, eyed his daughter-in-law's Brightkin from a throne in the North Hall. When she'd come into his presence the day before, he'd looked on Carys with silence and more than a little annoyance.

Now his dark gaze pierced her with curiosity and clear suspicion.

Carys cleared her throat and started to say something, but Robb glared, held up a finger, and she fell silent.

Say nothing.

Carys heard the dragon's voice in her mind. Gut instinct told her to listen to him despite having only just met the strange creature who seemed to be tied directly to the center of her being.

It was unsettling and comforting at the same time.

"Father," Lachlan started, then also stopped speaking when Robb's dark gaze swung toward him. Lachlan shut his mouth and looked at the ground.

Okay then. Lachlan was not going to help.

Robb cast his eyes across the curious crowd bunched into the room who were whispering in a mix of languages and accents. They were humans mostly, but a contingent of tall, richly dressed fae was also in the audience hall, staring at Carys with clear interest. A group of pale humans in foreign clothing murmured among themselves while a tall man with a dark gaze and a heavy beard stood in front of them, also staring openly.

It was by far the most attention she'd ever received in her life, and she immediately hated all of it. She looked for Duncan, but she couldn't see him because of the crowd.

Robb scanned the curious onlookers, then turned silently to his queen.

Lady Elanor rose to her feet and addressed the gathered crowd. She spread her arms and spoke in a gentle voice. "Friends and fae." She nodded at the fae party, and they nodded back. "Visiting lords and ladies." She looked at the pale people guarded by the dark behemoth. "This is a family matter, and the high chief requests privacy for our kin. If you would excuse us at this time, we would be most grateful. We will return to the high chief's regular audiences as swiftly as possible."

It was a very diplomatic "Get the fuck out of here," but the crowd listened. Dozens of people shuffled out of the hall—the castle guard serving as their ushers—leaving Carys in the middle of the room with Lachlan and his family on the thrones sitting above her, Aisling and Duncan waiting in the wings, and a massive, nearly seven-foot-tall man towering behind her.

Some of the stares might have been for him.

The dragon's name was Cadell, and the heat from his human form felt like the only thing keeping Carys warm under the frosty glare of Robb's blue eyes.

"So," Robb finally muttered, "the dragon is back."

In his human body, Cadell sported a shock of short, sandy-brown hair. His skin was pale and ruddy from the wind, and the angles of his face were sharp, severe cheekbones and a prominent, straight nose giving him the unmistakably wild air of a bird of prey. His dark eyebrows cut a broad line over his brilliant gold eyes, which were the same as in his beast form.

She couldn't say Cadell was handsome. He looked exactly like a dragon—somehow—just with a human face. When he'd transformed, he'd been clad in sleek leather armor the same color as the dark emerald dragon skin that molded to his body. His muscled arms were bare, but he didn't look cold. In fact, every now and then Carys thought she saw a flicker of a glow shimmering at his throat.

It was as if dragon fire lived inside him no matter what body he wore.

The dragon hadn't said a word out loud, though Carys could hear his voice in her mind.

The Alban chief is deciding what to do with you. Say nothing.

Carys didn't think she could speak to Cadell in her mind. She'd tried projecting questions at him, but if he heard her, he didn't respond. She was desperate to get away from the hall and ask Cadell a million questions, but instead, she was trapped in a stone chamber with Lachlan's family staring at her like she was a strange bug.

Lachlan was sitting next to his father, watching the dragon. "Cadell, how did you come to fly to our court?"

The dragon finally spoke, and his voice sounded just as it did in her mind, like a low rumble of distant thunder. "I felt my lady's presence."

"Carys is not your lady." Lachlan's voice was rough. "Seren was your lady."

"I know who my lady is, Lachlan of Moray."

A muscle jumped in Lachlan's jaw. "She is of the Brightlands. She cannot be nêrys ddraig."

"But she is," Cadell said. "How that came to be is for human minds to worry over. She is my lady now."

Carys turned to Cadell and whispered, "What does that mean?"

He spoke into her mind. *I am your dragon, Lady Carys. I will protect you with my life, and no being, human or magical, shall harm you unless they kill me first.*

Well, that was... intense.

"How are you my dragon when we've never even met before?"

I will explain later.

Duncan was sitting off to the side, lounging on a bench with his legs kicked out. "The kelpie and the unicorns."

Aisling turned to him. "What about them?"

Duncan lifted his head, his voice gruff as he looked at Carys. "She was touched by magic yesterday. A kelpie attacked her, and the unicorns healed her." He looked directly at Cadell. "That's when you started to feel her presence, isn't it? Yesterday afternoon."

Cadell nodded to Duncan before he turned back to Carys.

Forgive me, Nêrys, for not coming to you sooner. Do you want me to kill the kelpie? I will hunt it and destroy it, leaving its bones as an offering to Llŷr, the sea god who created it.

She quickly whispered, "That's really okay." She reached up and patted Cadell's shoulder. "I'm... good. No bones needed."

"Whatever Carys is," Duncan said, "she can't be *entirely* of my world. Not if she can hear dragons."

Carys glared at him like the betrayer that he was.

Duncan shrugged and raised an eyebrow but said nothing more.

"My lady's arrival in the Shadowlands has already been reported to the Cymric court," Cadell said. "High King Dafydd is readying a party to fly north. I will wait with my lady until he arrives."

Lachlan sat up. "Just a moment. Carys was born in the Brightlands no matter what anyone says. She doesn't belong here and she's not safe. People are already asking questions about her connection to Seren. She's now going to attract attention from the fae and the wolves. She *needs* to go back with Duncan."

Carys glared at Lachlan, but he pretended to ignore her.

"It's freezing!" Lachlan wrapped his arms around her. "We've got to get you inside. You're soaking wet, Carys."

"It's fine." She held on to him, elated by his declaration in the forest. "Tell me again."

"I love you."

He loved her. Through grief. Through loss. Through depression. They were better together. They were happy. "I love you too."

"Do you?" Lachlan asked softly. "Am I that lucky, Carys? Did the gods smile on me twice?"

"What luck?" She threw a blanket over his wet hair. "You told me yourself, we're meant for each other."

"Because we are." Lachlan's embrace was nearly painful. "You made me want to live again."

Carys pressed her cheek to his chest. This was her happy ending. She knew it.

And now Lachlan was looking at her like he barely knew her.

"I want to see my father." Carys swiftly corrected herself, but not before she saw Lachlan's eyebrows go up. "My uncle, I mean. My father's brother. His... twin. Shadowkin. I want to see my father's Shadowkin."

Robb narrowed his eyes. "Why?"

"In the Brightlands, her father is dead," Lachlan said. "He died in a car crash."

"The metal carriages that burn oil," Duncan said.

Robb muttered, "I know what a car is."

"I just want to see his face." Carys glanced at Lachlan. "And perhaps he would like to see mine."

Elanor spoke. "We understand your sentiment." She reached for Robb's hand. "It's perfectly understandable, my king."

Robb looked long at his queen, then back to Carys. "Our grief over Seren's death is shared, Carys Morgan. My son has told me of his meeting with you and about your... relationship." Robb shifted on the carved wooden throne. "But I am of a mind to agree with him. Whatever your sentiments may be, this place is not safe for you."

"Why would that be, Robb?" Duncan's voice was scathing. "Are you afraid of the fae? Court gossip? Or are you uneasy because you let her sister be poisoned in your own castle?"

Aisling gasped.

Carys froze. "What?"

"Silence, you interloper!" Robb rose and motioned to the guards. "Get this one out of my sight."

"I'm not leaving." Duncan leaned forward, his elbows leaning casually on his knees. "You know you can't get rid of me no matter how much you hate me." He gave the king a self-satisfied smirk. "Unless you want to anger him."

"Seren was poisoned?" Carys turned to Cadell. *"Poisoned?"*

The dragon's face was frozen in a mask.

Carys turned to Duncan, but he was looking at the ground, a grimace lingering behind his beard. She glanced at Aisling, whose hand was over her mouth. She was staring at Carys with round, shocked eyes.

Her sister had been *murdered?* And not a single one of them had shared that very important fact?

No one here had mentioned a single thing about how Seren had died, and Carys had assumed it was some kind of sickness. Lachlan had said she'd been ill. But *murder?*

"No one was going to mention this to me?" she shouted.

"And how, exactly, would this rumor affect you?" Robb asked. "Because despite what my son's Brightkin may say, it is only a rumor. A cruel, vile rumor with no basis in reality."

It is not only a rumor, Carys heard in her head. *The cross human is correct.*

Robb looked to the wings of the throne room. "You can ask Aisling —she is our castle healer and would know if anyone had wanted to harm our daughter-in-law."

Aisling stammered, "I-I—"

"Robb, please do not put Aisling on the spot," Elanor said softly. "We were all devastated by Seren's death, and sometimes when a young person dies, we look to blame. That does not mean blame is warranted."

Elanor's quiet words seemed to calm the tempers in the room.

"No matter what you believe happened to Seren, I am here now." Cadell stepped forward. He spoke silently to Carys. *I left Seren to tend to my young, believing she could come to no harm in her home. If she was under threat, she didn't tell me. I will never make that mistake again.*

Cadell reached his hand out toward Carys. "No harm will come to my lady, and Carys will leave this place when she wishes to and no sooner."

Robb's eyes burned. "You dare question my authority, beast?"

Cadell narrowed his eyes. "I am not one of your tame unicorns, Robb of Moray." The dragon stepped forward, and his figure grew taller before Carys's eyes. His chest expanded, and she could see the red fire glowing at his throat. "My lady does not answer to your authority any more than the cross human does."

Carys felt the situation escalating again. "Cadell, wait." She put a hand on his arm.

"Nêrys, step back."

"My love." Lady Elanor spoke again. "My Lord Dragon. It would please the queen if you both gave me the courtesy of your attention."

Cadell stepped back, still shielding Carys from Robb but calmed by Elanor's voice. He stood at attention, hands clasped in front as he blocked Carys from Robb's view. "Lady Elanor, you are wise. Speak."

Robb sat down too. "My queen, the hall is yours."

"Carys is Seren's sister." Elanor's eyes turned to Carys, who stepped from behind Cadell's back so she could see what was going on. "Seren's *Brightkin.* To even see her face is a happiness I could not imagine in this life. Carys Morgan, you will always be welcome in my home. The circumstances of Seren's death hang over us all, and we may never know the whole truth. *That* is a tragedy, but it is no one's fault."

Robb grunted, and Lachlan looked like he wanted to speak, but he kept silent as his mother continued.

"Cadell has said that King Dafydd is readying a party to come north." Elanor looked at Robb, then Lachlan. "Carys is Dafydd's niece. We should wait until he arrives before anything is decided."

Robb took a deep breath, and while his eyes still bored into Carys, the expression in the cold blue had softened. "I do hear your words, my queen."

Elanor said, "Of course, the final decision should remain with Carys alone. My dear, what do you want?"

It was the first time anyone had asked Carys that in days, and her heart immediately softened toward the regal woman. "I'm grateful, Queen Elanor. I would like to stay until my uncle arrives."

"Very well." Elanor smiled and turned to Robb. "My love?"

"She stays." Robb glanced at Lachlan, then back to Carys. "Until we have some answers, she will stay."

CHAPTER FOURTEEN

Duncan caught her arm as she started walking out of the hall. "Carys—"

Cadell turned on him, a throaty hiss vibrating through his body and shaking the air.

Duncan dropped his hand. "Carys, we should talk."

"Why?" She kept walking, feeling Lachlan's eyes on her back. She didn't like being the center of attention, and that entire episode had given her the shakes. Now she was walking through a crowd of whispering courtiers who stared at her with questions she didn't want to answer.

Added to that, she also had a nearly seven-foot-tall dragon at her back, glowering at everyone around her like he was seconds away from breathing fire on the lot.

"You know why!"

Carys stopped when she had passed the crowd of courtiers. This was Duncan. If there was anyone in this upside-down place that could relate to her, it was him. And she had questions.

She had a *lot* of questions.

Carys looked at Cadell, then Duncan. "It's fine. Duncan, follow us. Cadell needs fresh air."

She had no idea how she knew that, but she did. The effort of keeping his human form when he was emotionally wrought was taking a toll. His shoulders were broader, and the fire didn't calm in his chest. Even though he walked on two legs, he seemed far more animal than human to Carys.

She didn't know how the connection with Cadell had formed so immediately and completely; but she could feel his emotions almost as if they were an extension of her own.

Did he feel the same about her? How?

She trusted him. Completely. But she'd just found out her sister had been murdered and Cadell had been off duty at the time.

So she had questions for him too.

Carys, Duncan, and Cadell walked out of the castle and into the courtyard through the door where they had entered, the guards stepping back and clicking their heels as they spotted Cadell.

"You're like a knight," she murmured.

Cadell heard her. "Your knight. I answer only to you, Lady Carys."

"Please just call me Carys."

"I answer to you, but you do not command me, Lady Carys."

"I'm not a lady."

"You are to him." Duncan came to walk next to her. "The bond between a dragon and their nêr is like that."

"Nêr?"

"Nêrys is the female form of the address. Your uncle is a nêr ddraig, a dragon lord. You are a nêrys."

"But what does that *mean*?" Carys kept her voice low as they crossed the courtyard, every eye on them, from the weird little man to the laundress hanging clothes in the grassy common to the blacksmith who paused at his forge to watch them and nod at Duncan. "No one will explain what any of this means."

"Patience." Duncan sounded exasperated.

Carys wanted to hit him. "And how is my uncle getting here so quickly?" She asked the question that had been brimming in her mind. "Do dragon lords *ride* dragons?"

Cadell stopped dead in his tracks and turned to her, his stern gaze rocketing between confusion, irritation, and something that hinted at embarrassment.

Duncan cleared his throat and tried to hide a smile.

"Does a nêrys ddraig *ride* a dragon?" Cadell's eyebrows drew together. "No, Lady Carys. A dragon is never *ridden*."

Okay, so clearly that was a foot-in-mouth situation. "I... I'm sorry; I didn't mean to offend you."

Duncan cleared his throat again. "She asks because the popular tales and dramas in the Brightlands tell stories of humans riding drag-ons. There are plays, movies, books—"

"Do I look like a horse?" Cadell stared at Duncan.

"No." Carys was quick to jump in. "Again, I am so sorry. But from the way people talk, it seems like dragons definitely do help some people move faster. So I was just wondering... how?"

Cadell, seemingly mollified, started walking again, his massive boots squelching in the mud of the courtyard. "When you fly with me, you will ride in a coracle of course."

As far as Carys knew, a coracle was a small round Welsh boat used in rivers and calm seas. "How—"

"It's a little like an air carriage," Duncan tried to explain. "Round on the bottom, high sides, large center post with a grip the dragon can carry as it flies. They're designed to tip as they land so the dragon lord and whatever warriors are with him can run into battle."

"There are royal coracles as well," Cadell said. "For peacetime, which all dragons prefer." He looked down at Carys. "Unlike wolves, we do not seek war."

They left the castle gates with not a single guard stopping them. It looked to Carys like once she had a dragon at her side, no one was really worried about her security.

Had that been Seren's mistake?

"Cadell, tell me about Seren's death." She glanced at Duncan. "Unless you think Duncan might have…"

Duncan put his hands on his hips. "Might have what?"

Cadell stared down his nose at Duncan. "Lachlan's Brightkin was not in the Shadowlands when your sister was killed. He is not a suspect."

Duncan narrowed his eyes at Carys. "You think I'm a murderer?"

"Not if Cadell doesn't," Carys said.

"Low, Carys. That is low."

"I don't trust anyone right now." She looked at Cadell. "Except for him, and I don't even know why."

"There." Cadell pointed himself toward a hill just outside the village where a stone tower dominated the skyline and sheep were grazing on the slope. "You can trust me. Because I am your bonded dragon, Carys of the Brightlands."

"How? Because I am Seren's Brightkin?"

"Yes." Cadell frowned. "And no. I cannot explain it any more than you can, but the moment the magic of this place touched you, I felt you. From hundreds of miles away. I felt the heat of Seren's death as if it were a spear piercing my heart." He turned to face Carys, and his golden eyes were filled with emotion. "Yesterday I felt a new root grow in the hollow Seren left. The moment I felt it, I knew that you were in our world."

"Yes." A root. That was exactly how it had felt to Carys too. Not a string or a chain but a living, growing vine that connected this magnificent creature to her own soul. "Does it always happen this way?"

Cadell smiled. "Yes. Dragons live very long lives. We can go centuries without a nêr calling to us, but once that connection is made, there is no doubt."

Duncan spoke up. "This is all very moving, but can we get back to why it would even cross your mind that I might have murdered Seren? After everything we planned, Cadell—"

"I believe Seren was poisoned" —Cadell kept his eyes on Carys—

"but this human was not in the realm when it happened, and he has no magic."

Duncan crossed his arms over his chest. "I contribute in other ways, dragon."

The dragon's glance was withering at best. "You can trust the cross human and me, my lady. Everyone else could be a danger to you."

The landscape before them opened up, and Cadell stretched his body out, a fiery shimmer glowing over his skin. The human form disappeared, revealing Cadell's true body, an iridescent dragon the size of a small jet with two muscled back legs and two wings folded back from his front legs.

"You're a wyvern." Carys smiled. "Not like on the flag."

The four-legged beasts are depicted in paintings, but all my kind take this form. There is some variation in other populations, but I am dragon.

She walked around his body and her hand reached out, but she paused. "Do you mind?"

My lady. He nodded his great serpentlike head, which bore a row of spikes that almost looked like a crown. *I understand my form is new to you. You may examine me if you wish.*

She ran her hand along his pebbled skin, olive green and shimmering under her fingers. The top layers were translucent, giving Cadell the appearance of striking iridescence and allowing the fire at his throat to glow.

His skin seemed to ripple as she touched, and Carys had the strangest sensation that she had done this before. "Did I dream about you?"

It is possible, Nêrys. Brightkin can dream of their Shadowkin.

"Do you mind?" She put both hands on his neck and rested her cheek against his skin. "You're so warm."

No human has touched me since Seren died. The voice in her mind ached with grief.

"I am so sorry, Cadell." The tears that came to her eyes were hot and fast. How could you cry for a sister you never knew? Seren's death felt fresh when she heard Cadell's voice.

She continued to walk around him, fighting back tears and giving this strange dragon the touch he seemed to crave. "Do all dragons live in Wales? Cymru?"

No, there are dragon populations spread across the world. Our kind need large territories to keep peace among ourselves.

Duncan cleared his throat. "In the Shadowlands of Western Europe, the dragons all live in Cymru, but there are other pockets that I've heard of. Eastern Europe. Persia. China, of course. A couple in the Americas, I think."

"How big is the Shadowlands?"

The Shadowlands are everywhere, my lady. Wherever your world exists, our world does too. We are the hidden and the magical in every place human imagination has lived.

"Big," Duncan said. "Very big. It's everywhere."

"Are they connected?" She turned to Duncan. "Like, could I take a boat to Shadowlands France?"

Duncan shrugged. "If you want to brave the leviathans."

"Sea monsters," she whispered. "Of course there are sea monsters."

"The sea holds more monsters than any on land." Duncan walked to a grey stone jutting from the grass and stretched out, his back to the rock. "You won't catch me on a boat in this place."

The monsters of the sea are frightening, but some are kind. Dragons have a good relationship with the selkies and the whales.

Selkies, dragons, kelpies, unicorns. It was a lot to take in, but as she ran her hand over Cadell's warm body, she felt safe in a way that she hadn't since she'd walked through the fae gate. "Are all dragons as beautiful as you?"

You flatter me, Nêrys. Dragons are built for survival and battle, not for beauty like a one-horned horse.

She smiled. "Do you not like the unicorns?"

Duncan chuckled. "It's an old rivalry but a friendly one. Unicorns can be ferocious in battle when they're roused."

The cross human is correct.

"They saved me from a kelpie, you know."

Then I must offer them a boon for protecting you before I could.

Carys turned to Duncan. "Why didn't you tell me Seren was murdered?"

"I was trying to get you to go home," he said roughly, "not pique your interest with a mystery."

"Why?"

"Why should you have gone home?" He frowned. "You found Lachlan. You knew the truth. And because your sister was *murdered*." He rolled his *r*'s hard over the word, clearly angry. "And not a damn one of them in this place would seek out the truth. They all made excuses for it, and I knew something was dirty."

"You don't seem too concerned about me staying now." She ran her hand over Cadell's warm skin, scratching along the ridge of his spines the way he liked. "You were baiting Robb in the throne room. Why the change of heart?"

"Well, you have a dragon now, don't you?" He stared at Cadell. "Which makes no sense at all, I might add. You shouldn't be able to speak to him. He shouldn't have been able to feel you." Duncan narrowed his eyes. "I don't like things I don't understand."

"Sounds like a personal problem to me," she muttered.

Cadell laughed softly in her head.

She patted the dragon, walking around him, wanting to know every curve of his body and every ripple of his beautiful skin. He had a large scar on his side, as if a sword had slashed through his hide. "You said you're built for battle, but you don't like war."

We like to be left alone. Our numbers are not great, and though we live a long natural life, that is shortened by human and fae wars.

"Do the humans and the fae battle here?"

The fae are the whisper of war.

Duncan added, "With few exceptions, the fae play humans against each other for amusement, Carys. You'll very soon find that most conflict in the Shadowlands has a fae component."

Seren's mate comes. Cadell turned his head toward the castle. *He has feelings for you.*

"Does he?" Carys's wonder turned to resignation when she realized Cadell was talking about Lachlan. "Or is it all for my sister?"

I am not a sentimental creature. I see what I see. Seren's mate has an emotional attachment to you. It is evident, but you cannot trust him.

Carys blinked. "Why not?"

Because you cannot trust anyone here.

───

LACHLAN SAT ACROSS FROM HER, his back to the same rock where Duncan had been sitting before he stomped down the hill, muttering something about getting back to work now that Cadell was around.

The dragon was stretched along the top of the ridge, his tail wrapped around his body and his eyes closed. He wasn't sleeping. He was fully focused on her but trying to afford her and Lachlan a level of privacy.

"Cadell likes this place." Lachlan looked at the dragon. "It's good to see him."

"Was he always with Seren?"

"Not as a child." Lachlan cleared his throat. "Aisling told you that she was raised here. And Seren was too. The three of us and my cousin Harold from the Anglian court."

"You told me you grew up together."

Lachlan nodded. "We all played together as children. I have two siblings, you know."

Carys shook her head. "How would I know that? You only ever mentioned Duncan."

"Because I know him better than my brother and my sister." He pulled at the grass beside him. "Nora is in Éire and Rory is in Cymru."

"Because of this pact thing."

He nodded. "So I had Duncan and Seren. Aisling and Harold. But when Cadell found Seren—"

"What do you mean, when he found her?"

"Dragons know when a human is their nêr. It usually happens around... eleven or twelve, I think?"

Cadell spoke softly in her mind. *Seren was the sixth nêr I served. You are the seventh.*

"Seren was ten," Lachlan continued. "Cadell sensed her and flew here." He nodded at the round tower. "Right here in fact. All of us were playing and we heard thunder in the distance. Harold knew exactly what it was, and he ran screaming." Lachlan's eye twitched. "They see more dragons in Anglia; he was afraid."

"But not Seren?"

"No." Lachlan smiled. "She was a Cymric princess. Her father is a nêr ddraig. She'd been raised with dragons from birth. For Seren, dragons were her protectors. Her nannies even."

"So she wasn't afraid."

He shook his head. "She climbed to the top of the tower and stretched out her arms." His eyes drifted to the rocky ruin, lost in the memory. "She held out her arms like she was waiting for him. I'd never seen her more excited. She knew. As soon as he appeared, she knew he was for her."

"And he stayed here?"

"No, he took her." Lachlan looked at Cadell. "He wrapped his giant claw around Seren's little body and snatched her up like an eagle hunting a fish. Aisling was screaming and Harold had already run, but I tried to climb up and save her. I didn't know what was happening." He blinked and looked back at Carys. "My father explained when I ran home. I was crying. I thought the dragon would kill her." He shook his head. "I didn't understand why she had to leave."

"Where did she go?"

"Back to Cymru. To Caernarfon. Another Cymric lord's child was sent to fulfill the Queens' Pact."

"Just like that?"

"Just like that." He picked up a rock and tossed it down the hill. "Dragon takes your friend away. No worries, have another."

She saw the loss written over his face. "You missed her."

"She wrote us letters. Aisling and I. She trained in Cymru with Cadell. All nêr ddraig have to be trained as warriors, not diplomats like her training with my mother had been. She'd been learning languages and fae lore and history, but after Cadell came, she had to learn how to fight and shoot. How to attack from a coracle in battle."

So her dead sister wasn't just a princess but a badass too. Carys felt proud and jealous all at once. "The guard in the courtyard this morning said she was a good fighter."

"She was incredible." Lachlan smiled. "And frighteningly good with a dagger in close combat." He smiled. "Kind of terrible with a sword though."

Why did that make her feel better? It wasn't as if she was good with a sword. Carys was good with a reference library, a web search, and a PowerPoint presentation. She could solve a mean jigsaw puzzle, but she couldn't lift a sword.

"But she came back. At some point she came back."

Lachlan stood and walked to her, holding out his hand for Carys to take. She gripped it and came to her feet, and she didn't pull away when Lachlan kept her hand firmly grasped in his own. They started to walk toward the tower.

"She came back when she was seventeen, I think? She came for a state visit with her father, and it was…" He put his hands up to his temples, miming an explosion.

"Tell me about your wife."

Lachlan looked over at Carys with sleepy eyes. "You're asking me to tell you about my late wife while we're in bed?"

Carys scooted closer to him, pulling the heavy blankets with her. "Sure. It's not like she's an ex-girlfriend. She was your wife. And she's still a part of your life; she was important."

His expression turned from a slight frown to a soft smile. "What a beautiful heart you have, Carys Morgan."

She nestled into his shoulder and played with the hair on his chest.

"Well, you've done a very good job ensuring I am not insecure in this rela-tionship."

"Seren was the girl next door. Our families had known each other for generations. I don't remember not having her in my life. She went away for school when we were eleven and was gone for years. Then when she came back..." He let out a low whistle.

"She had boobs."

He threw his head back and laughed. "She did. I did notice those; you're right."

Carys laughed with him. "So you fell in love when you were a teenager."

"Yes, and we married young." He pressed a kiss to the top of her head. "Our parents were... not thrilled to be honest. They both had different plans for us, but in the end they gave in. They saw how much we meant to each other."

"Wow." She kissed his shoulder. "That's beautiful. But no kids?"

"No, it wasn't..." He frowned a little. "You know, we had busy lives. It just didn't happen. And then she was gone."

"You left a few things out of the story."

He leaned forward. "And how was I going to explain all this? Would you have believed me if I told you everything?"

"You never gave me the chance."

Lachlan looked at Cadell. "I don't want to only speak of Seren because I know you think that my feelings for you are based on my memory of her and it's not true. I went looking for you for the same reason you want to see your uncle. I missed her desperately, and I thought I'd be satisfied just seeing you alive, seeing some echo of the woman I loved still living in the Brightlands."

Her smile was bitter. "But all that changed when you saw me in a bookstore? You expect me to believe that?"

"It's *true*, Carys. I loved Seren, but you're a different person entirely. My feelings for you weren't what I expected." A smile stole across his gorgeous face. "I came looking for Seren's twin, but I fell in love with a completely different person. And you're wonderful. You're smart, loyal, brilliant…" He swallowed hard.

Carys drew her hand away. "But?"

Lachlan took a step back, holding her hands in both of his own. "But you were *not* trained in battle. You were *not* trained with a blade or a bow, and the danger here—"

"Seren was trained in all those things and she was poisoned anyway."

Lachlan looked as if she'd slapped him.

"Her warrior training didn't help save her life." She looked at Cadell. "I have *him* now, and I have Duncan."

Carys couldn't read the expression on Lachlan's face, but she could tell he was struggling.

"Duncan?"

"Your brother has been honest with me," Carys said. "Well, mostly honest."

"Forget Duncan," Lachlan said. "I trust Cadell, but I'd still prefer you go home. Cadell and Duncan both say Seren was poisoned, and I believe them. I do. I know Cadell would never lie about that, but whoever killed Seren could be in the castle. They could see you as a threat."

"Why? You said yourself I'm nothing like her."

Lachlan shook his head. "We don't know why she was killed, so I have no idea if that makes a difference. Go *home*, Carys. Seeing your uncle's face isn't worth your life. Would your father and mother want you to put yourself in danger that way?"

Carys turned to Cadell and saw him with one eye open, watching her.

I see you, Nêrys.

She turned back to Lachlan. "I'm staying. And I may not have warrior training, but I have a brain." She pointed at Cadell. "And now I have a dragon."

"Carys—"

"I'll figure out the truth. So no, I'm not leaving. I'm not going back home until I figure out who killed my sister and why."

His face turned stormy, but he didn't say another word. Lachlan turned on his heel and left.

Carys watched him leave, and a cool resolve settled in her mind. "Cadell?"

Nêrys.

"I'm staying."

Of course you are, my lady. And I will stay with you.

CHAPTER FIFTEEN

She was not as confident the next morning. "What was I thinking?"

They were walking to the unicorn forest the next day, and Carys was full of doubts.

She wasn't a detective. She barely liked true-crime podcasts. Sure, she was good at puzzles—and apparently she could talk to dragons—but did that really mean anything when it came to solving a murder that had happened two years ago?

"What?" Cadell looked down at her. "Do you want to go back to the Brightlands? If you do, I will fly you to the fae gate now."

So a giant dragon could follow her home to Humboldt County. That would go over so well with the forest service.

Carys shook her head. "I'm not going home until I meet my uncle and figure out who killed my sister."

"You're conflicted."

She looked up at him and took a deep breath. "Of course I am. This is scary as hell. But life is full of conflicts. I'll figure this one out."

They walked through the forest, and she brushed her hands along the trees, taking comfort in the soft brown bark covered in moss.

The morning was pearl grey again, and the day was as light as it got in the Shadowlands. It was like a grey overcast sky that never cleared. Carys found herself missing the ocean fog she'd grown up with. At least that usually burned off by the afternoon and the sun peeked out.

"Why are we doing this?" Carys tugged at her collar. She was dressed in finer clothes than the day before, and they were not nearly as comfortable. The wrapped trousers were fine, but the boots that covered them were shining black leather that Elanor's maid had delivered to her room, and while they were better than Duncan's oversized boots, they were *not* comfortable.

Her tunic was heavier than the light wool she was quickly learning to appreciate, and her cloak felt like she was dragging a weighted blanket through the woods on her shoulders.

"Is this fur?" She glanced at her shoulders. "I think this is fur."

"It's warm." Cadell remained in human form as they walked through the forest to meet Darius and Yasmin. "Your clothes are fine, Nêrys. Stop fidgeting like a child."

"It's fur. Animals died for these pelts. That is not okay."

"Animals die from all sorts of things." He frowned. "Fur is *warm*. Warmth is important for humans. You can die from cold."

She had to admit the fur-lined cloak was toasty warm. "Wool is warm too."

"You're the niece of the king of Cymru going to formally meet the unicorn chief of the Blessing of Moray; you're not going to wear spun wool to meet a chief."

Cadell himself was wearing a leather cloak over his armor. Since he emanated heat, it was more for looks than necessity, and it looked completely badass.

Carys, on the other hand, had her hair braided with ribbons, uncomfortable boots, and a cloak made of little furry creatures she didn't want to think about.

"I already met them," she said. "And they seemed pretty casual if you ask me."

"You met them when they saved your life; now we are going to meet them formally as I am a magical creature returning to their territory, and I am also in their debt because they saved your life." He held up a basket wrapped in velvet. "We are bringing gifts, and we are wearing nice clothes."

"Fine." At least she'd get to see Azar again. The memory of the bright little girl—unicorn—was enough to bring a smile to her face. "You're right. I know you're right."

"Of course I'm right."

The forest was darker than it had been two days before. The shadows were dense, and the light was grey and flat above the trees. Though the birds sang in the canopy and she could hear little creatures hopping in the branches, without a bright child perched on her shoulders, it felt more menacing.

She glanced at the basket. "What gift are we bringing?"

"A collection of herbs from Elanor's garden, some incense traded from the East, and I added a dragon scale as a personal token of my thanks."

"Okay, two thoughts. One, a dragon scale?" Carys's mind raced. "I feel like that has so many magical uses, right? Potions? Spells? Do the unicorns do spells? Their magic seems very elemental, and that seems like it would be connected to fae mythology but—"

"Fae are not myths." Cadell looked slightly annoyed. "Two?"

"Two what?" Carys frowned.

"You said you had two thoughts. Save your questions for another time."

"You pulled off a scale? From where? Did it hurt?" She looked at his backside, then caught Cadell staring at her. "I'm sorry, that might be none of my business."

The corner of his mouth twitched up. It almost looked like a smile. Almost.

"We shed scales from our tails. And to answer one of your questions, yes. Dragon scales and dragon teeth are useful in healing potions. Yasmin will appreciate it. We do not often give them as gifts."

They came to a fork in the path, and Carys found herself drawn to the right path. "Is it this way? I think I remember—"

"No." Cadell grabbed her arm before she could set foot on the path. "Not that way."

She looked at him with alarm, then back at the path. "There's something bad there, right? I felt it the other day."

"Look." He nodded toward the dense trees where the path led. "*Really* look."

She peered into the trees and noticed that the light seemed more muted there. Birdsong stopped and the brush was silent.

Bright red hawthorn berries were her first warning. They peeked through the shadows like the lure that they were. As she kept her eyes trained on the path, the darkness grew, and the trees seemed to swallow any glimmer of illumination. Blue lights flickered in the space between the dark trunks, and the faint sound of childish laughter reached her ears.

"Wisps." She blinked. "Is this a gate?"

"No, but it is an old fae fort," Cadell said. "You need to watch where you're going. The fae will try to draw you in. You're a curiosity to them now."

"What if I turn my clothes inside out?"

He frowned. "What would that do?"

"Can I carry bread?"

"To eat?" Cadell shrugged. "Of course. Are you hungry?"

Okay, so most of the myths and old wives' tales she'd read were probably nonsense, but a few things did seem to hold true. "But they don't like iron, right?"

Cadell nodded. "Very true, which is why they do not allow humans to mine it."

Don't allow didn't mean it didn't exist. "But you're more powerful than any fae, right? You have physical strength, *and* you have magic."

"I have both those things, but a powerful fae with strong magic can ward against me and hide you from my sight."

"What?" She turned to him. "I've never read anything like that. How could the fae keep you away from me?"

Cadell led her down the path to the left, and soon Carys saw the silver-washed loch through the trees. The light grew a little brighter, and the birds started singing again.

"This isn't a book or a story in your world, Nêrys. This is real now. We are creatures of magic," Cadell said. "As they are. Magic works against magic. Though no human being or creature could keep me away from you, my lady, a powerful fae could hide you from my senses and I would not be able to find you. Be *careful* where you walk."

"Carys!" A bright shout from the trees ahead made her turn. A familiar grubby face ran toward her. "Mother said you were visiting us today."

She caught the little girl up in her arms, and Azar quickly climbed around to Carys's back. "How did she know? We just decided to come out here this morning."

Were unicorns precognitive? She'd never read anything like that in texts.

"Yasmin knows things." Cadell's face was soft when he looked at Azar. "You've grown, little one. Do you remember me?"

She shook her head. "No, but I know you're dragon." She bared her teeth. "Rawr."

"You are fierce." Cadell smiled. "I am dragon, and I am in your father's debt. He saved my lady."

"Is Carys your lady?" Azar hugged her around the neck. "So you *are* magic. I knew it." She looked up at Cadell. "Do you know my mother?"

"And your father, little star. I held you when you were first foaled."

Her little chin jutted out. "I'm not a baby now."

Cadell nodded deeply. "I can see that."

Azar scrambled down and ran ahead. "Mama!"

Carys looked up at Cadell. "You're good with kids."

"I should be," he muttered. "I have six of my own."

"Holy shit, Cadell."

He frowned. "Shit is the least holy thing I can think of."

"Mrs. Cadell must be busy." She cocked her head. "As were you."

He smirked. "Dragon hordes are not like human families. Our breeding is not romantic. Our seers decide which dragons should mate and when. Our children are all raised communally."

Carys whispered, "Dragon babies."

Cadell raised an eyebrow. "Are hidden until they are quite large."

"Even from me?" She gave him wide eyes and a hopeful smile.

"Even from you."

"Please let me see the dragon babies. Please, please, please."

"Absolutely not."

"Carys Morgan!" Yasmin's sweet voice sang through the trees. "And Cadell, my old friend." Next to Yasmin was the great golden stallion with a fearsome horn jutting through his forelock. He lifted his head and tossed it back with a loud whinny.

"Still posturing for guests, are we?" Cadell leaned back on his right leg. "Darius of the Blessing of Moray, I come bearing gifts from my lady and a personal token from the Horde of Eryri." Cadell offered a deep bow.

Darius transformed into his human form. The gold sigil on his forehead seemed to glow as he approached them. "Cadell of Eryri, you are welcome, and your lady needs no introduction as she saved the life of my child. She enjoys the favor of the blessing and will always be welcome."

Cadell glanced down at Carys. "I am glad to hear it, because she's been complaining about her boots for an hour."

Darius threw his head back and laughed before he turned to Carys. "Then Carys Morgan, take off your boots and make yourself at home."

CARYS SAW Aisling as soon as she entered the clearing. The delicate woman was sitting on a log bench on the other side of the flower-filled meadow, speaking with a man holding a flowering branch.

Cadell caught her stare. "The young mage is consulting with one of the unicorn potion masters. Unicorns are skilled in healing arts."

Carys watched Aisling wave a hand over a bundle of herbs, then turn to the unicorn and smile. The two were easy with each other, giving all the appearance of serious colleagues.

"Does Aisling have magic?" She looked at Cadell. "Duncan said that Lachlan was 'fae-touched.' That some Shadowkin have a little natural magic, like I can talk to dragons."

"You can talk to *me*," Cadell said. "Out loud. And you can hear when I speak to you. But you can't hear or speak to every dragon."

"Okay. What about Aisling?"

Cadell nodded at Aisling. "I don't know if she is fae-touched, but she has trained herself to use magic. Most Shadowkin are able to wield magic if they try, but most of them do not. It is a practice that takes strict discipline and years of study."

"So Aisling is training as a mage?"

"And an alchemist."

Carys looked away from the healers, not wanting to stare. "Why would she do that? She's royal, right?"

"Lady Aisling is the youngest daughter of the third daughter of the Éiren queen. Her parents are likely hoping she will marry someone… notable. For political reasons. More likely she will end up marrying a minor lord or a wealthy merchant for trading reasons."

"And she doesn't want that." Carys glanced at Aisling again.

Aisling was rapt, listening to another unicorn who had joined the healers, a woman who lifted a vial of some glowing blue liquid and was explaining something to Aisling and the man. She nodded seriously, and the three remained deep in conversation.

"Yeah," Carys muttered. "I don't see her being happy married off."

"I believe she prefers a scholar's life." Cadell started walking through the long grass. "It is a wise course. If she can prove her skills, she may avoid an unwanted marriage."

"And she was Seren's best friend?"

Cadell didn't answer right away. "They were more like siblings.

They grew up together, so they were close. I would call them sisters more than friends."

Carys thought about Laura and her sisters. "So they fought."

"Oh yes." Cadell kept his voice low. "Not as much after Seren returned to Scotland when they were older, but Seren told me they fought quite fiercely as children."

Sisters could be brutal against each other but also fiercely loyal. "Do you think Aisling could have harmed Seren?"

"I think anyone could have harmed Seren." Cadell glanced over his shoulder. "Except the cross human. He's quite trustworthy."

"Duncan? He lied to get me here, so I don't know if I agree about that."

Cadell frowned. "Did he?"

Carys opened her mouth, then closed it. "Okay, he didn't directly lie, but he definitely didn't tell me the whole truth."

"I haven't told you all my truths either, but that doesn't mean I'm a liar."

She narrowed her eyes at him. "What are you hiding, Cadell?"

"Many things. Aisling has spotted you."

Carys turned and saw the wave that Aisling was giving her. "We'll talk about this later. Hello!"

"Carys." Aisling walked across the meadow, her long skirts dragging in the tall grass. "Isn't it wonderful here? I don't know why it's always warmer in the unicorns' part of the forest, but it is. It's like they carry sunshine. I mean, I imagine. I've never seen sunshine, but Lachlan says it's very warm." She spotted Cadell and gave him a polite bow with her head. "Lord Dragon."

Cadell returned the gesture. "Lady Aisling. I believe the unicorns have elemental magic that they don't talk about freely, and that is why their dwelling places are more temperate. That is just a theory, however, and has no basis in true knowledge."

Aisling smiled brightly. "I suspect you're right! I missed you, Cadell."

"My lady." He nodded deeply. "Seren would be glad to see you thriving at court."

Aisling's gaze darkened, and Carys took note.

Sorrow for a lost friend? Guilt over her death? Cadell had told her she could trust no one, but Carys had a hard time imagining one sister wanting the other dead. Slightly maimed, perhaps, but never dead.

Aisling forced a smile to her face. "I get lost in my grief sometimes. Seeing you with Carys is haunting, I cannot lie." She turned to Carys. "You're identical, you see? Especially in formal clothes like that. The memories of Seren are sharp." She frowned and looked down. "Even though years have gone by, the loss still feels fresh."

Carys's doubt flew away. "Of course. I can't imagine how I'm going to feel when I see my uncle, and my father has been gone for six years. My wound isn't fresh, but I'm sure it will be overwhelming."

"I hope..." Aisling frowned. "I do hope you'll give all of us grace. Lachlan especially. It's hard seeing a loved one come back from the dead." She quickly added, "But not. Because obviously you're not Seren, but you can only imagine how it feels to see you."

"Lachlan..." Carys didn't know how much she wanted to say. "It's complicated."

"I'm sure it is. I know that he cares deeply for you." She glanced at Cadell. "He lost Seren. I know he doesn't want to lose you too. That's why he's been so adamant that you return to the Brightlands. I suspect he fears for you. That's all."

So Lachlan had confided in Aisling. Interesting.

"I know." Carys looked at Cadell. "But Cadell is here now, and I feel very safe with him. Lachlan is going to need to calm down."

Aisling started walking toward the trees, and Carys fell into step beside her. "Lachlan is usually very calm. He was even-tempered even as a child." She smiled. "And well-traveled. He tells the best stories in court. Most of us aren't like Lachlan. We don't go back and forth to the Brightlands."

"Why not?"

Aisling looked surprised. "I don't know who would take me.

Duncan? He's the only Brightkin I know, and he would never take me. He only takes Lachlan."

"Not anyone else? Ever?"

"No." Aisling's face was cautious. "It's a strange place for us. Stories of giant machines made of metal and bright screens with false images. No magic. No familiar magical creatures. To most Shadowkin, the Brightlands are fascinating but frightening."

Her friend Laura had asked Carys once if she'd ever go into space if she could. Carys hadn't even thought about it. Being an astronaut sounded a little like the way Aisling described the Brightlands. Theoretically possible, but so out of the realm of reality that it was hardly worth thinking about.

Carys asked her, "Have you ever wondered who your Brightkin is?"

"Yes!" Aisling's face brightened. "That I do wonder about. I wonder what kind of life she has. What it must feel like to be burned by the sun." She touched the edge of her chin. "Does my twin have children? What is my opposite nature? I think every Shadowkin wonders what kind of life we would have on the other side of the gates. But the reality of it is far more intimidating than the idea."

If Aisling's Brightkin was her opposite, she'd be bold, jovial, and possibly crass; Carys kind of wanted to meet her. "Where were you born? Maybe I can find her."

Aisling laughed. "Hardly a good use of your time."

They reached the far edge of the trees, and Carys spotted the silvery loch in the distance.

"I heard you met the kelpie the other day." Aisling shuddered. "Frightful creatures. We learn very young which bodies of water they haunt, but the signs might be foreign to you."

"I've studied mythology in my world, but I don't know how much of that lines up with the reality of your world. And I've spent the past few years teaching at the university about common threads in *world* mythologies, so—"

"You're a university professor?" Aisling's eyes brightened. "That's wonderful."

"Yes." Carys sensed a kindred spirit in a fellow academic. "I teach a class on introduction to world mythologies, so it's about myths and legends from all over the world and common threads between different cultures."

"That's fascinating, but I can see how that might not help much in Alba." Aisling gestured to the water. "Take kelpies. Most of them hunt in more remote areas, but this one has settled here, maybe to be close to the blessing for some reason."

"And do kelpies behave differently in Alba than in Ireland—in Éire?"

Aisling nodded. "They do. And different still are the northern nokkers and nixes. I've never been to Nordland, but my cousins in Anglia are familiar with them."

"There is water horse mythology in Asia too," Carys added. "It's a common legend that shows up in many parts of the world."

Aisling smiled. "Not a legend here."

"No, I guess not." Carys stared at the loch, her memory flashing back to the terrible equine monster that had nearly taken her life. She didn't want to think about even more monsters living in this strange world, but if she was going to stay here, she'd have to start believing every myth she'd ever studied might be reality in the Shadowlands.

She watched a small group of unicorn children dancing and playing in the meadow. "Why would this kelpie want to be close to the unicorns? To trap them?"

"I doubt it. Kelpies feed on human energy. I suspect it's something relating to Cadell's theory about elemental magic. Everyone is drawn to unicorns." She turned to face the lively clearing with unicorns in human and animal form. "They're all ridiculously beautiful of course. They're warm. They're innately good."

Cadell added, "And they're true. In the Shadowlands, that is a valued trait."

"An excellent point," Aisling said. "Like dragons, unicorns do not lie or conceal who they are, though they do conceal themselves. They're quite shy individually."

Carys spotted Azar. "Not that one."

"Isn't she darling?" Aisling's eyes glowed. "She's such a sprite. Her parents were double blessed by the gods."

Carys looked at Cadell. "I've heard that a couple of times now. 'By the gods.' Who are the gods here? I'm sure they're different than the ones in the Brightlands."

"The gods here are old," Cadell said. "And varied. They wear many forms, and humans serve the one that calls to them. Some appear as storms, some as spirits or energies. Many take animal forms when they want to wander the Shadowlands."

"Like Aengus Óg," Aisling said. "When he flies among the birds. Or Epona taking the form of a mare to walk with the horses."

"The Éiren people have many gods," Cadell said. "The Cymric do as well. They usually have different names, but they're often the same gods."

"Are the fae considered gods?"

"No," Aisling said. "But they're perhaps... closer than humans are."

Carys looked back at Cadell, but he inclined his head toward Aisling.

"Lady Aisling would be more expert in fae customs and culture than either me or Lachlan," he said. "The fae favor her people."

Aisling's cheeks turned rosy. "The Éiren court and the fae court are closely connected. Queen Orla took a fae noble as her consort long before I was born, and that has led to very close relations."

"As her consort?" Carys looked at Aisling. "Like she married a fae?"

"It's not unheard of," Cadell said. "Fae often become enamored with mortal beauty and will take human lovers. The queen of Éire is a powerful woman and known for her beauty."

"It's said that if a fae and human union is blessed by the gods, it might even produce a natural child." Aisling's hand clutched her skirt. "Can you imagine?"

"A child who belongs in neither world," Cadell said. "I would not envy that offspring."

"But imagine the power," Aisling said. "I might envy that." She quickly looked at Carys. "For using magic, I mean. Cadell is right. A child such as that would be neither human nor fae and might be shunned by both. Though it would be treasured by its parents, I am sure."

"That's right," Carys murmured. "Humans here can't have children."

Sorrow flickered across Aisling's face.

Cadell quickly said, "Nothing in the Shadowlands is born but by magic. While it is true that human and fae unions sometimes produce natural children if the gods approve, magic is still involved."

"And how do you know if the gods approve of you?" Carys looked at Cadell.

He shrugged. "How does anyone in any world know that? We should get back to our visit with Darius and Yasmin. I believe they have prepared a feast to welcome us, not that there will be anything for me to eat there."

Carys frowned. "What?"

"Unicorns do not eat flesh," Aisling said. "They will not willingly take the life of any living creature."

"And dragons *only* eat flesh," Cadell said. "Luckily I went hunting this morning."

* * *

THEY WERE HALFWAY BACK to the castle when Cadell shifted into dragon form and took to the sky overhead, letting out a great roar and flying in circles.

They approach.

"Who is they?" Did Cadell mean her uncle?

"The dragons are coming." Aisling watched him in the air. "Cadell's people are solitary by nature, but they always react this way when their kin approach." She took Carys's hand and picked up her speed. "Come on. You're not going to want to miss their landing."

Go, my lady. Cadell spoke from the air. *I will fly overhead and keep you in sight.*

"Okay." The fancy boots were squeezing her feet, but Carys pushed past the discomfort and started to half jog up the path to the village.

They ran up the hill toward Tower Ridge—the backbone of rock that overlooked the castle where the old tower stood—then down through the town where the rumor of approaching royalty had already spread. Villagers rushed from houses and shops up to the castle as the sky grew cloudy and the wind picked up.

Aisling guided Carys up to the first parapet along the castle walls where archers lined the defensive structure, though they seemed to be at ease.

The crowd gasped, and several people in the crowd turned and pointed to the sky.

The beasts appeared on the horizon, emerging from a bank of dark clouds, three winged forms, two of them carrying pendant-like coracles in their clutches.

"Do you see, Carys?" Aisling grabbed Carys's hand and pointed to the massive field that sloped down from the south side of the castle walls. "They'll land here. If they're coming in peace, they'll land in the town common."

What about if they're coming in war? She didn't voice the question because it was clear from the elation she felt from Cadell that the dragons were coming in peace.

"Let's stay here." Aisling was looking around, Carys's hand still clutched in her own. "It's not too crowded up here, and you'll have the best view."

The great beasts circled overhead, a ruby-skinned dragon with nothing in its claws, a fiery-orange dragon carrying a small coracle, and a massive black dragon with a gold-layered coracle that had to belong to a king.

The dragons spiraled overhead, growing closer and closer as they descended, and the black dragon let out a roar that shook the leaves on the trees and made the crowd shout and mill around.

"Gods save us if they were coming in war," one of the archers murmured.

Carys felt no terror but a vibrant thrill in her chest as she watched the red dragon descend, sweeping the field just a few feet over the grass with its red throat glowing, arrowing past the castle, and coming to rest on the crest of Tower Ridge.

The orange dragon came next, flying low and gently dropping the coracle, which tilted forward as it touched the grass. A large door dropped open with a mighty thunk! and a squad of guards wearing dark green leather poured onto the field, all of them marching in formation and forming a semicircle while the orange dragon flew past the castle and landed next to the ruby.

Behind the soldiers, three figures in light green cloaks emerged from the coracle.

"My aunt!" Aisling clapped her hands. "She traveled with the queen's guard in the green." Aisling pointed at the soldiers who followed them. "I wondered if Regan would come." Aisling started to wave from the parapet. "She's been with my Aunt Eamer, your step-mother—Seren's stepmother, I mean. She's my teacher, and it's been months since she visited. We'll be able to continue lessons if she stays for a while."

One of the cloaked figures drew back her hood to reveal a waterfall of flowing black hair much the same color as Aisling's.

"There's Regan." Aisling waved her arm higher.

Regan looked up, and her eyes landed on Aisling. She was younger than Carys had expected. Her face was unlined, her eyes a brilliant blue, and a stark strip of pure silver hair flowed from her temple down to her shoulder. She gave Aisling a short nod and then drew her hood up again.

"We'll meet her at the castle later," Aisling said.

The other two cloaked figures looked around but didn't stop, walking past the soldiers and heading to the gates while the soldiers clad in green waited in formation. None of them spared a look for Aisling.

Aisling's smile fell a little. "I'm sure she's tired from flying."

A growing trepidation grew in Carys's chest. Her father's twin was flying closer, circling the castle in the claws of a dragon, and she would see him soon. He would see her.

Of all the unreal things she'd seen since stepping through a fae gate, seeing her father's face seemed the most unreal of all.

Carys asked Aisling, "Have you ever flown?"

She shook her head. "Seren tried to take me, but I was too afraid."

The black dragon descended, the beast letting out one more ferocious roar before the gold coracle landed on the field, rocking forward to release the door. Immediately another squad of guards wearing bright red emerged while the black dragon beat its wings and flew back to the clouds, circling the castle with Cadell.

Behind the second group of guards, a dark-haired man of medium height emerged, marching toward the guards and speaking quietly to a courtier who followed on his right.

The crowd cheered in welcome, and a group of children ran past the castle, flying brightly colored kites as a group of courtiers from the castle stepped forward to greet the king's party.

A woman, clad in a deep blue cloak, stepped forward, bowing deeply, and the dark-haired man looked up.

Carys's breath caught in her throat. He wore a beard, and he had a barrel chest and thick arms muscled in a familiar way. He was older than her father, aged by life and years. He nodded at the courtiers, then scanned the crowd, waving to the people gathered to greet him. His eyes traveled up the castle walls, a frown marring his strong forehead.

The moment their eyes met, he froze.

Carys felt tears start to well up at the look of recognition.

Dad.

She blinked them away.

No, not her father, though he was the mirror image. A little older, a little harder. His expression was more severe, but his features were the same.

She saw him mouth a name. *Seren.*

She put a hand to her chest and shook her head, and the man closed his eyes.

He nodded. Not Seren. Not his daughter.

"Hail, King Dafydd!" someone shouted from the crowd in English. "Welcome to the king!"

The man turned from Carys and held his hand out to a tall woman who fell into step beside him, graceful in a green velvet dress and fur cloak. Her hair was covered, but Carys could see that it was nearly as long as her dress, dark as a raven's wing, and braided behind her in an intricate woven pattern.

"That's Eamer, the queen consort of Cymru."

"Your aunt?"

Aisling nodded. "And Seren's stepmother. She would be something like an aunt to you since she's married to your father's Shadowkin."

Eamer's eyes also found Carys in the crowd, but the woman was carefully expressionless before she looked away. The king took her hand and walked toward the castle as the crowds cheered and the dragons circled overhead.

"Now imagine that entrance on the battlefield" —Aisling spread out her arms— "with the dragons spewing fire and clearing the field before a flood of Cymric soldiers poured from their coracles and attacked."

"Good Lord." No wonder no one challenged them.

A few of the guards shot Aisling dirty looks but quickly looked away.

Aisling ignored the guards. "And don't forget the archers in coracles overhead, shooting from the air."

"Remind me not to make King Dafydd mad."

Aisling laughed. "I don't think there's a chance of that." She took Carys's hand and tugged it. "Come. You've seen the grand entrance. Now you should go and meet your uncle and aunt."

CHAPTER SIXTEEN

By the time Carys and Aisling reached the castle yard, the crowds had grown even bigger, with villagers rushing around and children running out to stare at the two massive beasts that had come to rest on Tower Ridge, waiting like great birds of prey on the horizon.

"I don't see Cadell."

Aisling was pushing through the crowd, Carys's hand gripped in hers as Carys tried not to panic.

"Aisling," she shouted, "do you see Cadell?"

"He won't have gone far." She kept Carys's hand gripped tightly. "Step back! Lady Carys and Lady Aisling to the castle!"

The crowd loosened, but it didn't disperse.

I'm here.

Cadell's voice came from behind her, and when Carys turned, she saw he was in human form again. This time he was walking next to a woman with black hair, light brown skin, and beautiful gold eyes like his. She was as tall as he was, her curly hair cropped short along the sides and longer on top. She was wearing the same leather armor, but hers was in pure black with gold details.

"My lady." Cadell stopped and spread his arm toward the other dragon. "This is Mared, Lady of Eryri and your uncle's dragon."

Mared gave Carys a short nod. "Lady Carys, we will escort you to the keep." With Mared taking the lead and Cadell safe at her back, the crowds parted, and she and Aisling were able to cross the yard with no further problems.

They walked through the inner courtyard where the Cymric soldiers were making camp, assisted by the Alban guard. The men and women shouted back and forth, mostly in English—which seemed to be the common language—teasing their compatriots with good-natured insults and more than one lurid proposition.

"The Dragon Guard and the Moray Guard are very often in the same places," Aisling said. "The soldiers in Lord Robb's castle here are the ones he travels with, so most of the men and women know each other."

"That makes sense."

The soldiers fell silent as the dragons passed. None of them engaged with either Mared or Cadell with more than a respectful nod.

"Lady Dragon Mared." The Alban guard at the double doors snapped to attention as they approached. "King Dafydd has requested an audience with Lady Carys in the portrait gallery."

"Understood." Mared turned to Aisling. "You must leave us now."

"Of course." Aisling turned to Carys and, after a moment of hesitation, gave her a quick embrace. "I'll meet with you later. Good luck."

Good luck. I hope you don't hate them.

Good luck. I hope they don't hate you.

Good luck. I hope you don't burst into tears when you see the face of your dead father.

All of that was running through Carys's mind as she followed Mared through the castle and into the same long hall where she'd spoken with Lachlan right after she'd arrived. The flickering blue lights were the same. The oppressive darkness of the walls was the same. But this time, instead of feeling alone and confused, she had Cadell at her side.

Carys wasn't alone anymore, but she was still confused.

Mared drew back a thick red drape and ushered Carys into the portrait gallery.

"Lady Carys." She nodded and stood at attention but did not walk farther into the room.

Dafydd, king of Cymru, was standing alone in front of Seren and Lachlan's wedding portrait when Carys walked into the gallery.

He turned, and Carys didn't burst into tears but it was close.

They stood frozen, both of them looking at each other for a long time.

Dafydd finally spoke in a low voice. "You look just like her."

"You sound just like him." She blinked back tears.

She wanted to run to him and hug him, but the man in front of her was not her father. His face was older and harder. He wore armor and a circlet of bright gold on his forehead. His hands were scarred from battle, not from carpentry.

Dafydd walked toward her slowly. "They tell me that my Brightkin died. Passed into the otherworld over six years ago."

She nodded. "His name was Gareth Morgan. My mother's name was Tegan. They died in a car accident. Do you know what that is?"

His eyes were pained. "I do, child."

"Did you feel it?"

"I think so." Dafydd frowned a little. "I had a bout of melancholy that I attributed to missing my daughter, but now I think that must have been his loss."

"He was a wonderful dad."

"I hope I was the same." Dafydd's eyes warmed. "Will you sit with me a moment, Carys Morgan? I would like to know my daughter's kin."

When Carys nodded, Dafydd held his arm out, ushering her to a pair of benches sitting in front of a lit fireplace that warmed a small circle near the hearth.

Mared and Cadell stood on either side of the doorway, guarding the gallery from interruptions. She thought of Cadell, reached out and tugged on the vine she felt wrapped around her heart. Cadell must have felt it. He turned and their eyes met.

Do you need me, Nêrys?

She shook her head.

"It is comforting, is it not?" Dafydd said. "To have that calm voice in your mind."

"It is. Right now?" She took a long breath and let it out slowly. "Very comforting."

Dafydd stretched out his legs and leaned forward. "I readied my coracle the moment Mared got the message from Cadell that you were here. I knew that Lachlan had a relationship with *his* Brightkin. It happens sometimes, particularly with children who grow up around the fae gates, but it never occurred to me that he would go in search of *you* when Seren died."

Carys took a deep breath. "I'm still trying to figure out how I feel about that."

Dafydd's eyes narrowed. "Yes, I imagine you are. In case no one has told you, you're allowed to feel however you feel. You're Seren's twin, but you have no obligation to Lachlan or to me. You have your own life, Carys Morgan."

"I appreciate you saying that."

"I can see Cadell's bond to you, and I can't explain it, but I'm glad for it." He cast his eyes toward the stoic woman standing across from Cadell. "Mared has been my truest companion and my closest confidante for over fifty years, not that you can tell by her grand expressions of devotion, mind you." He smiled and looked toward the archway. "I trust her more than anyone in my life—even my own wise queen—and she has never betrayed me."

"That's amazing." Carys wondered how old Cadell was. It hadn't occurred to her to ask.

"It's not in their nature, you see? Dragons will be brutally honest, but they will never hurt intentionally, and their loyalty goes far beyond anything that humans understand."

"I do trust Cadell." She frowned. "I trusted him immediately, and I can't really explain why. Maybe it's something about hearing his voice in my mind."

That's probably part of it.

She turned toward him and gave him a smile, but Cadell's face didn't even flinch from his soldier's stance. "He reminds me of a loyal knight."

"It's not a bad comparison, but they are knights who choose their commander. Dragons live for hundreds of years and can bond with multiple humans or none in that time. They choose us, not the other way round."

Carys frowned. "Why?"

"Why do they choose one human over another?" He shrugged. "No one knows."

"No, why do they choose us at all?" She glanced at Cadell, then back to Dafydd. "What do we give *them*?"

She felt Cadell start and knew her dragon was listening.

"A wise question," Dafydd said. "And one I cannot answer fully. Purpose, perhaps? Humanity, though I can already hear Mared's opinion on that." He smiled, reminding Carys of her dad. "The bond between a nêr and their dragon is a gift of the old gods, so it is beyond our reckoning, but we do know it is a sacred trust that we must honor."

She stared at Cadell for a long moment as he stood at attention and pretended to ignore them both. "I'll never take it for granted. Not ever." She looked around the cold stone walls. "Even with Duncan and Lachlan here, this place feels very... foreign."

"Because of the magic?" He raised his eyebrows. "Myths in your world are real in this one, while automobiles and skyscrapers are only tall tales here."

"Everything is different." She shook her head. "Even though I was born in Wales, I didn't grow up there. And I'd never been to Scotland until a week ago. I have a degree in mythology, but it seems like most of what I know only touches the surface of the reality here."

Dafydd frowned. "It will be dangerous for you here. You must not be afraid to lean on Cadell. He will guide you."

Carys leaned forward. "Did you ever wonder about my father? You're a king. Were you ever tempted to find him?"

"No." Dafydd shook his head. "I had no right to intrude on his life. But I did wonder about him. Sometimes when I went near the gates, I used to think I could feel him. Feel our connection."

"I like that idea," Carys said. "I like that maybe Seren knew about me, felt me a little bit. Even though we seem so different."

"I like to think your father was the steady, logical part of me." Dafydd crossed his arms over his chest. "I feel that he must have been sensible since I am so often not."

Carys grinned. "Yeah. He was sensible. Very *pragmatic.* Fun though."

"But tell me, Carys Morgan." Dafydd leaned forward and narrowed his eyes. "Could he tell a good joke?"

Carys burst into laughter and nodded, tears pricking her eyes through the pain of memory. "Yeah. Dad could tell a great joke."

"Good." Dafydd reached out and took her hand. "So my wildness gave him something too."

"I'd say so." She took the back of her hand and wiped her eyes. "This place is something else."

"Remember, all of humanity has its light and dark. And darkness isn't bad." The corner of his mouth turned up. "Though some here take our shadow nature as permission to act on their worst impulses, we know that it is not." His eyes darkened. "That is never an excuse."

Carys could see the grief hidden behind the man's kind expression. At the end of the day, he might be a king, but he was still a father.

"I remember when my parents died that people avoided talking about them around me," Carys said. "When that was the last thing I wanted. I wanted to talk about them all the time."

"I'm sure they loved you very much," Dafydd said. "I think my greatest fear when Seren died was that people would forget her. I'm an old man." His voice grew rough. "When I die, who will remember that wonderful child?"

"I won't forget her. I'll never forget her." Carys sat back and looked at the portrait on the wall. The proud chin and the confident eyes. "She was strong, wasn't she?" Carys spoke under her breath. "Sometimes I don't feel very strong."

"She was strong." Dafydd looked at the portrait. "And ornery."

Carys cocked her head. "Headstrong, maybe. Not ornery."

"Are you trying to defend her?" Dafydd huffed a little. "Seren was an *ornery* child. Contrary." Dafydd's eyes lit up anytime he said his daughter's name. "And passionate. Affectionate. Loyal. Her birth was quite unusual. Usually the fae give children to the Shadowkin of their mother, but I had no wife."

Carys frowned. "Eamer—"

"Queen Orla and my father were in negotiations for years about our marriage. I was a young warrior leading my father's army. I was still living in the barracks with my men! When Seren appeared at my door, *everyone* was shocked. I wasn't ready to be a father, but thank the gods my mother was still living." He smiled at the memory. "We managed somehow, that contrary little girl and me."

"That's so strange." Where was her mother's Shadowkin? Why hadn't Seren been given to her? Was she one of the blue lights lost in the fae forest? "What did your parents think of you suddenly having a baby?"

"Oh, in this place you don't question the arrival of any child. They are a great blessing because their arrival is the will of the gods."

"You don't see very many children here."

His expression darkened. "Only ever what the fae allow." He shook the shadows away. "Anyway, I wouldn't have cared what *anyone* thought. I took one look at Seren and fell in love." Dafydd held out his hands. "Those round cheeks and all that dark hair. She was a restless baby, always judging me with those brilliant blue eyes." He winked at her. "She made everyone laugh. Her grandmother was in raptures."

Dafydd's stories reminded Carys of her own father's anecdotes about her childhood. The same delight. The same pride. "I can see how much you loved her."

His chin lifted. "I'm sure your parents felt exactly as I did, Carys Morgan."

"They told me they did." She swallowed the lump in her throat. "I miss them every day, so it's really wonderful to see your face."

Dafydd stood. "I should take my leave. I am a king newly arrived in an ally's court, and there are many things I need to do." His eyes shone and his voice was rough. "But seeing my daughter's face again..." He swallowed hard. "Looking at your face is like seeing the sun shine."

Carys stood. "Can I hug you?"

He didn't even wait a moment but surrounded her with an embrace that loosened the flood of tears Carys had managed to hold back. She allowed herself to weep, her body shaking as Dafydd held her up.

Cadell ran toward her, but she didn't want to leave Dafydd's arms.

"I am not your father," he said quietly. "And you are not my daughter. But we loved them, and we lost them. Maybe we can help each other find peace."

CHAPTER SEVENTEEN

Carys spent the rest of the day in her own rooms, writing down everything she'd learned about Seren, about the Shadowlands, about the kings and people she'd met, about the myths that were real and the lore that was not. She was trying to organize her thoughts so she didn't feel lost. When the sky was dark and Bonnie came in to tend the fire, Carys saw Duncan waiting in the hallway by her door.

"Knock, knock." He leaned against the doorway. "How are you? You weren't at dinner."

She scrambled out of the bed, throwing a wrap over her shoulders. "It's cold. Come in and talk to me." She walked to the table. "I forgot about food."

"I noticed." Duncan stepped into the room and stood with his arms crossed, staring at her. "You can't skip meals here. It's cold and your body has to work harder. You walk more. The environment is harsher. There are no cars or elevators or bicycles."

"Oh, no way." She pointed down. "Are you saying that my e-bike isn't waiting in the garage downstairs? That's wild—I just ordered it online."

Duncan glowered. "Very amusing."

Bonnie shook her head. "It's like you two are speaking another language entirely."

Duncan turned to the maid. "Bonnie, would you be a dear and fetch Carys a tray with some bread and cheese?"

"There are some cold pies stored in the larder as well, Lord Duncan." She nodded. "I'll make a tray, and she'll eat it." She stood, dusted off her skirts, and looked to Carys. "What would you like to drink, my lady?"

"Just water is—"

"Wine," Duncan said. "Or beer. It'll be easier on your stomach."

Carys sighed. "Right. Wine please, Bonnie."

"I'll be back in two shakes of a duck's tale." She looked at Duncan. "And you?"

"Beer."

Bonnie rolled her eyes. "Why did I even ask?"

The maid walked out, and Duncan came to sit at the table across from Carys.

"How was your meeting with Dafydd?" he asked, his arms still crossed over his chest.

"Good. Emotional." She shrugged. "Kind of expected that."

"Did he try to take you to Caernarfon?"

She frowned. "He didn't bring it up. Why?"

"The Cymric think their country is the greatest in the world."

"Because it is. Obviously."

"Dear God, save me from Welsh pride." He rubbed his eyes. "Every person in this blasted place thinks their country is the greatest in the world. The Albans, the Cymric, the Anglian, and dear God, especially the Éirens. It nearly makes me appreciate the union a bit." He held his fingers close together in a pinch. "A *tiny* bit."

Carys set her journal on the table. "So I've been making notes about everything and—"

"Where'd you find that?" Duncan leaned forward. "That journal. Paper can be hard to come by here."

Carys pointed to the wardrobe. "There was an empty journal in the back of the chest. It took me a minute to get the hang of the fountain pen at the writing desk, but I managed."

"I forgot about Seren's journals," Duncan muttered. "I wonder if Lachlan has the rest."

Carys's curiosity was piqued. "Seren kept journals?"

"Meticulously." Duncan sat back. "She was known for them. Wrote everything down, that one."

"My dad was that way." She mused. "He always had a notebook on him. Was always writing. My mother had her sketchbook, and my dad had his notebook."

"And you?"

"Nothing." She shrugged. "I'd rather have a book to read. I don't need everything written down. If I don't remember it, it probably wasn't that important." She squinted. "That may explain a good portion of my problems at work."

Duncan smirked. "Seren recorded everything. She'd write down names of people she met, how the crops were looking, what the women wore to court banquets—there's one tomorrow night, by the way. You can't forget that one, because it's the welcome dinner for Dafydd and Eamer."

Carys smiled. "I'd say I'll write it down, but I won't."

"Being aware of your negative traits doesn't excuse them." He cocked an eyebrow at her. "Bonnie will remind you; just don't leave the castle." He looked at the journal again. "What are you writing?"

"It sounds like I'm being a little like Seren, but only for organizational purposes." She folded down a corner of the book. "There's so many people and so much new information."

"I was young when I learned all of it," he said. "A sponge. It probably seems a bit overwhelming."

"Seems? No, it's very overwhelming. And I wish to hell I'd brought my old Celtic mythology textbook because I've been studying more American mythology the past five years, so I'm in way over my head."

"I'm sure there are books in the library here, but they're mostly going to be in Gaelic."

"Not superhelpful." Carys stared at the journal. "Mostly I'm trying to figure out who had a reason to kill Seren. And I'm thinking there's a lot."

Duncan sat up straight. "You're trying to figure out who... Why would you do that?"

"Because I'm going to figure out who killed my sister," Carys said. "Obviously. I already told Lachlan and—"

"You told Lachlan about this, and he approved?" Duncan's face was a storm. "That reckless bastard—"

"He didn't approve, but I don't care."

"Did you tell Cadell?" Duncan frowned. "Where is Cadell?"

"On the roof." She pointed up. "He just curls up there like a cat, I think."

Not at all like a cat, Nêrys.

She nodded. "He's close."

"This is ridiculous." Duncan stood and started pacing. "Lachlan was right. You're going back to the Brightlands. Tomorrow."

"Absolutely not." She crossed her arms over her chest. "You're not my boss, and neither is Lachlan."

"I took responsibility for you when I brought you to this place. You have friends, Carys. People who love you and are going to be waiting for you. You need to think of them and not the ghost of a dead woman."

Carys did think about Laura and Kiersten, but she also thought about Laura's sisters. About Lachlan's face when he talked about Seren. About Dafydd's grief.

"I know there are dangers." She uncrossed her arms and leaned forward. "And I understand why you and Lachlan want me to go." She took a deep breath so she didn't overreact. "I know you're worried. But as you correctly pointed out earlier, I have a *dragon*. Cadell and I have a unique opportunity to get justice for my sister."

Duncan looked up. "I suspect Cadell wants you safe more than he wants to know who killed Seren."

I want both.

"He wants both."

I am on the roof above you and will burn down the castle, grab you, and fly you to our horde if need be, Nêrys.

"Yeah, he's got me covered." She patted the journal. "And I have you, even though we don't really... get along."

"It's not my job to be your friend—it's my job to get you back to Scotland in one piece." He looked at the door. "Where is Fiona? You need food."

"Not Fiona," Carys whispered. "Bonnie."

Duncan growled and muttered something in Gaelic.

"Cadell says I can trust you," Carys said. "He calls you the cross human, which is..."

"Accurate," Duncan growled.

"Fairly accurate, yeah." Could Lachlan and his twin be more opposite? "But I respect that grumpiness and I appreciate the honesty, okay? Cadell trusts you. That's good enough for me. I think between the two of us, we can figure out my sister's murder."

"What?" Duncan stopped pacing, walked back to the table, and sat, propping his elbows on the table and staring at her. "Why do you think we could possibly—"

"Because we're both smart, and all English language speakers have been subjected to more true-crime entertainment than most of us ever wanted or needed," Carys said. "We probably know more about solving crimes than the police here."

"There are no police here."

"See?" She spread her arms. "We're already the best candidates to do this."

"Why?" His expression and his elbows hadn't moved. "Why should we?"

"Because she deserves justice."

He leaned forward and narrowed his eyes. "*Why*, Carys?"

"Because…" Carys's voice dropped to a whisper. "I love Lachlan. I do. But—"

"Part of you wonders if he killed his wife?"

"No!" She bit her lip. "Yes?"

Duncan raised an eyebrow.

"A very tiny, teeny-tiny part." She held her fingers together. "Like… *microscopic*."

"I'm not going to tell him you think that because it would *crush* him. Why do you think Lachlan could have—"

"I don't think that!" That tiny, *tiny* part of her wondered, but only because Cadell didn't seem to trust Lachlan and Lachlan hadn't told her his wife had been murdered. He didn't even seem sure that she *had* been murdered.

But what husband wouldn't wonder if his previously healthy wife suddenly keeled over? Didn't police always suspect the husband first? Or was Carys watching way too much TV?

"I suspect *everyone* right now," she said. "If you hadn't been in a completely different dimension when Seren was killed, Cadell and I would suspect you too."

"You should. *I'm* a bastard." He drummed his fingers on the table. "But Lachlan is nice and charming and not me at all. And he loved Seren madly."

It stung even though Carys already knew it.

A muscle in Duncan's jaw twitched, and she could feel the irritation rolling off him, but he let out a small sigh and the determined set of his mouth softened just a little.

"Fine. I will help you solve Seren's murder, but I'm doing it for her. She was a good woman, and she deserved a long life."

He cared for her too. Cadell's voice echoed in her mind. *And he cares for you.*

Carys ignored the strange twist she felt in her chest. It didn't matter that Duncan cared for her. And he was right.

Seren had deserved better.

Her twin had a father who loved her. Friends who depended on her. A dragon who was tied to her very soul. Seren had deserved a long life flying through the Shadowlands with her dragon and husband at her side. One day, if Carys had children, her sister might have raised their twin in this world. Their lives were inextricably linked, and Carys felt a low, burning fire of anger when she thought about Seren's life being cut short.

"Okay then." Carys opened her journal. "Tell me everything about Seren that you remember. I want to know it all."

THE NEXT MORNING after Bonnie helped Carys dress, Duncan met her in the foyer of the castle where two arms of a grand staircase met like two branches of a stone river, curving around to meet a statue of a rearing unicorn.

He was holding a chicken leg wrapped in paper and shoved it at her. "Eat."

It smelled amazing, and she realized she'd forgotten to eat breakfast. "Why are you always trying to feed me?" She squinted. "And why do you look all..." She waved a hand up and down.

"What?" Duncan took a step back and looked down.

"You look... fancy."

"Fancy?" He snorted. "Hardly."

Duncan was dressed in the same wrapped leggings most of the men in the castle wore, a kilt in weathered brown and blue with red details, and a wool knit sweater on the top. His beard was freshly trimmed, and his wavy red-brown hair was slightly tamed.

He looked good. He looked... handsome.

Really handsome.

Dammit, there was that strange twist in her chest again. There was a part of her—a small part—that acknowledged that if she was attracted to Lachlan, it was natural to be attracted to Duncan as well. That made sense because she was in love with Lachlan and Duncan looked exactly like his brother, and that had to be normal.

Right?

She didn't want to think about it, so she took a bite of the chicken leg. "Thanks," she muttered around the bone. "This is good."

The corner of his mouth lifted. "My *lady*. Your table manners befit your lofty station."

"Shut up." She gulped down the bite and wiped her mouth with the napkin. "Okay, I guess I was hungry after all."

"You ate like a bird last night, and you need to take care of yourself."

Carys took another bite. "I don't like steak-and-kidney pie. My dad loved it, and my mother would make it, but I just never—"

"In this place, you eat when there's food." He took an apple from his pocket. "Finish that and then eat this apple. I packed some cheese too. I know you like cheese."

"Who doesn't like cheese?" Carys scoffed. "Sociopaths, vegans, and people who hate happiness?"

Duncan stared at her. "Unicorns."

Touché.

"Okay, but they're herbivores, obviously, so that makes sense." She walked at Duncan's side as they turned right down a corridor to the left of the stairs. "Unicorns are, like, the opposite of sociopaths. Where are we going?"

"Aisling's work room. She'll know who has Seren's journals."

"Can't you ask Lachlan?"

"Couldn't find him this morning," Duncan muttered. "He's avoiding me. I think he's avoiding everyone since you arrived."

"Right." Carys frowned. "Could Aisling have them?"

"Possibly. I don't really know what happened to Seren's things after she died. I imagine some of them were taken back to the chamber you're staying in, but Lachlan probably kept most. Maybe some were sent to her father. Her journals though..."

"Journals are really personal."

"Exactly."

"The good thing is, if we can find them, they'll give us more insight to what was going on in her life than anything else. Unless they're all about crops and ladies' dresses, of course." She finished the chicken leg, wrapped it in the napkin he handed her, and took the apple Duncan held out. "So why are you all dressed up?"

He raised a single eyebrow and took the chicken leg in the cloth. "I'm not dressed up."

"For you?"

He huffed. "Elanor commanded me to clean up for the banquet tonight. I expect she'll have clothes picked out for you too. When Elanor commands you, you don't ignore her."

"Okay, but actually she seems really nice."

"She's a formidable queen," Duncan said. "Born in Briton. Fostered in France—called Gaulle here. Not within the Queens' Pact, but something similar. She's highly educated, and she's a good match for Robb. She was like another mother to me as a child, so I treat her like my own."

"And she was Seren's foster mother," Carys said. "So she knew her better than her stepmother probably."

"Not probably. Definitely." Duncan pointed them down another hallway.

Carys couldn't figure out how he knew where he was going, but she imagined it had something to do with the paintings on the walls because all the corridors looked the same. She caught a familiar image from the corner of her eye and stopped. "Hey."

He halted immediately. "What?"

Carys pointed to the painting just past the corner. "That painting..." She frowned. "It looks like my mother's work. But not."

He walked over and stared at it. "It's a landscape. I don't know enough about art to tell one style from another, but I do know this one was painted by Efa of Eryri. She was a painter in a religious cult of some kind."

"How do you know?" She couldn't stop staring at the snowy peaks of the mountains in the painting. It wasn't just *like* her mother's work —it was startlingly similar in brushstroke and perspective. The use of light was different, but that would be expected in a dimension without a sun.

Duncan pointed to a small gold plaque in the frame. "It says it right here. Efa of Eryri, Daughter of Epona. Eryri is the name for the Snowdonia region in North Wales. Epona is a goddess."

"She's a Celtic fertility goddess, if I'm remembering correctly." Carys leaned closer to the painting. "Efa of Eryri. Eryri is where Cadell is from."

"I'm no art expert, but I've heard her name before, so she must be fairly well known."

"She's still living?"

"I don't think so. From the date on this painting, she'd be well over a hundred by now if she was still living." He nudged her back down the hallway. "Maybe she was related to your mother's Shadowkin."

"Oh, you're right!" Something like that definitely made sense. "Very cool that she was famous though." Carys smiled. "My mother would love that."

"Was your mother well-known in America?"

"Not really. She rarely sold anything; she mostly painted for herself and for friends. She did behind-the-scenes work in Hollywood for a while. She made a lot of money doing that when they first moved. Mostly storyboards. Costume sketches. That sort of thing."

Duncan looked impressed. "Amazing. She must have been talented."

"Have you heard of Javier Torres, the film director?"

Duncan halted. "Are you serious? Of course I have. His films are some of my favorites. I loved *Army of the Underworld*."

Carys smiled. "My mother did the storyboards for that. For a number of his films. Javier considered her his visual muse. I still talk with him and his wife sometimes. They always send me a very cool Christmas card."

"Fuck me," Duncan muttered. "Do all Californians know famous people?"

Carys laughed. "Hardly."

They turned another corner, and Carys could feel a draft coming from an open outer door at the end of the hall. They were near the courtyard, and the chilly morning air gusted into the castle.

"We're closer to the working part of the place now," Duncan said. "Alchemy can be messy. Aisling works here."

Carys kept her voice low. "Cadell said that she learned alchemy because she probably wouldn't make a good arranged marriage. Is that true?"

"Oh." Duncan shrugged. "Maybe with *her* family, yes. But she's a brilliant woman. I think she always preferred books to politics."

They approached the end of the hall, and Carys saw a wooden door cracked open. Two voices were raised inside.

"...don't think that's appropriate, Lachlan."

"Why not? I think Seren would want you to get to know her better. After all, she's her sister."

"You're not just talking about me getting to know her. You're talking about—"

"Company." Duncan pushed the door open, uninterested in eavesdropping the way Carys would have. "Lachlan, Aisling."

Aisling was standing in the middle of the room, her arms crossed, looking uncomfortable with Lachlan standing across from her. She was wearing a plain blue dress and a white apron that looked like it had seen burns and tears aplenty.

Lachlan was wearing clothes Carys hadn't seen before, wool leggings like Duncan, but his jacket and kilt were fitted, and his boots reached up to his knees. His hair was bound firmly at his neck, and he wore a leather vest over his chest.

His eyes landed on Carys immediately, and he turned to face her. "Carys."

God, he was so beautiful she wanted to weep. She wanted to run to him and kiss him good morning. Her body wanted to know why he wasn't waking beside her. She wanted...

She wanted him so much.

"Lachlan," she said his name quietly. "How are you?"

"Better for seeing you." His eyes spoke volumes that weren't for others to hear.

Aisling wore a stiff smile, and Duncan cleared his throat.

"Duncan." Lachlan frowned. "Why are you holding a chicken bone?"

Duncan grunted but he didn't answer.

Lachlan spoke to Carys. "I was just telling Aisling that I think it would be nice for her to spend some time with you while you're here." He glanced at Aisling, and the look they exchanged made all of Carys's antennae go up.

"After all," he continued, "she and Seren were like sisters."

"That part is true." Aisling uncrossed her arms and smiled brightly. "Good morning, Carys. I'm so glad Duncan brought you. I was hoping I could lure you into my lair."

CHAPTER EIGHTEEN

Aisling bustled toward them while Lachlan hung back. "Watch the floor just there. It's a mess."

Carys glanced at the spot where she was pointing and saw a steaming liquid spilled on the floor. It looked as if it was eating away at the stone.

"I dropped a bottle of acid when I was working earlier," Aisling said. "I was about to clean it up when Lachlan interrupted me." She tossed a handful of something that looked like grain over the steaming liquid. "You can go, Lachlan. Let me show Duncan and Carys my workroom."

Aisling's castle workroom looked like a wizard's laboratory, and Carys was more than a little jealous.

"This is so cool," Carys murmured.

"Cool is good, correct?" Aisling smiled as she worked. "I believe I have that right, that you're not speaking of temperature."

"Cool is very good."

There were long bookshelves all along the front wall where they'd walked through the arched doorway. The shelves were piled with various manuscripts, scrolls, and more than a few piles of loose papers.

There were assorted specimens in jars, many of which Carys didn't want to examine too closely, and pots of trailing ivy cascaded from various nooks and crannies.

There was a row of sizable windows along the outer wall, pushed out from the chamber so shelves could be built into them to catch the cool light outside. They were lined with different potted plants, clippings in jars, and tubes holding roots and bulbs.

"I love your laboratory." Carys turned in circles, taking everything in.

"I'm glad you came to visit." Aisling had a smudge of dirt on her cheek, and she wiped her hands on her apron. "It's my favorite place."

Lachlan's eyes were fixed on Carys. "You're looking well this morning, Carys. How did you sleep after your meeting with Dafydd?"

She glanced at him. "I slept well." Her irritating heart raced to see his admiring stare.

"Will you be at the banquet tonight?" Lachlan's voice reminded her of lazy mornings in bed.

"Of course she will be." Aisling shooed him out the door. "Go. I imagine your father is already on his horse. Go put your arrows to good use, Lord Lachlan. Your guests will be hungry tonight."

Lachlan sent Carys one last look before he left the high-ceilinged room.

"He's going hunting with Lord Robb and King Dafydd." Aisling narrowed her eyes at Duncan. "Weren't you invited, Duncan?"

"I was, but I'm useless with a bow." Duncan wandered over to the wall of plants and looked into the courtyard. "Give me a shotgun and I'd be helpful."

"Ah, but the fae would have none of that." Aisling looked at Carys and winked. "We're limited on what metals we're allowed to mine and we have no access to gunpowder, though I have heard the Shadowlands in the Far Eastern world have it."

Carys looked at a row of jars, tubes, and simmering cauldrons on the worktable. "So you're a chemist?"

"Alchemist." Aisling called out, "Nate?"

A young man came from behind a set of bookshelves. "Yes, Lady Aisling?"

"I'd clean up that spill, but I have guests. Can you get it for me? I don't want any accidents."

The young man bowed. "Of course, my lady."

"Use the boar-leather gloves." She motioned Carys toward the windows where Duncan was standing. "It's my own space and I love it. I brew practical things for the castle and the town mostly. Potions, healing salves, teas, and tinctures, of course. But I do experiment with rarer ingredients when I can get them, and I practice my spells, of course. Regan will be with me later when she's rested."

"Where does your aunt live most of the time? Is she close by?"

Duncan muttered, "Thank God, no."

"Regan lives here and there." Aisling laughed a little. "She's not married, so she can do as she pleases."

"Regan travels with the fae," Duncan said. "Be careful talking with any of her companions. They'll be like Dru."

"Right."

Aisling waved a hand. "Duncan is suspicions of anything fae. I grew up with the Good People in my grandmother's court, so they don't bother me."

"Yet." Duncan surveyed her plants. "Your herbs are looking well. I'm impressed you can grow rosemary inside."

"It's always a challenge to get them enough light." Aisling pointed to a system of mirrors hanging along the walls. "I use those to amplify the natural light. We don't have a sun, so growing anything indoors is a challenge, particularly warm-weather plants."

Carys frowned. "With no sun, how do you grow anything at all?"

"We have light." Aisling pointed to the windows. "We have... I suppose it doesn't make much sense to you."

From the moment Carys had arrived in the Shadowlands, the lack of a sun had nagged at the back of her mind. The light grew brighter in the morning and the sky was illuminated by stars at night, but that was the only familiar light. It was as if the sky was constantly covered by a high fog that blocked the heavens.

"Magic," Duncan said. "There's no other explanation. It's not very satisfying for our scientific minds."

Someone spoke from the doorway. "Magic is its own kind of science."

Aisling turned, and the smile that spread across her face was slightly frantic. "Regan. I didn't expect you this early."

Carys turned and saw the raven-haired woman from the coracle walking into the room. She was dressed in severe clothing, wearing a long tunic, leggings, and a fur cape with a streak of red at the shoulder. A fox pelt.

It was impossible to say how old Aisling's aunt was. She could have been fifty or thirty. Her face carried a slight blur over it, as if it might change depending on the angle that you looked.

She stared at Carys and spoke to Aisling. "I wanted to start your lessons today, Niece."

"I'm ready." Aisling took off her apron and hung it on a standing rack by her worktable. "I have my most current spells worked out, and if you'd like to look over them before I add them to the grimoire, I can—"

"You're Carys Morgan." Regan walked toward Carys, bright blue eyes fixed on her face. "You really are her twin."

Aisling's hands were gripped in her skirt. "She's Seren's Brightkin, Regan. Of course they look alike."

"How... alarming." Regan's eyes didn't blink.

"Not to me." Everything about Regan put Carys on alert. "You knew Seren?"

"Of course she did." Duncan angled his body so he was ever so slightly between Regan and Carys. "Lady Regan."

Regan looked up and smiled seductively. "Duncan Murray. Blacksmith of the Brightlands." Her tongue hissed on the last syllable. "You know I am no lady."

"In that we're in agreement."

She cast a ravenous look from his boots to his beard. "Let me know when you've changed your mind, Brightkin."

"Not fucking likely."

Aisling tried to keep the mood light. "Let me introduce you properly. Regan, this is Carys, Seren's Brightkin. Carys, this is my aunt and teacher, Regan, Lady of Ulaid. She is the daughter of Queen Orla and a very talented mage."

The young one feels guilt. The older one feels nothing.

Carys spotted Cadell from the corner of her eye. He was standing in human form on the other side of the workroom windows. He wasn't looking at her but at Regan.

Carys turned to Aisling, startled by the mix of emotions playing across the woman's face. She was a bundle of nerves. Guilt or worry?

Why? From her aunt? From Carys and Duncan? From her aunt meeting Carys?

"We should go," Carys said. "I don't want to interrupt your time with your aunt, but we'll see you at the banquet tonight, right?"

"Of course." Aisling let out a quick breath. "And if there's anything you need before tonight—"

"Seren's journals," Duncan said. "The record books she kept. Do you know where they are?"

"Oh goodness." Aisling looked down and blinked. "Uh, probably with Lachlan? I would think they'd be with Lachlan. Check with him."

"Are you okay?" Carys asked. "You seem..."

Guilty. Cadell was right. Aisling looked guilty.

"Perhaps it is the sight of your face, Carys Morgan."

Carys turned to Regan, who had perched herself on a stool near Aisling's worktable.

"Why?" Did Aisling have something to do with Seren's death? Was she feeling guilty about something Lachlan had asked her to do? What was she hiding?

Cadell's voice came to her mind again. *She's hiding something.*

"Don't be silly." Aisling shook her head. "Carys, of course it's not the sight of your face. It's still a bit startling to see you, but—"

"She couldn't save her." Regan stared at Carys, and her voice was cold. "Can you imagine failing like that?"

Duncan sucked in a breath.

Regan continued to tear down her niece, piece by piece. "My niece trained her whole life to be a healer. She studied so hard, and yet she couldn't save her best friend."

Carys looked at Aisling, but the soft young woman was frozen. Her cheeks were red, and she stared at the ground in front of her feet.

"Does she have a lover? A family? Even a pet?" Regan continued. "Of course not. She sacrificed everything, and yet when her dearest friend was dying, she couldn't even save her." Regan offered Carys a smirk. "Makes one feel quite useless, doesn't it?"

Regan's voice dripped with cruelty, but Aisling was silent. She gripped her tunic in both hands, her body stiff and her shoulders tense.

Duncan was the one who broke the silence. "You tried, lass. Pay her no mind. Everyone in the castle knows how hard you tried."

"No, she's right." Aisling's voice was barely over a whisper. "Regan is right. I couldn't save my closest friend." She blinked hard, and her hands released her tunic. "Carys, Duncan, I'll see you tonight." She lifted her eyes, and her expression was carefully blank. "I should start my lessons now."

* * *

I HATE HER. Carys gritted her teeth as they walked out of the laboratory and into the courtyard to meet Cadell. She glanced at Duncan, then back at the windows into Aisling's laboratory. "She's cruel."

Duncan nodded. "Aye, she's that."

"Why does Aisling—"

"We can't pick our family, can we?" He looked straight ahead. "There's no helping it, dove. The moment Aisling decided to study magic, Regan was her only option. The Éiren queen wouldn't allow

Aisling to be trained by anyone outside the family, and Regan is the most powerful mage in Éire."

"So she has to just... deal with it?"

Duncan stopped when they reached Cadell's side. "We all have our burdens to bear."

Cadell spoke out loud. "Regan is a venomous snake, but she was far away in the Anglian court when Seren was killed. I checked."

Duncan lifted an eyebrow. "And does that make a difference when magic is involved?"

"She would have to be an extraordinarily powerful mage to kill someone from that distance, and I don't see that power in her," Cadell said.

"What if she hired someone to kill Seren?" Carys wasn't ready to eliminate Regan when the woman was so obviously evil.

"Then she would have killed that person to cover her tracks," Cadell said. "It's possible. I will ask Mared to look into it."

Duncan said, "Something tells me that if Regan wanted to kill someone, she'd do it with her bare hands. And she'd enjoy it."

"She makes no attempt to hide her malevolence." Cadell turned and walked toward the gates. "In that, at least, she wears an honest face. Nêrys, what are your wishes today?"

Carys fell into step beside him with Duncan bringing up the rear. "There's a banquet tonight, but I don't have to do anything for that. Aisling said Lachlan might have Seren's journals, but he's out hunting for tonight. So..." She looked over her shoulder. "Any ideas?"

"I have one." Duncan glanced at the dragon. "But you're not going to like it."

Cadell turned. "What?"

"Carys is determined to stay here and find out who killed Seren with your help." He looked at Carys. "That means she's here for more than a couple of days. More than a weekend camping trip." He raised an eyebrow.

Carys understood immediately. "I have to go through the horrible fairy murder forest again, don't I?"

The woods were just as dark as she remembered, but with more context, they seemed even more menacing. Carys and Duncan stood on the edge of the forest where Cadell waited.

They'd walked for an hour to get there, declining the dragon's offer to fly them in his massive claws.

Carys wasn't quite ready for that yet.

"I should not go with you." Cadell paced along the boundary of the forest path. "I will attract more attention than if I remained here. Within the gate, attention is perilous."

He clearly wasn't very pleased about the situation.

"I'll be fine, Cadell." Carys stared into the darkness between the trees. "What's in there? Really?"

"Dark fae," Duncan said quietly, wrapping clothes around his hands. "And their creatures. The wisps you know. Pixies, which are not as nice as their name. Trolls, of course, they're the hungriest. And sluagh." He spat out the last word.

"Slow-uh what?"

Cadell answered, "The sluagh are the souls of the angry dead. Most of the wild souls who don't become Shadowkin turn into wisps." His voice was as gentle as she'd heard it. "They'll trick you, lead you away from the path, but they're not dangerous in themselves."

"The sluagh are different," Duncan said. "They're furious they were never given life. Full of spite. Do you remember Dru's face after we walked through the first time?"

Carys nodded.

"That's the sluagh."

Cadell took a deep breath. The light behind him was pearl grey and luminous, but his face was dark. "Perhaps it's a mistake to let Carys go through without me."

"No, you were right the first time," Duncan said. "I've walked this path more times than I can count. Now they know her footsteps too." He looked at Carys. "You'll be fine with me. Just don't stray."

Carys nodded and looked at Cadell. "Your magic won't work here, right?"

"No." He glared at the trees. "The dark fae wards sap my power."

"Then it's better to leave me with Duncan, right? Like you said, a dragon in the gate will attract attention."

With an angry huff, he stepped back over whatever barrier he'd crossed, stretched his body into his dragon form, and crouched in a nearby clearing, his wings folded back and steam escaping from the sides of his massive jaws.

"And that's what a dragon looks like when he has a tantrum," Duncan whispered. "Come on then. Do you have your gloves?"

"I grabbed my wool ones from your cottage when we stopped." She pulled them on, covering her skin. "So the sluagh will ignore me? Is that what tried to grab me before?"

"I don't fully know, but stay with me and you'll be fine." He held out his hand. "And just maybe I can convince you to stay in our world."

"Nope." She looked over her shoulder. "Besides, do you really want to deal with Cadell if you came back without me?"

The big man glanced at the dragon, who let out a rumble like low thunder.

"I'll bring her back." Duncan grabbed Carys's hand. "Probably."

They started into the forest, and Carys kept her hand tightly gripping Duncan's.

Whispers came to her ears, the fluttering, clicking sounds of winged insects she couldn't see. The sound of pebbles dropping on dusty ground. Invisible creatures that fluttered past her ears and face, snagging her hair and laughing before they flicked away.

She kept her eyes on Duncan's back as he forged his way through the forest, stepping where he stepped, walking as close to him as she could without tripping. At one point Duncan took her hand, wove their fingers together, and wrapped her arm around his waist, drawing Carys close so her body was pressed against his and their joined hands were firm on his abdomen.

They walked deliberately through the underbrush, Carys matching Duncan's steps.

She felt her body react. It was impossible not to. He smelled like a campfire and whatever fragrant oil they'd used on his skin when they trimmed his hair that morning. Spicy and intoxicating. His clothes were rough when her cheek pressed against them, and the wool scratched against her skin, relieving some of the pressure that seemed to build the farther they walked.

Duncan didn't speak, but after interminable minutes of primeval clicks, menacing laughter, and distant music that tempted them off the path, she heard him speak softly.

"Nearly there."

The light grew, and Carys could see blue between the trees.

"Stars." She smiled. "I can see stars."

"Yes." His hand spread and pressed her palm to his abdomen. "We've crossed the threshold to home."

Duncan heaved a breath, and she felt his shoulders relax. The hand that pressed her palm to his body relaxed and he cleared his throat. He slowed and released her from his grip.

"Probably safe now." He didn't look at her but glanced back at the forest and the dancing blue lights that called to Carys. "Ready?"

She looked at the blue lights and found herself wanting to join them even though she knew the danger. "They make me sad."

His voice was soft. "I know."

Duncan and Carys walked down the path, and she could see Murrayshall House in the distance.

"I'm on sabbatical from my job," she said. "But what about you? Can you afford to take time off?"

The corner of his mouth turned up. "Sabbatical? Are you writing a book?"

"You didn't answer my question."

He sighed. "I'm disgustingly rich. It's the one thing my father actually gave me before he died. I don't really have to work. I just keep busy at the forge because I like it, and Andy keeps me busy here." He looked down. "But none of it will fall apart without me."

He kept looking at her, and Carys knew it was her turn.

"I'm not writing a book." She bit her lip. "I probably should after this, but I'm on medical leave."

Duncan frowned. "Medical what?" He froze. "Because you're sick? What are you doing here?" His voice rose. "Carys, do you need a doctor?"

"Not that kind of medical leave." She huffed a breath. "I've been depressed for the past two years. I think it was because of Seren's death."

"That shouldn't be debilitating." His forehead was creased with worry. "Why would that be so bad that—"

"Maybe because she was poisoned, okay?" Carys threw out her hands. "I don't know. Maybe because magic was involved. But yes, maybe that's part of the reason I want to figure out what happened to her, all right? Maybe her soul can't rest. Maybe she's..." She pointed back to the forest. "One of the sluagh now."

"Don't even joke about that—it's a horrible fate." He stared at her. "For what it's worth, you don't seem depressed to me."

Huh.

Carys thought about how she was feeling.

Confused. Conflicted. She looked at Duncan's broad shoulders. Maybe very conflicted.

But she didn't feel depressed. Not at all. The exhaustion was gone. She was sleeping better. She was focused. Determined. The brain fog had lifted.

"Honestly?" She sighed. "It started getting better when I met Lachlan. I don't want to say that love heals depression or anything silly like that, but—"

"Lachlan was tied to Seren." Duncan's voice was soft. "He's literally magical." He started walking down the path again. "It makes sense, Carys."

But it wasn't just Lachlan.

She glanced back at the dancing lights and realized that something that had felt missing in her life wasn't missing anymore.

Because she did believe in fairy tales, and now she knew why.

"I'm fine." She reassured Laura and Kiersten over the phone. "I promise, things are actually... well, it's complicated, but they're good."

"So you're talking to him?" Kiersten asked. "You two are figuring things out?"

"We are." She tried not to lie. "I've made some really good friends here, and I'm spending time with them too. I feel like... It's hard to explain, but I feel really at home."

"Well, it's close to where you were born, right?" Laura offered. "Maybe your genetic memory needed a refresher or something."

"I definitely felt something special when I visited Norway the first time," Kiersten said. "And I wasn't even born there."

Carys suddenly realized that both her best friends had Shadowkin hanging out somewhere in the woods of Northern California. Were they friends there?

It was such a weird thought.

"Okay, it's so late here," she whispered. "But I wanted to call so you didn't worry. I know it's been a while."

"So what's the plan?" Laura asked. "When are you coming home? Is Lachlan coming with you?"

"We're still working on that. About the future." She took a deep breath. "I'm probably going to be scarce for a while though. I'm trying to unplug a little bit."

That was an understatement.

"We're camping a lot around the estate. Talking and... stuff." She glanced at Duncan, who was standing at the door. "So I'll be here. It's Murrayshall House in Scone. If you can't get ahold of me, you can call Mary—she's the housekeeper here—and she can take a message."

Duncan nodded solemnly and gave her a thumbs-up. *Good idea*, he mouthed.

"Are you still having to deal with the asshole twin brother?" Kiersten asked.

Carys cringed and glanced at Duncan from the corner of her eye. "So the thing is—"

"I cannot believe that Lachlan didn't tell you he has a *twin*," Laura said. "Is he really as hot as Lachlan? It's kind of mind-boggling to think there're two of them."

"I'd say you should share," Kiersten said. "But I've already had my share of hot assholes."

"Uh..." She glanced at Duncan again. "He's okay. A little rough around the edges is all."

Duncan raised an eyebrow and put a hand to his chest. *Me?*

She couldn't suppress her smile. "It's good. I don't want you guys to worry. Everything is good right now. Just leave a message with Mary if you can't get ahold of me. She'll know where I am. Cell phone connection is as bad here as it is at home."

"Got it," Laura said. "It's good to hear your voice."

"Good to hear yours too," Carys whispered. "I should go."

"I'm sure you're exhausted," Kiersten said. "Go to sleep. Love you, Carys."

"Love you girls too." She hung up and set down her phone. "That was weird."

"I'm sure it was, but we should get out of here. I already left a note for Mary and Andy." He nodded at her phone. "They'll keep an eye on your phone, carry it around a bit so it doesn't look suspicious to your friends."

"Sounds like a plan." She stood. "Let's get back to Cadell. We have a banquet to attend."

CHAPTER NINETEEN

The welcome banquet that night would be held in the grand hall of the castle, the guests a mix of local lords, light fae, unicorn guests, and visiting dignitaries both from the north of Anglia and the southern part of Alba. Over two hundred people would be in attendance to greet the Cymric king and queen according to Bonnie.

Duncan and Cadell waited outside her door while Bonnie and the lady's maid finished preparing her hair. It might not have been as long as most of the women's in the castle, but the maid had managed to make her dark waves look magical, twisting them up and into an elaborate knot on her head, threaded with ribbons and flowers.

She was wearing a green-and-red velvet gown in honor of King Dafydd, and a gold dragon pin with green eyes had been delivered to her door by one of Dafydd's men. Bonnie pinned it to her shoulder, securing the warm, fur-lined cape in place.

"I'm guessing that hall is going to be freezing cold, isn't it?" Carys asked.

Bonnie nodded. "The great rooms are very difficult to heat. There will be fires, but keep your cape on and drink some wine to warm up.

Try to dance if you can figure out the steps. Duncan has a fine step, so I'm sure he'll lead you."

"Duncan?"

"Oh yes, he's a wonderful dancer." Bonnie nodded curtly. "Does that surprise you?"

"Yes." She glanced at the tray of bread and cheese he'd had delivered to her room an hour before. "How about the food? What kind of food will be there?"

The lady's maid asked Bonnie something in Gaelic, Bonnie responded, and then the girl left the room.

"I've heard from the cooks that there will be roast boar and venison that the hunters shot this morning. Breads and cakes. Pies aplenty. I promise you won't go hungry, but try not to eat too much so you can dance."

"So eat, but drink too, and keep your cloak on, but dance if you can figure out how to dance, but don't eat too much," Carys muttered to herself. "I'm going to do something horribly embarrassing, aren't I?"

"You'll be one of many humans there, my lady. You're not the guest of honor."

"Thank God." That was her nightmare. "How did Seren do these things?"

"Your Shadowkin was raised in a royal court, Lady Carys." Bonnie smiled a little. "Formal banquets would have felt as natural to her as breathing." The maid stepped back and looked at Carys in the rippled mirror. "There. You're beautiful, but I dressed you in a very different style to Seren. You'll want to distinguish yourself, I think."

"Good idea. And thanks." The last thing Carys wanted was people screaming, thinking she was her dead sister come back to life.

Then again, that *could* reveal some secrets.

"I'll call the dragon and the man." Bonnie patted her shoulder. "Don't forget, if you get a bout of nerves, Cadell is always there."

She was trying not to cling to her dragon too tightly, but she had to admit she'd have run screaming from the Shadowlands by now if Cadell hadn't come along.

"It's time." Bonnie walked to the door and opened it. "She's ready, my boys. Take care of her tonight or you'll hear it from me."

Carys stood and suddenly realized why dancing might be an issue. The velvet dress was heavy, and the boning around the bodice was stiff. How did anyone dance in dresses like these?

She glanced at the mirror and marveled. The velvet bodice might have been stiff, but her posture was a thing of beauty. "My mother would be thrilled."

"You look very appropriate." Cadell walked into the room, his leather armor the same as it always was, though his hair was perhaps a bit more tame and he wore a green-and-red cloak that matched Carys's colors. "Colors of Cymru. And King Dafydd has given you the brooch of the nêr ddraig to wear." He nodded. "Well done, Bonnie."

The maid nodded. "My lord."

"Nêrys, we should go."

Duncan looked her up and down. "You look bonny. Let's go before the dragons eat all the roast venison."

Cadell cast him an irritated look. "We already hunted today."

"Will the other dragons be there?" Carys's heart jumped. "The three from Wales?"

"Yes, of course." Cadell took her arm and ushered her down the hallway with Duncan bringing up the rear. "Many of the unicorns from the Moray blessing will also be there, along with a party of light fae and a few local fae who were invited by Darius and Yasmin. I'll warn you that a few wolves from the Borderlands are accompanying the Anglian lords."

"Wolves?" She tried not to shudder.

"They'll be in human form for the banquet," Duncan said. "You won't mistake them for anything but what they are."

"Nothing will happen to you at the banquet," Cadell said. "It is the safest place to encounter a wolf."

"But two hundred people?" She was never going to remember any names.

"Not counting the fae," Duncan said. "Because there's no telling how many will show up."

"The fair folk love parties and will often come to human gatherings even if they're not invited," Cadell said. "Keep in mind who you are dancing with, because they are attracted to anything or anyone who is a novelty. Do not go anywhere with anyone but me or Duncan."

She glanced over her shoulder at Duncan. "Are we sitting together?"

"I imagine so," Duncan said. "Elanor would have put you near people you know. Your uncle will be at the high table with Robb, Elanor, and Lachlan, but Aisling will probably be seated with us."

"Unless her aunts want her at the Éiren table," Cadell added.

"That's possible too."

They reached the top of the stairs, and the sound of voices mixed with the sound of music echoed through the castle. There was clanging and the clatter of crockery. Guards were stationed five deep at the doors, checking all the guests as they entered the castle and made their way around the massive statue of the two rearing unicorns that dominated the entryway.

The herald at the bottom of the stairs spotted them and called out: "The Lady Carys, Lord Dragon Cadell, and Lord Duncan of Moray."

Multiple faces turned to them as they walked down the stairs and into the entry chamber; Carys clung to Cadell so she wouldn't trip. Many of the faces wore curious expressions, but just as many glanced at her and Duncan, then turned back to whomever they were speaking with before or continued walking into the dining hall.

The crowd was a glittering mix of faces, voices, accents, and finery, a rainbow of styles and colors that filled the entryway and flowed into the hall.

They turned left at the foot of the stairs, and Carys got her first view of the great hall decked out for a formal dinner.

There were giant banners hung from the ceiling, blue and white on one side, red and green on the other. Thousands of blue-white tapers were glowing overhead, suspended by magic to illuminate the darkness while four hearths blazed with fire to warm the hall.

Blue lights danced overhead, and sparkling lights spun in the air like constant confetti.

There were tall, willowy fae men and women, their large eyes and long hair shining in the candlelight; pointed ears peeked from behind their shimmering hair, and rings decorated their ears, noses, and hands. They wore gold jewelry in abundance along with cloaks of glittering fabric adorned with jewels that winked as they moved.

"Beautiful." She nearly lost her breath to see a group of them en masse.

"Dangerous," Duncan murmured.

"Seductive by design," Cadell added. "Some of it will be glamour. Much of it is real."

The unicorns who greeted them as they walked through the crowd to find their table also towered over the human guests, their beauty as majestic but their faces warmer.

They were broad shouldered and strong, wearing flowing tunics with no apparent notice of the cold. Their long hair was a mix of soft waves, riotous curls, and every color in the rainbow.

Carys noticed that both the fae and the unicorns varied in their features more than the humans did, their features a mix of ethnicities from all around the world. Eyes of every shape and color, skin of every tone from deepest ebony to pale white ash.

The living tapestry moved in graceful dancing that dominated the center of the room while human and fae musicians played from a platform near the high table at the front of the room.

There were tall people with dark hair and weathered skin that Carys immediately identified as the wolves that Cadell and Duncan had spoken about. Stoic in expression, they stood along the borders of the room, speaking only with each other, their eyes and hair ranging from dark brown to pale grey.

"Wolves?" she murmured.

"Yes." Cadell leaned down. "A wolf's hair will always match their eyes. Grey and grey. Brown and brown. They mimic their animal form in this."

"And dragon eyes are gold."

Cadell nodded. "Yes, Nêrys."

The wolves wore blue-and-red jackets and had the most military bearing of any of the magical creatures. Like the dragons, they appeared somewhat discomfited in human skin.

Cadell spoke to Carys quietly as they walked. "There might be unicorns seated with us, so be mindful of how much meat you eat," he said. "They do not judge humans, but it's rude to wave a dead creature in their face. That's why dragons don't eat at human banquets."

"Because you consume entire deer in one swallow?" Duncan asked.

"Only in our natural form," Cadell muttered. "Do you enjoy provoking me?"

Carys tried to distract them from the bickering. "Are all the wolves here men?"

"There are male and female wolves in attendance. They are some-times hard to tell apart. They don't differentiate gender in dress."

"Neither do dragons," Carys said. "You all wear the same armor, correct?"

"Correct."

Musicians filled the room with the sound of pipes, harps, flutes, and drums. Dancers were already spinning in front of the head table where a wide floor had been cleared so the king and his guests could watch as the dancers reached the front, bowing to the royal table before they parted and moved to the back.

Robb sat at an elevated table at the front of the room, King Dafydd beside him, their queens on each side. And next to Queen Elanor, his face glowing and his burnished hair falling in glorious waves to his shoulders, was Lachlan.

By the time her eyes found him, he was already watching her.

"Lachlan saw me." She gripped Cadell's arm.

"He sees no one else." Cadell urged her to the left. "We'll be sitting at the front, near your uncle."

She couldn't take her eyes off Lachlan. He was dressed in a dark-blue-and-green tartan thrown over his shoulder, and his cape was made of black fur. His reddish-brown hair gleamed in the candlelight, his jaw was clean-shaven, and his lips were full as he reached for a goblet of wine.

He watched her as he drank, and Carys could feel the memory of his lips brushing over her breast. His skin would be warm at her neck, and her body ready for him.

Carys. Cadell squeezed her arm and spoke in her mind.

"Sorry."

You love him. She did too.

It was a harsh slap in the face that reminded Carys what she was doing at the banquet that night and why she'd decided to stay. Yes, she needed to sort out her feelings for Lachlan, but she needed to solve the mystery of Seren's death too, and this was the perfect place to people-watch.

She turned to Duncan. "Did you ask Lachlan about the journals?"

"I did. He claims that Aisling has them. She packed up all of Seren's books and put them in storage. He says the journals were among them, but she didn't put personal information in them. It was a schedule of her work more than a confessional."

"So he says." Carys glanced at Lachlan and saw him watching her and Duncan. "Aisling may not have realized that Seren's journals were mixed in with her books."

"That was my thought as well." Duncan glanced up at his brother. "Do you want to make him jealous?"

Carys blinked. "What? No, that's not what I was thinking at all. I just wanted to—"

"Dance, I think." Duncan slid his fingers between her hand and Cadell's arm. "Dragon, I will dance with the lady while you find our seats."

"Happy to avoid the dance floor." Cadell disappeared into the crowd.

Carys found herself pressed to Duncan's side. "I wasn't even thinking about dancing. I'd rather—"

"It's a banquet." His voice was uncharacteristically playful. "You have to dance. It's expected."

"I don't know how to do any of this."

She hung back as they approached the whirling, spinning dancers on the floor, weaving in and out in lines and circles that made her dizzy. The music had changed from a slower, lilting melody to a raucous reel.

"Duncan, I don't know—"

"Oh lass" —he linked her hand with his— "you've got to be the bravest woman I know. Don't be afraid of a little bit of dancing now. Just follow my lead."

And with that, Duncan hooked her arm in his and spun her around, holding her at the waist before he whirled her out and back again, their bodies touching only briefly before he spun her around again.

"What are we doing?" She couldn't keep the smile from her face.

"Haven't ye ever been to a ceilidh?"

Carys shook her head. "No!"

The music was loud enough to drown out everything but the stomping of boots on the ground, the slapping of hands, and the laughter from the humans, fae, and unicorns around them.

She spun from Duncan's arms and into the arms of a man standing next to him, a grey-headed man with twinkling blue eyes and a long beard.

He whooped out loud, turned her around, and sent her right back to Duncan, who grasped her around the waist and turned them in circles.

"Go with me now." He bent down and his mouth was at her ear.

A column formed, two rows of dancers standing across from each other, clapping in rhythm as couples bowed and danced between them.

Duncan took her hand, knit his right with her left, and put his other at the small of her back as the clapping company raised their arms up and she tripped and skipped between them, trying to follow Duncan's lead, his pleasure like a great warm cloak thrown over her. Her heart felt light in a way that it hadn't since she'd crossed into the Shadowlands.

This was magic. This was *fun*.

As they reached the end of the column, Duncan spun her away, landing her in the line across from him and next to the grey-haired man. He stomped and whistled as the next couple came through the line, roaring with laughter as the man stole a kiss from the blushing woman before he came to stand beside Carys, throwing her a wink before he shouted something in Gaelic to his lady.

"Are you having fun?" Duncan shouted.

Carys grinned. "I didn't know I could dance!"

"You can with me." He grinned at her and looked back at the dancers, singing along when the men's voices rose and joined the instruments.

She could hear voices all around the hall as the song got louder, celebratory clapping and hearty shouts as joy filled the dark night and cold room, and Carys felt—for the first time—her blood stir as if the song meant something to her. Not as a curiosity. Not as an observer.

She felt a part of the music, a part of the magic of the dance, and felt the lure of this mysterious place. It was light and joy stolen in the middle of darkness, a shining star glistening in a velvet black night.

Just then a hand landed on the small of her back and an arm slipped around her waist. She gasped for a moment until she smelled his familiar scent.

Lachlan.

She turned and saw the set of his jaw and the furious expression in his vivid green eyes.

"You're trying to make me jealous." He stole her away from the dance floor, rushing her toward a curtain on the far side of the banquet hall. "He's trying to make me jealous, and it worked."

CHAPTER TWENTY

"Lachlan, what are you doing?"

"I can never seem to get you alone, can I? You've time for audiences with the king. Meetings with the unicorns, the dragons. Even a *kelpie*, for fuck's sake. And gods know my brother, the blasted—" He flung the curtain back and shouted at the servants who were loitering in the small chamber. "Out!"

"Sorry, my lord." They scuttled out, and Carys wrenched herself out of Lachlan's arms.

"What are you doing?" She pointed at the curtain. "Do you realize that Cadell is going to burst through that curtain any moment and tell you to go to hell?"

"Not if you tell him to stay away." Lachlan stepped toward her, pressing in with his body. He backed her up to a wall and halted only inches from her face. She felt the heat of his breath on her lips. "Tell him to stay away, Carys."

Her body was screaming at her. "Cadell," she whispered. Would he be able to hear her through the tumult of the banquet hall?

I am here, Nêrys.

She sighed in relief when she heard his voice. "Stay away. Just for a while."

Call when you need me.

She closed her eyes, and Lachlan's forehead fell toward her, their brows touching as she felt him heave a great sigh.

"I miss you every day," he whispered. "Every *night*. Do you think my body has forgotten yours? You being here and not being in my arms is torture."

"You left me, Lachlan. You *left*."

"But I would have done anything to stay. I nearly *bargained* with the fae who came for me, Carys. I nearly gave them..." He shuddered. "I only went because I knew that if I didn't, they would have hurt you."

Carys shook her head. "Did you think they were going to just let you go? You're the prince."

"I don't care!" He choked on the words. "I was happy with you. I felt like I could breathe again. And then in the blink of an eye, my future was gone. *Again*."

She saw the mix of grief and love in his eyes and she was tempted. So tempted. In the confusion and the magic and the chaos of this new world, being alone with Lachlan felt blessedly normal.

She halfway believed that she'd push the curtain to the side and step into her own cozy house in California with Lachlan beside her, teasing her about her crazy dream.

"I love you." He pressed her hands to his chest. "Tell me you believe me, Carys. Tell me you know."

"I want to believe you." She pulled her hands away. "But do you understand why that's hard? Every moment I'm here, I'm surrounded by her. Seren's memory shadows everything I do, Lachlan, and the more I learn about her, the more I realize we were nothing alike."

"That's what I'm saying!" His face brightened, and he pressed her hands closer. "My feelings now are for you. Not Seren. I'll always love her, but I want a life with *you*."

Carys was still trying to wrap her mind around the idea of Lachlan loving her—truly loving her—when he seemed to have been in love with Seren his entire life.

"I need time," she whispered. "All of this is new and—"

"You need to leave," he whispered. "It's not safe here. I'll come and find you and we can run away. We can hide from them and start a life together. We don't have to play their games."

"And let Seren's murder go unanswered?" She shook her head. "Lachlan, you're dreaming if you think your father would ever let you go. Duncan was right: you have responsibilities here. Seren understood that. She knew—"

"Seren knew I had no intention of taking the throne!"

Carys blinked. "What?"

"I gave that up the moment I married her," Lachlan continued. "My father refuses to believe me, but there was no way I could have remained married to the queen of Cymru and stayed here on the throne. Dafydd has *one* heir. My father has three. For me to remain on the high chief's throne would mean uniting two kingdoms, and that would completely alter the balance of power in Briton. I was always going to give up the throne to Rory, Nora, or one of the clan chiefs. Always."

Carys's mind was whirling, not only because of Lachlan's passionate proclamations of love but because she'd just realized why someone might have wanted her sister to die.

"I need to go back." She drew her hands away from Lachlan's and walked to the archway covered by the curtain. "Both of us need to go back."

Carys sat woodenly at the banquet table after a massive dinner of venison, roasted game, and candied fruit while the two kings made speeches singing the other's praises and complimenting Queen Elanor on her hospitality.

She was curious to examine Eamer, Dafydd's wife, but there wasn't a chance to mingle at a royal banquet. Everyone seemed to acknowledge that Seren and Eamer had not been particularly close. Aisling had mentioned it more than once, and Lachlan never spoke about her.

The woman in question was the tall lady she'd seen step out of the coracle behind King Dafydd. She was taller than her husband, though not as tall as Robb. Her hair was dark and braided back from a severe and dramatically beautiful face. She had a strong jaw, deep-set eyes, and a sculpted mouth that was pursed and painted deep red to match the velvet dress she wore to complement her husband's finery.

A gold crown was set on her forehead, and though her eyes flitted to Carys every now and then, she mostly seemed to avoid looking at her.

Eamer of Tara, second daughter of the High Queen Orla of Ireland, and by most accounts, the mildest of the four. Married to Dafydd of Cymru for the past twenty-three years.

Carys kept her voice barely above a whisper, grateful that Cadell always seemed to hear. "Twenty-three years? So Seren was in Alba when they married?"

Yes. Elanor was the only mother figure that Seren knew as a child.

"So Seren and her stepmother didn't have much of a relationship."

Things were cool between them. Eamer respected Seren's role as Dafydd's daughter, but they were not close. Seren had no warmth for Eamer but was always ready to compliment her work as queen.

"Got it."

On the other side of Eamer were three willowy fae whose skin seemed to glow from within. One was a fair-skinned man with braided hair the color of pure gold and a gold hoop piercing his nose. The next fae was a dark-haired woman with olive skin and vivid blue eyes, her flowing hair rippling over her shoulders like ebony water.

The third was another man, his skin brown as hazelwood and his dark gold hair falling in soft waves to his shoulders. His eyes were vivid green, but his mouth settled into a firm, straight line. He wore a dozen golden piercings in each ear.

The fae lords from the Borderlands. They control the gate through which you arrived and have been watching you all night.

Carys tried not to squirm. "I didn't notice them."

If you had, I would be surprised. Do not be alone with them.

While servants cleared the dishes, a lone singer stood at the foot of the head table and started a song, accompanied by a harp.

Carys didn't know what to make of the singer, who was clearly not human but was very short for a fae. She had warm brown skin, black hair twisted in coils and decorated with gold beads and flowers, and eyes the color of sunlit water. She sang with the clearest, purest voice Carys had ever heard.

"Sing me a place where sea becomes sky
Where stone swallows mountain
Where this world goes to die"

She is also fae, Cadell whispered in her mind, *but not of the Borderlands.*

Carys felt the dragon's eyes on her.

Do you recognize her, Nêrys?

Carys shook her head. "No. Why would I?"

Her name is Naida.

Carys was transfixed, frozen in her seat, but she sat up straight when she realized that she knew the melody the strange fae woman was singing. It was the same song Dru had been chanting through the woods as Duncan and Carys made their way into the Shadowlands.

"Write me a poem of heather and firth
Where forest touches night and night becomes earth
The shadows they call you when life becomes still
They call you to taste them
They tempt you to thrill"

Was it intentional? A popular song? What did it mean? She glanced at Duncan, but he was deep in conversation with Darius on the other side of the table. She let her eyes drift to Lachlan, whom she'd been trying to ignore since they returned, and he was staring straight at her, his eyes full of a longing she could hardly dismiss.

The singer continued her mournful song.

"The darkness it holds you
Don't try to turn back
Its wild weathered places
Are all that you lack
The Shadowlands offer the life that you miss
And the ruddy wind whispers
A dark prince's kiss"

Lachlan's lips parted, and she could taste the memory of his kiss. Carys closed her eyes, her body aching for him, only to open them again when the hall burst into applause for the singer and the harpist.

"Lachlan!" someone shouted. "Lord Lachlan for the harp!"

The hall erupted in applause, and Carys looked around to see every eye on the high table. When she turned back to Lachlan, he glanced at her, then forced a smile and nodded at a young man who ran for the side of the room.

"Lachlan has a beautiful voice."

Carys turned to see Duncan watching her. "He does," she said. "He sang a lot in California. Loved it. Absolute magic on the guitar."

"He learned that from me." The corner of Duncan's mouth turned up. "They don't have the same instruments here as we do at home. I taught him the basics when we were young, but he's a far better player than I ever was."

The young man came back to the table, holding a harp that was small enough to fit on the player's knees. Lachlan walked out from behind the table and down the stairs, settling himself next to Naida, who leaned toward him and whispered something. Lachlan gave a slight nod, and the woman waved a gentle hand over Lachlan's throat, then another hand over his harp.

"What was that?"

"Lachlan has some magic in his voice," Cadell said, "but Naida's power is greater than his. It will amplify his voice since the hall is so large."

Carys nodded. "Right."

Lachlan cleared his throat and took a sip from the goblet his servant held out. "A song for our guests tonight." Though his words included the Cymric court, his eyes landed on her and didn't leave as he began to pluck the harp, drawing a flood of melody from the gold-inlaid wooden frame.

Duncan leaned toward Carys. "There are many kinds of magic that humans practice in the Shadowlands. This is Lachlan's kind."

He plucked the strings with such skill and speed Carys forgot where she was and that others surrounded her. All she could do was watch Lachlan as he filled the hall with his harp and his voice. All murmur of conversation stopped, and the lights around the hall seemed to dim.

As Lachlan started to sing in Gaelic, there were soft gasps around the hall. Whether it was Naida's magic or his own, Lachlan's voice sounded like it was coming from right next to her.

For a moment, Carys was at the pub in Baywood, listening to Lachlan entertain her friends with folk songs and holding the small crowd enraptured. Carys had felt as if he was singing just for her when he lifted his eyes from the guitar and smiled across the room.

She had no idea what he was singing to the audience in the great hall, but there were tears in more than one eye. And just like that night in the pub, the entire time he sang, he looked straight at her, his gaze never wavering.

His voice was a seductive whisper in her ear. The pure deep tone of his song curled around her, threading through the air that touched her neck, his breath a feather across her lips, the vibration of the harp echoing through her body.

He sings for you. Cadell's voice in her mind.

"Only for me?" she whispered.

For you, Nêrys. Seren didn't have patience for music.

She couldn't take her eyes off him.

Until she had to. The song finished, the magic drifted away, and the crowd applauded. They rose to their feet to praise the magical young lord, and in the tumult of the crowded hall with everyone vying for Lachlan's attention, Carys slipped away.

SHE WAS DRESSED in her nightclothes, staring at the burning fire in the hearth and wrapped in heavy wool blankets when she heard the knock at the door. She could feel Cadell overhead, curled in dragon form and resting on the roof of the tower when she rose and walked to the door.

Nêrys?

"It's probably Bonnie," she said. "Or Duncan trying to get me to eat more."

It is not. Cadell's voice drifted away. *I will leave you to your privacy, my lady. All you need do is call.*

Carys frowned as she opened the door, only for understanding to ring clear when she saw Lachlan on the other side.

His jacket was loose, and his shirt was untucked, wine spilled over the collar. His eyes were locked on her face. "You left."

"It was crowded. You know I hate crowds."

"Yes."

Tension rocketed between them, and she glanced at his hands, feeling his fingers on her skin the same way he'd caressed the harp at the front of the hall, wrenching the aching music from its body the same way he'd once touched her.

"Please," he whispered. "Please, Carys."

It was too much. She pulled him into the room, wrapped her arms around him, and lifted her head to meet his lips as he kicked the door closed.

His hands, his hands, his hands were everywhere, fisted in the heavy cloth that covered her, ripping away the blanket around her waist and gripping her hair at the nape. He tugged her braid loose and spread the dark waves over her shoulders, a groan catching in his throat as he walked her back toward the bed.

"I missed you." His voice was hoarse. "I missed you so much."

Lachlan touched her body as he always had, as if they'd been lovers for years. Nothing about him was unsure or hesitant. He knew exactly the curve where her back arched, the spot on her neck that made her cry out.

He lifted the dress over her head, lifted her and placed her in the bed, drawing the bed curtains around them. Then he ripped off his jacket and threw it to the foot of the bed before he started to fumble with his leggings.

Carys sat up, drawing the sheet with her to keep her from freezing in the cold air, then carefully lifted the tartan from his shoulder as Lachlan grew still under her hand.

"You never wore a kilt in California," she said softly. "I asked about it, and you said it was an old-fashioned thing."

"It is." He sat back on his heels, watching her as she slowly undressed him.

"It's beautiful." She unwound the heavy wool from his narrow hips and set the yards of woven fabric to the side, leaving him in nothing more than the long tunic stained with wine.

"Were you drinking?" He didn't seem drunk, but Carys wanted to make sure this was what he wanted in his cold, sober mind. "Were you drinking a lot?"

The corner of his mouth kicked up. "No, Dafydd spilled his wine on me. I probably smell like a wine barrel."

"No, you smell like you." She leaned forward and pulled the tunic over his head, leaving him bare in the darkness, his body as glorious as it ever was but his scars making more sense now that she knew the truth.

He had a knife wound on his shoulder. A childish prank, he'd told her. Carys leaned forward and put her lips on his warm skin, her tongue flicking out to taste the raised flesh. Lachlan's skin vibrated under her mouth.

"What was it really?"

"A training accident with my father's soldiers."

"A sword?"

"Bronze blade. Heavy."

Her fingers traced across his chest, the gold hair sprinkled over the corded muscles, to the gash a few inches down on his ribs. "And this one?"

"Hunting accident with a very drunk Anglian lord." He gripped her hair in his right hand and pulled her head back to expose her throat. "Give me your skin."

"You have it," she whispered.

Carys closed her eyes as her hands remained on Lachlan's shoulder and ribs. He kissed her with the hunger of lost months and lonely nights, his lips bruising in their pursuit. He leaned forward, nudging her back onto the pillows before he crawled next to her under the bedclothes and their naked bodies were pressed together.

He was heat and life, and she'd missed him so much she had tears in her eyes. Lachlan kissed her like the lover she'd known, cherishing the taste of her mouth, then peppering kisses over her cheeks, fluttering soft lips over her eyelids as she held him close.

"I missed you so much." His body grew harder and his voice rougher. "I missed you every moment of every day and especially every night. I couldn't sleep for days after I came back." He swallowed hard as his mouth left hers and he kissed down her neck. His fingers were rough, the tips callused from playing the harp, and the rough skin scraped across her nipples when he caressed them, making Carys shiver.

It was pleasure-pain that he followed with his mouth and teeth, ravenous to taste her body. His knee parted her thighs, and he pressed up, exposing her sex as one hand left her breast and felt for the heat between her thighs.

"You missed me too." His breath was hot on her skin, his fingers coaxing pleasure from her sex. "I can feel it."

"Lachlan." She ached for him, gripping his shoulder with her hand as her other reached for the hard erection she felt pressing against her thigh. "Lachlan, please."

Her hand closed around Lachlan's hard cock, and she arched her back, the pleasure rising as he coaxed her body to release. His touch was magic, the rhythm of his fingers as delicate and relentless as they had been on the harp strings.

She closed her eyes and saw a wash of gold beneath her closed lids as the first crest of pleasure made her cry out. He silenced her with a hard kiss, his tongue dancing with hers as he moved up, bracing himself over her as he took her hand from his erection and nudged her legs wider, his cock finding her heat as he slid inside and seated himself to the hilt, his hips pressed against her parted thighs.

Oh God. He was everything. She needed him and he felt incredible. The climax he'd coaxed from her continued to roll through her body as he drove himself into her sex over and over again, the pleasure building with every thrust.

"Carys!"

"Come." She dug her fingers into the small of Lachlan's back, her shoulders pressed down as she rolled her hips up. "Please come."

She needed him to come. She needed the memory of them together, the sweet release of the bed and the heavy weight of him holding her down as her mind flew.

Lachlan came with a shout and a groan he muffled in her shoulder, his body pressing up and holding, holding inside as his cock continued to release. A shudder tore through him. He panted against her neck, wrapping his arms around her shoulders and rolling them to the side. He slid one leg under hers, pressing her to his chest and wrapping her body completely with his own.

It was the same way he always held her after they made love, as if a climax wasn't enough and he had to bind her in his arms to make sure she wouldn't slip away.

"I missed you," he murmured into her shoulder. "I missed you so much, Carys. I love you."

She didn't know what to say. Her mind was as overwhelmed as her body.

Making love to Lachlan was necessary and right and she didn't regret a moment of it, but while Lachlan was holding her the same way he always had, Carys couldn't find the same peace in his arms.

"Can I sleep here tonight?" he whispered. "At least for tonight?"

"Yes." She couldn't turn him away if she wanted to. She needed it as much as he did, her body craving the comfort of his familiar embrace. "Sleep. Let's both sleep."

We can talk in the morning.

CHAPTER TWENTY-ONE

When Carys woke in the blue light of morning, she immediately felt the warmth of Cadell's presence overhead and the cold sheets in the bed beside her. She opened her eyes, but Lachlan was gone.

There was a pang of disappointment followed immediately by a creeping sense of relief. Her body felt loose and worn and fantastic, but she was also confused.

Carys had fallen in love with Lachlan in the Brightlands, the wandering, good-natured Scotsman with a quick smile, an amazing sense of humor, and kindness oozing out of his pores. He was hardworking but not ambitious. Easy but entertaining. He was the perfect boyfriend.

But now she was seeing Lachlan where he was born, a land called Alba ruled by powerful fae and scheming humans raised in the shadow of magic, myth, and monsters. A land where children were sacrificed to forests, dragons carried kings, and ancient magic touched everyone from the lord in the castle to the farmer in his field.

This was where Lachlan was raised. This was the world he was born into. This was the place that had made him. She didn't know

Lachlan here, and she didn't know herself. Carys had been making love to a memory of what they had been, not the reality of who they were.

She turned to Lachlan's side of the bed and found the journal she'd been taking notes in open to a blank page.

Shit.

She grabbed for her journal and saw a scribbled note from Lachlan.

I didn't want people to start talking. It would make you uncomfortable. I left before the maid could come.

There was another line farther down the page, underlined for emphasis.

I did not kill Seren.

"Shit, shit, shit, shit." She flipped to the page just before the note and looked at the rambling notes she'd scribbled down two days before.

Who might benefit from Seren's death?
Regan—seems super evil
Eamer—things were cold between them, maybe jealous
Robb—ambitious, would be threatened by power
Aisling—fought like sisters
Elanor—doubtful but big unknown
Unknown fae enemies
Unknown human enemies
Not Dafydd, impossible
Not unicorns
Do the wolves have anything to do with this?
Lachlan?

His was the only name she'd written a question mark after because the thought of Lachlan killing his wife seemed utterly ridiculous to her when she wrote it down and even more ridiculous after their conversation the night before.

According to Lachlan, he'd wanted to give up the throne. Carys knew from details Duncan had mentioned that the Alban throne wasn't like the Anglian or the Cymric. There was a chief chosen from among the clans, but it wasn't a strict a hereditary title. The capital was in Sgàin for military and trade reasons, but if Robb ever displeased the other clan chiefs, he could be replaced, and he would be.

So the idea that Robb's son would give up the throne to be the consort of the Cymric queen wasn't a revolutionary idea.

Except maybe to Lachlan's father.

Robb immediately went to the top of her list. He struck Carys as an ambitious person and far more likely to believe that Dafydd's daughter should give up her crown instead of his son. Or why give up the crown at all? Maybe Robb envisioned a combined kingdom, uniting two old allies.

She jotted down another note.

Who rules Anglia, and could they be involved?

She needed to meet with Dafydd and find out what he knew about his daughter's marriage and future plans, but she needed to speak to Lachlan first and reassure him that he'd dropped off the suspect list.

I did not kill Seren.

Would he even talk to her after seeing her notebook?

"Shit." She took a deep breath and let it out slowly. "Okay, so the sex was probably a mistake."

Her body didn't agree. Her body felt loose and satisfied and... powerful somehow. Her body was ready to get out of bed, do a naked booty-shake in front of the fire, and saunter down the hall to get a cup of hot coffee.

God, she missed coffee.

A knock came at the door, followed by Bonnie's voice. "Here to light the fire, my lady."

Carys pulled the blankets over her shoulders and dragged the bed curtains closed. "Come in. It's not locked."

She could feel Cadell resting above her on the roof. "Cadell?"

Nêrys?

"I want to speak with Dafydd today if I can. Can you talk to Mared about that?"

I will communicate with her right now.

Carys felt the loss of his constant presence and turned her attention to Bonnie, clutching a blanket around her shoulders so it wasn't obvious she was naked when she poked her head from behind the curtains. "I bet there's a ton of cleaning to do today, right?"

"Oh, not as much as you'd think." Bonnie glanced at her as she made the fire. "You turned in early. The girls said you asked for a maid to help you out of your gown when the music was still going strong. Not much for parties, are you?"

"It was a lot to take in." She ducked back behind the curtains. The room was freezing cold. She missed her woodstove. She missed her house and her bed and her central heating.

And coffee. She could not emphasize that enough.

Bonnie seemed slightly sympathetic. "I imagine it was a new experience for you. Lord Duncan was up bright and early today. I think he already ordered a tray from the kitchen for your breakfast, so that will suit you. No need to go down to dine with the ladies in the morning room if that's coming up."

"Great." Carys peeked her head out from behind the curtains. "Wait, am I supposed to be dining with the ladies in the morning room?"

"If you like." Bonnie glanced at her, noticed her bare shoulders, and her eyebrows went up. "Then again, maybe not. Good thing Lord Duncan ordered that tray."

Why was he always trying to make her eat?

"Yeah, that was... thoughtful." Or intrusive. No, it was thoughtful. The last thing she wanted was to look everyone in the face this morning after she'd run out of the party. "Bonnie, did people seem to notice that I left early?"

"I wasn't there, was I?"

"People talk, and you have ears."

Bonnie turned. "They noticed, but they were talking about Lord Lachlan more. He seemed upset. Queen Elanor was trying to speak to him, but he looked a bit stormy until he spoke to his brother."

"Right." Duncan butting in again. Carys sighed. "Can you pull some comfortable clothes out for me if you have the time? I'm absolutely freezing, and my head is swimming."

"Too much wine." Bonnie's voice was brusque. "I'll set out some day clothes for you. What are your plans for today?"

Find Lachlan and apologize for doubting his innocence.

Talk to Aisling and look for Seren's journals.

Find out what Dafydd thought the future had looked like for Lachlan and Seren.

"Just wandering around."

CHAPTER TWENTY-TWO

Dafydd met her on the hill where the dragons rested during the lightest part of the day. On one side of the ridge was Sgàin Castle, the village, and the Borderlands beyond, dark even in the pale light of the Shadowlands midday. Beyond that forest was a dim suggestion of rolling hills and green fields dappled by forests and multiple rivers and streams.

On the other side of Tower Ridge, the land sloped down to the silver-blue loch and the unicorn's forest, more wilderness than settled land. Beyond the forest was a sea of green, rolling hills, and higher peaks in the distance, covered with snow.

The whole of the Shadowlands was washed in blues and greens, more suggestions of color than a punch of it. It made her soul yearn for light.

Dafydd was the first one to speak. "I feel questions churning inside you like too much wine on an empty stomach."

"That's a vivid mental picture."

Dafydd chuckled a little. "Ask anything you wish. I'll do my best to answer."

"I was just thinking that I miss the sun." She stared at the watercolor land in front of her, as beautiful as it was distant. "The light touches this place, but I can't see the source. It's like…"

"Living in a shadow?"

She turned to him. "I guess that's the point, isn't it?"

His smile was wry. "Your sun is a powerful thing. It burns the skin, but it makes flowers bloom with such vibrance it made me want to weep." Dafydd stood next to Carys, turning his head to look at the four dragons who rested at the top of the ridge in their natural form. "I wish Mared could bathe her scales in its heat, but it's not possible."

"Why not?"

"Ah, the questions begin." Dafydd began to walk along the ridge. "Dragons can travel to the Brightlands, but they cannot take their natural form there. They must remain human. But they crave heat. It's one of the reasons they tend to hide their young near volcanos and other rips in the earth."

Mared opened one golden eye and peered at Dafydd.

"I'm not revealing secrets, Mared. She's nêrys ddraig. If she'd been raised here, she would already know these things." He smiled at Carys. "All dragons are secretive, but the females most of all since they lay the eggs. Though the males brood them, so maybe it's just Mared."

"Have you seen a baby dragon before?" Carys glanced at Cadell.

He has not, the dragon whispered in her head. *Stop poking, Nêrys.*

Dafydd shook his head. "No one sees them until they're roughly the size of a small elephant."

"You've seen an *elephant*?"

Dafydd grinned. "I actually saw my first elephant when I went to your realm. Being on an airplane was a new experience. Mared hated it with a passion."

"I'm surprised she went with you."

"I was too, but she loved the sun. We both did." Dafydd's expression was bright. "We took an expedition there with the help of a Brightkin I trust. Not my own, obviously, but the twin of my steward. He's quite a wealthy man on the other side. We do have some connections in the Brightlands. Maintaining them is of strategic importance."

Carys poked a little bit. "Did Eamer go with you?"

"No, she has no desire for it." He looked out over the landscape. "I'm sure you've heard she and Seren weren't close. But they got along well enough for my sake."

"What about the fae? Do *they* have connections in the Brightlands?"

"You saw them at the banquet last night." His eyes narrowed. "What do you think?"

"I have a hard time imagining that they blend in like you could."

"Very true. And they lose almost all their magic. What is a fae without their magic?" He looked at her from the corner of his eye. "Did you notice their attention last night?"

"Yes."

"They were fascinated by you, weren't they? I noticed that as well." His expression was grim. "Fae gates were created by… No one knows really. The oldest gods probably. Fair folk who no longer exist perhaps? Magic itself? There are many theories."

"But no one knows."

"Not really." Dafydd turned and looked across the valley and the dark forest beyond. "On this side, the fae and others of their kind control everything. Our mining. Our farms. The weather. Our children, more than anything else. But when it comes to entering the Brightlands, they have their limits."

Carys followed Dafydd's eyes, watching the forest and the murky landscape beyond. "So fae can't go into my world without help?"

"It works the same way as you coming here. Once the gates recognize you, you can travel somewhat freely. I understand it was fae mercenaries who… fetched Lachlan from your world."

Carys nodded. "That's what he tells me."

"But if you've never been into the Brightlands as a magical creature, you need an escort who is native to that realm." Dafydd's eyes drilled into her. "So on this side of the gates, you hold a particular kind of magic, Carys Morgan. Be cautious of who tries to befriend you."

"I didn't think I had that kind of magical power here. I mean, other than talking with Cadell, but I can't say spells or anything." Carys felt powerless and stupid much of the time. "Dafydd, why didn't you and Eamer have more children? Did the fae ever tell you?"

"No. They don't answer questions about that." A flicker of darkness in his blue eyes, and he stared at the ground. "We hoped for more, and I admit I was surprised when we did not receive another child. Eamer is of Éire, and her mother a consort in the fae court there. Most of her people are blessed with many children. It's one of the reasons Queen Orla has always been able to marry off the women of her family in powerful unions. My own father met Eamer and assumed we would welcome many children into our court."

"But it didn't happen?"

Dafydd's great shoulders lifted and fell. "We are given only what we are given. For me, Seren was always enough. Do you know if your parents ever wanted more children?"

She smiled sadly. "I always felt like they wanted more, but maybe it just didn't happen, you know?"

He nodded. "So perhaps the same fate was for us. And while Eamer and I were never blessed with another child" —Dafydd's eyes creased in pleasure— "we have fostered many and taken great joy in raising them as our own."

Carys looked to the castle in the distance. "It must have been hard letting her go."

Dafydd's smile fell. "The Queens' Pact demands it even when a king only has one child. Most regents have more than one and keep their oldest at home, but I only had Seren. So when she was only five, I sent her to be fostered here. Robb and I have always had a close rela-tionship. I trusted him the most. His son Rory was raised in Cymru with us, but Seren could only spend a few months at home each year until Cadell was called to her."

Carys couldn't imagine the pain of having a child and then being forced to give that child to another family. "I wasn't raised in Wales either."

Dafydd frowned. "Yes, I was told your parents moved away. Do you know why?"

"There was some kind of fight in their family, I think. They didn't talk about it much." She gripped her hands as they walked, resisting the urge to throw her arms around a stranger with her father's face. "We moved to North America. A place called California. Do you... know where that is? There's a Shadowlands California, right?"

Dafydd's eyes twinkled, reminding Carys of her father again. "There is, and I have visited the place. The nêr ddraig travel broadly, often to visit other dragon territories. It's one of the reasons Cymru has been so successful maintaining our independence despite the Anglian wolves."

"Are the English here as imperialistic as they were in the Brightlands?"

Dafydd smiled. "Pay no attention to our good-natured jokes. King Edgar is an ally and a peaceful man. He believes in conquest through trade, not war. He desires Cymric maps more than our land."

Okay, that answered one question. Apparently someone named Edgar ruled Anglia. "What's so special about Cymric maps?"

"Anglia is a seafaring country, and Cymric maps are some of the most extensive in the Shadowlands. Far better than the fae's, though they'll never admit it."

Carys's eyebrows went up. "Of course. Because of the dragons." She glanced over at the four beasts who had silently shifted, still bathing in the milky light. "But if people can go back and forth between the fae gates, why not just steal maps from the human world to use here?"

Dafydd let out a great laugh. "Now you're sounding like Seren." He cleared his throat, but a smile stayed on his face. "That becomes complicated. It's a mirror world, but things aren't quite as exact as you might think. The magic does what it wants at times. Borders shift. Islands rise or disappear. The Shadowlands shift in ways that the Brightlands do not."

"I hadn't thought about that." Carys continued walking toward the old stone tower, remembering Lachlan's story and imagining the child

Seren reaching out for the fire-breathing beast when other children would have hidden. "She was never afraid of him. Cadell, I mean."

"Were you when he found you?" Dafydd's eyes were intent on her face. "Did you feel any fear?"

"Not even a hint." The corner of her mouth inched up. "Do you have any idea why he came to me?"

"None." Dafydd shook his head. "As Lachlan and Duncan know each other, twins from opposite sides do meet. In some places the fae gates appear to be a little..." He pursed his lips. "Thinner. More fluid. But none of those Brightkin have ever shown any ability to use magic. Not that I've ever heard of."

"So you have no idea why I can speak to Cadell?"

"None, Carys Morgan." He reached out his hand and she took it. He lowered his voice and glanced at Mared, Cadell, and the other two dragons. "I would take you back to Caernarfon with me, but Robb seems determined to find out more about you. What do you want?"

"I want to stay here."

"Why?"

Carys didn't know what to say. Dafydd probably thought his daughter had died of a fever like everyone else.

"Carys?"

"Someone killed Seren," she blurted. "And I want to know who."

Dafydd's eyes flashed with anger, and he turned away.

"Dafydd?" She walked in front of him. "You're not surprised by what I said, are you? You knew—you suspected anyway."

"Of course I did." His voice was rough, but he finally looked at her. "When Robb told me my daughter had died, he said it was from a fever. And she had been ill. I knew that."

"But?"

"Mared and I always suspected we were not getting the full story. Seren *had* been ill with an infection. That's why she sent Cadell away when his children needed him even though she normally would have gone with him. But she was recovering and she was strong. Then when she died..."

"Why didn't you pursue it?"

Dafydd took a slow breath and let it out. "We could never know for sure."

"Do people just die here for no reason?"

"Yes." He looked at her. "Not for no reason, but life here is much more precarious than life in the Brightlands. We don't have hospitals. We don't have the same medicine. Healers are very skilled, and magic is powerful, but people can die very young." He lifted his chin. "Why are *you* certain?"

"Because of the way that everyone reacted when Duncan said it," Carys said. "Whatever happened to Seren, there's more than they're letting on. Why hide anything if it was natural causes?"

Dafydd turned and looked at the castle behind them. "Eamer thought that pursuing the truth might endanger our relationship with the Alban court. She didn't…" He frowned. "She cared for Seren, but she never loved her as I did. I thought she was thinking more rationally and I was blinded by grief, so I let it go. Now I see that I should have pursued it more."

"We can find the truth." Carys lifted her eyes to meet his stoic gaze. "I think we can figure it out."

Dafydd said nothing. He didn't agree. He didn't disagree.

He has many lives more than his to consider.

She turned to look at Cadell and realized that Dafydd's quiet might mean that he was speaking with Mared in his mind the same way she was talking to Cadell.

Dafydd is a king, Cadell continued. *Keeping peace means saving lives.*

Carys turned to Dafydd. "Was it true that Lachlan was planning to give up the seat of power here and leave Alba for Cymru?"

"Yes." Dafydd kept his voice low. "Seren told me that was their ultimate plan when she asked permission to marry him. They wanted to put Lachlan's brother Rory on the throne. It was a good plan, otherwise I could have never allowed her to marry him."

"They had to ask permission to get married?"

"Lachlan and Seren weren't farmers in the village. Those of our station do not marry for affection; we marry for alliance and political purpose. For Lachlan and Seren to wed, there were many meetings between me and Robb, between Elanor and Eamer. In the end, it was only the threat of them running away—and the knowledge that they could both disappear into the Brightlands—that made us allow it."

Carys nodded. "They'd both been across the gates before."

"And they had connections via Duncan," Dafydd said. "Robb has always resented Duncan for *existing*, but he knows that if he alienates Lachlan's twin, he'll lose his oldest son. And Duncan..." Dafydd frowned. "He has something over Robb, but I don't know what it is. Some power."

Carys tucked that away to ask Duncan about later. "Did Robb know that was their plan?"

"No, he was convinced I would pick another heir, and I let him think I was considering it." Dafydd shook his head. "It was the one secret I kept from Robb because Seren asked me to, and I still regret it."

"I think that maybe that secret might be what killed her."

"You think someone killed her so Lachlan wouldn't leave?" He stepped back. "But who would—"

"Maybe it wasn't because Lachlan was going to leave." Carys was quick to jump in because she could tell that Dafydd didn't want to suspect Robb of his daughter's death. "Maybe *not* telling people their plans made others think that Alba and Cymru would join kingdoms under Seren and Lachlan."

Dafydd's face grew pale. "And no one would want a united Alba and Cymru. The power imbalance would be too great."

"That's what I was thinking too."

Dafydd stepped back, clasping his hands behind his back as he walked toward Mared and Cadell. He walked in silence for a long time, staring at Mared in a way that made Carys think they were having some kind of conversation. A few moments later, he walked back.

"Mared and I will help you. I cannot question my daughter's death openly without risking the peace, but we will help you find who killed my daughter."

CHAPTER TWENTY-THREE

"You know, when you asked me the other day, it didn't even occur to me that Seren's journals would be among her books." Aisling was digging through a corner of the castle library where wooden crates were stacked. "I'm sorry I didn't think of it sooner."

"It's fine." Carys glanced at Duncan. "I'm just glad they weren't lost."

"Well, they were a little." Aisling brushed back a lock of hair that had come out of her braid. "Robb doesn't employ scribes like the Éiren court does, so the task of going through Seren's books was given to me, and I've just been so..." Aisling sighed.

"You're a busy woman," Duncan said gruffly. "They should get you some help."

"Ha!" Aisling's mouth turned up at the corner. "That would be a dream. If I were in charge of this grand library, I would employ an army of scribes and scholars, but alas..."

Carys smiled. "Not your call?"

Aisling shrugged. "All I have is one apprentice from the village and a few servants to clean up."

"That must be frustrating." Carys looked around the castle library, which was dusty and disorganized. If they were depending on Aisling to organize it, it would be an overwhelming task.

"But I do love being in the library," Aisling continued. "It's not really my job. And technically I'm only an apprentice mage myself, because to finish my studies I have to finish my grimoire and my amulet, and I can't really do that while Regan is jumping from one court to another, can I?" She popped her head up from the crates. "I apologize, these are my own frustrations and they're not your concern."

Carys saw in Aisling the echoes of academia at home. "No, I get it. When I was a graduate student, I felt like my desk was the dumping ground for every task no one in the department wanted."

"So it's the same in the Brightlands." Aisling returned to the crates. "Duncan, could you..."

"Of course." He stepped forward and gripped the heavy crate Aisling was pointing toward. He lifted the wooden box over his head like it was made of feathers, and Carys blinked when she realized she was staring at his back where it narrowed to his hips. It was too bad his kilt covered his backside. She'd love to see him in a pair of well-worn jeans that defined—

Fuck.

Carys looked at the ground, kicking a dust bunny that rolled across the intricately tiled floor. She cleared her throat. "This library is huge though. Clearly built by someone who loved books."

"Yes." Aisling answered her while lifting one book after another and stacking them to the side. "The former king—Robb's uncle—was married to an Éiren queen who invested heavily in bringing scholars to Sgàin. She had a musical school here, mages in residence. She had been trained as a scribe in Anglia, so she improved the library quite a lot. It was her passion."

"Robb didn't approve of all that," Duncan said. "Told Lachlan scribes, mages, and musicians attracted the fae."

"Is he wrong?"

"No." Duncan crossed his arms over his chest. "But if you're only concerned with hunting, farming, and war, what are you living for?"

Aisling pointed to another crate. "Duncan, can you—"

"Happy to, lass." He lifted the wooden box over his head, and Carys quickly looked away.

She was being an idiot. The last thing she needed was to be looking at Duncan that way. It was as if her night with Lachlan had switched on her libido, which was... idiotic to say the least.

She was a stranger in a foreign fae realm, trying to figure out who poisoned her magical twin, and she didn't need to be looking at Duncan's broad shoulders or the hard curve of his thighs under his kilt when he lifted that crate like it weighed—

Dammit!

"Found them." Aisling raised her head in triumph. "A whole crate of her journals right here." She pointed at it while Duncan stepped back into the confusion of wooden boxes. "I think I missed them because they were covered with some maps she was working on with Cadell." She cocked her head. "Land surveys from Northern Anglia, it looks like."

Carys cleared her throat. "Seren liked maps?" She remembered Dafydd mentioning Cymric maps.

"She adored them," Duncan said. "Collected every one she could find from the Brightlands when she'd visit with Lachlan. Even the old ones."

Aisling said, "On days she didn't have court duties with Lachlan, she and Cadell would just take to the air and..." Aisling's hand fluttered into the air. "She was an excellent artist too. Probably helped when drawing maps."

And Carys couldn't draw a stick figure. It was as if all her mother's talent in drawing had fallen into Seren's head and not her own.

"Let me know if you need help reading them." Aisling started restacking crates. "My Cymric is rough, but I could probably give you the basic idea." She caught herself. "Well, after Regan has gone. While she's here, we need to be working on my grimoire."

"Is that like your doctoral thesis?" Carys walked over and tried to help with the crates, but Duncan pushed her back.

"I don't know what that is, but when you're studying magic, you must study from the magical writings of others to learn, but you're only considered a true mage when you have written your own book of spells and demonstrated its usefulness to your teacher. For me, that's Regan."

"Yep, sounds quite a bit like a thesis," Carys muttered. "What about the amulet thing?"

"Older mages still use wands to channel their magic and center themselves," Aisling said. "But I think they're kind of old-fashioned. Most mages my age use an amulet or a talisman of some kind to practice." Her eyes lit up. "I heard about a mage from the court in Gaulle who was using a *ring*, and that seems very progressive."

"Mmm." Duncan nodded and stacked the last crate on the top of the pile. "I think a ring would be useful. Discreet like an amulet but directed." He shot his hand out. "Like a wand."

Carys barely stifled a giggle. "Yer a wizard, Duncan."

He narrowed his eyes and flipped her off, but Carys could only laugh.

"I had the exact same thought about using a ring." Aisling's face showed all the excitement of a true nerd, and Carys had never felt more at home. "But I don't know if Regan would even consider it. Amulets are preferred in Éire."

Carys could have stayed in the library for hours with Aisling, talking about magic and exploring the books, but she had a very large box of journals to read, and Aisling needed to get back to work.

Carys bent down and brushed a rolled map to one side, grabbing a book bound in red leather. "So these are my sister's books."

Duncan stared at the pile. "You're probably going to need your dragon."

"We'll take these to my house." Duncan had loaded the crate filled with Seren's journals into a wagon and covered it with furs and various household goods he'd collected from the merchants in the courtyard. "I think they'll be safer if we don't keep them at the castle."

"Good idea. Cadell and I can walk to your house when we want to read them."

"Can you read any Welsh at all?" He took the lead of the horse pulling the cart and urged the animal forward.

"I'm hoping some of it will come back. My parents usually only spoke Welsh when they were talking about my Christmas presents." She grimaced. "My mother spoke it more than my father, but he managed. It was her first language but not his."

"Neither of my parents spoke a lick of Gaelic," he said. "It's not common in Scotland, especially where I'm from. Even the old people speak English."

"I hear it here too." They walked over the moat and into the village. "The English, I mean."

"It's used for business mostly. You'll hear it around the castle because of all the traders and merchants." He nodded at a tall man with long braided hair sweeping in front of the pub. "That's Fionn," he whispered. "In Scone, his twin is named Javid and he's a petrochemical engineer in London."

"His parents must be thrilled."

Duncan clicked his tongue as he led the horse. "They brag about him at the corner shop every time I come in."

"And here he has a pub." Carys smiled. "So... Javid was born in Scotland, so his twin was too."

Duncan nodded. "That's how it works."

Carys looked at the dark-skinned man, at his angled face and thin build. "But his parents, maybe not?"

Duncan smiled. "Pakistan, I think."

"So *their* twins were born into the Shadowlands there?"

"I'd assume so."

"So…" Carys was thinking about a woman in a distant land, continents away from the child born in Scotland. "Who raised Fionn here?"

Duncan shrugged. "Whoever the fae gave him to. Families often look a little different here. People are accustomed to it, so it's not given any mind."

Just then a short round man with a long grey beard and a shock of white hair wandered out and pointed at something on the roof of the pub. Fionn walked over, listening and nodding.

"See?" Duncan shrugged. "There you go. Your dad is going to find something to criticize about your work in any realm."

Carys smiled politely at the people they passed, and Duncan quietly narrated a few more people he knew.

"That man's a baker here," he said quietly. "In the Brightlands, his twin sells real estate to corporations who build shopping centers on the edge of town." Duncan nodded at a woman they passed. "Hallo, Anna."

"Hallo, Duncan!"

He waited until she passed. "That's the mayor. I'm not joking, that's the mayor of my town, and here she and her husband own a tailor shop. She prides herself on the curtains in the North Hall. Tells everyone she made them."

"They're impressive curtains, Duncan."

He smiled. "That they are."

Carys tried not to stare as they continued walking through town.

"Where's Cadell?" Duncan asked.

"I can feel him around, but he's not focused on me right now." Carys shook her head. "It's hard to explain. If I called him, I know he'd be here in two seconds, but he's not hovering."

"It was always that way with Seren too. I used to tease Cadell that he was her butler." Duncan smirked. "He liked that."

"He did not."

"After I explained what a butler was, no, he didn't." He glanced at her as he continued walking beside the horse-cart. "You're really taking all of this quite well, Carys Morgan."

"No, I'm not. I ran out of the banquet last night, and Bonnie said everyone was talking about it." *And then I had sex with your brother.*

She mentally winced. It was none of Duncan's business. None at all.

Fuck.

"They might have been surprised you ran out, but they were more surprised you came at all, being a foreigner."

"Foreigner from the Brightlands or from America?"

"Both. Most of them have heard of America, but they've never met anyone from there. Even people from the continent are rare. Unless you command a flying creature like a dragon, it's a rare human in this realm who crosses the ocean."

"Right." She shook her head. "Sea monsters."

"Sea monsters."

They turned left at the end of the road, then right at the ribboned oak tree that led into the forest. Carys followed Duncan this time, knowing it was easy to get lost.

She thought back to the first time she'd run from the castle and the wrong turn she'd taken in the forest that led her to the loch and the unicorns. She must have walked far longer than she knew to get that far away from the village and human habitation.

"Why did you run?"

She blinked. "What?"

Duncan frowned. "Why did you leave the banquet so early? Avoiding another dance?"

Hardly. Her dance with Duncan had been the highlight of the party. She hadn't known he could be charming because he rarely was, but his playful demeanor on the dance floor and his light step had made her feel at ease.

She usually felt at ease with Duncan.

"Not the dancing." She looked at her feet. "You're a good dancer."

He grunted. "I'll let my mother know the mandatory classes paid off."

Carys couldn't help but smile. "Did she really?"

"Oh yes. Three days a week for several years before I went to school."

"Like, boarding school?"

Duncan nodded. "A grand old place where princes were educated, and my father was disappointed in me. I hated school."

"Did you?"

He glanced over his shoulder. "The only thing that saved me was rugby and rock climbing. And sneaking away when I could to watch the smiths near the stables."

"Is that when you got interested in blacksmithing?"

He handed the horse's lead to Carys and walked to the back to heave the cart over a rock in the middle of the path. "I'd always been interested in it, but yes. Here, of course, what I can do is very limited because of fae rules."

They had walked through the edge of the forest and to the other side where Duncan's cottage was hidden in a stand of ash trees. The moment she crossed the garden gate, her shoulders relaxed.

"So do you have a smithy here?"

The corner of his mouth turned up. "Of a sort."

"How do you work without iron?"

"More magic." He looked over his shoulder. "You can visit if you want. Meet Angus. He'll love you."

"Angus?"

"He's a..." Duncan frowned. "Better to meet him than to explain. Auld Mags is at the house, but unless you're there at night, you won't see her."

Carys stopped in the middle of the path. "I forgot you had a brownie. Brownies are powerful, you know. Way more powerful than people expect."

"Auld Mags wouldn't argue with you." He left the cart on the side of the cottage after unharnessing the horse, then lifted the crate full of Seren's journals into his arms. "Call your dragon and come inside. We have some reading to do."

Cadell set down another leather-bound volume and folded his massive hands in his lap. "This is also routine information that says nothing about why she was killed."

"The problem is that what we might think of as routine information could be the thing that got her killed," Carys said. "I can't explain it; I just have to read them." She sat back at Duncan's wooden table and huffed out a breath. "Which I can't do because they're in Welsh. Cymric. It's the same language, and I speak none of it anymore."

"I can organize them for you," Cadell said. "Put them in the order they were written. They start when she was very young, but she became more regular, writing in them when she returned to Caernarfon for training."

"That would be great. Thanks. But I will still need you to read them."

Cadell leaned forward and held up a small book bound in purple leather. "Do you truly believe that these journals are vital to discovering Seren's murderer?"

"I don't know for sure." She sighed. "But I think they're the best place to start."

Cadell looked grumpy.

"What do *you* want to do? Pick people at random, hang them by their toes, and torture them until they confess?"

"Seems like a better place to start than Seren's diary," Duncan muttered.

Cadell said, "I agree with the cross human."

"We're not torturing people!" Carys looked through another journal. "Yet." Her eyes were crossing as she tried to remember words she hadn't read in twenty years. "Okay, I'm useless with these."

Cadell looked over at Duncan, who was poking at the wood in the hearth. "We should ask your úruisg to translate them."

Duncan frowned. "What would Angus have to do with any of that?"

"Úruisg wield powerful magic. Old magic. Even older than dragons." Cadell pursed his lips. "Humans have such small minds."

"Dragon, I've never in my life heard of any úruisg having a gift for languages. The unicorns maybe, but—"

"Wait, what's a..." Carys frowned. "Oo-rishk? I've never heard that name before."

"Úruisg is the Alban name," Cadell said. "You might know it by another."

"Eh." Duncan shrugged. "They're not as common in tales as kelpies or unicorns. Not even by half. Most books would probably group them in with brownies or dobbies because they're household spirits. But they're not the same."

Carys's curiosity was piqued. "How are they different?"

"In the Shadowlands, a brownie tends to attach to a place." He nodded toward the chimney. "Auld Mags was here before I was. The cottage is more hers than mine in a way."

"And úruisgs?"

"Again, I don't know what it says in books, but in the Shadowlands, they attach to families. The older the family, the more likely they have an úruisg."

"But it's a kind of fae?"

"No," Cadell said.

"Yes," Duncan said. "As I actually know an úruisg, please ignore the dragon."

"The úruisg are very old magical creatures," Cadell said. "Who can be very wild and very solitary, but if treated with respect, they are extremely loyal to their families."

"They're also proud," Duncan muttered. "Opinionated as fuck. Good workers though."

"Angus is extremely loyal to Duncan, though I've never understood why. The Albans think they are native to this land, but they are not." Cadell looked at Duncan. "And they are not fae. Head and torso of a human, legs of a goat. Who does that remind you of?"

Duncan shrugged. "Angus."

"Pan." Carys sat up straight. "That sounds like Pan to me."

"The old gods would lay with anything that breathed," Cadell said. "Pan was the son of Mercury."

"And Mercury was Hermes," Carys continued.

"And who was Hermes before?" Cadell asked. "Old. Think very old gods."

Carys took a deep breath and thought about the pantheons of the ancient world. "Hermes likely came from the Egyptian god Thoth. Thoth probably had another name before that, but I don't know what it is."

Duncan shook his head. "I don't know anything about Thoth. And I've never heard Angus mention Hermes or anything like that."

"The old gods are tied together." Cadell persisted. "They take new forms as humans change. But they pass along powerful magic to their offspring."

"And Hermes was the god of *language*." Carys looked at Duncan. "The god of interpreters. If Angus's magic does go back to Hermes, he *could* translate Seren's journals."

"I agree, Nêrys."

Carys added, "And he could possibly guide us to the underworld too, but hopefully we won't need that."

"Mercury, Hermes, and Thoth may be interpreters," Duncan said, "but *Angus* is a crotchety old úruisg who lives in the stream by my forge and only works with me to piss off Robb. So if you think he can help you interpret Seren's journals, be my guest, but I think you're reaching."

"Lives in a stream," Carys muttered. "And bodies of water are passages to the underworld. Just saying."

Cadell stared at Carys. "You will interest him. You're of neither realm and both. A human born in the Brightlands who can speak with magic. If you bring him a gift, Angus may translate the journals into Anglian for you." He turned to Duncan. "What language does he speak with you? Gaelic or English?"

Duncan frowned. "English. But I know he speaks Gaelic too."

"And he speaks Cymric to me." Cadell rose to his feet. "I heard an úruisg complain once that all human language tasted like vinegar save for the language of flowers."

"The language of flowers?" Carys looked at Duncan. "Is that real here?" Delight fluttered in her chest. She loved studying the language of plants and the botanical connections between mythology and science. "Do magical creatures really use flowers to communicate here?"

"Yes," Cadell said. "Not dragons or wolves though. Flowers are meaningless to us."

And yet something about Cadell's face made Carys doubt he was telling her the whole truth.

"Angus *does* like flowers," Duncan said. "When I first moved into the cottage, Auld Mags told me to bring him daffodils on the New Year or he'd be offended."

"Daffodils symbolize new beginnings," Carys said. "That would be a good flower to take anytime you're going to introduce yourself."

"Auld Mags is a clever bwbach," Cadell said.

"Bwbach?" Duncan asked.

"It's the Welsh word for a brownie," Carys said.

Cadell looked at her. "Your mother was born in Cymru. Did she leave bowls of milk out at night?"

"Kind of?"

Not bowls, but there were mugs of milk left on the wood stove, and Carys had always thought it was her mother's superstition, but she didn't question it. Knowing that all of this was real added so many more layers to little things she'd always taken for granted.

"Mugs," Carys said. "Not bowls, but yes."

"She honored the bwbach." Cadell nodded. "Angus will know it. Human, do you have Queen Anne's Lace, tansy, and bluebells in the garden?"

"Probably," Duncan said. "Mags grows a bit of everything out there."

"She's smarter than you deserve. Magical creatures recognize flowers before words." Cadell reached out his hand. "Come. We'll bring some flowers and milk to Angus and see if he'll grant us a favor. Human, bring the journals."

"Not your servant, dragon." Duncan rose from the bench by the hearth. "But I'll bring them for Carys."

CHAPTER TWENTY-FOUR

They set off into the forest, Cadell remaining in human form and carrying a painted pitcher of heavy cream, Carys and her flowers at his side, and Duncan bringing up the rear with the crate of journals on his shoulder.

"Do you remember the way?" Duncan asked.

"How many times have I visited your forge, human?"

Duncan muttered something that Carys couldn't hear.

The part of the forest where they were walking was alive with birdsong, and as they walked, dead leaves crunched under their feet. She was glad she'd dressed comfortably that morning. The daylight was dimming, but she had no idea what time it was. Clocks didn't exist in the Shadowlands, and neither did the sun.

She glanced over her shoulder at Duncan. "How do you get used to the darkness?"

His eyes met hers. "I don't. That's why I don't usually stay in this place for long stretches."

It had been over a week that they'd been gone, and her one trip back had been at night.

"Does time pass like normal in the Brightlands while we're here?"

Cadell said, "Unless you're taken by certain people with pointy ears into one of their forts or hills, then yes. A week here is a week in the Brightlands."

"It was a good idea to go back and call my friends." The passing of time in this place felt longer and shorter at once. It was easy to get confused.

"Well, I already had one American woman descending on me and threatening to call the police—I didn't want Mary facing two more." He glanced down. "She knows what it's like to worry."

All this was no big deal as long as Carys returned to Scotland unharmed. But what if she didn't? What if she was delayed? "You said that time passes the same, but what if I'm taken by the fae—"

Cadell spun and swiftly put a hand over her mouth, stifling the words before they could leave her mouth.

"Christ, Carys." Duncan cursed loudly. "Watch your words."

Cadell looked to the left and right. He glanced up, then to the left again. The birds in the forest had gone silent, and something rustled in the underbrush.

He spoke directly in her mind. *You're human. Don't tempt them with questions like that or they'll think you're curious.*

When he released his hand, she whispered, "They're here?"

We are in the forest. Sprites and nymphs are the ears of the fae.

Carys nodded. "We should get on our way to see Angus."

Cadell looked down at his pitcher of cream. "I didn't spill it."

"You're acting like he's a fine fairy lord," Duncan grumbled. "He's Angus. He'd be happy with milk in a bowl. You didn't have to get fancy."

"We're asking the úruisg for a favor. Show the proper respect."

They passed over a small rise and then down again into a narrow hollow in the folded hills where Carys could hear a stream flowing. They walked over a small stone bridge, and the birds started singing again. A lightness filled the air despite the gloom overhead, and Cadell's shoulders relaxed.

"This is a good place." He nodded at Duncan. "You've warded it well. Safe from fae ears."

"It is," Duncan said. "But the wards are all Angus. I wish I had a bit of the magic that Carys does, but no spell works for me."

"I told you he was powerful," Cadell said. "How do you think they haven't found this place in the past ten years?"

Carys asked, "You've had this place for ten years?"

Cadell and Duncan exchanged a look but said nothing.

They walked down the hill, following a cobbled path set into the forest floor, and down into a grotto where high stone walls rose on either side. The air was damp and green, moss covered the rocks, and the scent of growing things overwhelmed the dry air and dusty leaves of the winter forest.

Carys frowned. "What have you been hiding and from whom?"

"How happy do you think the local fae would be to know a human smith was working in the Shadowlands?" Duncan turned to the right. "Angus!"

A stone archway appeared over a crack in the rocks, and standing under it was a creature like nothing Carys had ever seen. He had the legs of a goat, the muscled body of a human, and was dressed in hairy animal skins from the hood that draped over his twisted grey hair to the end of his long arms. Sheepskins if Carys had to guess. They were covered in sticks and leaves, as if he'd been rolling around in the forest.

"Angus." Duncan set down the crate. "I've brought you a guest. Carys, welcome to my very illegal forge."

Angus stepped forward, his loping gait reminding Carys of a man on stilts. His face, despite his hair, wasn't as old as she'd expected. He had a long, straight nose and deep brown eyes. His beard was wavy and stone grey, threaded with grass and flowers, and while his light brown skin was flecked with dirt, he smelled of fresh water and grass.

"Has Seren returned from the Annwn then?" the creature said. "Or is this her kin?"

"Her Brightkin," Duncan said. "This is Carys. She came to me looking for Lachlan."

"Ah." Angus glanced at Duncan from the side. "The spoiled boy has made a mess, I think." He leaned down and took a long sniff. "You have the smell of the sun and the shadow at once." The creature cocked his head at an angle. "And you have magic."

"She is nêrys ddraig," Cadell said. "Like her twin."

"Interesting." Angus stared at Carys for a long minute, examining her face.

Unnerved by his silence, Carys held out the bouquet of flowers. "I brought these for you."

"You're a clever one." Angus took the flowers and studied the bluebells and tansy. "You want a favor, Seren's twin."

"My friends call me Carys."

"I am not your friend." Angus looked up. "But I do find you interesting. You have the scent of Epona's daughters in your blood."

"I don't know what that means." Carys narrowed her eyes. "But you don't have an accent."

"I speak to all creatures in the language they understand," Angus said. "I don't need an accent."

"Wait, what?" Duncan crossed his arms over his chest. "You speak Scots English like me."

"He speaks Cymric." Cadell smiled a little. "Don't you, Angus?"

Angus waved a hand and hunched his back, dragging the hairy cape over his head. "Don't ask me questions, dragon. What do you want?"

Cadell held out the pitcher of cream. "I couldn't find silver or gold. Forgive me, but I was coming from the human's house."

"I don't have a silver pitcher," Duncan said.

"And I don't want one. I'm not a dragon." Angus took the pitcher of cream and lifted it to his lips, drinking it down so fast it dripped out the sides of his mouth and into his beard. "Milk from the earth. Clay from the soil." His eyes lightened. "My thanks to you, dragon. I don't need your gold or jewels." He turned to Carys and motioned toward the arch. "Come see, Brightkin. You can ask me your questions and I'll smell you a bit longer."

She looked at Duncan. "Smell me?"

He shrugged. "It's Angus."

Duncan's forge was little more than a covered shack with open windows, a wood-shingled roof, and a massive pile of firewood sitting outside to feed the great billowing beast of a fire.

Throwing off his sheepskin cloak, Angus worked the bellows, shirtless and sweating, his hair bound back in a long braid and his beard sizzling as the sparks from the fire flew out.

"How does he not get burned?" Carys asked Cadell, who was sitting far closer to the fire than she was comfortable with.

Cadell turned to her, his face glowing and flushed from the flames. He looked as happy as a pig in mud. "The water follows him. I don't think it's even possible for an úruisg to be burned."

"He can't be. Makes him the perfect partner." Duncan strode past her, his cloak also stripped away and his massive arms bare to the shoulder. "How is it?"

"Stubborn," Angus glared at something glowing in the coals. "Almost as stubborn as you." He took a pair of tongs and lifted a red-hot piece of metal from the fire. "It's thin; we could do with more if he was willing to give it."

Duncan turned to Cadell and held out his arms. "You're here."

Cadell glanced at Carys. "I don't want to scare her."

Angus looked at Carys from the corner of her eye. "That one doesn't scare easily. Her father made her brave."

Carys looked at the strange creature. "What do you know about my father?"

"No questions right now." Angus waved at Cadell. "Do it, dragon. We've been working on this thing for too long, and he'll need it soon."

"You'll have to melt the blade down and reforge it," Cadell said. "It will take time."

"Time I have," Angus said. "Do it."

Duncan walked to the forge and picked up the glowing metal with the tongs Angus had put down. He sighed deeply and leaned on a low stone wall. "Unfortunately, I agree with Angus. The extra weight will be worth it if you're willing to do it."

Cadell looked at Carys. "We've come this far," he said in a low voice. "But this is the last time."

"It's all we'll need," Angus said.

The dragon walked to a clearing on the other side of the forge and stepped out of his human skin and into his beast, spreading his wings and taking to the sky with a fantastic roar.

Carys's heart leaped in her chest as she watched Cadell soar overhead, his body breaking the sky as he flew back and forth, clearly stretching his wings.

She whispered, "He really hates being human."

Duncan walked over and looked up. "Aye, it's not natural for them."

She looked at Duncan, then at Angus. "So you built a secret forge so the fae don't know you're forging iron weapons."

"You guessed that in one," he said.

"Where are you getting the iron?"

Duncan said, "You'll find out shortly." He looked down. "Lachlan doesn't know about it either, so not a word."

"Why not?"

"He's shit at keeping secrets." Duncan glanced at Angus. "And this is a very big secret."

"I thought the fae wouldn't let any iron be mined or brought into Briton."

"We're not mining it." Duncan glanced at Angus. "I'd like to say I managed to sneak some from the Brightlands through the fae gate, but I'm not that clever."

Angus walked behind the forge and yelled, "He's definitely not that clever."

Duncan watched the sky. "Have you ever heard that phrase 'forged from the blood of my enemies'?"

Carys blinked. "I'd always assumed that was a metaphor because I'm not really a fan of mass murder to get tiny amounts of iron from human blood."

"Turns out you can forge iron made from the blood of friends too." Duncan watched the dragon flying overhead. "If that blood is willingly given."

"Oh my God." Carys got to her feet. "Are you telling me—"

"The amount of iron in human blood is minuscule compared to the amount in dragon blood." Duncan walked toward the meadow as Cadell circled closer.

The beast let out an awesome roar before he sprayed a column of fire into the air, circled once more, then came to rest in the meadow near the forge, his massive wings stretched out and his throat glowing with fire.

The air around them churned as he beat his wings in the air, rearing up to bare his green body and the iridescent shimmering skin beneath his wings.

"I'm not forging iron, Carys." Duncan stared at Cadell. "I'm forging steel. *Dragon* steel."

Angus approached the beast, dragging a large wooden barrel and a spear the length of a tall man.

Carys rushed toward Cadell, but Duncan caught her by the shoulder.

Hold, Nêrys. Cadell's voice came to her mind. *I give this willingly.*

She froze, but she couldn't tear her eyes away.

"Iron doesn't bother Angus. He doesn't love it, but it doesn't burn him. I suppose that should have been the primary clue that he's not really fae like Cadell said." Duncan watched carefully as Cadell leaned to the side and lifted his wing. "You may not want to watch this."

"I'll watch."

Cadell roared as the spear punctured his thick skin, and the rising fire in his throat glowed brighter than the forge.

Angus shouted something as he pulled the spear from Cadell's side and angled the barrel toward him. Dark red blood spurted from the wound, and Carys felt the ache in her side as Cadell's blood poured into the barrel.

"Carys?"

She bent over, nausea and pain sweeping through her as spots flashed behind her closed eyes.

Nêrys?

"I'm okay." She held her hand out as Duncan grabbed her to hold her up. "I can take it if he can."

Seren never felt it. Cadell sounded upset. *She said she never felt it.*

"Then she lied because it was important." She looked up at Duncan with tears in her eyes. "It's important, right?"

Duncan's face was a mask of anger. "Humans here have no defenses. No weapons that work against them."

The fae can never know. Cadell's voice was softer. *They must never know how this blade was forged. They must never know what we can do.*

"Enough!" Angus shouted. He pushed a heavy blanket into Cadell's wound. "Stay still, dragon."

A surge of power hit Carys's side, and the pain ceased immediately. A wave of soothing heat washed over her, then a growing burst of energy as the wound in Cadell's side knit together. Within minutes, Carys felt as if nothing had happened, and Angus was dragging the massive steaming barrel of dragon blood toward the forge.

"I'll bring the crucible," he muttered. "You feed the fire."

"How many times has he done that?" Carys asked. "Seren knew?"

Duncan walked to the woodpile. "It was her and Cadell's idea. Angus and I were forging the sword for Seren. When she died, Cadell and I decided to continue."

"So she could fight the fae?" Carys straightened herself. "Why would she need to do that?"

"I don't know, and I didn't ask." He started feeding more wood into the fire. "She knew I was a blacksmith and asked for my help."

"And you didn't think to mention this before?" Carys stared at the steaming barrel of blood. "This could be why she was killed, Duncan."

He shook his head. "The fae wouldn't kill with poison. When they kill, they want humans to know it was their doing. They don't know anything about this."

Angus walked over, carrying a large clay crucible. "I'll refine it like the rest." He eyed Carys. "She felt it?"

"Yes."

"So her sister did too." Angus's eyes gleamed. "I knew she was an impressive human."

"I need to read her journals." Carys wasn't interested in waiting anymore. "I need to find out who killed her and why."

Angus angled his head again, examining Carys like a bug under a microscope. "You came here to find your lover."

"And I found a sister instead. One who was murdered, and I want to know why."

Angus shook his head. "That's not all you want to know. And you don't love that one. Not really."

"What are you talking about?" She walked over to the crate of Seren's journals. "Do you know why Seren was killed? Can you translate these or not?"

"You have three questions, Brightkin." Angus crossed his arms. "You get *one*. Can I translate the journals? Do you love the king's son? Why did someone kill your sister? Pick the one you want me to answer, and I will answer it."

Carys felt the taste of a bargain ringing in the air. "You'll answer truthfully?"

Angus nodded. "I will."

"Do you know the answers to all those questions?"

"Perhaps yes. Perhaps no."

Carys didn't care what Angus thought about her love life, so she ignored the question about Lachlan. That left translating the journals or why Seren was killed.

Angus knew his own abilities, but she had no confidence he knew why her sister was murdered. He seemed like a hermit, and she doubted he was Seren's confidant.

"Can you translate the journals?"

The corner of his craggy mouth turned up, and he snapped his fingers over the crate of books. "Done, Nêrys Ddraig. I'll accept your dragon's blood in payment." Angus angled his body toward the forge and the massive barrel full of dragon blood. "I have work to do."

Duncan walked over to the crate of books and lifted one. He opened it and blinked. "They're still in Welsh."

"Give it to me." Would Angus lie? She didn't think so. When she opened the journal, the words swam in front of her for a moment before they settled into familiar shapes and sorted into words she recognized.

"I can read them." She closed one journal and took out another. The same thing happened. The handwriting was a little different, but she could read the heading at the top of the page.

Season of harvest, my fourteenth year.

Carys clasped the journals to her chest. "I can read them."

CADELL STARED into the fire at Duncan's cottage. "In a few moments, I will regain my strength and I can fly you back to the castle."

"Or we could walk." Carys hadn't experienced the thrill of flying in the claws of a dragon, and she didn't want the first time to be when she was cold, tired, and hungry and Cadell was recovering from blood loss. "I promise I'll walk fast."

Cadell didn't roll his eyes, but his expression said he wanted to. "Fine."

Duncan was stirring a pot that hung over the fire. "Angus said you smelled like Epona's daughters. Do you know what that means?"

Carys racked her brain to dig out her memories of Epona. "She's a Gallo-Roman deity. She was a fertility goddess associated with horses. A psychopomp as well."

"Psychopomp?" Duncan asked.

"A spirit or deity associated with escorting souls after death," Carys said. "Think Anubis, the grim reaper, the angel of death. Pan, in some of his forms. Valkyries. That type of spirit."

"Valkyries are..." Cadell blew out a breath. "Don't get me started."

Carys blinked. "Okay, there's a story there."

"They *revere* Epona in Kernow." Cadell ignored Carys's implied question. "You call it Cornwall in the Brightlands. That region is part of Cymru under Dafydd's rule, though the lords there are given much independence. They occasionally produce nêr ddraig, so politically they're considered the same people."

"Interesting, but what does that have to do with Epona? Who are Epona's daughters? I don't remember reading about Epona having any daughters within the Celtic pantheon."

"Not daughters of her blood, but there is a cult of Epona that exists among the humans of Cymru," Cadell said. "There are women who devote themselves to her worship, but they don't have daughters. The fae never give them children. Epona's daughters take vows of celibacy and live in isolation."

"What does that have to do with me?"

"Maybe your mother's Shadowkin is part of this group." Duncan stayed hunched over, stirring their dinner. "Seren was delivered to Dafydd and not your mother's Shadowkin. Maybe that's why."

"Ironic that servants of the fertility goddess aren't given children," Carys said.

"The fae hate Epona's cult," Cadell said. "They don't revere fae power or pay tribute, but Epona's magic protects her daughters so the fae are forced to leave them alone."

Carys nodded. "That's probably it then. My mother's Shadowkin is one of Epona's cult." She winced. "Such a negative connotation to that word even though I know—"

"Why is a cult bad?" Cadell frowned. "What do you call devotees to gods and goddesses in the Brightlands?"

"Religions?" Carys shrugged. "Worshippers? Faithful?"

"Then call them Epona's faithful if it makes you more comfortable." Cadell reached for Seren's journal. "The important thing is Angus translated the journals for you. Now you can read about the grain harvest and Seren's archery lessons." He set the journal down. "Fascinating."

"It might be." Carys scooted closer to the table. "I won't know until I read them."

Duncan stared at the fire, stirring away at the stew. "Why did Angus say you don't love Lachlan?"

Carys's breath caught. She cleared her throat. "I don't know. He's an old úruisg. What does he know about my relationship with your brother?"

The cross human is jealous.

Carys looked at Cadell, but the dragon had his eyes closed, so he missed Carys's mind-your-dragon-business look.

Duncan took a hook and pulled the stew off the fire, taking the steaming pot to the stove where three bowls were waiting. "Dinner is ready. Eat; then we should go back to the castle."

CHAPTER TWENTY-FIVE

They'd agreed to leave the journals at Duncan's house. It was only a thirty-minute walk from the castle, and now that Carys knew the route, she felt comfortable taking it on her own even when Cadell was sleeping in dragon form like he was that morning.

The day was as bright as the Shadowlands ever were, and the sky was a pale blue washed with drifting white clouds. Overhead, birds warbled in a riot of song.

It was one of the first things she'd noticed about this alternate realm. Birds were everywhere, filling the trees and swooping across the sky in massive flocks of starlings and songbirds. Raptors perched at the edge of meadows, watching for field prey to hunt.

Had the birds in her world once been like this? How many birds was she supposed to see in the forest?

She'd been reading that morning about Seren's training in Caernarfon, when she'd started keeping her journal in earnest.

Cadell and I flew through a flock of geese this morning, and one nearly bit my leg she was so angry. They were flying south to the warmer lands. Father says next year he and Mared will take me there. Anything to escape Eamer's nitpicking and angry glares. I hate her. I don't understand why Father ever married her. She's not even pretty.

Eleven-year-old Seren was full of bravado and excitement, the complete opposite of the shy bookworm that Carys had been at that age. She relished her training with Cadell and took quickly to the martial drills that all the young dragon lords had to participate in.

There had been only two other nêr ddraig born the same year as Seren, so there were three children her age training in Caernarfon. Their days consisted of schooling, drills, and flights with their dragons.

Seren swooned over Cadell, marveling at his wisdom and his strength. The way she spoke about him made Cadell seem like a cross between a big brother, a superhero, and a best friend. She reveled in flying, her small coracle clutched in his claw, or even sitting in the safety of his claws as he swooped over the mountains of Cymru.

She wrote about smearing lanolin over her cheeks to keep them from burning in the wind and tying her hair under a heavy wool cap. She wrote about the mundane and the thrilling with equal fervor, her childish delight in the world pricking Carys's heart.

She should have had a life.

A life with Lachlan.

She needed to talk with him. She needed to explain how confused she felt. If none of this had ever happened—if Lachlan had remained in the Brightlands—Carys would have happily grown old with him, sharing a life and building memories in Baywood, oblivious to the life he'd had here.

Now? She couldn't pretend she didn't know that he was her sister's husband. That he'd loved his wife so much that he'd crossed a world to search for Seren's Brightkin. And when he'd found Carys, he'd made her fall in love with him, pretending to be someone he wasn't. Pretending he was a normal human man and not a magical prince.

What should he have said? Would you have believed him?

Carys was lost in thought when she tripped over a root sticking up in the path. She looked down at her stubbed toe. A root?

Only then did she notice that the path she'd been walking through the edge of the forest had diverged and she was at the top of the ridge, looking down across the silver loch.

"Shit." How could she be so careless? Her mind was everywhere, but there was no excuse not to watch where she was going, especially when Cadell wasn't with her.

Carys looked around and sighed in relief when she realized she wasn't far off the cobbled path and she recognized the way back to the castle. She was about to turn when a movement on the edge of the loch caught her attention.

A woman sat on a log, her long dark hair flowing down her back and trailing on the ground. She was dressed in deep green, wearing a gown that looked as if it had been plucked from a medieval tapestry. Something about the woman was familiar.

Had she seen her in a dream?

Carys walked off the path and through the trees to the edge of the forest.

A dark man stood over the strange woman, his tall figure looming. His hair was long and hanging in his face, and his clothes looked like black rags. Was he a vagrant? A fae? Something about him felt other-worldly too, but nothing about the woman's posture spoke of alarm or fear.

The two figures were talking—Carys could tell that much—but they were too far from her to hear what they were saying.

She stepped closer.

The dark figure looked up, and she could see silver eyes glowing from behind his dark, stringy hair. The woman turned and her head angled when she saw Carys.

Without a word, the dark man drew a hood over his head and turned, stepping away from the woman and walking straight into the loch.

"Wait! The kelpie!" Carys started to run toward them, but her foot caught on a rock and she tripped, catching herself with her hands.

She scrambled to her feet, only to find herself alone on the edge of the forest, the woman gone, the loch clear and peaceful as glass. Carys looked around in confusion.

Nothing. The two figures were gone, as if they'd never existed, and Carys was alone.

⁂

BY THE TIME she got back to the castle, she had resolved in her mind that the two figures must have been fae and she'd be better off forgetting she'd ever seen them. The last thing she needed to do was eavesdrop on the fair folk, especially when she now knew a massive secret that could get Duncan, Cadell, and maybe even Angus killed.

It was lucky for her that she'd tripped in the first place.

"Lady Carys!" The guard snapped to attention at the gate and nodded. "How was your walk this morning?"

"Excellent." She hesitated before she asked the next question, but she pushed on. "Is Lord Lachlan in the castle this morning?"

"He is training with the Northern Guard in the inner courtyard, my lady." The man gestured toward the large gate that separated the outer courtyard from the inner. "Through the gate and you'll see them."

She walked across the muddy stones where wagons bumped, sheep wandered, and a pair of donkeys laughed at the busy humans around them. The Castle of Sgàin was a bustling place, more like a small city inside the walls than any kind of home. There were soldiers from Cymru still camped along the south wall, their tents set up with banners flying over them. On the north side was the constant traffic of merchants selling wares from the village and other regions of the Shadowlands.

Women walked by with baskets on their heads, men bartered in various languages, and animals brayed. Through it all was the occasional flash of the familiar. A man wearing a Mickey Mouse shirt under his worn woolen cape. A woman wearing a belt with bright beading and sequins. One teenage boy wore a New York Yankees baseball cap with fur-trimmed earflaps added along the edge.

Carys walked through the outer courtyard and entered the gate, where her fine clothing marked her as a resident of the castle. The guards eyed her with interest but said nothing as she walked into the inner courtyard to see Lachlan standing in the center of a group of men. Carys leaned against a wall in an inconspicuous corner so she didn't interrupt.

As Carys watched Lachlan, Seren's journals flickered in the back of her mind, coloring her own observations with her sister's childish ones.

I like Lachlan, but he's too quiet. He's not like the other boys who are rough with the girls. Harold is positively beastly! He tugs at Aisling's braids every day. It's not nice. Lachlan would never do that, but he doesn't stand up for Aisling either, and it's his own house. He should. The next time Harold bothers Aisling, I'm going to punch his big nose. Elanor will not approve, but it has to be done.

Lachlan was speaking to his men in Gaelic, so she couldn't understand him, but she could see the soldiers watching him with rapt attention as he demonstrated something with a bronze sword in his hand. He was stripped down to his sleeves, his shirt open at the neck, and he'd clearly been working, because sweat glistened on his face. He wore a leather vest with no decoration and a tall pair of boots with guards over the knees.

Another man stood across from Lachlan, his own sword in hand. He was dressed in a dark leather vest, his jacket also removed. The man had short dark hair and dark eyes. His skin was medium brown, and his posture was relaxed and confident.

The ranks of the Northern Guard were elite fighters who guarded the inner castle, the royal family, and the children of the Queens' Pact. They consisted of the best fighters from all the clans in Alba who were sent to Sgàin to serve the king. The men were a mix of complexions and hair colors. Pale skin and bright red hair, dark brown skin and black curling hair. There were a few women sprinkled in, but not many. They were kids that Carys would have seen on her own college campus save for the serious expressions on their very young faces.

Lachlan shouted something, and the man in the dark vest faced him. They parried with their swords, moving slowly so the soldiers watching them could follow what they were doing.

It was clearly a lesson, and Carys watched with rapt attention as Lachlan commanded the men and women. His movements were sure and smooth, clearly those of a master of whatever technique he was teaching.

So the musician is a warrior as well.

He was happy when he was singing, but Carys could see that he also reveled in this. He loved the attention on him, the admiration of the soldiers and the shouts of encouragement. It was a different kind of stage, but a stage nonetheless.

After they'd demonstrated the technique, the man in the dark vest stepped forward and spoke quietly to Lachlan. He looked over his shoulder, spotted her, and turned back to the man. He nodded and Lachlan said something to the soldiers before he walked away, striding toward Carys, whose mind suddenly went blank.

The last time she'd seen him, two nights before, he'd been lying naked beside her in bed. It felt like two years, but time had always been strange with Lachlan. The moment she met him, she'd felt like she'd known him forever. Their four months together felt like four years.

"Carys." He reached her and stood at a respectful distance. "How are you this morning?"

His expression was distant, and Carys remembered the last thing he'd written in her journal.

"I know you didn't kill her," she whispered.

A flicker of anger danced in his eyes. "My name was in your book."

"Because I had to—"

"Did you have a reason for seeking me out today?" He cut her off, his voice clipped and cold.

She felt his rejection like a stone in her chest. "I know you didn't kill her. Dafydd told me more about your plan to—"

"Shhh." Lachlan grabbed her by the arm, looked over his shoulder, and dragged her behind a stone pillar to hide them from view. "Whatever Dafydd may have told you, forget it."

"But that's how I know—"

"It doesn't matter, Carys." His eyes pressed closed. His jaw was tight. He opened his eyes slowly and took a deep breath. "Whatever Seren and I might have planned before she died doesn't matter now."

"How can you say that?" She kept her voice low to match his. "Lachlan, whatever is going on between the two of us, I can't ignore that my sister was murdered. Here." She put a hand on his chest. "In this place, her home, where she was supposed to be safe. It wasn't an illness. It wasn't a random fever. She was poisoned."

"How do you know?" He leaned on the wall, bracing his arm over her head. "Hmm? How do you really know?" He lowered his voice to barely a whisper. "There is *nothing* any of us can prove. People die here. We don't have penicillin and hospitals and modern medicine. We have magic and herbs and sometimes those do nothing, even when you beg the gods on your hands and knees to save the person you love most in the world."

She could see the pain of his grief again, and she wanted to hug him. She wanted to wrap her arms around his neck and press her lips to his skin and hold him until he didn't hurt anymore.

"Don't look at me like that." His voice was rough.

"I can't look at you any other way." She blinked back tears. "I can hear in your voice how much you loved her."

His chest was hard and warm beneath her palm. "I hate it when you cry. It makes me want to break something," he whispered.

"I'm trying to do the right thing here. This grief is poisoning both of us. Don't you see? This is why I was so depressed. This is why I couldn't escape that... pit. And if you don't resolve it, then nothing—"

"If someone really killed her, you're digging up secrets that are better left buried." Lachlan swallowed hard. "And it's only going to hurt you and the people who knew Seren and loved her most."

Carys blinked. "You don't want me to find out who did it?"

Lachlan leaned down and whispered, "I don't want you to *die*. This is reckless, Carys."

"I'm reckless? I'm not the one who crossed a fae gate and went in search of my dead wife's twin."

His eyes went wide.

"I'm sorry." She dropped her hand from his chest. "You did it because you loved her and—"

"I love *you*." Lachlan's jaw was clenched. "And I know you think I'm a liar." He closed his eyes and opened them slowly. "I know you don't believe my feelings, but they are real, and I don't want you hurt. You should return to Scotland with Duncan. I will find you when I can."

"That's it?"

"When I can leave the castle, I will come to you." He reached out and put a hand on her cheek. "Carys, this is what's best. It's dangerous here, and your having this magic with Cadell is... It's not natural. I'll speak to my father; I can make him see that it's for the best, and he'll understand that I need to come and see you."

She narrowed her eyes. "Come and see me?"

He let out a breath. "Come and *be* with you, Carys. It's not—"

"What do you think is going to happen? Do you think you're going to just pop in and out of my life when it works for you?"

"It won't be like that." He smoothed his thumb over her skin. "I haven't worked it out in detail, but if you moved to Scotland—"

She laughed a little and pulled her face away. "*Scotland?* I should move to Scotland? Just uproot my life to move across the world so you can... What? Come visit me when you get a break in your kingly duties?"

He stepped back and leaned on his sword. "I don't want this," he said softly. "You know I don't."

"Don't you? Because you looked really comfortable at that banquet the other night. Chatting with the fae and the unicorns, drinking in that applause." She tasted bitterness on the back of her tongue. "Here, you're... *you*. When you sing, everyone turns to listen." She smiled a little. "Life in Baywood must have seemed really small, huh?"

"No." He shook his head. "It was wonderful. Everything I wanted. You must know that."

Carys closed her eyes and took a deep breath. "You know, ever since I found out about my sister, I have wondered how the same man could fall in love with two completely different women. Just absolute opposites, you know?" She smiled a little. "I guess that's the point, right? My shadow self."

"Not as unlike as you think," he murmured.

"And I'm starting to understand it." She nodded slowly. "The life we had in Baywood? That was like your little dream, right? The quiet, simple life versus the big important life here with so many responsibilities and duties."

"Yes." He lifted one shoulder. "You're not wrong. They're different lives, but that doesn't mean one is better or—"

"The thing about dreams is that we wake up." Carys swallowed hard, forcing her words past the lump in her throat. "And I wonder if you would have woken up—because you *would* have woken up—and realized that you were tired of that simple life." She looked up and met his brilliant green eyes. "Because there is nothing simple about you, Lachlan, son of Robb, future chief of the Moray clan."

"None of that means that I don't love you." Lachlan lifted his chin. "Maybe all that means is the life you have in Baywood is smaller than you deserve. Maybe you do belong here with me."

"So you don't want me to leave after all?"

"I don't know what I want!" he whispered. "Except you. I want you. And I want you to be alive and safe, and I can't lose another woman I love. Do you understand how hard it is for me to not lock you in a damn tower so no one can touch a hair on your head?"

God, why couldn't it be simple? Carys shook her head and pushed back the tears that wanted to fall. "I believe you want me safe."

"I want you *alive*." He looked over his shoulder at the soldiers gathered in the courtyard. "And in this place, that is never a guarantee. *That* is why I want you gone."

She met his eyes and didn't waver. "I know you didn't hurt her, Lachlan. I know that in my bones. But I'm not leaving without finding out who did. If you don't want to help me, I understand."

He lifted his eyes to the sky and shook his head. His smile, when he managed it, was bitter. "You're more like your sister than you realize."

Lachlan didn't look at her again; he turned and walked away.

CHAPTER TWENTY-SIX

The following morning, Carys met Queen Elanor, Queen Eamer, and Aisling in a small room that looked over the formal garden. It was the queen's morning room, and there was a breakfast table laid out with boiled eggs, savory sausages, apples, pears, and berries, and pastries that looked as if they'd come fresh from a French bakery.

"Carys!" Elanor held out both her hands. "I am so glad you decided to join us."

She offered Elanor an apologetic smile. "Finally, right?"

Elanor smiled, and her eyes creased in the corners. "I would not say it. But yes. I've been looking forward to this." She was a beautiful woman with silver threading her blond hair and clear blue eyes the color of a summer sky.

"I am so fortunate to meet you," Elanor continued. "If you catch me staring, know that it is only because I loved your sister very much." A shadow of pain flickered across the queen's eyes, and she blinked rapidly. "But now is not the time to mourn. This is a celebration. Come and meet your aunt." Elanor motioned to where Queen Eamer was already seated at the head of the table next to Aisling.

Carys walked over and offered an awkward curtsy. "Your… Majesty?" She turned to Elanor. "I am so sorry—I don't know what's proper here. I am probably addressing you wrong too."

"We're not like humans in the Brightlands," Elanor said. "And you are family. Please." She motioned to a servant to pull out Carys's chair. "Eamer, this is your daughter's Brightkin, Carys Morgan."

Eamer, despite her pinched mouth, had kind blue eyes. "It's very nice to see you again, Carys. We didn't get a chance to speak at the banquet, and I have been busy with state business."

"I'm glad we can speak now," Carys said. "It's been wonderful to get to know King Dafydd a bit."

"I'm sure you have much to talk about," Eamer said. "And I'm sure you have many questions."

Aisling laughed. "Carys is full of questions. As much as Seren always was."

Eamer sent her niece a look, and Aisling went silent.

"That seems natural to me." Elanor sat down. "I'm sure if I ever visited the Brightlands, I'd have many questions as well."

As soon as Queen Elanor sat, the servants began bustling around the table, serving the food and filling goblets with water and cider. Carys took a portion of eggs and sausages, eager to fill her empty belly with food that smelled amazing.

She'd been sticking with the apples, cheese, and bread that Duncan brought most days. Cadell didn't want her eating much of anything unless he could smell it, and Cadell wasn't always around. But eating food from the queen's personal table seemed as safe as she could get.

Carys glanced at Aisling. "I feel like I know you a little bit already from knowing your niece, Queen Eamer. Aisling has been a great friend since I came to the castle."

Eamer looked at Aisling. "My niece has a true heart and a generous one. She trusts easily."

Aisling beamed. "Thank you, Aunt."

"I didn't say it was a good thing."

Queen Eamer was less intimidating on close inspection. She had a reserved demeanor and a quiet voice. Her hair was deep brown, the color of stained walnut, and she had blue eyes the same color as Aisling's set in an angular face.

Her features were dramatic at a distance but almost awkward on close inspection. She looked tired, tension evident in the fine lines around her eyes and mouth. Carys wondered if she was the type of person who didn't sleep well in a foreign bed.

"I understand there are a lot of meetings and things like that on a visit like this." Carys took a bite of sausage and nearly rolled her eyes in happiness.

"Indeed there are." Eamer glanced at Elanor. "The men always think they don't need our input, but if we left them to their own devices, I imagine not a single child in Briton would know how to read."

"Not a village child anyway." Aisling looked at Carys. "It was Queen Elanor's mother who pushed for public schooling funded by the local lords across Briton. She was well-traveled and worried that Anglian children were falling behind foreign populations."

"They were," Eamer said bluntly.

"So there are public schools now?"

"For boys and girls up to age fifteen," Elanor said. "After that, most of them choose to work, but there are some universities for higher learning and of course there are mage schools."

"The mage schools are very exclusive," Eamer said. "It's rare for them to take children not from high-born families."

"My aunts were both educated in the fae court." Aisling lifted her chin proudly. "As was my mother."

"The art and music of the fae surpasses anything that humans can produce," Elanor said graciously. "A very fortunate education."

Eamer asked Carys, "And where were you educated?"

"Uh..." She set down her water goblet. "I went to a... village school in Baywood, where I grew up, and my father was a teacher there. It was small, but the teachers were great. And I went to a university not far from where I grew up."

"A university." Aisling's eyes glittered. "No wonder you became a professor."

"Oh well." She glanced around the table. "I'm not a full professor yet. I teach though. And hopefully with enough experience and some more published work—"

"What do you teach?" Eamer asked.

Carys cleared her throat. "My specialty is world mythology and fantasy literature."

Elanor and Eamer both stared at her.

"The last class I taught was Introduction to World Mythology." Carys smoothed the napkin on her lap. "And I also teach a class on fairy tales and their influence on modern culture."

Aisling couldn't hide her smile. "You teach about us, you mean?"

"Uh... no." She smiled. "You're real people."

"But we're fairy tales to you." Elanor exchanged an amused look with Aisling. "Tell me, Carys Morgan, could you teach a class on the Shadowlands?"

"I don't think I'd dare." She took another bite and carefully swallowed before she spoke again. "It's one thing to read about something." She looked around the table. "To study historical trends and the movement of mythologies across cultures. How geography and politics influence the stories people in my world tell. But" —she smiled a little— "to be confronted with the reality is something entirely different. In my world, we tell stories about the kelpie or the rusalka or la llorona to scare children away from bodies of water that could be dangerous. Here, those creatures are real."

"Maybe they've always been real," Eamer said, "and humans in your world forgot about them."

"Maybe." Carys nodded. "Like I said, I couldn't teach a class on the Shadowlands. There's too much I don't know."

Elanor smiled. "A wise woman knows what she knows and what she does not."

"Indeed," Eamer said. "My Queen Mother would agree with you."

"May the gods bless her peaceful reign," Elanor said. "Carys, would you like more sausage?"

"Thanks."

Despite the awkward turn of the conversation, the air in the room was as warm as the light streaming through the windows, and Carys felt welcome.

That was until a cooler wind blew in with Regan's arrival.

"Regan." Elanor smiled politely, though there was tension around her mouth. "I'm glad you found your way to breakfast this morning."

"And miss the Alban queen's generous hospitality? Never." Regan sat next to Carys. "How could I miss spending a morning with the mysterious sister?" She cast her eyes toward Carys. "Carys Morgan."

Her name sounded sinister on Regan's tongue.

Carys smiled despite the shiver on the back of her neck. "Aisling, how is the progress on your grimoire going?"

"Good."

"Slow," Regan said. "She still has much to learn."

Two spots of red burned on Aisling's cheeks.

Elanor broke in. "And yet Aisling is such great benefit to our court. You'll be happy to know that she has gained a reputation for her healing knowledge. Even the unicorns consult with her on herbs and potions."

"Thank you, Queen Elanor." Aisling kept her voice low.

"High praise," Eamer said. "The unicorns are famed for their healing knowledge. I'm sure they've shared much with Aisling as well." She glanced at Regan. "Mother will be pleased."

Elanor's eyes cut from Aisling to Regan. "Perhaps you'll find more time to spend with your niece so that she may take on the full responsibilities of a mage. The king and I would both be in your debt, and it would allow her to take on a novice of her own."

"I'll consider it." Regan lounged in her chair. "My travels in Anglia consume me."

"What do you do?" Carys asked.

Regan turned to her. "What do *I* do?"

"Yes, what do you do in Anglia? Are you a healer like Aisling?"

Regan curled her lip, but Carys pressed on.

"Do you consult in political matters like your sister Eamer?" Carys kept her eyes wide. "You're the daughter of the queen of Éire, right?"

The corner of Regan's mouth lifted. "I am."

"So you must be busy." Carys lifted a goblet of water and sipped it. "Probably finishing Aisling's studies would free up some time. Less time traveling to places like Alba if there's already a mage in your mother's family living here."

"Aisling won't be here forever." Regan smirked. "Our mother will only allow her to be lovesick for so long."

"Regan." Eamer's voice cut through Aisling's quiet gasp.

Carys could see Aisling trembling in her seat, and Elanor must have noticed the woman's discomfort too.

"Aisling, I'm so forgetful," Elanor said. "I was going to give Carys a book that Seren gave me for my birthday a few years ago. It's in English, and I thought she would enjoy it. Would you be a dear and fetch it from the library for me?"

"Of course, Queen Elanor." Aisling immediately left the room, leaving Carys alone with Elanor, Eamer, and Regan.

Eamer said something to Regan in a language Carys didn't understand, and Regan slowly stood at the table, stretched her arms over her head, and grabbed a folded pastry and an apple from the table.

"This is boring. I'll find Aisling and work on her grimoire today." She glanced at Carys. "Enjoy your breakfast, Seren's kin. We will speak another time."

Aisling's absence and Regan's departure left the rest of the women at loose ends, and Carys could see that Eamer was itching to follow her sister. She decided to provide both women with an exit.

She scooted out her chair. "Elanor, would you mind if I got that book from you later? I forgot that I was going to meet with Cadell this morning."

Elanor nodded. "Of course."

"Carys Morgan." Eamer's sharp voice cut through the tension in the room. "I have a gift for you as well." She held out a box with a blue ribbon around it. "A memento of your sister from her childhood."

Carys reached out and carefully took the small box. "I will treasure it."

The queen offered only a stiff nod in acknowledgment before Carys left the room.

Carys sped to her room and opened the box from Eamer immediately. Inside she found a pocket mirror with a simple gold casing small enough to fit into a lady's purse. It was shaped like a compact, and on the front of the mirror was an engraved dragon with red enamel inlay. It was in perfect shape with hardly a scratch on it.

Clearly, looking at herself in the mirror hadn't been a high priority for her sister.

Carys flipped it to the back to see an engraved message in English.

> To Seren
> With joy in the eleventh year of your life.
> Eamer

It was a gift given almost as soon as Seren had returned to Cymru for her dragon training, a gold mirror for a rowdy warrior girl. Eamer must have given the gift with good intentions, the new wife of a beloved father, trying to curry favor with a daughter already half-grown.

And Seren had packed the fine gift away, a nêrys ddraig having little use for a present to enhance her appearance.

"You didn't understand each other." With the gift of distance, Carys could see how the two women—so very different—might have rubbed each other the wrong way.

Eamer struck Carys as a traditional woman who valued her role as queen and consort. She was involved in education and formalities while Seren had been a wild child who became a formidable adult, a warrior in her heart, raised in a wild place where she ran amok through the hills and forests of Alba.

"Not an easy relationship," Carys murmured. She opened the mirror to look into the glass and saw the edge of something white sticking out along the side. A thread from Eamer's purse?

Carys picked at it and quickly realized that it wasn't a thread at all but the edge of a paper sticking out from the backing of the mirror. Taking her fingernail, she pried up the polished metal to see a small compartment behind the mirror. A secret compartment containing a folded piece of paper. She set the mirror down and opened the paper.

> Meet me in the portrait gallery after dinner tonight.
> Please come alone.

Carys quickly stuffed the note into her pocket and put the mirror on the desk by the window.

What did Eamer want to tell her? And why did she want Carys to come alone?

THE BANQUET that night was the third one of Dafydd and Eamer's visit, though unlike the glittery finery of the first, this one was a more casual and music-filled feast held for the merchants, traders, and landowners in the area as well as some of the local lords.

Carys sat at the same table she had for the first banquet, but this time the atmosphere was much more relaxed. The music was lively, and she danced with Duncan again, then with Dafydd. Lachlan sat at the head table, but they were both avoiding each other's eyes.

"What's going on with you and my brother?" Duncan asked her the second time they danced.

The dancers around them were all speaking Gaelic. They were

taking a chance by speaking in English, so Carys kept her voice low. "He wants me to go back to Scotland."

"Oh aye, he would." The dance took them away from each other, but when Duncan reached her again, he continued. "He doesn't like conflict. He wants everyone to be happy. It's not a bad thing."

"It is when Seren's murderer is still roaming around the castle," Carys muttered. The more she'd thought about it, the angrier she got at her conversation with Lachlan.

What kind of husband didn't want to avenge his wife? What kind of lover was content to let his wife die without any questions?

"Cadell said you were at the cottage all day." Duncan ducked his head and spoke closely. "Any progress? She doesn't mention the forge, does she?"

"Progress, yes. The other thing, no. Still a lot of missing pieces." They ducked under a pair of arms, then circled around back to each other. "Cadell put them in order, and I've skimmed through them. I'm pretty sure the last journal is missing."

"Missing?" Duncan put his hand on her waist and spun her around before bringing her back to his chest. "As in gone?"

"Unless you think she suddenly stopped daily journal entries six months before her death, yes."

"Fuck."

"I had the same thought."

Duncan glanced at Aisling as they danced down the row. She was sitting at the head table. "Do you think Aisling missed one?"

"I can ask, but if they were all in one box, how likely is it that the journal Seren was keeping up to the day she died was *accidentally* misplaced?"

"You think her killer took it."

Carys was nearly out of breath. "Maybe they thought something in there would give their identity away."

"But to know that, you'd have to know what was in the journals. So the question is" —Duncan kept his voice low— "how many in the castle speak Cymric? Not many, I'd guess."

"Might not matter. The killer might have taken it on the off chance it contained something of value, whether they could read it or not."

Duncan frowned. "Good point."

Carys and Duncan danced down the front of the hall, passing the head table as they went. Lachlan glanced at her quickly, then looked away. Aisling was next to him, her face solemn. She stared straight ahead, her cheeks still a little red.

If she was anything like Carys, she was reliving her morning embarrassment. Over. And over. And over in her head. It was the curse of the socially anxious. Carys wanted to go talk to her, but she also didn't want to embarrass her further. She saw Lachlan lean over to Aisling, and the woman's expression brightened immediately.

Aisling won't be here forever. Our mother will only allow her to be lovesick for so long.

Carys looked at Aisling. Then at Lachlan. Then quickly away before they noticed her stare.

Oh, she was blind.

She was an idiot.

Was it Lachlan? It had to be Lachlan, didn't it? Regan must have been referring to him when she made the "lovesick" comment.

That was... complicated. And it added a whole new angle to Aisling's relationship with Seren. Maybe she was wrong. Maybe she was misreading the situation entirely. She looked at Aisling again. Lovesick for Lachlan? Or simply comforted by the goodwill of a lifelong friend.

Duncan had caught the direction of her gaze. "What's wrong with Aisling?"

The dance circled them around again, and the music got louder.

Too much to explain on the dance floor. "Regan said something to embarrass her at breakfast this morning."

"Oh aye, she would," Duncan growled. "That's a viper in the garden."

"Regan?"

He gave her a quick nod. "She should go to the top of your list. Seren never trusted her."

"Cadell said she was out of the country, remember?"

Duncan sighed. "Dammit. It'd be easier if she'd been the one. You wouldn't even have to convince anyone. Just say 'Regan killed Seren' and people'd believe ya. No one trusts her."

Carys made a mental note. "Why?"

Duncan leaned down and spoke into Carys's ear, the heat of his breath brushing across her neck. "Seren always said Regan smelled of the fae. She suspected Regan had a fae lover like her mother keeps."

"And that's a bad thing?"

Duncan kept his head close. "When someone is willing to align themselves with fae power, where do their loyalties lie? With the humans of this world? Or the ones who hold power?"

"Does this have something to do with your... extracurricular activities?"

Duncan pulled back, and the corner of his mouth turned up. "I'm going to remember that one. Extracurricular activities." He chuckled a little and led her through the alley of dancers, focusing on dancing for the last strains of the song.

For a few stolen moments, Carys joined him, reveling in the magic of the flaming hearth, the castle walls, and the stomping of the dancers in finery stolen from a fantasy novel.

Where are you, Carys Morgan?

She was in the middle of a fairy tale with all the intrigue, beauty, and humanity of her favorite stories. There were unicorns in the forest and fae in the shadows. There were kings and knights, and more wondrous than anything, there were *dragons*.

Carys threw her head back and laughed, catching Cadell's stern expression from the side of the room.

What would her mother say if she saw her here? Would the magic of the moment thrill her? Would the mystery intrigue her?

Don't follow the lights, my Carys. They want to lead you away from me.

The memory of her mother's warning popped into her memory the moment the music stopped.

Duncan cast a glance at the head table and took Carys's arm. "Lachlan looks like he wants to murder me."

"Don't joke about that."

Duncan lifted one dark eyebrow. "Oh? You think he could?"

Carys's breath caught at the danger in his voice. "No. I... I don't know. Let's try not to find out, shall we?" She looked around the room and noticed that Eamer was missing from the head table.

Meet me in the portrait gallery after dinner.

Oh shit. Not after the banquet, after dinner. Which meant she was late.

"Duncan, I need to go."

"Where?"

She looked for Cadell, who gave her a nod. "Cadell knows where I'm going, but I need to go alone. I'm meeting someone."

"Carys, who?" Duncan's fingers were firm on her arm. "Please don't—"

"It'll be fine, and I'll fill you in later." She looked up at Duncan. "I promise. Cadell will be listening for me."

Duncan looked like he wanted to say something, but he pressed his lips together and gave her a quick nod before he glanced over his shoulder. "Lachlan is watching."

"Fine." She heard her own voice. It was clipped and angry. "He can watch all he wants."

<h1 style="text-align:center">CHAPTER TWENTY-SEVEN</h1>

Carys drifted along the edge of the hall for a few long minutes, her eyes darting between Cadell, then to Lachlan, then to Duncan, then to the head table again, where Eamer was still missing.

She slipped out the door as a new song started and people were moving into position and grabbing partners for the dance. Ducking into the hallway outside, she maneuvered around a clutch of guards and through the curtains that separated the corridor from the portrait gallery.

She saw Eamer standing at the end of the hall, near the wedding portrait of Seren and Lachlan. She was staring at the portrait as Carys approached, her deep-set eyes trained on the image of her dead step-daughter.

Nêrys, I will remain in the corridor. If you need me, all you have to do is call.

With Cadell's voice in her mind, she approached Queen Eamer.

Eamer must have heard her, but she continued to stare at Seren's portrait.

The queen was wearing a velvet dress in a color that reminded

Carys of dense moss in a shadowy forest. The velvet curved down her back and trailed along the floor, mirroring her waterfall of dark hair. The deep brown was threaded with silver at her temples, and bright red rubies glittered at her ears.

"We were very different; she never called me her mother." Eamer turned to her. "I understood. Elanor was more a mother to her than I was. By the time we met, she was already ten years old. Within a year she was in training with Cadell."

Carys approached carefully. "And you had never trained as a warrior."

Eamer lifted her chin. "I am the second daughter of Queen Orla of Éire. I was trained in politics, languages, and foreign relations. From the time of my birth, I knew I would marry for political alliance." The corner of her mouth turned up. "So no. I never trained as a warrior. Fae guards protected me as a child, and fae-trained guardians followed me to my husband's court."

"And that's allowed? To have guards loyal to you above King Dafydd in his court?"

She cocked her head. "The Queens' Pact demands it. For political marriages and for children. Seren had a Cymric guard here in Robb's court as well."

"Good to know." Carys walked over to the bench where she'd sat with Dafydd the first time. "Why did you want to speak with me?"

Eamer joined her, sitting stiffly across from her. Carys didn't think she'd ever seen anyone with as straight a posture as Eamer's.

"You really are her twin." Eamer's eyes glittered in fascination. "I know I am Shadowkin. That I came into being by magic, the dark mirror of a human in your world. I know that somewhere in the Brightlands, my own twin exists, living a life with probably far more freedom than mine." She looked into the fire. "But I don't want to meet her. I don't want to know her. I have no need for her kinship or her regard."

"Did Seren?"

Eamer angled her head. "I never asked her. I would guess not.

There are those in this place who dream of the sun, but I was never one of them. I would guess Seren wasn't either. Who would choose sunlight over magic?"

Carys smiled a little. "So you have magic?"

"All Shadowkin are capable of magic, though some spend more time cultivating it than others. Earth magic belongs to all of us if we know where to look for it."

"That wasn't an answer."

Eamer lifted one eyebrow. "I don't owe you an answer."

Carys didn't know what to make of this queen. At first she'd read Eamer's severity as hostility, but she was starting to think that wasn't quite right. "Did you like Seren?"

Eamer took a long time to answer. She folded her hands on her lap and considered her words.

"Seren was not someone I would ever choose as a friend," Eamer said. "She was reckless and judgmental. Quick to anger and too passionate in my opinion. She was raised by a father who adored her and indulged her, then fostered by a court who also indulged her because she was the only child of a close ally."

Carys smiled. "You're really good at not answering questions."

"It didn't matter that I didn't like Seren. She was Dafydd's daughter, the future queen of Cymru. My like or dislike did nothing for her. I tried to teach her temperance, which she rejected." Eamer released her hands, which gripped each other on her lap, and ran her fingers over a seam of her dress. "Whether I liked her or not had nothing to do with my regard for her. I am not a violent woman, but I would have killed to protect her." Eamer's eyes met Carys's. "Am I telling the truth?"

Yes. Cadell's voice came in her mind.

"Yes." Carys agreed with him. "So why did you tell Dafydd to leave her death as an accident?"

"Because she was already dead, and finding who killed her would not bring her back to life. Destabilizing the peace of Briton is not worth vengeance for one life, even the life of a beloved daughter."

Carys was starting to understand. "But you know she was murdered."

"I have no doubt of it, and I never did," Eamer said. "That woman was healthy as an ox and suffering from a chest infection. There was no reason she shouldn't have recovered."

"But her death wasn't worth disturbing the peace?"

Eamer narrowed her eyes. "Have you ever seen war? Do you know what happens when society breaks?"

"No." Carys's voice was soft. "Not really."

"This place is not your world. Peace is not natural to the Shadowlands. We are magic and myth and every dark impulse that exists inside you. We must claw civility from the mud with power and domination. Because when peace breaks, good people become animals to survive."

Carys stayed silent. Eamer had clearly seen more than Carys ever had.

"When peace breaks," she continued, "who pays the price? Women. Children. The weak. But women and children most of all. No one wins a war. They are victors but never winners."

Carys was humbled by Eamer's clear passion for the vulnerable. "Is that why Seren was killed? Because she threatened the peace?"

Eamer sat back, and her eyes softened just a little bit. "Our island was at war for centuries. Millennia, maybe. The peace the queens brokered in this place has lasted for over a hundred years because good rulers and wise counselors put that peace over our own personal passions. Seren didn't understand that. Neither did Lachlan. They should *never* have married."

"But Dafydd said that Lachlan was going to hand the crown to his brother Rory."

Eamer nodded. "If they'd been successful in convincing Robb, the clan chiefs would have approved his younger brother, and a crisis would have been averted. But I don't know if Robb would have been convinced."

"Why not?"

"Robb was set on Lachlan being king. Determined to see it happen." Eamer's smile was rueful. "He should have left Lachlan in your world. Rory would be a far better ruler even though his father is loath to admit it."

"Why?"

"Dafydd raised Rory, and there is no finer man in this realm than Dafydd of Cymru."

"You love him." Carys felt herself soften for the stern woman who clearly loved her father's twin.

"Love?" Eamer lifted her chin. "I didn't marry my husband for anything as trivial as *love*. I married him out of respect."

"You've never answered my question, Queen Eamer. Why did you want to speak to me?"

"Because you're turning over stones that are better left alone." Eamer leaned forward. "I can't stop you, but I can warn you. Friendly faces are foes in the Shadowlands. Brutish honesty is the key to surviving here. Seren had no true friends in this place. Trust *no* one."

"Even Cadell?"

Eamer was quiet for a long time. "Who knows the mind of a dragon? Cadell was gone when Seren was killed. Have you ever asked him why?"

<hr>

CADELL WAS WAITING in Carys's room when she returned. The dragon was standing near the window, gazing out over the lights of the village and the twinkling blue lights of the forest in the distance.

"Cadell?"

"She's right." His face was a mask. "I never should have left her. It is my fault she died."

"Eamer probably doesn't know you went to take care of your children. She wouldn't doubt you if she knew that."

"It doesn't matter. I should have been here for Seren." His eyes were cold. "I didn't even suspect she was in danger."

"Cadell, she was poisoned." Carys spread her arms. "Did you taste all her food? Could you have healed her when she got sick?"

"Perhaps. With a dragon at her side, no one would have dared attack her. And I might have been able to heal her. Dragon scales contain powerful magic." He looked at the floor. "I would have shredded my skin to keep her alive."

The pain in his voice was palpable. Carys ran to the giant man and threw her arms around his powerful shoulders. He stood motionless, but eventually he lifted an arm and wrapped it around her.

"I'm sorry. I'm so sorry," Carys said. "If there was anything I could do to bring her back, I would."

I understand, Nêrys. I would not ask you to do the impossible.

"You were taking care of your children," Carys whispered. "Seren knew that. She knew that, Cadell."

"There are many who could have taken care of the children. Dragons raise all our young communally. We have a different concept of family."

The clinical voice told Carys that Cadell was back to himself. "Good. You should tell me more when you take me to see a baby dragon."

"Absolutely not." He walked to the table and lifted the journal Carys had been keeping. "I think you can cross Eamer off your list. She was never suspicious to me, but it's good to have confirmation."

"Agreed." Carys walked over and put an *X* after the queen's name. "Because even if she didn't approve of Lachlan and Seren's marriage, there is no way she would have killed Dafydd's daughter. It's not Eamer or Lachlan. That still leaves a lot of people who might have benefited from Seren's death."

Cadell read over her shoulder. "Why is Elanor on this list?"

"Because she was here, and she might have hated her daughter-in-law." Carys shrugged. "It was a long shot. I was writing down anyone I could think of."

"Elanor loved Seren like her own child. She raised her, and she has the same commitment to peace that Eamer has. You can cross her off."

Carys narrowed her eyes. "But wouldn't Seren's death *keep* the peace if it kept Lachlan on the Alban throne? If she and Lachlan had moved to Cymru and let Rory take the crown here, it might have caused problems."

Cadell nodded. "Because everyone expected Lachlan to rule." He stared at the journal. "And while Seren's death might keep the peace in Alba, it has shifted the Cymric throne into disarray. Dafydd's heir is gone, and there is no clear successor since Dafydd and Eamer were never given children."

"Oh shit. I didn't think about that." Carys sat down. "So keeping the peace in one country means instability in another one."

"I suspect neither Eamer nor Elanor would choose to keep peace by cultivating instability in a neighbor," Cadell said. "Therefore I do not think either of them would have killed Seren."

There was a loud knock on the door.

"Duncan is here," Cadell said. "And he is brimming with ideas." He walked to the door and opened it. "Whatever you're thinking, it smells of fae."

Duncan strode in. "How do you even..." He shook his head. "It does have to do with the fae, but it might be our only option to find Seren's missing journal."

Cadell came to attention. "Why?"

"Why do we need Seren's last journal?" Carys frowned. "Cadell, obviously the one she was keeping right before she died is going to have the most information about who might have killed her."

"She had no idea anyone was trying to kill her, otherwise she would have told me. You should not go anywhere near the fae."

Duncan stood in front of Cadell. "I can protect her."

"Clearly you can't. You're human and you don't even have magic."

"And you're dragon, which means that I'm her only option because the moment we go on fae ground, she's going to be invisible to you."

"Which is why she must never set foot on fae ground." There was a red glow at Cadell's throat. "You are stupider than I thought you were."

"She wants to find this journal? This fae can help her. She finds lost things."

The red glow got brighter. "Which might soon include you when I drop you in the loch."

"Okay, everyone, take a breath." Carys jumped between the two giant men. "Cadell, I do need to find Seren's journal."

His nostrils flared, but he remained silent.

"I trust Duncan, and so do you," she continued. "And remember, he has extracurricular activities."

The dragon's gaze never wavered from Duncan's face. "That makes no sense to me."

Duncan's expression was as stormy as Cadell's was. "She's talking about the sword, you great lizard."

Cadell's face moved ever so slightly. "Is it ready?"

"Almost, but I'm not going to go waving it about—that's as good as sending up a flare to the fae." He kept his voice low. "I do have... a dagger."

Cadell narrowed his eyes. "That's why the iron was light."

"It's bronze with a steel core, and Angus warded it. I can be *discreet*, but it will still work."

Cadell was silent, considering the idea.

"Added to the dagger," Duncan said, "Darius owes Carys a favor. We can ask him to help. No one is going to attack a human in front of a unicorn, not even a fae."

"I wouldn't count on that."

Carys raised a hand. "You know, I can probably help protect myself. I mean, the fae aren't usually ones to attack from the front. It's more likely to be a battle of *wits* than weapons." She looked between the two men. "Right?"

"The fae eat babies because they like the taste of human flesh." Cadell never stopped staring at Duncan.

Duncan said, "Not all of them do that."

"Keep telling yourself that fiction if it makes you feel better."

"I've made a decision." Carys closed her eyes. "We're going.

Duncan and I will go talk to this fae person, Darius can go with us, and you will stay as close as you can. I'm the niece of the Cymric king, right? They're not just going to kill me."

"I do not approve of this," Cadell said. "But clearly I have been overruled." He stepped out of the window, and in seconds, his skin fell away and he took flight.

CHAPTER TWENTY-EIGHT

"I just feel horrible." Carys could feel Cadell at a distance, but he was keeping out of sight as she and Duncan traveled north on horseback, through the forest and into the highlands. "I know he thinks this is a useless risk, but we're short on time. If this fae can help, it's worth it."

"He's not your father," Duncan said. "You don't have to ask his permission."

Darius had joined them at Duncan's request, walking next to them in unicorn form and guiding them through the mountain passes. He was bigger than Carys remembered, his shoulder far higher than their own mounts.

"I know, but he was feeling so awful about leaving Seren unprotected and then I did this."

"It's obviously important," Duncan said. "Since whoever killed Seren destroyed it or hid it, it must have something incriminating in it."

The idea that the journal had been destroyed had only just occurred to her. "What if it *is* destroyed?"

Duncan gave her a dark look. "That's the reason we're going to see this fae. She can find lost things even if they've been destroyed."

"She must be really powerful."

"She is." Duncan looked at the sky. "I do understand his anger."

Carys's horse tossed her head, tugging on the reins. "Eamer just threw it in Cadell's face that he didn't save Seren's life, and now I'm willingly going to meet a powerful fae." She tried to remember what Duncan had told her about how loose to hold the reins in her hand. "He must be so mad at me."

"What he is, is petty." Duncan glanced at the sky. "He's punishing you. He could have flown us by coracle faster, and then we'd have arrived in minutes instead of hours."

There was a shower of gold, and Darius appeared in human form. "Dragons are extremely petty." He looked at Carys, whose horse had stopped and was refusing to move. "Your horse is growing irritated with your inexperience and nervous as we approach fae land."

"She's growing..." Carys bit her tongue. "Okay, sure. So you want me to ride behind you?"

"No. I am too heavy for this animal to carry me and another."

In one movement, Darius scooped her off her horse's back and set her on the ground. He murmured something to the mare in a language Carys didn't recognize, then took the reins. "You will ride with Duncan."

"No." She looked at Duncan, then back at Darius. "I'll do better."

"Not without practice on flat land." Darius looked amused. "Ride with the human, Carys. He doesn't bite, but this horse will."

Carys walked back to Duncan on his horse. "Apparently my horse didn't like me."

Duncan tried to hide his amusement. "Give me your hand." He held his out and showed Carys how to mount the horse behind him. Then he scooted forward, keeping her hand in his and brought it around to rest on his stomach. "Scoot forward."

Her breath caught as she bumped up against Duncan's back, his firm butt resting right between her open thighs.

Her heart raced. "Okay then."

"Comfortable?"

"Yep."

Fine. It was fine. She was definitely not thinking about Duncan's hard abdomen under her hands or their legs pressed together or the warmth of his back or those very, very firm thighs.

None of that.

He glanced over his shoulder. "Are you cold?"

"Nope." Cold was the last thing she was.

Darius and Duncan guided the horses though the narrow trails that crisscrossed the highlands, climbing higher and higher as the hours passed. Duncan rewrapped his great kilt to cover Carys and protect them both from the mist. She hid her face against his back, drifting off to sleep more than once from the rhythm of the rocking horse and the long trail.

She woke from a dream of fog and whispers when she heard the cry of a hawk nearby. "How much farther?"

Darius answered her. "The Crow Mother lives on a mountain you will see when we ascend this ridge. There will be fog; you cannot see the top."

Crow Mother? Carys's mind whirled with the possibilities. Crows were associated with so many things in mythology, and most of them weren't good. Bad luck, portents of death, general dark deeds. They were also messengers, so she tried to keep an open mind.

"Will Darius go with us?" she asked Duncan.

"I will take you as far as I can," Darius answered. "She alone decides who may climb her mountain."

Carys's arms tightened around Duncan's waist. "So she might not let any of us up there?"

Duncan kept his voice low. "She'll want to speak to you."

She remembered the warning Dafydd had given her. "Because I'm from the Brightlands?"

"Yes." He glanced over his shoulder. "I'll be with you."

The unicorn slowed his horse to walk beside them. "You saved my child, Carys Morgan, so I will protect you as much as I can. But know that my powers are limited in fae strongholds. Just as the fae are less powerful among my people, I am less powerful among theirs."

"Got it." She nodded. "Thank you."

"Don't thank me." Darius looked to the sky. "And definitely don't thank her should you meet."

"I won't."

Carys peered around Duncan's broad shoulders as the hills around them gave way and the sky cleared for just a few moments. Below them was a wooded valley with a river running through it, and beyond the river rose a rocky hill. The summit was covered in fog, and a rumble of thunder sounded in the distance.

"It's beautiful."

"Aye." He put his warm hand over hers. "It is. Maybe someday you can come to Scotland and see the country the way you should have."

Her normal life seemed so distant that it was hard to respond. She swallowed the lump in her throat and nodded. "I'd like that."

Duncan didn't speak for some time.

"Do you still hate me?"

"What?" She looked at the back of his head. "When did I hate you?"

"You know when."

She reached back in her memory to the moment she discovered that Lachlan's dead wife was her mirror image. The moment she realized that her boyfriend's love might have all been an illusion.

"I did hate you a little."

"Am I lucky enough to hear a 'but' in that statement?"

She took a deep breath. "I'm glad I found out." Was she? Yes. She closed her eyes. She hated not knowing things. "I am."

"Are you convincing me or yourself?"

"Do you wish you didn't know about this place?"

Duncan's great shoulders shrugged. "I hardly remember *not* knowing Lachlan. It's not the same."

"I wish I'd known Seren."

"She was a handful." Duncan chuckled. "A firecracker. Bold as brass and unapologetic about it."

"So basically my complete opposite."

Duncan glanced over his shoulder. "I don't know you well, but I don't think I agree. I think you've absorbed some of Seren just by coming here. There's more bold in you than you admit, Carys Morgan."

"Caw!"

Carys looked to her right and saw an iridescent black crow perched on the low-hanging branch of a pine. It peered at their party a moment before it flapped its wings and flew away.

"She knows we're here." Duncan looked up. "Cadell is near."

Carys followed his eyes and saw the magnificent profile of her dragon on the hill above them. He took to the sky, circling the mist-covered hill before he swooped back over the river valley below.

The rumble sounded again, and Carys realized that it wasn't thunder at all but the burgeoning glow of fire in her dragon's belly.

Darius spoke up. "Cadell is giving the Crow Mother a display of his power to let her know that you are his nêrys."

Cadell's brilliant green wings spread as he cut through the clouds, and then he arrowed down toward the valley, his neck stretching out and his mouth opening wide as he blasted a column of fire across the tops of the trees, banishing the fog from the sky and sending a blast of heat up the mountain.

As high as they were, even Carys felt the heat on her cheeks.

For a brief moment, the fog on the mountain in front of them cleared and Carys saw a hint of an old stone castle, its towers jutting out of the rock like craggy fangs. A second later, the fog was back, swirling around the castle and the hill it sat on.

Cadell came to rest on the hill across the valley as Carys looked up, hoping to catch his attention.

"I'm doing what I think is right," she murmured.

I am here, Nêrys.

"Duncan is with me. So is Darius."

You will not be hidden from the unicorn as this fae has not warded against his magic. Be careful and stay close to him for as long as you can.

"I will."

It took a long time to cross the valley and ford the river at the bottom. Carys took her boots and stockings off to keep them dry, but her lower legs were soaked after the effort. Even Duncan's warm back couldn't stop her shivering.

At the base of the hill, Duncan pulled on the reins.

"This is as far as the horses should go. They'll spook once we cross her wards."

"What?" She waited while Duncan dismounted. "Why? Do the fae dislike horses?"

He helped her down and quickly led his mount to the trees as Carys found a fallen log and sat on it to put her stockings and boots back on. It helped with the shivering. A little.

"It's a complex relationship. Horses have their own gods and their own magic. Fae can't influence them the same way they can humans." He nodded at Darius. "It's part of the reason that Darius can see through their wards while dragons cannot."

"Strange."

You smell of Epona's blood.

Epona, the goddess associated with horses. The goddess that the fae didn't like.

Darius dismounted and walked over. "We leave the horses here."

"Agreed." Duncan guided his horse to a stand of pines. "We'll tie them up here and go the rest of the way on foot."

Darius lifted his nose and smelled the air. "I smell no predators nearby, but tie them loosely, human. They do not owe us their lives."

"Done." Duncan walked back to Carys. "Ready to do some hiking?"

She looked up at the pine-covered mountain shrouded in fog and shadows, then down at her newly warm feet. The sun had never seemed farther away, but she knew in her gut that clues to her sister's death lay at the top of that dreadful hill.

"Hiking is the one thing I can do in this crazy place." She nodded. "Ready."

***

THE WAY WAS narrow and rocky, but it curled up the mountain like a slow-moving twist of smoke, drifting back and forth over the face of the hill. Verdant green brush quickly gave way to dense pine and cedar, and the way was strewn with needles. Carys's feet were slipping on the damp forest path, so they had to move slowly.

Duncan took up the lead, his steel-core dagger hidden away in his boot. Carys walked behind him, glad she was an experienced hiker but wishing for her modern boots, which would have been a vast improvement over the stiff leather she was wearing. She had taken a jar of honey from her saddlebags and tucked it into the pocket of her tunic.

Bonnie had been confused when Carys asked for a dressy, embroidered tunic that morning to wear with a pair of practical wool trousers. Carys suspected that arriving in work clothing would be offensive to any fae, much less a powerful one, so she wore her dressier boots, the nicest leggings she could come up with, and she'd braided her thick hair into two plaits that fell over her shoulders. A fur-trimmed cloak both dressed up the outfit and kept her warm.

Darius brought up the rear, still in human form and wearing nothing but his linen wrap and a cloak over his broad shoulders. He said he preferred to climb mountains in human form as his natural form wasn't as nimble on narrow, rocky paths.

Crows and blackbirds visited them regularly, squawking from the trees as they climbed. There was no other birdsong on the mountain, and the quiet pressed against her.

"It feels like the fae gate," she said.

Duncan glanced over his shoulder. "There's a reason for that."

She looked through the trees, halfway expecting to see blue lights dancing in the shadows, but there was nothing to break the darkness, which was almost worse.

Skittering from the brush, a massive rat darted out of the bushes, making Carys jump back and nearly fall into Darius.

"It's fine," the unicorn said. "She has an affection for the creatures."

"Rats?"

Darius nodded. "They're smart and sociable, much like crows."

Okay, he had a point. That didn't mean Carys had to like them.

As they walked, her ears grew familiar with the quiet, and she perceived more and more rustles in the bushes. There was life there, though it was the scurrying, stealthy kind. Something climbed in the trees overhead, jumping from branch to branch. Carys didn't think it sounded like a bird.

She felt something over her shoulder, the sense of a predator watching them, but when she turned, she saw nothing.

"It's not a wolf," Darius murmured. "But you're not wrong."

The fog became thicker, blocking any view of the valley below and any glimpse of Cadell in the distance.

"This is what he meant, isn't it?" She looked at Darius again. "That he wouldn't be able to see me."

Darius looked around the fog, his eyes intent on the grey mist. "We have crossed her wards now. Even my own senses are dulled."

Duncan spoke from the front. "Good thing some of us haven't ever relied on magic to stay alive." He continued trudging up the hillside. He picked up a branch and gripped it, using it as a walking stick.

Darius called out. "Human, what are you doing?"

Duncan turned. "What?"

Carys looked back and saw that Darius's eyes were wide.

"You've taken something from her forest," he whispered. "I cannot protect you from that."

Duncan looked at the stick in his hand. "It's a stick."

"It's hers." Darius shook his head. "An unwise acquisition."

Duncan was still looking at the stick in his hand when Carys heard the rumbling in the distance. It took a moment to register, but then she looked at Duncan and felt her heart speed up. "Something is coming."

He turned to the low crashing sound that echoed through the trees. He peered into the darkness and stepped off the path, bracing his massive body on a pine trunk rooted to the sloped hill. "Carys, run. Back to the horses now. I'll distract it."

She looked at Darius, but the unicorn didn't move.

"What should we do?" She looked at Duncan. "We can't leave him alone with whatever that is."

"We can't protect him," Darius said.

Duncan's eyes were locked on the darkness. "Carys, go back to the horses. Now."

Whatever was coming through the forest was getting closer.

Darius said, "Run past Duncan. Up the hill."

"What?"

"Carys!" Duncan shouted. "Why aren't you gone?"

"She won't let you in a second time," Darius said. "If you want this visit to matter, keep walking and leave Duncan."

"Darius, what are you telling her?" Duncan shifted, lifting the branch like a baseball bat. "Get her out of here."

"Carys, run up the pathway." Darius urged her on. "Run now."

"What?" Duncan turned and glared at the unicorn. "Get her back to safety!"

"Do it." Darius's voice was steady. "Run past Duncan. Leave him here and go up the hill. Whatever is coming does not have a taste for you. Keep climbing."

Her heart was racing, and she looked from Duncan to the unicorn, back to Duncan.

Duncan's nostrils flared. "For God's sake, woman, run!"

Darius put a hand on her back and pushed her past Duncan on the path. "You heard him—run."

Carys's feet moved automatically, racing up the hill, past Duncan, past the monster coming through the trees, toward a vengeful, jealous fae who liked rats and kept monsters to attack anyone who took a stick from her forest.

"Carys!"

She paused, gripping a pine branch, and looked back at Duncan just as the monster broke through the trees. The bear's feral roar shook her bones as it reared on its hind legs, bellowing in anger.

Duncan jumped between the bear and Carys, holding the tree branch like a bat. "Darius, get her out of here."

Carys saw the bear's red, furious eyes. "No!"

Darius pushed her up the hill even though every instinct in Carys fought against leaving Duncan alone to fight the beast.

"It's going to kill him! That bear will—"

"Keep walking."

"Why are you so calm?" She wanted to scream. "That bear will tear Duncan to shreds. He has no gun, no sword. All he has is one—"

"It's not real, Carys."

She slipped and scrambled up the path, turning to snatch one last look at Duncan with her heart in her throat.

He was facing the animal, the branch still held up, as the bear snarled and batted at the branch.

"Come on, ya foul-breathed bastard," Duncan shouted. "Why are you looking at them when it's me who's angered your mistress?"

She yelled at Darius. "It looks pretty fucking real to me!"

"We're almost there." Darius yanked on Carys's arm and dragged her away from the fight. "Don't distract him and he'll be able to face the beast down. He knows the rules here; you don't."

He didn't fucking know the rule about picking up a stick though, did he?

Carys swallowed the lump in her throat and kept running up the path. She felt dread creep up the back of her throat as they reached the top of the hill. Fog still whirled around them, and the rain was pounding on their back. She was soaked to the skin and shivering from fear, adrenaline, and pure, bone-chilling cold.

When the fog cleared a little, she blinked. "What is that?"

While she was expecting a massive castle like the one she'd seen from a distance, the building that met them was anything but grand.

The cottage was thatch-roofed and made of stone, a round

chimney in the center of the building pumping out a stream of smoke that blended into the drifting fog that had grown suddenly still.

Crows flapped and squawked around the cottage, flying from tree to tree and eyeing Carys with interest. One flew over and dropped a shiny silver locket at her feet before he hopped away and watched her with a single shining eye.

"Don't touch it. She wants—" Darius's voice cut off as a shower of gold swept over him and turned him from human back to his natural form. The golden-brown unicorn reared up a little bit, clearly perturbed that the fae magic had taken his voice when she needed it most.

"Don't touch the locket," Carys whispered to herself. "Don't take even a stick." She swallowed hard. "I'll remember."

She put her hand in her pocket and gripped the jar of honey. She hadn't come empty-handed. She was visiting the fae, but she wasn't coming with nothing.

Darius tossed his head and whinnied.

She turned back to the stone cottage when she heard the door creak open. Whatever this building was, it seemed to be inviting her in.

Carys gathered her courage and walked to the door.

CHAPTER TWENTY-NINE

At first the passage from the dim light outside the cabin to the darkness inside was jarring, but within a few seconds, Carys's eyes adjusted to the warm glow of the fire in the center of the room. There was a round stone fireplace with a large open hearth, slate grey and hung with pots, spoons, and clay bowls that dangled from hooks pressed into the mortar between the rocks.

Something that smelled delicious was bubbling from a pot hanging over the fire, and a woman with dark curling hair was bent over, stirring it.

"You're cold." The woman stood and turned, a warm smile resting on her face.

She was middle-aged and matronly, a homely apron covering her woven green dress. She wore a kind of bandanna in her hair that covered her ears and held back the dark curls that fell to the middle of her back. Her hands appeared rough and callused from work.

Hardly the powerful fae that Carys had been expecting, but that was likely the point.

"Can I get you a bowl of stew?" the woman asked. "I prepared it this morning."

"No." She didn't even think of thanking her or taking food from a fae. "You are kind to offer it, but no."

The woman's dark eyes glittered. "You smell of the sun and redwood trees and green and growing things, human."

"You know redwood trees?"

"Most nêrys ddraig smell of smoke and bronze and blood." The woman turned back to the pot on the hearth. "You're not what I expected."

"You're not what I expected either."

"I'll take that as a compliment." The woman swung the arm holding the pot away from the fire and rested on the bench placed in front of the hearth. She motioned to the stool across from her. "Sit if you would like. Your feet are sore."

Did this count as accepting hospitality? It probably didn't matter because Carys felt her feet move to the stool, almost against her will. She was exhausted and afraid.

"Your friend took something of mine."

Carys looked to the door, but she couldn't seem to find it in the shadows of the cottage. "He borrowed a walking stick to help him on the path."

"Hmm." The woman pursed her full, rosy lips. "Perhaps he will explain that to Orick."

Carys felt the same floating sensation in her head that she remembered from the pub in Scotland when she sat across from Dru and reached over to pinch her wrist to keep her mind clear. The sharp pain did the trick, and the floating sensation went away.

The woman caught the motion, and her dark eyebrows went up. "You don't trust me, but you come to ask me for a favor."

Carys sat across from the woman. "What can I call you?"

The fae woman smiled. "You may call me Crow Mother, which is the name I use on this mountain. Or you can call me Branwen, a name beloved by your people."

"Is Branwen your name?"

"Of course it isn't." Branwen leaned forward. "But you knew that already. What can I call you?"

"Nêrys works." Nêrys was a title, not her name. That was a safe option to give the fae.

"But your name is Carys, and you're the Brightkin of Seren."

Carys racked her brain, trying to figure out how to reply. "Seren was my sister."

"She *is*. She's only in the underworld, dear." Branwen kicked out her feet. "It's not that bad a place. No dragons though. I'm sure that's driving you crazy. Driving *her* crazy." The woman waved a hand. "I have difficulty telling the two of you apart, which is interesting."

Was it?

Carys thought about how to proceed. "Have you met my dragon?" Questions seemed to be a safe bet as long as they were polite. It never paid to be rude to the fae. "Seren's dragon?"

"Cadell of Eryri?" A smile curved the corner of her lips. "Son of Ffion the White? Brother of Emyr the Great? I know your dragon, Nêrys. Do *you* know him?"

Carys answered carefully. "I am getting to know him."

"A Brightkin with magic." Branwen leaned forward and sniffed. "You smell of more than just the sun and old giants." She narrowed her eyes. "What a fascinating thing you are."

You have the smell of the sun and the shadow at once. It was what Angus had told her, and Carys found it interesting that this powerful fae also perceived something different about her scent.

"I do love the smell of humans," Branwen continued. "The older ones are too tough for my palate, but the young?" She smiled. "Delicious."

Carys's stomach turned, but she knew the fae was trying to get a reaction from her, trying to stoke her anger. "Your house is very comfortable."

"How do you find your time in the Shadowlands? Is it very different?"

"Yes." Carys looked out a small window, but there was nothing but grey fog visible through the milky glass. "I miss the sun."

"The sun." Branwen's eyes glittered. "I would like to see the sun."

Would you? It surprised Carys that the powerful fae hadn't seen the sun before. Then again, maybe she'd never found a human to take her through a gate.

Carys brought the jar of honey from her pocket and placed it at Branwen's feet. "I brought you a gift. I'm looking for something. You might know where it is."

Branwen picked up the honey and eyed the fine white jar that Duncan had stolen from the kitchen. "Honey is a good gift. I am pleased."

"I'm glad you like it."

Branwen's smile crept around the corners of her mouth. "You seek your sister's murderer. I cannot tell you who it is."

"And I wouldn't ask you to," Carys said. "My sister kept journals. One of them is missing."

Branwen played ignorant. "What a pity. It might have been lost. Or destroyed."

"It's possible that it's gone," Carys said. "But someone told me you are skilled in finding lost things."

Branwen leaned back and hummed in the back of her throat. "My crows find many things as they fly. Babies, rings, broken things." She cocked her head. "If they were to find something that belonged to Seren, I would give it to you."

"Why?"

"Because you are her sister."

"And what would you want from me?"

"A simple exchange. Your service to me for a year and a day." The woman reached over to the stew and stirred it. "A very reasonable trade."

A year and a day could mean anything to the fae. A year in a fairy fort could be a thousand years in the human world. Even if Carys were willing to give up a year of her life, she knew not to take that offer.

"I don't have that time to spare," Carys said. "I'm trying to find my sister's killer."

"Pity." The woman looked over at Carys from the corner of her eye. "Perhaps my crows have already found this thing you seek. It would be a shame to lose it when your sister's killer is close."

"Is he? Or she?"

The woman only smiled. "Your firstborn child then. Give it to me and I will hand over the one who poisoned your sister. You will have no need of a journal if the murderer's head is delivered to you."

Carys's eyes went wide. "What?"

"I won't eat the child," Branwen explained. "If I wanted to eat a human child, I could just go to the gates. I would take good care of it. Like a pet. But I have need of a natural child born in the Brightlands, so I will take that in exchange."

Carys blinked, pushing back the fog that seemed to gather around her. "Does anyone actually agree to a bargain like that?"

Branwen's eyes shone. "Kings and queens have agreed to that bargain, Nêrys Ddraig. My gifts are a powerful lure." She looked Carys up and down. "You're young and healthy. Surely you could have many."

"All the same, I can't offer you a child."

"One eye then." Branwen pursed her lips. "Only one. Your eyes are blue like the sky in the Brightlands. I would like to keep one."

"I am not giving you an eye."

"Hmm." Branwen seemed disappointed. "Honey is a pleasant gift, but what about the bees' queen? Can you bring me the queen of all the bees?"

The queen of *all* the bees? Branwen was asking for the impossible. "I can bring more honey and ripe apples. I can bring you fresh milk. I can bring you a cow so you would have milk every day."

Duncan would help her find a cow. Right?

She thought about offering one of Cadell's dragon scales, but that wasn't something of her own, and who knew what a fae could do with a dragon scale?

"Apples?" Branwen looked interested. "Your lover's Brightkin has apple trees behind his house, does he not?"

Carys tried not to show her surprise at Branwen's knowledge of Duncan. "Yes, my friend has apple trees."

"Then I will take whatever little bird sits in the apple tree behind the Brightkin's house." Branwen smiled innocently. "Surely one little bird is a good exchange for a valuable journal that belonged to your Shadowkin."

Carys remembered an old folk story of a promise made to a trickster, only instead of a bird in the tree, a farmer had lost his daughter, who had climbed into a tree to pick some apples. Who knew what was in Duncan's tree right now? Whatever was in there, Carys was betting that it wasn't a robin.

The fae wouldn't take a cow. Honey wasn't enough. She definitely wasn't giving her a year of service, her firstborn child, or one of her eyes.

Do it. It's the only thing of value you have.

Do it for Seren.

"You want to see the sun." It was the one thing that Carys could offer, the one thing that belonged to her that a powerful fae might want.

Branwen's eyes lit up. "I do want to see the sun."

What could one fae do in the Brightlands? Even a powerful one wouldn't be able to use magic. And Branwen would hardly be the only fae to cross the gates. The soldiers who had taken Lachlan were fae mercenaries, but they'd had to use force, not magic.

It was Carys's single bargaining chip, and she was using it, but she knew she had to be specific.

"I am not looking for just anything that belonged to my sister," Carys said clearly. "I am looking for the journal that Seren was writing at the time she died. Only that journal."

"And if my crows found this journal, what would you give me in return?"

"If you bring me Seren's last journal, I will take you through the fae gate to see the sun."

There was an eager murmur from the shadows of the cottage, but Carys refused to look. She kept her eyes on Branwen, who met her gaze.

"Then we have a bargain." The fae woman smiled. "You're a clever human, Carys. And you *do* look like your mother."

Carys's eyes went wide. "What did you say?"

Smoke from the fire billowed through the cottage, but it wasn't smoke, and it wasn't a cottage after all. She felt her stomach drop as the world dissolved around her. The fog unfurled, wrapping cold fingers around her throat and choking off any shout she might have made. It held her in its cold grip for a few seconds, and then it drifted away with a sharp breeze, leaving Carys at the summit of the hill, a crumbling stone castle on the other side of the clearing and a unicorn waiting near the trees.

A familiar voice whispered in her mind. *I will see you soon.*

SHE SHOOK her legs loose from the chill of the fog and started walking toward Darius, who was still in unicorn form, just as Duncan ran panting to the top of the hill.

Carys's heart leaped. "You're alive!"

"What were you thinking?" He ran and gripped her by the shoulders. "What were you thinking, Carys?" His face was twisted in torment, and a deep claw mark scraped down the side of his face.

"I..." She frowned. "I talked to her. That's what I came here to do. I didn't want—"

"You shouldn't have faced her alone!" He shook her by the shoulders. "What did you promise her?"

Darius eyed them, tossed his head, then turned to walk down the hill, leaving them in his dust.

The fog wrapped around Carys's legs and arms, chilling any piece of exposed skin. "Can we walk back? I'm freezing."

"Not until you tell me what you promised her," Duncan growled.

"Here?" Exhaustion was quickly overtaken by anger. "Right here?" She wrenched herself away from him and turned to survey the broken castle. "Right here in the middle of her hill? Really, Duncan?"

He swallowed hard, released her shoulders, and turned, holding his arm out to the side and motioning toward the path. "My lady."

He said it to antagonize her, but she refused to take the bait.

They walked in silence, passing the clearing where the bear had attacked him.

"Carys, wait."

She turned to look over her shoulder, and Duncan's face was grim.

"Let me go first," he said. "Please. In case something is on the path."

He walked past her, limping a little; the wound on his cheek was red and angry.

Her anger died down when she saw him trying to hide the pain. "Do you have anything for that cut?"

"Aisling will have something back in Sgàin." His voice was clipped, and he didn't elaborate how he'd survived the bear, how he'd managed to fight his way to the top of the hill, or what he might have promised a fae-powered bear named Orick while she'd been meeting with the Crow Mother.

The stick that had caused the attack lay at the base of a pine tree, covered in blood. There were black marks in the soil and blood smeared on the rocks.

"I'm glad you weren't hurt too badly," she said quietly.

"Are you?" he snapped. "Maybe you should have gone back to the horses when I told you then instead of being a stubborn, reckless—"

"I wasn't being reckless." Anger banked at a slow simmer quickly rose to a boil. "I was listening to Darius, who told me I might not get another chance to meet the Crow Mother. It's not my fault you picked up a fucking stick in a fairy murder forest!"

Duncan spun, stepping back up the path until they were face-to-face. "Do you even know what could have happened to you? You could have disappeared for a hundred years. You could be dead. You could have given away your only child to be her snack for tea." His face went pale. "Oh God, please don't tell me you—"

"Do you think I'm that big an idiot?" She shoved his shoulder. "Do you think I don't know even a little bit about how to talk to the fae after all the books I've read and all the stories—"

"A week and a half ago, you thought all that was fiction!" He grabbed her hand. "I never should have brought you here. I should have kicked you out and dealt with the police and told them you were having a mental breakdown if they came calling. God knows I should never have brought you here."

"Oh, fuck you!" She tried to walk past him, but he had her hand in an iron grip. "Let me go."

"No."

She leaned in. "You think I would have given up if you told the police I was a lunatic? Then you don't know me. At all."

Duncan's face twisted. "You really love Lachlan that much?"

"I wanted to know the truth!"

You don't love that one. Not really. She blinked at the memory of Angus's words, but she didn't break her staring match with Duncan.

"So you found the truth." Duncan dropped her hand and spread his arms. "And all of this along with it. Ready to play queen yet? Ready to fall into Lachlan's arms and live your life in this place? Ready to abandon our world like he wants you to?"

"No!"

Duncan lifted his chin. "Oh wait, he doesn't want you to do that, does he?"

Carys could feel the heat pouring off Duncan's body. Steam rose around his neck, and the brilliant green eyes that usually towered over her were directly in line with her own because of the slope of the hill.

They were face-to-angry-face.

"He wants you on the side." Duncan gritted his teeth. "Because he *will* marry again, Carys. You know that, don't you? He'll have to. Robb isn't going to leave that political opportunity in the dirt." Duncan shook his head. "Lachlan will take another bride, and it's not going to be you."

The truth of it hit her like a punch in the gut. "Fuck you. I may not know how I feel about your brother right now, but—"

"So why did you sleep with him?" Duncan yelled. "After everything he's put you through! After all the lies he told you. Lachlan—" He bit back the words.

Carys blinked. "How did you..." She frowned. "Are you *jealous*? You don't even like me."

"Fuck you." He laughed a little. "Fuck *you* for being so damn blind, Carys. Just..." He let out a growl of frustration and lifted his arms, gripping his neck.

Carys could see his knuckles were bruised and bloody. Part of her wanted to hold them because she couldn't imagine the pain, but she was so angry it burned in her chest.

"What?" She scoffed. "You think because Lachlan and Seren loved each other in this world that I owe you—"

"You owe me *nothing*." He drilled his brilliant green gaze into hers. "You owe neither of us a damn thing." He stepped closer, his broad shoulders blocking the cold wind that swept up the mountain path. "But... yes. How could I not wonder?" Duncan lifted his hand and his cold, bruised fingers hovered over her cheek. "All the years seeing them together, seeing how much they *loved* each other. I wanted..."

"You wanted?" Carys's mind went blank. She wanted to feel his fingers on her face. They would be callused and rough, and a deep, yearning part of her wanted to know the scrape of those calluses on her skin.

"Souls are drawn together," he said softly, "in this place." He searched her eyes. "Call it fate or destiny or—"

"You're saying..." She felt a strange tug in her gut. "You're saying that you and me? You think *we* should have been—"

"It doesn't matter what I thought." He shook his head. "It doesn't matter."

But something very deep in Carys's soul told her it did matter. Very much.

"Do you feel it?" His words were slow and halting. He held his hands back, not quite touching her face as he leaned closer. "Here. Now. Even a little?"

His lips hovered an inch from hers, their breath frosting out and mingling with the dense fog that blanketed the forest. They were lost in the woods, strangers in the shadows, and he felt solid and real like nothing else did.

"Yes." She spoke the word, and a moment later Duncan's lips were on hers, his hands still holding back. His mouth was bruised and bloody, but that didn't stop him from commanding the kiss from the moment their lips met.

She put her hands on his warm neck, and his skin was so hot she nearly felt her fingers burn. He flinched at the contact but pressed harder into the kiss, opening his mouth to deepen his taste. When their tongues touched, she tasted his blood.

"No." Carys drew back and closed her eyes. "You're hurt and we can't do this."

Duncan's dark eyebrows drew together. "You owe him *nothing*. He lied to you in so many ways."

She took a step back and put a fist over her chest. "But he's still *here*."

Duncan took another step back, and his smile was bitter. "In all the years Lachlan and Seren were together, I never went looking for you." Duncan swallowed hard. "I thought if it was meant, you would find me." He lifted his hand and looked at it, frowning at the blood and the dirt that caked his knuckles. "But he found you first."

Carys was confused, and part of her was still angry. Angry with Lachlan for the lies, angry with Duncan for... she wasn't quite sure what. Angry with herself for being some kind of prize between two competing brothers.

"I'm not doing this." She stepped back and shook her head. "Yell at me some more if you want, but um..." She swallowed hard. "I did what I had to do to find my sister's journal." She stepped past him and walked down the path, her broad strides eating up the distance to the bottom of the hill. "And I'm not going to apologize."

The moment she crossed the fae wards, Cadell swooped down and plucked her up in the grip of his massive claws.

CHAPTER THIRTY

Riding in the claws of a giant dragon over the highlands of Alba was as absolutely frigid and terrifying as Carys had thought it would be. She was clutched in the open-air cage of Cadell's massive talons, secure from falling but not at all shielded from the wind. She glanced below once, but luckily the clouds covered the landscape.

He won't drop you. He won't drop you.

The dragon gave a giant heave of his wings, and they rose higher in the air.

The cross human has upset you, Cadell said in her mind.

She could barely speak for her teeth chattering. "He thinks that s-since Seren and Lachlan l-loved each other in this world, that he and I should have f-fallen in love in the Brightlands." She wrapped her cloak around her as much as she could, grateful and also horrified at how fast Cadell could fly.

He is not wrong. Fate is not written in stone, but souls draw together on either side of the gates. Many Shadowkin marry the same person as their Brightkin in your world.

"That d-doesn't mean we're… f-fated or anything."

Your fate is your own, Nêrys. And somehow you hold qualities of the sun and the shadow. This is why we can speak. That means your fate is far more fluid than most.

"So I f-fit n-nowhere. G-great."

You are cold.

"I am freezing."

This is why coracles were invented.

"Well, we don't have one r-right now, d-do we?"

A moment later, she saw Cadell's belly begin to glow with fire, and his skin radiated a massive heat that didn't cut the bite of the wind, but it did make the flight tolerable.

They flew over the hills and dipped down in the valleys, making the journey back to Sgàin in minutes rather than hours.

"Duncan said you were being petty, making us take horses to see her."

I do not know this word.

She had to smile. "Yes, you do."

They circled over the castle, but instead of landing in the courtyard like she expected, Cadell banked to the left and swung back, heading to the Tower Ridge where she saw three other dragons waiting. Beside them, standing near the tower, were two figures dressed in long, dark clothes and heavy cloaks.

Carys spotted Dafydd and Eamer from the air.

"He brought my aunt?"

Eamer insisted on coming with him. She has great concern for you.

Cadell swooped down and gently placed Carys on the ground before he circled again, landed, and went to settle next to Mared and the other two dragons.

"Cadell said you went to see a fae queen." Eamer was the first to speak. "Why would you do that? Did you bargain? What did you bargain for?"

"Seren's journal. Duncan said she can find lost things even if they were destroyed."

Eamer's eyes glittered. "Then you have spoken to the Crow Mother."

"Do you know her?" Carys remembered that Eamer had a greater knowledge of the fae realm than either Duncan or Cadell.

"I know *of* her. She takes many faces, and in Alba she keeps to herself." Eamer's eyes were troubled. "I have my suspicion about who she really is, but I don't want to speak that name unless I am sure of it. What did she ask for?"

"A year and a day of service."

Dafydd reached out and gripped her shoulder. "Tell me you didn't."

"Of course not." Carys looked between her uncle and Eamer. "She also asked for one eye and my firstborn child, but I traded one passage to the Brightlands."

The queen frowned. "I didn't know she had lost passage, but... maybe she is not who I thought." Eamer considered for a moment before she nodded. "It was a good bargain, Carys. The best you could have hoped for."

She felt relief at hearing Eamer say it. "Duncan and Darius went with me."

"Darius? The chief of the Blessing of Moray?" Dafydd asked. "How did you get a unicorn to escort you to the fae?"

"I saved his daughter from a kelpie," Carys said, "like on the first day I got here."

"You have seen many dangers in your short time here," Dafydd said. "I truly wish you would come with us to Caernarfon. You would be protected there."

"Robb will not let her leave." Eamer looked at Carys. "He may not be probing you for answers yet, but that is only because Lachlan restrains his curiosity and he fears offending Cadell. Plus he knows the servants are watching and giving reports to Elanor."

Carys blinked. "They are?"

Eamer gave her a withering look. "Always, Carys. *Always.*"

Dafydd looked at his wife. "Robb is convinced he'll find answers about Carys's magic if she stays in Alba, but her mother's Shadowkin *must* be in Caernarfon. Any answers that might be found would be in Cymru, not here."

"That may be, my king, but she wouldn't be able to find Seren's killer if she leaves Alba." Eamer put her hand on Dafydd's arm. "And I am beginning to think we were mistaken in letting that offense pass." She looked at Carys. "I have heard from sources in Anglia. There are rumors swirling about Lachlan's future and about the balance of powers now that the throne of Cymru has no heir."

Carys remembered Duncan's words on the hill.

Robb isn't going to leave that political opportunity in the dirt. Lachlan will take another bride, and it's not going to be you.

Carys shook off the troubling thought. This wasn't about Lachlan and her—it was about Seren and her death. "Have they heard about me yet?"

Eamer nodded. "Yes, and word has spread that you have bonded with Seren's dragon, but many do not believe it."

She looked at Dafydd. "I need to stay."

"Carys, it's too—"

"You deserve answers, Uncle. And Cymru needs answers too."

"Agreed," Eamer said. "I should return to Caernarfon to see to matters in the court, but Dafydd will stay here. I will tell his lords that he stays to visit his daughter's Brightkin. No one will question it."

Dafydd nodded. "And I will take my leave of Robb's castle with Eamer, but Mared and I will stay close. Cadell will be able to call for us if you need our help."

"A good plan, my king." Eamer turned to Dafydd and nodded. "Cymru will have the answers it deserves."

Carys had the urge to hug Eamer before the woman turned away, but she pushed back that instinct and nodded respectfully at the woman in the dark fur cloak. "I won't forget what you've told me."

Eamer opened her mouth, then closed it again. She nodded once before turning back to the castle, and the flame-colored dragon transformed and walked behind her.

THE CROSS HUMAN knocked on Carys's door later that night.

She opened the door, saw him, and closed it immediately.

"Carys, please." He kept his voice soft.

Cadell was resting on the roof overhead. *He is still your ally. If he comes to make peace, you must hear him.*

She hadn't told Cadell about Duncan's kiss on the fairy hill or the tangle of emotions that was wreaking havoc in her heart.

You don't love that one. Not really.

Why were the words of a grumpy goat-man pinging around in her brain on a loop? She knew her feelings for Lachlan were complicated, and they had been ever since she'd discovered who his wife had been.

But to say she didn't love him?

Hell, maybe she didn't love him. Maybe she loved the memory of him. How he'd made her feel and the way that he'd charmed her back to life. The way he'd pursued her and the way he loved her friends and her simple life.

Everything about her life had seemed to delight the man, from her cozy house in the forest to her books and the paintings on her walls.

Was her life a quaint novelty to the prince?

And then there was Duncan.

Grumpy, horrid Duncan who was rude and pushy and angry more than he was charming. Who was constantly forcing her to eat food she didn't like and stuffing her feet into boots that didn't fit. Duncan who'd dragged her into a world that could easily kill her.

Because that's what you wanted.

Carys opened the door to see him patiently waiting, leaning on the wall across the corridor. "Hello."

Duncan pushed himself upright. "Hello." He looked to the left and the right. "Could we have this conversation inside instead of in the corridor?"

She stepped back and opened the door a bit, but Duncan still had to angle his shoulders through the narrow passageway. She closed it behind him and walked to the table where a bowl of forgotten apples was sitting in the center next to her journal.

"You didn't come down for dinner, so I ordered a tray for you." He eyed the apples. "You're still not eating enough."

"I'm not hungry." She noticed his face. "The cut is almost gone."

He touched his jaw with absent fingers. "Aisling is good at what she does."

"I'm glad." She waited for him to sit.

Duncan perched in the wooden chair, looking a little like a bear on a tricycle. "The leaving banquet for Dafydd and Eamer is tomorrow. You'll need to come to that one or it'll be considered rude."

"I know. I will. Bonnie already told me."

He grunted, then cleared his throat. "Carys, about this morning—"

"We don't need to talk about it. We were both angry, and there was probably some magic swirling around up there and she messed with our heads." She swallowed. "Probably."

Duncan frowned. "The fae weren't interfering with my thoughts or my emotions."

Fuck you for being so damn honest, Duncan Murray. I was trying to give both of us an out.

"Right." She sighed. "Okay, so I don't know how—"

"Will you forgive me for being so forward, Miss Morgan?"

Carys blinked. Duncan's tone had lost his usual roughness, and the overt lairdly accent was back in force. She pictured him in the drawing room of his mansion back in Scotland, dressed in luxurious knitwear and freshly showered with the stern countenance of his ancestors watching over his shoulder.

"Forgive you for being so..." She blinked. "Did you suddenly turn into a Jane Austen character or something? Forward? I kissed *you*."

His green eyes turned stormy. "Aye, that you did."

Aaaaand the courtly laird was gone again.

Carys stood and started to pace. "Angus said I didn't love Lachlan, and maybe the old goat-man is right, but that doesn't mean I don't have feelings for him even when I'm severely pissed off at the man—which I am. I'm pissed off at both of you for different reasons, and honestly?" She turned to face him. "I'm tired of it. I'm tired of feeling like an emotional ping-pong ball, and I'm... tired. I'm just tired." She swallowed hard. "And I'm sad that I found out that I had a sister I never knew because I was a really lonely kid. I wish I had known her."

The corner of his mouth turned up. "She was easy to love. And irritating as hell, but she was a cracker."

"Yeah." She blinked back tears. "And someone killed her. Someone she thought was a friend. And this *isn't* a Jane Austen novel, and someone could definitely kill me even though I have a giant dragon literally sitting on me right now." She pointed to the roof where Cadell was resting.

I am not sitting on you.

"You're sitting on my roof, Cadell. It's kind of the same thing."

Duncan smiled and looked at the table. "I never questioned the bastard's taste. That's for damn sure."

"What?"

"Nothing." Duncan stood. "You're right. The important thing is to find out who killed your sister. And the political maneuverings of the royal courts here aren't your problem either. I'm sorry I dragged you into this."

"You tried to convince me to forget him. It's not your fault." A thought froze Carys and glued her feet to the floor.

Duncan had tried to get Carys to forget Lachlan. He'd tried to convince her to go home and move on with her life, undoubtedly knowing that if she'd done that, he never would have spoken to her again in his life.

The woman he thought might be his destiny.

Duncan would have given up any chance with her to keep her from the Shadowlands. To keep her safe.

"Carys, what's wrong?"

She shook herself out of her frozen realization. "Nothing." Her voice was barely over a whisper. "I forgive you. I mean... there's no need to even ask. It's fine. It's just not the time to think about all this and—"

"Exactly." He nodded. "I agree. The priority is finding Seren's killer." He rose and started walking to the door.

"Yeah." She nodded. "That's the most important thing right now. And after we figure out what happened—"

"It's not important." He glanced at the table. "Please make sure to eat something tonight. It's only been a week and a half, and I can see you getting thinner. This place is hard on a body."

"I will." Her voice caught a little bit. "And I think it's important."

Duncan turned at the door, his hand on the bronze latch. "What is?"

"Figuring out how I feel about you. And about Lachlan."

His face went blank. "You don't owe either of us anything."

She frowned. "Aren't you worried about me getting my feelings about you and your brother confused? I mean, right now I wonder if Lachlan fell in love with me or just with the woman who looked like Seren."

Duncan couldn't stop his smile. "Oh, I don't worry about that." He walked slowly to where she was standing by the table and gently lifted a hand to her cheek.

She could feel the heat of his body in the cool room, the subtle humming of his massive energy, vibrating within his stillness.

He didn't touch her skin, but he tucked a piece of her hair behind her ear, his hand hovering at her temple. "You never liked me from the beginning. If you ever give me a chance, Carys Morgan, it'll be because I earned it."

CARYS WALKED to the library the next morning, looking for a book in English that might tell her more about Briton history and the Queens' Pact.

Or a spy novel, but that was probably hoping for too much.

She was trying not to think about how much she missed her mobile phone and what that said about her. She'd thought she had a healthy balance with technology when she was at home—not being one of those people whose face was always stuck to a screen—but she was starting to realize that when you had hours and hours of nothing but your own thoughts swirling around your head, solitude could be tedious.

She opened the double doors to the massive castle library and caught Aisling rummaging around in the stack of crated books.

"Carys!" She looked up with a slightly panicked smile. "How are you? I heard you had an adventure with a bear yesterday." She wiped her face, only to leave a smudge of dirt behind.

"Yes." She looked at the pile of crates, which appeared to be the same ones where Seren's journals had been stored. "Can I help you look for something?" Why was Aisling looking in Seren's books?

"Oh, could you?" Her quick relief dispelled Carys's suspicions. "Ages ago, I loaned Seren a book about fae history and I think she forgot to return it, and now Regan is asking for it and I don't know where it is, and books here aren't like books in the Brightlands." She sniffed and started to rummage around again. "They're still mostly handwritten, so they're very valuable."

"Sure, I'll help you look." She walked over. "Point me to a crate."

"Try this one." She patted a wooden box. "It's mostly books on dragons and flying and such, so it's probably not in there, but she wasn't the most organized person."

"Right." Carys pulled the crate over to a stool and started to sort through the books, none of which were labeled on the spine. "What language?"

"Anglian." Aisling nodded. "So anything not Anglian, just set to the side." She started digging through her crate again. "Regan is moving forward on helping me with my grimoire. Finally."

"Good." Carys glanced at her as she set aside something that was clearly in Welsh. "So after that, you'll leave Alba?"

Aisling nodded. "Yes. It's time. It's past time, of course, but..."

*Aisling won't be here forever. Our mother will only allow her to be lovesick
for so long.*

Regan's words came back with a vengeance along with the
memory of Lachlan and Aisling at the banquet.

"Won't you be sorry to leave?" Carys asked. "You've been here your
whole life."

"Exactly. It will be better..." She shook her head. "It will be better
for me to leave. Seren and I used to talk about it all the time. Once I'm a
mage, there will be positions available to me in other courts."

"That would be amazing," Carys said. "Everyone here raves about
your work. You would be an asset."

"Exactly." Aisling's nod was a little desperate. "We used to talk all
the time about what I could do away from Sgàin. I'd meet new people. I
might even travel to the continent if I could fly by coracle. Seren
promised..." Her smile was bitter. "I always said I wasn't brave enough
for sea travel, but if that was the only option to get away from
Alba, I—"

"Is it Lachlan?" Carys kept her voice quiet.

Aisling's face went pale, and she stared at the crate. "I don't know
what you mean."

"It's terrible to love someone when they don't love you back." Any
doubt that Aisling was in love with Lachlan fled when she saw the
poor woman's expression.

Aisling couldn't look at her. "I promise you nothing ever happened
between us."

"I didn't think—"

"Of course not. He loves you," Aisling's voice was barely a whisper.
"He loved Seren. And I loved them both. I would never..." She looked
up at Carys, blinking rapidly. "I only wanted them to be happy. I
promise."

It was a lie, but Carys couldn't judge her for it. Aisling was probably lying to herself. How could she not have hoped that Lachlan
would someday turn to *her*—to the woman who had loved him

constantly—and suddenly see that *yes*, she was the one? How could she not have wanted Lachlan to return her feelings?

"I know." Carys nodded. "I don't blame you. I understand."

Aisling's delicate features crumpled in pain. "How could you? You have a good man who loves you. I just want to get away from this place, and my aunt" —she let out a sound that was halfway between a laugh and a cry— "my aunt is too busy meddling in the Anglian court to train me. She's finally agreed, and it's only because..." Aisling glanced at Carys. "It's not important. I'm sorry I'm unburdening myself on you."

"It's fine." Why was Regan meddling in Anglian politics if she was the daughter of the Éiren queen? Is that what mages did? Why was Regan now willing to move her niece from the attentions of the prince of Alba?

Would Regan have killed Seren to give her own niece a chance with Lachlan?

Maybe, but she was the only one besides Duncan with an alibi.

Carys nearly missed it with her mind whirling, but she looked down to see a green leather-bound volume with the title *Fae Martial History through the Third Age* when she opened the cover.

"Found it."

Aisling looked up, wiping her eyes and spreading more dust on her face. "Oh, that's it. Thank the gods." She reached for the heavy volume. "Regan would murder me if I lost it." She snatched it from Carys's hands. "Bless you. For everything. And I'm sorry."

"For what?" Carys felt the urge to reach out and take Aisling's hand, but she knew it wouldn't be welcome. "We can't help who we love, can we?"

Aisling nodded, looked at the book, and tried to smile, but it was painful. "No. We can't."

CHAPTER THIRTY-ONE

The banquet that night was a festival of light and music. There were a thousand blue-lit torches hanging in the air, suspended by fae magic, a gift from the same fae lords of the Borderlands who had been at Dafydd and Eamer's welcome banquet. They were there again, eyeing her with even more interest as she sat between Duncan and Cadell.

Cadell had changed his leather armor into a set that was black and threaded through with silver. His shoulders were tense, and his eyes continually swept the banquet hall, moving from the fae attendees to the wolves and back again.

"Something is in the air," he murmured. "Human, do you feel it?"

Duncan leaned forward. "Are you talking to me?"

They were the only guests left at their section of the table as the rest of the revelers had taken to the dance floor.

"Of course I'm talking to you."

"Not really 'of course.' Carys is human too."

"Not according to the rumbling of the fae at the king's table." Cadell's eyes never left the golden-clad group. "They're speaking among themselves, and they heard about her bargain with the Crow Mother."

Carys kept her voice low and tried to conceal her staring with her wine goblet. "What does that mean? They don't think I'm human? Of course I'm human."

"They don't think you're Brightkin."

"Of course I'm Brightkin. Seren was my Shadowkin, and they all knew her, right?"

"There is something about that bargain..." Cadell looked at Carys, then at Duncan. "Dance with her. I want to observe them."

Duncan cleared his throat and squirmed like an eleven-year-old boy. "Cadell, I don't think Carys—"

"I'm tired." Just the thought of being in Duncan's arms was... complicated. "And my feet hurt from the other day—"

"Exactly, her feet." Duncan gestured toward the floor. "I don't know how she didn't break an ankle climbing that mountain."

Carys frowned. "I'm a very experienced hiker."

"I'm just saying that your ankles are quite..." His cheeks flushed a little. "Delicate." He pushed back from the table. "Excuse me."

Duncan stood and stomped away, his burly shoulders disappearing into the crowd.

"Not him too," Cadell muttered.

She could feel her cheeks warming. "I don't want to talk about it."

"Lachlan was bad enough, but the cross human—"

"Excuse me" —she pushed back from the table too— "I should go find—"

"Lachlan." Cadell lifted his chin.

"I should find Lachlan?"

"No need." Lachlan's low voice was behind her.

Carys turned and looked up. "Oh."

"I already found you." He held out his arm and smiled. "Shall we dance?"

She looked at Cadell, then at the fae clustered at the head table, whispering among themselves and not pretending to hide their stares.

"That's fine." She nodded. "Good. Yes, we should dance."

I see that your feet have magically healed themselves. Astonishing, Nêrys.

Carys shot him a look that said shut up.

"Excellent." Lachlan took her hand. "We haven't had a chance to dance yet."

"No, we haven't."

As soon as they reached the dance floor, the music changed abruptly from the rousing, foot-stomping pipes and fiddles to a drawn-out waltz that wept with aching strings as the fae singer Naida, who sang on the first night, began a new song.

Lachlan swept her into his arms and guided her into the stream of dancers in the center of the floor. "Do you remember?"

It was the one dance he'd taught her back in Baywood, and it was impossible not to be thrown.

"Yes." Her voice was barely audible, and she found herself looking up into Lachlan's vivid green eyes.

"We danced to this in the living room," he said. "That beautiful night that it was snowing and the moon was full."

"Of course I remember."

It had been like magic, a rare early snow falling on the cedars and the redwoods around the house, the meadow that stretched from the picture window to the forest slowly growing white with drifts. Blue light peeked through the clouds, illuminating the clearing around the house and casting shadows in the trees.

"You told me the story of how your parents met." She glanced at Robb and Elanor, who leaned together at the front of the hall, conspiring and smiling like sweethearts. "You might have left a few things out."

"I didn't lie. It was a match arranged by their families."

"But not to join two powerful companies." She stared at the strong line of his throat. "How did you hide so much, Lachlan?"

"I didn't want to." He leaned closer, touching his forehead to hers. "But do you see how impossible it would have been for me to explain all this?" His arm swept out, and he dipped her back.

Carys was struck dumb, staring at the floating blue candles, the sparkling gold confetti drifting in the air, and the ceiling of the great hall, which had somehow turned to delicately falling snow that smelled of cedar and moonlight.

"Lachlan."

He drew her up slowly and leaned forward, whispering into her ear. "Do you still believe in fairy tales, Carys Morgan?"

She was silent because there was nothing to say. She rested her head on Lachlan's shoulder, dancing under the magical snow and whirling under blue lights that danced over her head.

Don't ever follow the lights, my Carys. They want to lead you away from me.

Carys took a deep breath and centered herself, remembering the touch of her mother's fingers on her cheek. The gentle voice in her ear. *Don't follow the lights.*

"Someone told me," she started, "that you would marry again. That you would have to."

Lachlan's steps faltered a little. "Who told you that?"

"Does it matter?" It probably would have been better if he'd loved Aisling all along. She would make the perfect queen. "Alba needs a queen, doesn't it?" She glanced at Elanor, who was watching Lachlan and Carys with soft eyes. "Your mother has a big job."

"It's one you'd perform excellently." He twirled her around, changing rhythm as the music moved from the waltz to something more lively. "Maybe we've both been focused on the wrong thing." His eyes locked with hers. "Who better than a mythology professor to be queen in a fairy-tale world?"

She scoffed. "What are you saying?"

"When was the last time you missed Baywood?"

"This morning."

He didn't respond to that.

"I miss my friends. And I know they miss you," she whispered.

"What am I supposed to tell Laura and Kiersten when I go back without you?"

"I don't know." He turned them in fast circles, wrapping the rhythm of the music around them both. "Maybe you won't have to go back without me."

"Really?" She looked at Robb and Elanor, both of whom were watching the two of them dance. Elanor was beaming and Robb... and he was almost not frowning. "You think they're going to let you go to the Brightlands?"

The music stopped and Lachlan leaned down, his lips inches from hers. "You think they're going to let *you* go? After they already lost your sister?" He put his arm around her waist and guided her through the crowd. "And what of Dafydd? Eamer?"

"They know my life is there. My home is—"

"What about Cadell?"

Cadell? The idea of leaving the dragon—*her* dragon—pierced Carys's chest like an ice pick. What would Cadell do when Carys returned home? "I don't know. I haven't thought about that yet."

"You told me that I was reckless once." Lachlan pressed his cheek to hers and whispered in her ear. "You walk through this world thinking you leave no footsteps, Carys Morgan. But your path here could change everything." He pulled back and stared into her eyes. *"Everything."*

THINGS WERE BEGINNING TO BREAK. There were cracks in the air around her, like ice splintering on the surface of a pond. Carys walked through the woods near the unicorn's territory and felt tendrils of magic whispering through the trees.

It was the first time she'd walked in the trees since her bargain with the Crow Mother, and something felt different. Birdsong was quieter. The rustling and snapping felt less ominous and more familiar. She saw lights in the distance, but for the first time in her life, they didn't scare her. They danced like friends, calling her to play in the shadows.

"You're different now."

Carys looked to the left and saw a familiar figure kneeling at the base of a twisted oak tree. She had long dark hair curling past her shoulders with braids woven through it. Her flawless skin was a warm golden brown, and her eyes were brilliant blue.

The fae wore a string of golden hoops up to the tips of her pointed ears, but her clothes were plain and practical. Work clothes, if Carys had to guess.

"I know you." Carys's feet were off the path, and the ground beneath her boots was soft and springy. "Your name is Naida."

"That is what some call me. And those same call you Carys."

"Yes." Carys stepped closer. "You sang at the banquet with Lachlan. You used your magic to make his voice louder."

She was cautious speaking to the fae, but there was something warm and earthy about Naida that welcomed questions.

Careful. She heard Cadell's warning in her mind.

The fae woman looked up. "I mean her no harm, dragon. This land isn't even warded."

"Wait, can you hear him?"

Naida smiled and sat back on her heels. "I'm not like the others here. And yes, I did sing at the banquet. But you are wrong that I sang with Lachlan. The prince needs no one to sing with him. That's where his magic lies."

Carys blinked. "Wait, really?"

Naida pinched a bright blue flower and added it to a woven basket by her knees. "Lachlan was quite jealous of his brother once, but he has learned to use the magic he was gifted." The fae stood, and Carys realized that despite her presence, she was tiny, even shorter than Carys's height.

"I thought all fae were tall."

Naida's eyes danced with amusement. "And I thought all Brightkin were mundane."

"Trust me, more than one of my professors has said my work was plenty mundane." She looked around the forest. "Wait. Where am I?"

Naida reached to the trunk of the oak and pressed her fingers into the bark. "Near an old fae fort, Nêrys. You don't remember walking here?"

No. Carys didn't remember walking off the path to the blessing, but apparently she had and she hadn't even noticed. Why hadn't Cadell warned her? She glanced up.

"The dragon doesn't see me as a threat." Naida knelt down in another spot. "I told you I'm not like the others."

"What are you doing here?"

"Gathering herbs. And mushrooms." She glanced up and took out a small, curved bone knife. "The knife is for the herbs and the flowers. The herbs that grow over old fae hills are stronger than others."

"Is that why Aisling gathers them around here?"

"I don't know the mageling's habits," Naida said. "But probably." She took the knife to a bunch of wild yarrow, then hooked its tip around a large mushroom that she added to the basket. "What are you doing in the forest?"

"Why did you say that I was different now?"

Naida sat back on her heels. "An answer for an answer?"

Carys nodded.

"You're different because you smell of the Crow Mother," Naida said. "She has marked you." Naida cocked her head. "You smell of someone else too."

"What does that mean?"

Naida raised a single arched eyebrow.

"Right," Carys muttered. "An answer for an answer. I'm in the forest because I'm going to the blessing to talk to Darius. He did me a favor the other day, and I wanted to offer my appreciation."

"And you wanted to escape them."

Carys frowned. "The unicorns?"

"The humans in the castle." Naida smiled a little. "They do not know what you are. Humans don't like that."

"Right." Carys knelt down and snapped off a mushroom growing among the oak tree's roots. She held it out to Naida. "For you."

"A gift." The fae woman smiled. "I am grateful." She put the mushroom in the basket and turned back to Carys. "Other fae will sense the Crow Mother's mark; they will leave you alone. No fae would harm you with Branwen's mark on your skin."

"Wait, is Branwen actually her name?"

"It's a name she uses where I come from."

"You're not from here?"

Naida smiled but said nothing.

Carys tried to put pieces together. Naida was shorter than the fae in the Borderlands, and her speech was different too.

Wait.

The fae woman's hair was dense and curly. She could hear Cadell's voice, and she was small, muscular, and clearly at home in the forest. Her mother's stories came back to her from a hundred different nights. Mysterious creatures hiding in her canvases, fairies who looked much like Naida.

A familiar warmth grew in Carys's chest. She'd missed seeing Naida for who she was because the setting was wrong. But fae traveled too, and if Carys was right, this one was far from home.

Carys smiled slowly. "Ellyllon." The woman before her wasn't a fae of Alba but one of Cymru. "You're far from home."

Naida's eyes lit up. "It pleases me to hear our name in Cymric even if your accent is not very good, Nêrys Ddraig."

Carys sat across from the elf. "Why are you here? Is that rude? My mother—"

Naida's eyes glowed. "Did your mother tell you stories of the ellyllon in the Brightlands?"

Carys's smile was impish. "An answer for an answer."

"You learn quickly, Nêrys." Naida set her bone knife down. "A heart will travel great distances for love." She leaned closer to Carys and breathed in. "But when I smell you, it reminds me why I remain here."

"My smell..." She frowned. "Lachlan?"

Naida's laugh danced through the trees. "Not the human." She wrinkled her nose. "Definitely not a human."

What other fae had she been around? Was the bear a fae trapped in an animal's body? It certainly wouldn't be the first time something like that had happened in a story. Carys racked her brain but came up with nothing.

"Yes." She remembered to answer Naida's question. "My mother loved telling me fairy tales." She leaned back against a tree trunk. "I think she liked fairy tales more than facts."

"Perhaps fairy tales *were* facts to her."

There was a great rumbling roar in the distance like thunder and shrieking rolled into one.

"What was that?" Something about it reminded Carys of the fae bear, and goose bumps rose on her arms.

Naida looked toward the trees. "The water horse is restless today."

Through the trees, Carys could see the silver of the loch glistening in the low light that illuminated the forest. "I saw a woman near the loch once. She was talking with a dark man, and he looked angry."

"He is always angry." Naida stood. "Even Epona's grace will not soothe him."

"Epona?"

"I must go." Naida stood, picked up her basket, and walked toward the oak. "Blessings of the day to you, Nêrys Ddraig."

"But wait, what does Epona…" Carys walked around the oak tree to peer into the forest, but the small fae was gone. "Naida?"

The ellyllon had disappeared into the trees like a shadow melting into night.

"I just don't see it." Duncan had his feet up by the fire, his boots sitting on the hearth while he warmed his wet socks near the flames. "I don't see Aisling capable of murder. Even if she loved Lachlan, I don't see it."

"Loves." Carys stood and walked over to the fire to hold her hands near the flames. "Very much present tense. And as Naida reminded me, a heart will travel great distances for love."

Duncan stared at the fire. "We both know that's true."

It was raining and the shadows of the night pushed at the shutters in Duncan's cottage at the edge of the forest.

"Aisling loves Lachlan. I kind of think she's loved him her whole life."

"God, that's miserable." Duncan's voice was thick with compassion. "Looking back, I can see it, but she's always been such a quiet thing. A sweet heart in that one." Duncan looked at her. "It *can't* be Aisling."

"I agree with you."

"Can you imagine? Growing up in the same court, always being there, loving someone and knowing they were in love with someone else?" Duncan looked away. "It's miserable."

Was it? Was Duncan talking about Aisling or something else?

Carys stepped away from the fireplace. "All that, and she can't leave without causing an international incident. It's awful."

Duncan raised his voice a little. "She's in love with your boyfriend, you know. Still pity her?"

"Boyfriend?" She cleared her throat and walked to the table. "Do we really want to call Lachlan..." She shook her head. "I'm not jealous of Aisling. I feel for her."

"Och," Duncan rumbled. "I hope you didn't use that tone with her. Pity's worse than hatred to a proud heart. And she does have a proud heart."

Carys stared through the cracks in the window, but the rain didn't seem to let up even a little. "Do you think Cadell can fly in all this?"

"God above, he's a dragon, not a wee bird." Duncan stood and walked over to join her at the table. "Stop fussing over the beast."

"If he's cold and uncomfortable, he'll just be crankier when he gets here."

Duncan picked up a red leather journal and started to page

through it. He turned to a page that Carys had already examined. "What's this?"

Angus's translation of the books only worked for Carys. "That's Seren's second-to-final journal, but the sketches are from a survey run she and Cadell did on the islands to the west. She has some notes about how many of them are inhabited. The current populations. That kind of thing."

Duncan frowned. "I don't recognize these."

"Really?" She looked at where he was pointing. "Which ones?"

"The ones she's highlighted in this sketch." He angled the page toward Carys. "Look here. These are the Hebrides." He pointed to the islands west of Alba but north of Éire. "But look down here. The ones she marked in red. There are islands south of the Hebrides that don't exist on maps of Scotland. North of Éire but jumping east toward Alba."

"Are these islands old? Maybe they weren't eroded in this world but they were in ours."

"But why highlight them?" Duncan raised an eyebrow. "What does it say?"

Carys read the tiny notes in the margins of the sketch. "Nothing much. Just notes on people and livestock, I think. Uh... 'Forty houses. Fifteen flocks. Five herds.' She was counting sheep and cattle, I think."

"On islands that don't exist on other maps." He frowned. "Who could create land? And how?"

"The fae?" Carys took the journal. "They have elemental power, right? Maybe links with sea deities?"

"Or a very powerful mage." Duncan lifted an eyebrow. "Humans can have powerful magic here. Don't underestimate them."

"Do you know a mage with that much power?"

Duncan shrugged. "I don't, but I don't know many mages at all."

Carys thought about the one mage she knew. "Regan's a mage."

"Yes, and she has an alibi for when Seren was killed."

"But what if she hired someone?" Carys lifted the red journal.

"You'd do something that extreme if you were trying to keep a big secret hidden."

"Okay." Duncan nodded. "Is she capable? Of course she is. She's a menace. But how could an assassin have gotten close enough to try? Seren would never let down her guard around someone she didn't know."

"I don't know." Carys deflated a little bit. "I'll read through them again. Look for any mention of Regan's name. Or anyone who was new to the castle."

There was a quiet tapping at the door at odds with the fury of the storm outside. Carys turned to Duncan. "Expecting company?"

He narrowed his eyes. "Auld Mags isn't bothered by the weather most times, but maybe there's a leak in the shed."

"You make your brownie live in the shed?"

"She *wants* to live in the shed." Duncan scowled. "She has the run of the place when I'm not here. It's hardly even my house." He walked to the door and cracked it open. A lash of rain swept across the threshold and gusted damp leaves inside.

On the stoop there was a package wrapped in oiled cloth and bound with leather straps. Duncan picked it up.

"What is it?"

He picked a black feather from the leather bindings. "I think your fae bargain came through."

CHAPTER THIRTY-TWO

S he fell asleep in Duncan's bed that night, the black leather journal that had been the last her sister wrote lying next to her pillow. She tossed and turned, her sleep fitful as the storm outside lashed the forest and rain beat on the heavy thatched roof.

In the middle of the night, there was a hand on her shoulder.

"Peace, Carys."

The hand was warm and heavy, smelling of ash and oiled leather.

She stilled, and the low voice that sang to her lulled her into a deeper sleep.

Carys stood on the edge of the forest, watching her mother.

"Don't," she whispered. "Daddy says it's dangerous."

Tegan Morgan turned to look over her shoulder. "Your father isn't like us, cariad." She turned back to the forest where a doe with two small fawns slowly padded from between the trees. "The animals don't know him like they know us."

Carys stood frozen as the doe walked slowly toward her mother, who held a hand out to the creature and murmured something under her breath.

The deer turned toward Tegan, putting her snout into the woman's waiting palm. The animal bent her head and gave her mother a not-so-gentle headbutt.

Carys walked closer as her mother petted the animal. The deer angled its head to spy her before it turned back to Tegan. All the while, the two spotted fawns waited near their mother on wobbly legs.

"See?" Her mother smiled and stroked the deer. "She doesn't fear us."

"Why not?"

"We smell of wild things, my treasure." Her mother whispered something in Welsh that Carys didn't understand.

Her parents only spoke Welsh when they didn't want her to understand something. Carys knew a few words, but not like her mother. Welsh was the language her mother dreamed in. At least that's what Tegan said.

"Come." Her mother held out her hand. "Come say hello."

Carys walked over and saw a flock of finches flitting from branch to branch, moving closer to the deer on the edge of the forest. Within minutes they had landed on branches in the cedar tree above them, darting up and down and flying in circles around Tegan's head.

"Pretty little things," Tegan murmured. "Do you see them, Carys?"

"Yes."

More birds gathered around the edge of the forest, a small army of song-birds and snappy blue jays hopping and fluttering along the border of the trees, flashing their bright feathers as they swarmed Tegan, Carys, and the three deer.

"We should get them some corn," Carys said. "At school, the teacher said deer like corn."

"No, they don't need that." Tegan stroked her hand down the doe's neck. "She needs wild food to feed her babies. Leaves and soft twigs. Mushrooms and ferns."

"And your flowers from the garden?"

Tegan's laugh tinkled in the sunlight. "Yes, and definitely those too."

The doe lowered her head and nudged her fawns closer.

Carys stayed very still. "She's showing you her babies."

"I am honored, mother." Tegan whispered to the deer again. "She will bless you with a safe summer, sister. I know it."

"Who?" Carys wanted to get closer, but she heard her father's cautious voice in her mind, warning her that wild animals were wild, not pets. "Who will bless the deer?"

"The forest," Tegan said. "Mother Nature. The spirits of this place."

"Like ghosts?"

Tegan smiled. "No, not at all like ghosts." She patted the doe's cheeks once more before she stepped back and waved her arms for the deer to go. "Ghosts are of the underworld. The dead world. And we are very much alive, aren't we?"

Carys lifted her arms as her mother swooped down and picked her up, swinging her around in the middle of the meadow while the birds fluttered and chirped around them.

"My daughter." Tegan kissed her cheeks as she set her feet back on the ground. "My gift. My perfect, perfect gift."

CARYS WOKE, and dim light was peeking through the shuttered windows.

"You slept hard." Duncan stood near the fire where he was feeding more wood into the flames. "Were you warm enough?"

There were heavy wool blankets piled on top of her, more blankets than she remembered when she went to sleep.

"Yeah." She sat up. "Sorry I took your bed."

"It's fine. I slept by the fire." He stood and brushed the ash from his hands. "The storm was ugly last night, and we need to take the journal to the forge this morning so Angus can translate it. No use going to the castle just to walk back in all that mud." He pointed to the table. "Apples and cheese. No bread, I'm sorry to say, though I could run into town and grab some if you want."

She rubbed her eyes and yawned. "From a baker who's a software engineer in Scotland or something?"

Duncan smiled, muffling a yawn of his own. "No, she's a midwife for NHS."

"Buns in the oven," Carys said. "One way or another."

Duncan chuckled a little. "I'm going to remember that."

Carys slid out of the bed and walked to the table, carrying the journal with her. "I had a dream about my mother. It was so vivid."

"Hmm." He glanced at the bed. "It took you a while to get to sleep."

"I was tired, but I couldn't make my brain shut off."

"I never sleep well in unfamiliar places," he muttered. "Don't blame you. I think Cadell is sleeping on the roof."

She looked over at Duncan. He was rumpled, his short hair mussed in the front and his beard tangled. He'd taken off his heavy wool sweater to sleep, and the shirt beneath it was open at the neck.

"Keep looking at me that way" —his voice rumbled like soft thunder— "and I'll forget all my strict rules about patience."

She looked away. "Sorry."

"Remind you of him?"

"No." She couldn't say it fast enough. "I wouldn't worry about my ever getting you and your brother confused."

"I could say the same thing about you and Seren."

She looked up. "That's the point, right? Our Shadowkin are our secret selves. Our opposites. The *feral* twins."

Duncan stepped closer. "Are they? Tell me, Carys Morgan, who's the more feral? Lachlan or me?"

She opened her mouth, then closed it. She picked up an apple and the journal. "We should get going to the forge."

<hr>

THE ÚRUISG STARED at the journal that Carys held out, examining the ruined pages. "It was thrown in the loch."

"Possibly," Carys said.

"No, definitely."

"Can you make it readable?"

"Can Epona revive her daughters?"

Carys narrowed her eyes. "Yes?"

Angus shook his head. "That was a rhetorical question, Brightkin. But one you should think about." He snapped the book closed and handed it back to her. "Here."

"You're not going to translate it for me?"

"I did." Angus trod on his graceful goat legs over to Duncan. "The dragon isn't with her."

Carys immediately flipped open the journal, then closed it when she recognized the words. She didn't want to be rude and read in front of them.

Well, she *wanted* to, but she wouldn't. Duncan had warned her that úruisg were easily offended, so she didn't want to chance it.

"Carys is safe with me right now, and being human tires Cadell." Duncan was plucking hammers from the wall and hanging them in different places. "Why do you live to irritate me?"

"Because you put them in the wrong places." Angus snatched a wooden tool from Duncan's hand. "Stop playing with my forming hammers."

"This is *my* forge, Angus."

"Of course it is." The úruisg hung the wooden hammer back on the wall. "And I organize it for you."

Duncan muttered something under his breath.

Carys tried to be polite. "How is the progress on the sword? Is it… swordlike?"

Angus stared at her through his ropy grey hair. "You're an odd human. I'll be finished soon. The blade is done."

"Is it?" Duncan's head swung around like a startled owl. "Let's see then."

Angus scowled. "It's not a sword yet."

"It's a blade. I want to see it."

"So do I." Carys felt oddly territorial over this sword now that she knew where the úruisg and the blacksmith were getting their iron. "It's Cadell's sword too."

"Like the dragon needs another weapon," Angus muttered. He ambled over to a blackened set of shelves piled with stones, random glass and pottery, and stacked leather scraps. He flipped down the back of one shelf and withdrew a wrapped object around a yard in length.

Carys sidled next to Duncan. "Do you know how to fight with a sword?"

"Surprisingly yes." Duncan glanced at her. "But it'll be better when I can train with this blade. Bronze has a different weight than steel, and I'll have to adjust." He reached out and took the wrapped object from Angus. Then he lifted it, holding it balanced on one palm. "We were right to add more weight."

"Take it out of the leather, you idiot. You can't tell anything right now."

Duncan set the blade on the worktable and carefully unwrapped the sword. He took a deep breath and looked at Angus. "This feels... important."

Angus huffed. "It took over three years to gather the iron for this blasted thing. Of course it's important."

Duncan pulled back the cloth to reveal a dull grey blade that Carys hardly thought was very impressive, but by the look on Duncan's face, he was pleased. He held his massive arm out straight from his body, the metal in one hand.

"It's good, Angus. It's perfect."

"The balance is exactly right for your height and weight." The creature loped over to Duncan and looked the weapon up and down. "Give me two days to finish it and wrap the handle and you'll have a blade the fae will hate you for."

"Excellent."

"And why are we trying to antagonize the fae again?" Carys looked from Angus to Duncan.

"Why not?" Angus shrugged.

Duncan lifted the sword and held it up. The grey blade looked more than sharp. It looked lethal, and so did Duncan.

"Because the Shadowlands is a fae realm at the end of the day, and they play with humans like we are puppets." Duncan stretched the sword out straight, feeling the weight of the blade in his hand. "I may not have magic. But I'll have this."

CARYS WANTED nothing more than to hide in Duncan's cottage and read Seren's final journal immediately, but she knew that after a full day being gone, her absence would be noted. So she carefully packed the last journal into her bag and walked back to the castle with Duncan and Cadell.

A messenger came running as soon as they arrived. "Lord Duncan, the king requested your presence in the south hall as soon as you returned to the castle.

"Great." Duncan looked at Carys and Cadell. "I'll see you later." He glanced at the bag over her shoulder. "Be careful."

"I will." She looked to her left. "I have Cadell."

I am here.

Though the dragon didn't speak, he nodded solemnly at Duncan.

Cadell was clearly annoyed that he had to stay in human form, but he was also determined to remain near Carys, especially now that she had Seren's final book hidden in her bag.

"Good." Duncan's gaze lingered on Cadell for a moment before he turned back to Carys. "Send a messenger if you need me."

"I will." Carys started up the stairs, glancing at the massive statue of the twin unicorns in front of the great hall. "Why does Robb summon Duncan when he obviously dislikes him?"

"I think Robb finds the cross human useful." *It is the úruisg.*

She frowned. "What?"

The reason that Robb will never banish Duncan from Sgàin is because of the úruisg. Angus is fond of Lachlan's Brightkin, and úruisg are known to be very loyal. If Robb drove Duncan away, Angus would abandon the Moray family, and Robb believes that would cause them bad luck.

Carys reached the top of the stairs with Cadell and turned left. "Is he right?"

Likely yes. I also suspect that Robb knows that Duncan is secretly forging iron.

"That's not good."

It is immaterial. Robb is power hungry, and he will see iron as an advantage. As long as he can plausibly deny knowing about it should the fae ever find out.

"So he's antagonistic to Duncan in public." She kept her voice low. "But secretly he wants him to be here."

"You're perceptive, Nêrys."

"Oh." She laughed a little. "Trust me, nothing is more political than a university campus. This is practically straightforward compared to budget fights in the humanities department."

"I do not know what that means."

"And you should pray that you never do." She reached her door and opened it, only to find Lachlan waiting inside.

Cadell turned to Carys and gave her a brief nod. "I will go stretch my wings."

"That's..." She tried to say it wasn't necessary, but the stormy look on Lachlan's face told her that some privacy was probably a good idea. "Okay. I'll see you later."

Call for me and I will come immediately.

"Cadell." Lachlan nodded to the dragon before Cadell stepped out onto the ledge outside Carys's window and transformed.

The gust of wind shook the windows, and Carys set her bag down on the middle of the bed. "Hello, Lachlan."

He was pacing and trying not to. He kept walking, then stopping. It made him look like a windup toy running out of energy. "You spent the night at Duncan's."

"Yes. I didn't want to walk through gale-force winds and driving rain. Call me soft."

That made him stop and stare. "You're saying it was only because of the weather?"

"And you're assuming it's not?" She felt exhaustion creeping up on her and her patience was thin. She took a deep breath. "You're jealous of your brother."

"Of course I am." He bit out the words. "I see how he looks at you."

"Do you?" Carys narrowed her eyes. "You're perceptive that way? Because I'm beginning to think you're kind of clueless."

"What does that mean?" His jaw tensed. "I'm clueless?"

"Aisling."

He lifted his chin, rearing back slightly at the name. "Sere— Carys." Lachlan quickly corrected himself, but the slip was impossible to miss.

Carys's jaw dropped. "Oh." She stepped back. *"Ohhhh."*

His face went carefully blank. "I misspoke. You know I'm talking to you."

"Do *you* know you're talking to me?" She let out a sharp breath. "Wow. I was wondering when that was going to happen. I mean, it happened a couple of times back in California, but I didn't really think anything about it because of course you were going to misspeak sometimes. You were married for years. I excused it because..." She let out a long breath. "I didn't know."

"Carys." Lachlan strode over and took her by the shoulders. "I love you. And I loved Seren. You accepted that once without question."

"When I didn't know she was my twin," Carys said. "Do you seriously think that doesn't change anything for me? How could it not?"

"How could you look at Duncan the way you do?" His hands tightened, and he dropped them from her shoulders. "I thought you disliked him. Do you... Don't you see what he's doing? He's always been jealous of me. He's trying to come between us."

"I'm not going to talk to you about Duncan." She felt her cheeks grow warm. "I don't know how I feel about either of you right now. I want to talk about Aisling."

"Aisling..." Lachlan let out an exasperated breath. "It's an infatuation, Carys. It doesn't mean anything. She's had this affection in her heart since we were children."

"Lachlan, she's nearly thirty years old." Carys spoke softly. "This is not an infatuation. The woman is in love with you."

"It doesn't matter. Seren saw it as clearly as you, but she knew that I've never felt that way about Aisling. I couldn't. I loved Seren. Always." He walked toward her, his hands held out. "And now I love you."

"Because she's not here." Carys closed her eyes even as Lachlan took her hands in his.

"Who? Aisling?" He scoffed. "Aisling is nothing to me. A sister more than a woman."

"No, you don't..." She swallowed the lump in her throat and stared at Lachlan's chest where it rose and fell with his breath. "Do you ever wonder what would have happened if I'd met Duncan before I met you?"

Lachlan was silent.

Carys looked up. "Do you?"

"I..." He closed his eyes and shook his head a little. "I don't know why you're asking that. You didn't meet him first, you met me. It makes no—"

"Cadell tells me that souls find each other. That souls are drawn to their lovers on either side of the shadow. That's why so many marriages are the same here and in Scotland. So if you and Seren were meant here, does that mean—"

"Did Duncan tell you this? Did he put this idea in your head?" Lachlan bent down and forced her eyes to his. "He's trying to confuse you."

"Is he?" Her voice was quiet. "Or is he trying to protect me?"

Lachlan stepped back. "So that's all then?" He lifted a hand, clenched it in a fist, then let it drop. "That's all there is for us?"

"I don't know." He was getting her off track. "Talk to me about Aisling and Seren."

"You think Aisling killed my wife?" Lachlan let out a rueful laugh. "Aisling, of all people. Aisling *adored* Seren. They were as close as sisters."

"Sisters fight." She didn't know from personal experience, but she'd seen Laura and her siblings. No one fought more viciously than siblings. "Brothers fight."

"Brothers are going to fight about this," Lachlan muttered. "Forget Aisling. As soon as Regan is finished with her mage training, Aisling will be married to some minor but strategic Anglian lord to shore up her family's trade position. Nothing you or I say will change that. She's Orla's granddaughter; that's her role."

Carys frowned. "What? I thought she was going to be a mage."

"That may be what Aisling *wants*—that's what her mother wanted —but that's not going to happen. Aisling's mother was married off to a boorish Anglian, and her daughter will be too."

"That's not what Aisling said."

Lachlan crossed his arms. "Well, that's what's going to happen."

Carys remembered Aisling's bright eyes when they spoke in the library. *Seren and I used to talk about it all the time. Once I'm a mage, there will be positions available to me in other courts.*

Had Aisling only been wishing? Did she know her fate like Lachlan claimed, or was she clinging to hope that things could be different?

Maybe Aisling had other plans.

Maybe Seren had been part of those plans.

Seren and I used to talk about it all the time.

Like Lachlan, Seren must have known what would happen to Aisling once she was of no more use in Alba. She hadn't tempted the Alban prince, but she could always be married off to another. It didn't matter what Aisling wanted.

I might even travel to the continent if I could fly by coracle. Seren promised...

What if Seren's promises were what got her killed? If Seren—heir to the Cymric throne—had made plans to get Aisling away from Alba and spoil her family's plans for her, that would have been an international incident of massive proportions.

"Where's Aisling?" Carys asked Lachlan. "Where is she right now?"

CHAPTER THIRTY-THREE

The sky was unnaturally dark for midday, awash in deep blue and moody purple. The forest loomed in front of her, beckoning with narrow paths that ran through the trees. She strode down from Tower Ridge, glimpsing the silver loch in the distance and arguing with Cadell as he flew overhead.

Let me put on my human body and come with you.

"She won't talk if you're there." Carys knew it in her gut. "She'll talk to me. I'm Seren's Brightkin, but she won't talk to you."

I do not like this. The sky is ominous.

"The sky is…" She looked up. "There's probably another storm coming and it's dark because there's no fucking sun in this place and I swear if I don't see some actual sunlight soon, this pale skin is going to become translucent." She started to stomp. "If you want to be helpful, just hang back up by the tower and wait for me. You'll be close enough for me to call, right?"

There has not been a moment since I found you that I have not been close enough to call save for your reckless trek to see the fae sorceress.

"You call it reckless, I call it productive." She patted the journal in her pocket. She'd left her bag in her room at the castle, but she wasn't leaving Seren's last journal unguarded. Luckily the tunic she was wearing had deep pockets sewn into the front. "Stay close and let me talk to her."

You truly think that Seren's plans to help Aisling escape marriage might have been the reason she was killed?

"Aisling has hopes and dreams and... talent. Seren saw that." A quick skim of the last journal had made that clear. "There was no way that my sister was going to let her closest friend here get married off if she didn't want it."

Political marriages are the fate of the ruling class. Personal arrangements are usually respected because of it.

"What, like having a mistress on the side?" Carys scoffed. "That's a risk men can take, not women."

Here it is an option for both.

"So you say."

Think for a moment. Women here have no risk of bearing a lover's child. They can take any man or woman they want as a lover, and they do. Aisling has that option.

She'd never thought about that, but no risk of pregnancy in this world was probably the reason she saw female soldiers and so many diplomats even though much of the Shadowlands felt as if it was stuck in the past.

"I'm not saying you're wrong." Carys neared the edge of the forest. "I'm saying Aisling doesn't want to get married." She corrected herself. "Aisling doesn't want to marry anyone but Lachlan, but that's not an option. Seren knew that, and I think they had plans to fly away from here and someone found out."

Who?

"Regan is the most likely." Carys paused at the edge of the forest and looked up.

Regan was in Anglia. As much as I would like to blame her for Seren's death, she couldn't have killed her.

Cadell was gliding overhead, circling her and coming perilously closer with every circle.

"Please," she whispered. "Let me talk to Aisling on my own. She needs a friend right now, not an inquisitor."

Are you saying that I am not sympathetic?

"Your human form is the size of a garden shed, and I've never seen you smile."

I smile.

"Is that what dragons call it when they breathe fire?"

He didn't have a comeback for that.

"I'm going to the meadow by the old fae fort," Carys said firmly. "That's where her assistant said she was gathering herbs. It's not occupied. There are no wards. If I need you, you can be with me in minutes."

She's more powerful than she appears, Nêrys. Be careful.

"Right now I think she's feeling pretty powerless." Carys turned to face the path. "She needs a friend, so just keep your distance."

For now I will comply.

Carys turned and walked into the forest, weaving between trees that reached up to the sky, oaks and ash and beech that whispered in the wind, their bare branches crisscrossing the blue-and-purple sky.

Forests had always been Carys's refuge even when she was a child. She'd run through the redwoods and pines, touching their trunks like other children greeted friends. She delighted in the blossoming of the dogwood, the smell of cedar in the fog, the soft ferns that carpeted the forests around Baywood.

As she turned a corner in the path, the dome of a giant oak rose in front of her, its bare branches layered and twisting across the stormy sky. Its roots were blanketed in verdant moss, and a party of black-and-white-crested songbirds jumped among the raised roots, searching for food.

Carys walked slowly toward the massive oak, drawn to the life she felt from its center.

"Hello." She realized she'd been neglecting these trees because they felt foreign, and it weighed on her mind. "I'm sorry I haven't spoken to you before."

Birdsong chorused around her, and the crackle of wind in the winter branches grew louder.

"My mother would have loved to meet you. She told stories for the trees." Carys walked over to touch the trunk of a regal grey oak. "When she painted in the forest, she would tell stories about elves and fae and dragons and great wild boar. She sang to them."

The bark felt warm beneath her fingers, and its energy touched the surface of her skin. Despite its age—maybe because of it—this forest felt very alive.

"You're beautiful." She looked up at the gnarled, bare branches of the oak. "And you make a home for so many creatures."

Carys could feel joy rustling in the trees around her. The forest was proud of the birds that nested in it, the moles and creatures that dug underneath. The badger's den and the trotting lynx. They all made their home in the ancient trees.

She was welcome.

Carys smiled as she walked around the oak tree, running her fingers along the bumpy bark. On the other side, the trees opened up and she saw a path bordered by red-berried rowan trees twisting through the forest.

Rowan tree and red thread keep the witches from their speed.

It was an old saying her mother had whispered as she planted the mountain ash trees around the border of their house in Baywood.

The rowan will protect you. It's good luck.

"Is this for me?" Carys took a step toward the path. It appeared to go off in the same direction as the more familiar one, but she was hesitant to take an unfamiliar path in the forest when she knew where the other one led.

"I give my gratitude to the forest." She pressed her fingers to the oak trunk. "But I should take the way I know." Carys walked back around the tree, but the old path had disappeared. "Or... not."

A harsh caw sounded from the branch above her, and Carys looked up to see a crow sitting on a low-hanging branch. It angled his head toward her before he flew around the trunk of the oak and swooped down the rowan path.

"Cadell."

Yes, Nêrys.

"I'm taking a new path to the fae fort."

I do not advise this.

"Doesn't matter." She carefully stepped over the oak roots and walked toward the rowan path. "The trees showed me this path, and the other one is gone."

Nêrys, stay where you are. I'm coming.

She was tempted to say yes, but when she looked up, the branches that had crisscrossed happily across the blue sky seemed to draw closer, blocking the light.

"I don't think the trees want you here right now."

The branches eased back.

"Yeah, they don't want a dragon here."

This is dangerous.

His voice was louder in her mind. A part of her suspected Cadell was right and she should make a break for the edge of the forest while she could still see the loch, but the other part of her reached out for the rowan trunk and felt its sap run up to greet her.

"I think it's okay." These trees knew her. Somehow they knew her. "There's something familiar about this forest."

It was planted over a hundred years ago. The oak you were touching was a gift of the Cymric queen.

"Maybe that's the connection." But why would an oak tree planted a hundred years ago by a Cymric queen show her a path in the forest? "Okay, I'm taking the rowan path now."

The old fae planted rowan around their forts to guard against hostile magic.

"Then it looks like it's leading me in the right direction." She didn't tell Cadell about the crow. The dragon would probably set the forest on fire and swoop down to grab her.

Carys walked between the rowan trees, going deeper and deeper into the forest. The crow flew before her, waiting on each branch for her to catch up before he continued flying up the path. After a few minutes, she couldn't see the sky.

THE PATH through the forest grew narrower, and the sky was blocked overhead, but nothing about the forest felt ominous. The ground beneath her boots was springy and soft, the stones layered with moss and dry leaves. Pine needles on the ground swallowed the sound of her footsteps as she approached something that looked like a great green wall.

It rose in the distance, a round hill of deep forest green dotted at regular intervals with craggy grey standing stones jutting from the mound.

"The fae fort." She'd seen the path that led to it and the meadows on the other side, but from this direction she could see how vast it was. So large, in fact, she wondered why it wasn't visible from the top of Tower Ridge.

"Cadell, why couldn't I see this structure from the top of the hill?"

It sits in a fold of the landscape, hidden from Castle Sgàin. It was designed that way, but I can see it.

"Good."

The rowan path led straight to the fort, and the damp air grew chilly as she approached. There was a rill flowing across the path, and she hopped across a pair of stones to stay on track.

Nêrys. Cadell's voice was cloudy but still there.

"Hey." Carys stopped and looked around. "I crossed a stream, and your voice is quieter."

You have crossed over the old wards, but you are not hidden from me. Be careful.

"I will." She walked to the left, following the path that led around the base of the fort. She could hear someone speaking in the distance, and she noticed the birds had grown quiet.

"...not sure what you mean."

"She knows something."

"You're wrong."

"It's obvious you..." The wind snatched the other words away. "...so it's time."

Aisling was in the meadow, but there was someone with her. Carys paused, debating whether she should leave and find Aisling another time, but as she turned, a branch cracked under her foot.

"Hello?" Aisling called out. "Who's there?"

Carys kept walking, and as she rounded the fort, she could see Aisling in the meadow, standing by a wide-leafed dusty-grey plant and holding a bone knife in her hand. Carys looked around, but she didn't see anyone with her.

"Hi." Carys lifted her hand and waved. "It's just me."

"Carys?" As soon as she saw Carys, Aisling's shoulders relaxed, and she put her bone knife in the basket. "What are you doing here?"

Carys wondered if she'd mistaken personal musing for conversation. "I was taking a walk. I... I realized that I hadn't really said hello to the trees properly, and my mother would judge me if she knew."

Aisling smiled. "Well, if you want to help me cut some mullein before the rain starts, I'd love the help." She looked up. "I can tell the clouds are going to let go soon."

"Sure." Carys scanned the meadow as she walked closer, but she couldn't see anyone. "What's mullein?"

"An herb." Aisling knelt down and started digging in the soil around the base of the large plant. "I collect it here because things grow in this meadow even in the winter." She lifted her eyebrows. "Old fae magic I think."

"What do you want me to cut?"

"Here." Aisling reached into her basket and grabbed another knife. "Use this and cut some of the leaves off near the base. The medium-sized ones are good. The big ones are too old."

"Okay." The mullein leaves were soft and bore a feathery texture. "What's it for?"

"The leaves?" Aisling grunted as she dug. "The leaves are good for respiratory illnesses, and there are several sicknesses racing around the castle right now. I also read a letter from a mage in Anglia recently that mullein roots can be used to treat skin rashes, so I was going to experiment."

"You're really good at this stuff, aren't you?" Carys completely understood why Seren didn't want to see a mind like Aisling's locked into a political marriage in a place that wouldn't appreciate her. "In the Brightlands, we have all these different medicines, and here you use magic and herbs to heal people."

"Duncan says that many of the medicines in your world are derived from natural sources anyway." She pushed back a piece of hair that had fallen into her face. "So maybe it's almost the same thing."

"And we don't have magic."

Aisling smiled, but it was an absent kind of smile. "No, you don't."

"Yeah, my doctor in America has never used a spell to clear up a cough, so you have her beat there." Carys sat back on her heels, watching as Aisling dug up another root.

She looked around the clearing and saw the sprawling oak where the fae woman Naida had been gathering mushrooms. The grass in the meadow seemed a little brighter. The sky a little clearer. "The magic here is still strong, isn't it?"

"It is." Aisling looked up. "Can you feel it? Seren avoided this place. Cadell didn't like it when she was here. He can't stand the fae."

"Yeah, he's overprotective." She reached out and felt for the dragon's presence. It was faint, but it was there. "Any progress on your grimoire?"

"I'm close to finishing, and Regan agreed to stay until I'm done." Aisling's face was blank. "I'm ready to move on from here. I've heard that the medicinal knowledge in the Near East is much more advanced than what we have. If I'm able to find a position on the continent, maybe I'll meet mages from—"

"Lachlan said your family is going to marry you to an Anglian lord like your mother." She didn't know why she blurted it out like that.

Fuck. Carys immediately regretted it.

"They're not." Aisling's face was pale. "Eamer says... She says my grandmother..." Aisling sat back and her shoulders were tense. "Why were you talking to Lachlan about me?"

Carys desperately searched for the right words. "I found Seren's last journal."

Aisling's face went pale.

"She knew you wanted to get away from here." Carys spoke quickly. "That you wanted to work in foreign courts, and I thought maybe your family wouldn't have liked that and—"

"How did you find her last journal?" Aisling slowly rose to her feet, the bone knife clutched in her hand.

A crow shrieked from its perch on a craggy standing stone partially tilted to the side. Aisling's eyes darted to the crow and went wide. She looked back at Carys, then at the crow again.

"No," she whispered. "You didn't." Aisling's chest heaved as she stared at the crow. "Tell me you didn't."

"I just found it." Carys stood and stepped back slowly. "Why do you—"

"You shouldn't have been *able* to find it." Aisling gripped the bone knife, and her face drained of color. Her skin was pure white, and her lips stood out like blood-red flowers on snow. Her mouth thinned, and her eyes moved from Carys to the crow and back again. "What have you done?"

"Cadell?" Carys reached out, but the voice that came back was dull and nearly silent.

Nêrys... what...?

"No." Aisling raised her hand and pressed her palm out. Her voice was an icy gust scraping across the silent meadow. "No!"

Carys felt something hit her, like the rush of wind from a passing truck. "What did you do?"

"You will *not* call the dragon." The warm woman's face had turned into a blank mask.

"What did you do?" Dread snaked through Carys's stomach, and a horrified realization dawned in her mind. "She was your best friend."

Aisling bared her teeth. "I threw that journal in the loch, weighed it down with stones! You *never* should have looked for it, you stupid woman!"

Nêrys, where are you?

"Cadell?" Her neck whipped around the clearing, searching for his voice. "Cadell!"

The shadows were darker and deeper. The air was silent, and the space between the trees seemed to shrink until there was no way between them.

She looked back at Aisling. "What's happening? What are you doing?"

"I didn't know what she might have written." Aisling's knuckles were bloodless as she gripped her blade. "It was in Cymric, and I couldn't read it. I couldn't take the chance."

There was a dull roar like beating wings in the distance and a growing thunder as lightning cracked overhead.

"Take what chance?" Silent tears fell from Carys's eyes. "Chance what, Aisling? Please don't say—"

"Oh gods!" Aisling's face flickered between fear, guilt, and pure rage. "What did you do, Carys? What did you—"

"Shut up, you idiot." Regan stormed out from behind a standing stone, crossed the meadow, and struck Aisling across the cheek, sending the young woman to the ground where she lay still.

"You." Carys turned in circles as Regan raised a hand to her. "You were in Anglia when she died."

Regan smiled. "You think I killed her?" She whispered something under her breath.

Carys tried to run, but her feet felt rooted to the ground. The air around her grew foggy and dull, and the roaring in the distance fell silent.

Regan sighed and walked to Carys. "You're more like your sister than I realized, you persistent, annoying bitch." She raised her hand again, and Carys braced for a physical blow, but instead, everything went black.

CHAPTER THIRTY-FOUR

When Carys woke, she was in a stone chamber with no windows and only a few candles lit. There was a fire burning in a corner fireplace, and a dark figure hunched over it.

She wasn't bound, but she was sitting in a chair and her legs felt heavy, as if weights had been tied around her feet. "Where am I?"

The dark figure in the corner moved, but it didn't speak.

There was a scuttling along the wall beside her, a clicking sound somewhere behind, and Carys turned her head to see what was there, but nothing permeated the relentless darkness of the cave. There was a faint blue light coming from somewhere, but nothing in her line of sight was clear. It was as if a filter had been cast over her eyes.

"Where did you bring me?" Her vision wasn't the only thing that was foggy. Her limbs were heavy, and her reflexes were dull. Her own voice sounded like it was coming from a great distance.

"Did you... drug me?"

"No." It was nearly a whisper. "This will help you."

Carys blinked and saw a sturdy wooden table in the middle of the room. On it was a candlestick, an open book, and a basket.

Aisling's basket.

"Aisling?" Carys looked up and saw that the blue lights were wisps caught along the low ceiling of the cave, dancing and flying around the room, blinking in no particular pattern.

Souls. Little souls of the lost. Wild twins lost to the fae, consumed to feed their magic. Carys felt tears come to her eyes.

"If you're going to kill me, just do it." She'd be with her mother. Her father. Maybe with the sister she'd never known.

Would Lachlan and Duncan know what had happened to her, or would she just disappear? Laura and Kiersten would go crazy, but who else would care? She had no family. No job. No students. The college would hire someone to fill her position. They'd forget about her eventually.

The heavy weight of despair made her head slump to the side.

"I told you." The whisper came again. "This will help you."

The shadow moved, and Carys closed her eyes, willing whatever was going to happen to happen softly.

Please. At least give me that.

Let death be soft.

"Carys?"

She opened her eyes, and Aisling was in front of her. Carys's vision cleared a little. Aisling's face was still pale and her lips blood red, but the chaotic emotions she'd displayed earlier were gone, replaced by grim determination.

Carys forced her lips to move. "Where are we?"

"In the fae fort. Regan left to reinforce the wards so Cadell can't find you."

"I'm in the fae fort?"

Aisling walked back to feed the fire more wood, and the light grew brighter.

Carys looked around the room, and pieces of her shattered consciousness slowly put her surroundings and situation together.

She was being held in some kind of workroom or kitchen. There were cauldrons of various sizes hanging on a wall. There were shelves holding dusty glass jars, so dirty that Carys couldn't see what they contained. The fireplace was the only part of the room that seemed well maintained.

"Regan works here sometimes when she wants to hide." Aisling knelt down and stirred something bubbling over the fire. "She won't work magic within the castle walls, and the unicorns don't watch this place. Only a few local fae even visit here, but they don't come inside. They say it's *contaminated* by human magic. Can you believe that?" She glanced over her shoulder. "They teach us, but they hate us too. Even us."

Aisling walked toward the table and snapped her fingers in the air. The old sconces on the wall began to glow with a cool white light. The wisps still swirled overhead, dancing on the earthen ceiling like fireflies. As the room grew brighter, Carys could see more.

The chamber had clearly been abandoned long ago. Mushrooms grew from cracks in the mortar, and moss was slowly overtaking the floor. Despite all that, there was a thick veil of magic that lay heavy in the air, making it hard to think.

"Cadell can't feel me here, can he?"

"Cadell will be able to see the fort from the air" —Aisling's voice was rote as she looked at the large grimoire open on the table— "but if he approaches, it will appear to move. You're hidden from him now. Dragons are visual creatures, and they don't use magic the way we do."

"The way you and your aunt do, you mean." Carys fought for her anger, shaking off the despair that threatened to creep up her throat and choke her.

"The spell Regan cast was only short-term." Aisling turned back to the cauldron that was simmering over the fire. "The wards won't hide you for long, so she went back to strengthen them. She'll have to find a sacrifice, but she's an excellent hunter."

"What kind of sacrifice?"

Aisling's eyes drifted upward to the glowing blue lights hanging above them. "The same kind the fae used to make this fort."

"No." Regan was going to sacrifice more souls to keep her. "Don't let her, Aisling. Let me out before she kills—"

"You think I'm in control of this now?" Aisling shot Carys a look over her shoulder. "I tried to protect you, just like I tried to protect Seren."

"You killed Seren." Carys forced the words out. "Didn't you?"

"Regan trapped me too." Aisling walked back to the table, ignoring Carys's question. "I don't know what you want me to do about it."

Carys's eyes landed on a small black book next to the grimoire.

Seren's journal.

She kept her voice soft. "Why did you kill her, Aisling?"

The woman's face was blank. It was as if the life had drained from her, though she was still moving. "The fever killed her. It wasn't me." Aisling glanced at Carys before her eyes returned to the book. "Seren came to me for a potion, and I gave her one. I was the only one she trusted. She wouldn't even take potions from the unicorns."

"She trusted you." Carys swallowed with difficulty. She felt like there was a mass of stones in her mouth, blocking her tongue from making a sound. "And you killed her."

"It wasn't like that!" Aisling slammed her hand on the table. "You don't understand anything. You've been here a few weeks and you think you know anything? I loved Seren!"

"But you loved Lachlan more?"

Aisling curled her lip. "Lachlan should have been mine. If Seren had stayed away with her dragon, he would have grown to love me. I *needed* him to love me. The whole reason they kept me in this court was so I could be his queen."

"I read her journal." Carys blinked and looked back at the black leather book sitting on the table by the large open volume and the candle. "She loved you too. She wanted to give you a life away from here. She knew—"

"She knew I loved her husband, and she wanted me gone." Aisling's cold facade cracked. Just a little. "At least she didn't pity me like you. Like Duncan. Like *all of them*! I hate it. They think I don't see it? I do."

"She was your best friend."

Aisling's blue eyes turned frosty. "Friendship? What is friendship? If she loved me, she would have left when she saw him falling in love with her. They never should have been together. It was bad for everyone, Carys."

"She was in love."

"She was selfish," Aisling spat out. "She only thought about herself. Not Lachlan. Not the Queens' Pact. Selfish."

Carys blinked back tears. It was obvious that Aisling had rationalized her betrayal. "And you weren't? It wasn't selfish to kill your best friend?"

"I needed to take some action." She walked back to the fireplace and the cauldron. "Regan sent a raven from the Anglian court. She said that with Seren sick, I could do something about my situation. She said I was being... pathetic." Aisling's face went blank again. *"Pathetic."*

"Seren didn't think you were pathetic."

"Lachlan did." Aisling's lip curled. "I heard the pity in his voice."

Duncan had called it. There was nothing worse than pity.

The mental fog was clearing as the light grew brighter. "You poisoned her, didn't you?"

"It wasn't poison! The fever was bad." Aisling frowned. "It *really* was bad. I looked in Regan's old grimoire for something to help and... I found it."

"Found what?"

"It was only a spell. One spell I added to the potion recipe. I wasn't trying to *kill* Seren." Aisling walked over and stared at the waterlogged journal. "I *wasn't* trying to kill her. I wasn't. I just wanted to kill the love between them."

Carys was no magic user, but she could easily see how a spell to kill the love between two people could quickly morph into a lethal curse. "Kill their love?"

Aisling looked up, her eyes distant. "Don't you see? If their love died, Lachlan would see *me*. That was all I needed. For him to not love *her*. Then there would be room in his heart for me."

"Love doesn't work that way."

"It does for Lachlan!" Aisling's laugh was manic. "Don't you think? Seren died, so he went to the Brightlands to find you." She wandered over to the table and flipped through the leather-bound grimoire, a bitter smile marring her beautiful face.

"Lose one Seren; find another," Carys whispered.

"Even the foreigner can see it." Aisling's voice dropped to a low growl. "Easy as anything for a prince with passage through the gate."

Despite the fog that permeated Carys's mind, the words still stung.

"So what happened?" Carys forced out the words. "Did you make the potion wrong? You didn't kill their love; you killed the woman."

"Oh, I made it correctly." She flipped a page and ran her finger down the book, her eyes glittering in anger. "Despite Lachlan's disregard and my family's blindness, I am a brilliant mage. The potion I made was *perfect*." Aisling looked up, and for the first time, there were tears in the corners of her eyes. "It was perfect."

Carys tried to play on Aisling's humanity. "But the potion recipe was Regan's, not yours. And Regan's idea of killing love was different than yours." She twisted her arms against her bindings. "Let me go, Aisling. I don't blame you. It was Regan who killed Seren, not you."

Aisling's expression fell away, and her face went blank again. "That's not... exactly true."

"What do you mean?"

Aisling's eyes were wide, staring at Seren's journal. "I could have made an antidote. When I saw what happened, I could have reversed the curse."

"What?" Carys's heart plummeted. "Then why did you let her die?"

"Everyone would have known." Aisling looked up. "They would have known my potion had made her sicker."

"So all you wanted was to save yourself?" Carys couldn't hide the disgust in her voice.

"I couldn't let him know." Aisling's voice was a soft whisper. "How would Lachlan ever love me if he knew? If I cured Seren, my life would have been over." She shook her head. "I have nowhere to go." She looked at Carys, and it was like a light switched on. "I have nothing if I don't have Lachlan."

Carys knew that Aisling was correct. If she'd been caught poisoning the heir of Cymru and the wife of the Alban prince, her life would have been forfeit.

The queen of Éire would have disavowed her own granddaughter to avoid a war, blaming Aisling for individual malice.

The one ally Aisling had was the person she'd killed.

"You don't have to kill me." Carys was starting to feel desperate. If Aisling could kill her best friend, killing Carys to hide her crime would be nothing. "I'll go back to the Brightlands. No one needs to know. Maybe Cadell..."

Aisling walked over and stood in front of Carys, looking at her with dead eyes. "Your dragon will kill me the moment he discovers what happened, and no power in the Shadowlands will stop him."

Carys was going to die because Aisling was one hundred percent correct.

"Please, Aisling." She shook her head. "Let me go. I'll tell Cadell that it was Regan. He'll believe me. *I* can stop him from hurting you. We can fly you away—"

Aisling put a hand over Carys's mouth. "I'm not going to kill you." Her voice was eerily calm. "That would cause far too many questions. But you need to forget." She lifted her hand away and smiled. "If you forget, then I can think up a story. I can fix all this, but you need to forget."

"What?" Carys blinked. "Forget... what?"

Aisling walked over and lifted the journal. "Forget this. Forget Seren. Forget the Shadowlands. Forget Lachlan and Duncan. If you forget all of it, no one has to know."

"What are you talking about?" Carys leaned forward, her eyes going wide. "I'm not going to forget everything just like that. And even if I did forget everything, how do you think you can get me home?"

"Regan can take you through a fae gate." Aisling's laugh was high and desperate. "She's crossed the gates before. She said so."

"You think I'm going to just wake up in the middle of a Scottish forest and not have any questions?"

Aisling's eyes were bright, nearly feverish, as she danced from the book to the cauldron and back again. "That won't be my problem, Carys. That will be yours."

"Aisling—"

"Regan won't kill you!" Aisling took a sprig of something from her basket. "Don't you see? If you don't remember, she won't have to kill you. It's the only way to keep you alive."

The woman was losing it. None of this made any sense. "What about Cadell?"

"If you're on the other side, the dragon will leave." Aisling threw an herb into the cauldron and furiously stirred. "He'll have to; the horde will call him back if his nêrys is gone."

"What about Lachlan? Are you going to make Lachlan forget me too?"

Aisling's eyes darkened at the mention of Lachlan's name. "Lachlan can chew on stones." She twisted her flushed lips. "I don't care about him anymore."

I don't believe you.

"Okay, what about Duncan? He's the most stubborn man I've ever met in my life. You think he's going to just let all this go? You don't—" She stopped short of telling Aisling about Duncan's dragon-steel sword. "He's dangerous, Aisling."

"I don't doubt it. And I don't doubt that he's in love with you—I see how he looks at you—but I don't care." She let out a slightly manic laugh. "They all just... *love* you. I don't know why. I'm more beautiful than you are. I was more beautiful than Seren too."

"You are!" It was true. Aisling was a stunningly beautiful woman.

"I'm quiet and reserved and... accomplished. I listen to their stories and their stupid, *stupid* jokes." Her cheeks grew flushed. "I did everything I was supposed to, and it didn't matter. He still loved her more."

"Aisling, you're a beautiful, talented, intelligent woman." *Except when you're trying to kill me.* "You deserve a life away from here. You deserve more than what your family has in mind for you. Just let me go. Help me get out, and I *will* help you."

"You're lying." Aisling walked back to the table, looked at the book, and took another herb from the basket. "But I can do this. I can make you forget."

"I don't want to forget." Carys blinked away tears. "I don't want to forget any of this."

Not even the fear.

The fog in Carys's mind was starting to clear. She didn't know if Cadell was breaking through the wards Regan had cast or if someone was working another kind of magic, but she felt the dense blanket of magic around her thinning.

"You and I, Aisling." She struggled, her limbs warming and growing stronger. "We can figure something out. Maybe you can come to the Brightlands with me."

"No." Aisling shook her head and ran to check the cauldron. "I'm running away, so it doesn't matter. I don't care."

"I don't believe that." Carys could see the woman's madness but also her pain. She cared. She cared very much. "What do you think Seren would want you to do? Ruin both our lives because you made a mistake? Because you loved Lachlan?"

"Seren!" Aisling spun and held up a shaking finger, pointing at Carys. Her eyes were wide and her lips flushed. "Don't talk to me about Seren. She was my best friend, and you never even knew her."

"What would she want you to do?" Carys pressed Aisling again, sensing a weakness. "Would Seren want you to do this to her sister?" Carys knew that Aisling was desperate, but she was clinging to a plan that was swiftly crumbling under her fingers. No matter how lovesick, guilty, and panicked Aisling was, she was also intelligent. She had to know that none of this was going to work.

"You're not her sister." Aisling shook her head and turned back to the cauldron. "I was her sister, and she took the man I loved."

"I can help you," Carys whispered. "I can help you get away. You could start a new life somewhere very far away."

"I don't believe you." Aisling turned and sneered. "You'll tell *Lachlan*."

"I won't."

"I don't believe you!" she screamed and swept the basket from the table. "Why are you distracting me?"

Because if Aisling managed to finish whatever potion she was working on, Carys might be fighting for her life without remembering who was a friend and who was an enemy. She'd be lost in her own mind.

A distant sound like stone grinding along rock rumbled through the earth around them.

Aisling froze. "Regan is back."

CHAPTER THIRTY-FIVE

Aisling ran to the table, grabbed Seren's journal, and ran back to Carys, stuffing the journal back in Carys's pocket. "Don't let Regan see it."

The grinding sound of stone ricocheted through the chamber, and an arched doorway appeared in the wall. Through it swept Regan, dressed in dark trousers, a leather vest, and a long royal-blue cloak that covered her head.

"What are you doing?" She stood at the mouth of the archway, her eyes fixed on Aisling, who was standing near the cauldron. "I told you to get rid of her. Can't you do anything right?"

"People will ask questions if we kill her." Aisling held up her hands. "If she forgets all this, it can all go back to how it was." She pointed to the fire. "I'm making a spell to erase her memories, Regan. You can take her back through the gate. You told me you could do that."

Regan shook her head sadly. "You silly little girl. Don't you understand what's happening? There is more at stake here than your lovesick mewling and stupid guilt."

She walked over to Aisling's cauldron and swung the rack away from the fire. Her skin sizzled where it touched the burning metal, but Regan didn't flinch.

Aisling covered her mouth as the steam died on the surface of the bubbling mass.

"And you." Regan turned to Carys. "The fae should have eaten you in the forest before you ever set foot in this realm." She cocked her head. "I might know one or two who would eat you now." She smirked. "And not in any pleasant way."

She turned away from Carys and walked to the table where Aisling's grimoire was sitting. "Where is the spell you wrote to blind the dragon?"

"What are you talking about?" Aisling's voice was small.

"You blinded that beast when you poisoned his mistress the first time, or he would have come back when she got sicker."

"What?" Carys looked at Aisling again and saw the truth written all over her manic face.

Of course. Of course she'd have to blind Cadell or block him in some way.

Aisling looked at Carys, her eyes glittering. "I had to. He would have felt Seren dying, and I couldn't have that."

Regan yelled at Aisling. "How did you do it? He's breaking though my wards."

Aisling had sense enough to look frightened. "Regan, if he's breaking through the wards, we should run. That spell isn't strong enough to—"

"Absolutely not." Regan snorted. "Not until I find that bitch's maps. If the kings see them, it's all over."

"I told you." Aisling's voice was brusque. "I looked through her things after she died. None of the maps in Seren's papers had anything about the western islands. They were property boundaries for local lords and one map of the Northern Sea. None of the western islands were on there."

Regan glanced over her shoulder at Carys. "Well, now you definitely have to kill her. She can't know any of that."

Aisling's eyes narrowed on Carys, but she said nothing.

"How about you?" Regan walked over and bent down, getting in Carys's face. "Do you know where your sister's maps are?"

Carys closed her eyes. "I think I'm going to throw up."

Regan heaved a sigh. "Seren was so superior to you. Despite the dragon, you're... nothing. Very boring."

"I don't have any maps," Carys said. "I'm going to puke."

"I think you're lying." Regan ran a finger down her cheek, scraping Carys's skin with a clawed nail. "Hand them over and maybe I'll feed you to the kelpie instead of taking you back to the forest. The kelpie will give you a quick death."

Carys kept her eyes wide and woozy. "I don't know what you're talking about."

Regan's eyes lit up and she stood up straight. "You're lying! How intriguing."

Carys *was* lying. She knew exactly what Regan was talking about. She was looking for the maps Seren had drawn into her journals, the ones that had been sitting in the old crates for years, not neatly drawn out on large scrolls like Aisling had been looking for but scrawled in a journal among crop reports and banquet menus. "I don't think Seren had any maps with her stuff. Not that I saw."

"You're a bad liar. If I wasn't going to kill you, I'd say you should work on that." Regan leaned down again, inches from Carys's face. "Your nosy sister was always taking off to snoop with that beast. She knew what was happening. I'm so glad Aisling killed her. It's the one smart thing my niece has ever done."

"Regan!" Aisling sputtered.

"Calm down." Regan's green eyes never left Carys's stoic gaze. "This one knows what I'm speaking of, don't you?"

"No idea," Carys whispered. "I do feel Cadell getting closer though. Might be a good idea to run. Dragons can be... burny."

Regan narrowed her eyes. "Some fae magic is breaking through mine, and I don't like it. I was given assurances that they wouldn't interfere."

"You got me there." Carys kept her eyes wide and innocent. "I don't really know any fae the way that you do."

When she'd first woken and realized where she was, she had been resigned to dying. But the more Regan talked, the angrier Carys became.

Fuck this sorceress. She wasn't going to die at her hand. Or at least if she was going to go, she'd make sure Cadell could take Regan with her. She felt his magic coming closer, like heat from a distant fire.

She reached out. She didn't know how, but she concentrated on that hot thread of anger, wrapping it around the tie she felt to Cadell... then she *yanked* on it in her mind.

Carys heard a distant roar of dragon fire. "He's coming."

Seren's journal lay heavy in the pocket on her right, but Carys tried not to think about it.

"Fine. If you don't know anything, you're no use to me." Regan drew a long bone knife from a scabbard at her waist. "Goodbye, lesser Seren."

"Wait." Carys needed to buy time. "I think there were maps in my sister's journals, nothing nicely drawn but sketches mixed in with a bunch of other stuff. I didn't really understand why she drew them, but they were there."

"What?" Aisling frowned.

"Her journals." Regan pressed the bone knife to Carys's neck. "Where are they?"

"They were in the library for years." Carys smiled a little. "Right under your nose."

Regan spun and stalked toward Aisling. "What have you been hiding from me?"

"I don't know." Aisling raised her hands. "You asked me for maps. I looked through everything. I gave you everything she had, and you said it was worthless."

"They're just sketches really." Carys spoke softly. "They were in her journals all the time."

Regan turned back to Carys and put the knife at her throat again.

"You're more clever than I gave you credit for. I thought you were a lovesick idiot like this one. Where are the journals? Never mind—they'll be at the castle. I'll find them."

The knife pressed closer, and Carys felt her skin break open.

"They're not there!" The pain nearly made her cry out, but Carys controlled it. "I hid them, and you won't find them without me." Tears fell from her eyes, but she forced her gaze to Regan's. "But others will."

The sting from Regan's knife broke through the rest of the fog. Her legs felt light and quick again. Carys could feel her toes, her ankles, the pain from the bindings around her wrists.

"Tell me where."

"And have you kill me? I'm not an idiot. Take me to the fae gate and I'll tell you where to find them. I'll go back to my world, and all of you here in the Shadowlands can go to hell for all I care. All I want is to go home."

Was there any way that Regan would believe her?

The woman stepped back and lowered the knife. Then she lunged forward, the knife raised.

Carys couldn't stop the flinch, but Regan halted inches from her face and laughed. Then she bent over, slid the knife between the bindings holding Carys's legs to the chair, and sliced through them. She stared at Carys, her eyes narrowing. "What is that smell?"

"Probably onions."

"At least you're funnier than Seren." Regan rose and motioned to Aisling. "Get her arms. She won't hurt *you*." She kept her eyes on Carys as Aisling came over and sliced through the bonds holding Carys's wrists behind her back.

Regan turned to the right, staring into the distance. "The dragon isn't alone anymore. Others have come."

Carys could feel the growing power. The fire was burning hotter. There was a magic surrounding them and the faint sound of feathers flapping in the darkness. She stretched her arms in front of her, and in the distance, she heard the faint call of a crow and Naida's voice whispering in her memory.

You smell of the Crow Mother.

Only other fae will sense it.

...they will leave you alone.

No fae would harm you with Branwen's mark on your skin.

"You should run." She touched the slice on her neck as she rose and stretched her legs. "They're coming for me right now. And you probably didn't hear the news, but I struck a bargain with the Crow Mother."

Regan's eyes went wide. "What did you say?"

"I owe her a favor, so unless you want to piss her off, you're not going to hurt me."

"You're lying."

"Am I?"

Regan clearly couldn't tell if Carys was telling the truth or not. The tension in her jaw told Carys that she was carefully considering the situation.

Dragon breaking though fae wards with unknown reinforcements with him.

A human protected by a powerful fae.

Dragon. Really big, really pissed-off dragon.

Regan was out of options, and by the anger burning in her eyes, she knew it.

"If you want a chance at finding Seren's maps, you better leave now. I may not know who that fae woman is, but you clearly do. Think she'll be pissed at you if you kill the Brightkin who owes her a favor? Take off, Regan. Leave me alone."

Regan's rage was clear when she screamed. The walls shook with anger, and the stones surrounding them shifted in their mortar. "I should kill us all now!"

"That seems counterproductive," Carys said.

"Regan, stop!" Aisling ran to her aunt. "She's right. We need to run. We have to leave now. Cadell will have raised the Northern Guard. Lachlan and his men are probably already outside."

"No." Regan grabbed for her niece, flipped her to face Carys, and pulled her to her chest. A second later, the tip of the bone knife was at Aisling's throat.

Aisling cried out, "What are you doing?"

Regan backed toward the archway, still holding the knife at Aisling's throat. "You're soft like Seren." She kept her eyes on Carys. "You won't want me to kill her."

"You think I care?" Carys shook her hands and slowly flexed her feet, which tingled and burned. "Aisling killed my sister. She tried to kill me."

Regan flipped the knife around with a quick hand, swung her arm forward, and sank the knife into Aisling's belly.

"Guh." Aisling's cry was soft and guttural.

"No!" Carys lunged forward but stopped when Regan dragged Aisling back.

"See? You're soft." Regan pushed the knife deeper. "Even though she did kill your sister. Tell me where the maps are or I will gut her in front of you."

Aisling clutched her abdomen with both hands, blood seeping between her fingers. Her eyes rose to Carys's. "Seren…"

"You're not leaving this mound with me, Brightkin. So tell me where the journals are or I gut Aisling like a fish."

Carys's mind flew in a hundred different directions at once. Aisling was bleeding in front of her, but she wasn't dead. Cadell was coming, but maybe not fast enough to save Aisling.

"Carys!" Someone in the distance was shouting her name, and there was the sound of stone and scraping metal. "Carys, where are you?"

Regan pressed the knife deeper, and Aisling's face drained of color. "Tell me, Brightkin." She whispered something under her breath, but Carys couldn't hear it.

"Seren?" Aisling's eyes had gone watery and blank. "Seren, help."

No matter what Aisling had done, Carys couldn't sit and watch her die under Regan's knife.

"The journals are at Duncan's cottage." Carys kept her eyes on Aisling's. "I hid them in an apple crate he keeps in the rafters. Now go and leave her with me."

Regan smiled and pulled the knife from her niece, letting the woman fall to the ground. "You're not a bad bargainer after all." She took a step toward Carys, but just then a crow flew through the black stone archway and perched on the table, angling its black beady eye at Regan.

"Caw!"

"Damn you to the deep," Regan hissed a second before she threw up a hand. The stone wall folded in on itself, creating a new passageway, and she fled through it, closing the wall behind her.

Carys rushed to the bleeding woman. With Regan's knife removed, her blood was pouring from her belly to the earthen floor. "Aisling?"

"I deserve this." The woman's lips were pale, nearly blue. "I know I do. Tell Seren I'm sorry."

"Seren's dead." Carys pushed her arm around Aisling's body. "But you aren't. Don't die, Aisling. Help me out here."

Bits of stone and moss were falling overhead, as if Regan's and Aisling's magic had been the only things holding up the chamber. Mushrooms grew up around Aisling's body, feeding on the dark red blood pouring from her wound.

"The fort is going to collapse." Aisling whispered a spell and tried to lift her hand, but it fell limp at her side. "I don't want to die in the earth. Can you take me... I want to see the sea. I miss the sea."

The crow cawed again, louder this time, and Carys felt a surge of power in her limbs. The bird flew out of the dark passageway where it had come.

"You're not dying!" Carys managed to get Aisling to her feet, dragging the woman toward the arch where the crow had flown.

She didn't stop even though the walls around her were pitch-black. She could see faint blue lights overhead and a dull white glow in the distance. She headed toward it, ignoring the wild shouting in her mind.

Nêrys!

"I'm coming out. Regan stabbed Aisling, and she's going to Duncan's cottage to find Seren's journals. Get me a doctor or a healer or... whatever you can find, Cadell. We need to save Aisling and stop Regan before she gets there."

There was a rumbling behind her, but Carys didn't turn to look. The crow in the passageway was joined by another, then another, then another until the cacophony of caws and shrieks drowned out the sound of shouting in her mind.

The black birds swirled around the glowing grey entrance to the fae mound, and Carys stumbled through them, falling to her knees as she reached the lush green grass of the meadow, and the birds flew away.

The fae woman Naida was standing at the entrance, her hand held to the ground and her face tight with exertion. Behind Naida stood a company of soldiers from the castle, Lachlan standing at the front, bronze sword at the ready, and beside him, Duncan was ready with a sword of dragon steel in his hand.

"Carys!" they both shouted.

"Thank the gods." Naida let out a breath and stood. "Regan's magic was so strong. If I didn't know better, I would think she's fae."

Carys tried to lay Aisling gently on the grass, but her arms grew weak as soon as the birds flew away and she dropped the dying woman.

Duncan and Lachlan rushed toward them. Lachlan dropped his sword and threw his arms around Carys while Duncan knelt at Aisling's side, driving his sword into the earth.

"Human, take that iron from this ground." Naida's face went pale. "I don't know where you forged that, but unless you want to make me your enemy—"

"She's dying." Duncan yanked the sword from the earth and slung it over his shoulder, into a leather scabbard. He looked up in supplication. "Naida, she's dying."

Cadell roared overhead, joined by another dragon carrying a coracle.

Naida looked up at the dragons overhead. "I will try to heal her." She looked at Carys, who was limp in Lachlan's embrace. "Nêrys, calm your dragon before he burns down the forest. He smells your blood."

"You're bleeding?" Lachlan asked.

"Cadell!" Carys pulled away from Lachlan and ran to the center of the meadow, waving both her hands overhead. "I'm here. I'm safe."

Nêrys?

She ran to the edge of the forest and waved her arms. "Cadell!"

The dragon came wheeling down overhead.

"Carys!" Lachlan and Duncan ran after her.

"What are you doing?" Duncan yelled as Cadell's roars came closer.

"Regan is going to your cottage." She held back her hair as it whipped around her face. "We have to keep her from getting Seren's journals. There's something about those maps."

"What are you talking about?" Lachlan yelled. "What maps?"

"I'll explain later."

Cadell landed, his massive wingspread blocking the sky from view.

Nêrys. He bent his head. *Bring your wound to me.*

"Cadell." She ran to her dragon as he bent his head and threw her arms around him. "I'm so sorry I went without you."

You were betrayed by a friend. Don't move. He breathed out, his exhalation searing her skin.

Carys flinched, but she held still as he'd told her and felt the wound at her neck disappear. "Can you heal Aisling too?"

Naida is tending to her, and I hear the unicorns approaching.

The pain in Carys's neck was a memory when she turned back to Duncan and Lachlan. "It was an accident." It was enough of the truth for the moment. "The potion came from Regan, and Aisling didn't know it would hurt Seren."

Lachlan's face went pale. "Aisling?"

"Regan's going to Duncan's to get Seren's journals. We need to get them before she does."

Duncan looked up at Cadell. "Can you carry me and Carys both?"

I can carry two humans. He flexed his massive claws. *We must go now.*

"He says he can take us both." Carys stepped back. "Let's go."

"Don't be ridiculous," Lachlan snapped. "Duncan, you're not trained."

"I have iron." Duncan held up the sword.

"And no training in it and no defense against magic." Lachlan scowled. "This isn't a contest. We have to be smart. Regan is an immensely powerful mage."

Duncan gritted his teeth, and Carys looked up, spotting Mared and Dafydd in the distance. "Both of you can go." She waved her arms at the dragon soaring overhead. "My uncle and Mared can take one of you—the other can go with Cadell and me."

"I'll go with you." Both Duncan and Lachlan spoke at the same time.

"Not the time!" Carys yelled.

Duncan stepped back even though his face was a storm. "Fine, go."

Carys cast one last look at Duncan as Cadell heaved his body into the air, grabbed Carys in one claw and Lachlan in the other.

Then they were flying and everything was wind.

CHAPTER THIRTY-SIX

Cadell carried them over the loch, circling the fae forest in the distance before he turned back to land in the meadow closest to Duncan's cottage.

"I can already feel her magic." Lachlan dropped to the ground, and his sword was in his hand. "Carys, stay behind me."

"Got it." She wasn't an idiot. Lachlan was a trained soldier, and she wasn't.

Cadell transformed into his human form and ran with her.

"Nêrys, you're still weak from her spell."

"I'll be fine." She was lightheaded, but there wasn't enough time to recover.

Behind them, Carys heard Mared's coracle drop with a wooden *thunk*, and two pairs of footsteps came running out.

"Mared will watch from the sky." Dafydd was huffing as he ran, and he carried a bronze axe in his hand. "If the witch has called for reinforcements, she'll tell me."

"The wards are already up around the place." Lachlan started running toward the cottage.

"She's one woman," Duncan said. "How powerful can she—"

The force of an invisible barrier slammed into them and cut Duncan off.

Carys hit the ground as if she'd run into a wall. She felt sick to her stomach and turned to retch, but nothing came out.

"What is that?"

"Black magic," Lachlan muttered. "She's more powerful than we knew."

Dafydd narrowed his eyes. "I feel fae magic too, my boy."

Duncan walked back and forth along the edge of the shimmering barrier, which flexed and pulsed with power. "Fae magic, is it?" He drew his dragon steel from the scabbard at his side and plunged the tip of it into the earth.

There was a scream in the distance and a shuddering groan as the earth lifted and the ground shook.

"What is that?" Dafydd growled.

"You know what it is." Duncan left the sword in the ground and nodded at Lachlan. "See if you can get through."

Lachlan nodded at his brother and pressed his shoulder against the shimmering barrier, which flexed and wobbled for a moment before he pushed through and stumbled to the other side.

"I'm in." Lachlan looked at Dafydd and Cadell. "Come on."

Cadell stepped forward, pushing through the shimmering barrier before he turned and helped Carys through, then Dafydd.

Duncan pushed through the barrier, his hand on the sword's hilt, then he pulled it from the ground behind him and the earth shook again, but Lachlan and Cadell were already running.

I will kill her, Cadell said into Carys's mind. *I will kill her, Nêrys.*

She'd never heard Cadell's voice so cold.

"Come on!"

Duncan ran past a copse of hawthorn trees and stopped. "Mags?"

The body of a small creature lay on the ground. It was dressed a brown dress and a green cap. Its ears were pointed, and it was barely over two feet tall.

"Mags!" Duncan knelt and touched his fingers to the small body. "What has that bitch done?"

The body moved a little bit but not much.

"She was protecting the cottage," Cadell said. "The bwbach have old power. That this Regan could hurt your brownie means she is more than a human mage."

Duncan stood and looked at Carys. "Angus. He'll be in danger."

"We need to get to the house." She looked at the tiny body. "Cadell?"

"She's alive," Cadell said. "The best thing we can do is kill the mage so Mags can heal from her familiar energy."

"I'm sorry, old girl." Duncan placed her gently under the hawthorn trees and they kept moving. "I'll be back."

The ground angled up even though the cottage sat on no hill or rise in the earth. Nevertheless, the way forward meant they were climbing over rocks and thorny ground as they approached the cottage.

"How did she do this?"

Dafydd answered. "She's using fae magic, but I don't know how."

"The fae can make a mountain out of flat land?"

Lachlan panted. "How do you think they built their forts?"

Carys slipped and fell as the sky opened up and they were pelted with icy rain. The soft grey clouds turned black as they approached the cottage, which was now perched on top of a mound. The air cracked with lightning, and Mared roared in the distance, covering the sky with fire and black smoke.

"Dragon fire cannot banish this magic," Cadell said. "She's channeling fae sorcery."

"But how?" Lachlan wiped the rain from his face. "She's human!"

"Is she?" Dafydd's mouth was set in a firm line. "Orla's consort is fae."

Duncan and Lachlan looked at each other.

"What does that mean?" Carys blinked back the rain, trying to shield her face from the weather as driving rain turned to sleet.

Cadell stepped between Carys and the rain. "Nothing is born in the Shadowlands save by magic."

"You're saying that Regan isn't a Shadowkin?"

"Children can be born here," Lachlan shouted. "Fae and human *can* have children."

"We would have known," Dafydd said. "If the queen of Éire bore a fae child, the entirety of Briton would—"

"It doesn't matter right now. Whatever Regan is, she's powerful and she's dangerous," Carys said. "And we have to stop her."

Duncan lifted his dragon-steel sword. "If she's part fae, this will kill her."

"We need to keep going." Lachlan pressed forward.

THEY CLIMBED the hill to the top and stumbled over the edge where a strange calm enveloped the cottage that Duncan called home. There was light grey smoke curling from the chimney, coming in rapid puffs.

"She's burning the journals." Carys bolted for the cottage door.

Duncan and Lachlan shouted behind her. "Carys, no!"

The door swung open, Carys tumbled through, and the door slammed shut.

Regan was sitting by the fire, paging through Seren's journals and casually tossing them into the flames. "It took you long enough."

Carys wiped the rain from her face as Cadell pounded on the door. "You can't hurt me."

"I might." Regan looked up, closed the journal she was reading, and tossed it into the fire.

"No!" Carys lunged for the fireplace, but Regan lifted a hand, and she froze.

"What did you see?" Regan narrowed her eyes. "I opened these books and saw nothing. Blank page after blank page. What magic are you playing with, Brightkin?"

Carys blinked. "What?"

"See? You're not lying." Regan stood and leaned against the table, picking through the crate of journals. "Which irritates me. I hate not knowing magics. Some spell has been put over these books, but I can't discover their magic. It's not fae. It's not human. I should be able to read them, and I cannot." She wrinkled her nose. "This smells of the old gods."

More pounding at the door, and then glass shattered and Cadell reached a massive arm into the cottage before Regan lifted an arm and shoved him back.

"How did you get so strong?" Carys was still frozen, but she didn't fear Regan, not with the smell of the Crow Mother on her. "My uncle thinks you're half-fae."

"Does he?" The corner of Regan's mouth turned up. "That would be quite the *scandal*, wouldn't it? The daughter of Queen Orla a halfling mutt?" Regan's mouth twisted in a bitter smile. "Unwelcome in human courts or fae. What kind of abomination would she be?"

"You are." It was clear as day. "Nothing is born in the Shadowlands save by magic."

"And dark magic at that," Regan hissed in her face. "A hybrid creature that belongs nowhere. Sound familiar, Carys Morgan?"

"I'm not fae," she said. "Nothing about me is fae."

"But you're not entirely Brightkin either, are you?" Regan stared at her, lifting her chin and gazing into Carys's eyes. "She was such a plain girl, your sister. But she had a scar on her neck." Regan ran a finger down Carys's throat. "Did you know that? A battle scar. The scar made her interesting at least. You have nothing."

"Yep. Super ordinary." She tried to move her feet and couldn't. "You should leave me and take off."

"I should—" Regan blinked. "What is that?" She stepped back, and her shoulders curled inward. "What is that?" She screamed as her eyes locked on the door.

There was a thunk, then another one.

Thunk.

Regan gasped and threw a hand out.

Thunk.

Craaaaack!

"Who did this?" Regan screamed. "Who brought iron into this place?"

"Not iron." Carys felt her feet loosen as Duncan's sword broke through Regan's wards. "Steel."

"No!" She waved a dismissive hand in Carys's direction, flinging her into a wall.

Carys flew through the air and hit the stone wall, crumpling to the floor.

It hurt. Every part of her body was screaming, but she scrambled to her feet, moving through the pain. She lunged toward the fireplace and the other journals sitting precariously near the flames. She grabbed them as the door cracked open and the walls of the cottage shook.

The ground thrust up beneath her and she fell, cracking her forehead on the slate hearth, but she managed to grab Seren's journals and hide them under her body even as coals rolled out of the fire and singed her skin.

She cried out, and Cadell roared from the window, breaking through the warded glass with a massive fist.

"Carys!" He pushed inside, shoving the stones around the window to widen the space as the cottage door fell inward.

Carys rolled away from the fire, the journals clutched to her chest as she scrambled under the table and all hell broke loose.

Duncan broke through the doorway with the dragon-steel sword, taking a knee and bending low as Lachlan leaped over his back with his bronze sword drawn.

"Brother!" Duncan flung the steel sword toward Lachlan, who dropped the bronze, grabbed the steel, and charged Regan.

The sorceress pulled down a heavy wooden rafter, knocking Lachlan away before he could strike.

The roof of the cottage tilted precariously as the foundation shifted and the rafters rained down. Thatch, dust, and wood fell around Carys.

"Stay under the table," Cadell shouted.

Duncan stood and lifted his arms, holding up a falling rafter with his massive strength to keep the cottage from collapsing in. "Cadell!" He roared. "Get her out of here!"

"Regan!" Dafydd shouted from the doorway. "You murderous hag!"

"And?" She bared her teeth as Lachlan climbed over the rubble to get to her.

"You're dead." Lachlan's face was pale with fury. He swung the iron toward Regan, who had nothing but magic to defend herself.

And fae magic didn't break steel.

She screamed as the sword slashed down, cutting across her body with a burning slice. Acrid smoke filled the air, and shimmering red blood sprang from the wound across her chest. Regan fell back, collapsing into the rubble of the rapidly disintegrating cottage.

"Cadell!" Duncan shouted, his chest heaving as he held up the ceiling. "Get. Carys. Out!"

"I have her, boy!" Dafydd ran over and grabbed for Carys's arm as Cadell covered her body with his own. "Run!"

Regan threw out a hand, and blood spurted from Lachlan's mouth and eyes, but he didn't yield. He slashed again, cutting Regan across the legs and sweeping with an upward angle, slicing her belly with a killing cut.

Regan grunted and fell to her knees, silver and scarlet blood mingling as her belly burst open and her entrails fell to the rubble-strewn ground.

Lachlan didn't stop but stepped over a fallen timber, and just as Cadell and Dafydd hustled Carys from the room, she saw cold determination on his face as he raised the dragon steel one last time, swung downward, and cut Regan's head from her body.

A pulse of magic burst from the halfling's broken corpse, shattering the wards that had held up the cottage as the roof of the building collapsed and everything before Carys's eyes went dark.

CHAPTER THIRTY-SEVEN

S he was lying on the damp ground and the sky was grey and cold, but the rain had stopped. Someone was gently wiping something from her face, but she reached out in the darkness for Cadell.

Cadell?

You can speak to me in your mind now.

Am I?

Yes. You haven't woken from the shock yet.

How?

How anything, Nêrys? You don't seem content to follow any rules.

She tried to think about that, but her mind was too tired.

Is Lachlan alive?

Yes. Dafydd already had you out the door, so I went back for him.

Duncan?

Not even a house falling on him could kill that one.

And Seren's journals?

Buried very safely in the rubble. You secured them under the table, so we can dig them out when the cottage is secure.

Is Regan dead?

Very dead, Nêrys.

She let out a relieved sigh, and she felt Duncan's hand on her cheek.

"Wake up, Carys." His voice was urgent and low. "For the love of God, wake up."

She felt his lips touch her forehead.

Cadell?

Yes, Nêrys.

I'm really... confused.

Understandable, my lady.

She knew she needed to open her eyes, but the thought of returning to fire, rubble, death, and two quarreling brothers made her keep them closed for just a moment longer.

But she wasn't alone.

You'll never be alone again, Cadell said in her mind.

Carys opened her eyes and Duncan grabbed her, clutching her to his chest. His shoulders shook, and he rocked her back and forth.

"Thank God. Thank God," he whispered fervently.

"I'm okay." She dug her fingers into his massive shoulder. It was a little like trying to comfort a brick wall. "I'm fine, Duncan."

"You scared us, girl."

Dafydd's voice made Carys look to the side. The old man's face was creased with worry and covered in dust and blood. He had a cut over his right eyebrow, and blood ran into one of his bright blue eyes.

"Aunt Eamer is going to be pissed at me for cutting up your pretty face," she whispered.

Dafydd threw his head back and laughed.

"Trust a Welsh woman to make a joke five minutes after she almost died," Duncan muttered. He lifted Carys and carried her to a grassy spot that wasn't covered in rubble. "I'm going to set you down here," he said. "Are you okay?"

She nodded.

"I'm going to look for Mags." He glanced at the ruins of the cottage. "She's going to be in a full-on rage for what we've done to her house."

Carys looked up to see Cadell and Mared flying overhead.

"What are they doing?"

"Waiting to take us back. Mared says there's a fight brewing at the loch."

"Fuck." Carys's eyes searched for Lachlan, who was kneeling by the smoking ruins, Duncan's steel sword in his hand. "He left an army on the edge of unicorn territory."

"That he did."

Carys forced herself to her feet and limped over to Lachlan, who was staring at the ruins with silver and red blood spattered on his face, blood dripping from his eyes, and dust and rubble in his russet-brown hair.

"Lachlan?" She knelt and put a hand on his shoulder.

He looked up and frowned. "She killed my wife."

"Yes. And you killed her."

"It's not..." His jaw tensed and his face crumpled. "It doesn't make it hurt any less."

"No." She blinked back tears and knelt beside him. "I don't think it can."

Lachlan let out something halfway between a groan and a cry. His shoulders curled in, and he leaned on the steel sword in his right hand, which was dug into the earth.

"Carys, I'm sorry." He shook his head. "I'm so sorry."

"For what?"

"For everything." His eyes were hollow. "Duncan was right. I never should have gone looking for you. I never should have drawn you into..." He looked at the smoke and stone. "All of this. You had a good life."

"Yeah." She sat back on her heels and took a deep breath, letting it out slowly. "I did."

Carys thought about her life. Her friends and her job. The family she'd lost and the one she'd patched together for herself. All that was important. It was precious.

But it wasn't everything.

"Because you came to find me, I have you. And I have Duncan. I found out that I had a sister who was really amazing." She smiled a little and looked over her shoulder to where Dafydd waited. "I have an uncle. And an aunt. I have family again."

Lachlan nodded.

"And I have a dragon." She looked up at Cadell, who was circling slowly overhead. Watching. Waiting for her.

Always, Nêrys.

Lachlan laughed a little. "Admit it—the dragon is your favorite."

She gripped his shoulder in her hand. "I can't answer that right now because we need to get back to Aisling and stop your army from going to battle with the unicorns."

"Oh fuck." He hoisted himself up and wiped his eyes with the back of his hand just as Duncan came running up the hill.

His eyes scanned the rubble. "Is she here?"

"Who?"

"Mags."

"Not here." Lachlan handed his brother the sword. "That thing is too heavy."

"Not for me." Duncan took the sword, hastily slid a cloth over the blade, and secured it in the scabbard. "You didn't even clean it."

"Not the time." Carys tried not to yell. "Wounded friend. Unicorns. Remember?"

Dafydd raised his arms and sent a sharp whistle into the sky. Seconds later, Mared swept down and grabbed Dafydd and Lachlan in her claws.

"Cadell!"

I am coming.

Her dragon flew down with a roar, opened his claws, and grabbed Carys and Duncan in a single dive. She felt the cold security of Cadell's grip around her and the warm radiance of the fire in his belly.

Duncan was clutching Cadell's leg, his eyes closed and his mouth muttering something she couldn't hear.

"Are you praying?" she shouted.

"This is mad!" He looked up, then back at Carys. He started to smile. Then to laugh. "Absolutely mad!"

"Where was Mags?" Carys shouted. "She wasn't there?"

"I couldn't find her," he shouted back, "but I'll get Angus looking when I can." He looked at the ground. "Is Aisling still alive?"

"Cadell?"

She's alive, the dragon's voice said in her mind. *But she's very, very weak.*

WHEN THEY LANDED, Lachlan was already kneeling in the meadow at Aisling's side, and Naida's hands were on her. The army of Sgàin waited a short distance away, standing down as their leader knelt by the dying healer and the small fae woman.

The unicorns stood among the trees, watching the soldiers with cautious eyes while their chief knelt beside the dying human.

She's still alive. But barely.

Darius and Naida were speaking softly and urgently in a language Carys didn't recognize.

"I need to talk to her." Carys walked over, leaving Duncan with Lachlan's men.

Lachlan was holding Aisling's hand. "Let them heal you," he said. "They say you're blocking their magic. Why?"

Aisling shook her head. "Where is Carys?"

"I'm here." Carys knelt in the grass.

The corner of Aisling's mouth turned up. "You're safe."

Naida looked at Carys. "Convince your friend. Darius and I *can* heal her, but she won't let us through. She's lost blood and she won't survive long."

"Aisling," Carys said, "you need to let Naida heal you. You can trust her and Darius."

Naida bent down to Aisling's ear. "You will owe me nothing, mage. I do not tally favors as other fae do."

Aisling shook her head and coughed a little, a smear of blood visible on her berry-red lips. "No."

"Who did this?" Lachlan gripped Aisling's hand and looked at the vicious, bleeding wound. "Was it Regan?"

"I did this to myself." Aisling looked at Carys. "Is she dead?"

"Yes." Carys didn't say who had killed Regan, and Lachlan didn't either.

"Good." Aisling stared into the sky, her eyes resolute. "Lachlan, please."

"I'm here."

"Leave."

"What?"

"Please. Just for a moment." She blinked back tears. "I want to speak with Carys."

Lachlan stood, and a blank expression fell over his face. He stepped back to give them privacy.

"Aisling, don't do this." Carys scooted closer and took her hand, speaking urgently to the dying woman. "I didn't tell them."

"But you will. You *should*."

Carys said nothing. Regan's spell or not, Aisling *had* killed Seren. And she'd refused to heal Seren to cover her own crime. "But you can live."

"Lachlan will blame me." Aisling started crying. "When he thinks about it. When the battle rush wears off and Lachlan thinks about what's happened, he will blame me." She shook her head slowly. "This is better."

"No, it's not." Carys's eyes filled with tears. "None of this is better. *Life* is better."

Aisling was a killer. She was also a victim of a family who had only used her. She was Seren's closest friend and her murderer.

"I loved them both." Aisling's voice was barely a whisper. "She never should have come back to Alba. I can't..." She sucked in a shallow breath. "You have to listen to me."

"Aisling—"

"Shadowkin, Brightkin," she whispered. "The two of you are different. You *always* were. Regan and I both saw it." She seemed to have trouble breathing. "You already know it."

...some hybrid creature that belongs nowhere. Sound familiar...? Regan's whispered accusation came back to her.

"I'm human," Carys said. "I'm like you."

"More than you know." Aisling smiled, her lips fading to blue.

"What are you talking about?" Carys could barely see for the tears streaming down her face. "I don't understand."

Aisling motioned for Carys to come closer. She put her ear to Aisling's lips.

"*Nêrys ddraig,*" Aisling whispered. "You are creatures of the Annwn. Find a way there, Carys, and you might find them both."

"Aisling?" Carys pulled back. "Aisling!"

"There is a way." She closed her eyes. "Enough."

"Aisling?"

Naida shook her head. "She's dying."

Aisling's eyes flickered open again, but there was a blankness behind them. "Lachlan?"

He ran over and dropped to his knees to take her hand. "Stop this. Stop this now, Aisling." He looked at Naida. "Is it too late?"

Naida said nothing, but she took her hands from Aisling's body.

The dying woman blinked, staring into the sky. "I'm so sorry, my love." Tears dripped from the corner of her eyes. "I loved you. Please believe me."

"I know. I..." Lachlan swallowed back whatever he'd been about to say. "My friend, what would you have me do?"

Aisling smiled a little. "Take me to the loch. Don't let me die on the earth."

"But the kelpie."

Her voice was barely a breath on her lips. "I do not fear him."

Lachlan fixed his expression into a mask of resolve, reached down, and lifted Aisling in his arms. He walked with long strides through the trees, past the unicorns, and toward the water. Carys, Duncan, and his men walked behind him.

She heard the soft sound of hooves padding through the forest as they broke through the trees and the dull, heavy beat of wings overhead.

Cadell flew down over the loch, breathing a stream of fire that touched the surface of the water, turning it to steam.

"What's happening?" Carys reached for Duncan's hand. "Why does she want to go to the loch?"

Duncan said nothing but folded her cold hand in his warm palm and held it to his chest as he watched his brother carry the girl who had grown up at his side and the woman who had loved him all her life.

When Lachlan reached the edge of the water, the surface stirred in a great whirlpool along the edge. A moment later, the kelpie rose out of the water, screaming in rage at the humans and unicorns violating his territory.

"No." Lachlan stepped back. "Not like this."

"Hold." Aisling held out her hand and spoke in a soft voice. "I see you."

The kelpie stopped screaming and dropped to its black hooves, the water still swirling around it. He stared at Aisling, snorting out steam.

"I *see* you," she said again.

A second later, the otherworldly horse disappeared and a darkly beautiful man rose from the loch. He wore grey clothes drawn from the water itself, and his coal-black hair was woven with long grass and weeds. His eyes were storm grey, the color of a mirror reflecting the winter sky, and his skin was as pale as the dead.

"Aisling?" Lachlan held her to his chest even as her blood started dripping down the front of his clothes. He backed away from the kelpie. "Please don't—"

"Leave me." Her voice was clear and strong. "Let me go."

"I've seen him." Carys pulled away from Duncan's hand and walked forward, drawn to the water's edge. "I've seen you."

He was the pale man she'd seen on the shoreline talking with the woman. He turned to Carys, and his lips curled back; she saw the fearsome pointed teeth that filled his mouth. Dread curled in Carys's stomach as the air along the edge of the loch seemed to still.

The dark man stepped from the water and onto the rocky shore.

Time froze. There was no sound. No birdsong. No whinnying of worried unicorns or creak of leather armor and bronze blade. The world around her slowed to a crawl, and even Cadell's voice felt murky and distant as the man walked across the smooth grey rocks toward Aisling.

Carys breathed in and out, caught in the liminal space between water and sky, life and death.

"I see you, son of Lir." Aisling's voice was a clear bell in the preternaturally still air. "If you take me back to Éire, I will grant you a favor."

The man spoke, but his lips didn't move. "What favor does Orla's blood have to offer me?"

"My willing life."

The dark man angled his head. "You come to me willingly?"

"I am a murderer and a betrayer. I do not want to die on land," Aisling said. "Take my life and deliver my soul to Bríg that I may ask for her mercy."

"If you come to me willingly, your wish is granted." The man reached for Aisling, and Lachlan was still as the dark man took the dying woman from the prince's arms.

Aisling and the kelpie's eyes met for a moment, and then she closed her eyes, let out a breath, and allowed her head to fall against his chest. Her face turned white, and her lips were blue.

The air was still as the water horse turned back to Carys with Aisling in his arms. "I see you too, blood of Rhiannon." The man's lips didn't move, and his voice came as a whisper in her ear. "The goddess's daughters walk between worlds."

Carys blinked. "What?"

The dark man turned to the loch. The second he stepped back into the water, the air around Carys released, sound filled the air again, and Aisling and the man were gone.

"What happened?" Lachlan spun around, hand on his sword hilt. "Where is she? The monster took her!"

"Calm yourself, son of Robb." Darius stood in human form in front of his people and stared out across the water. "The mage woman asked the kelpie to take her. There is nothing here to avenge."

CHAPTER THIRTY-EIGHT

Carys sat on the edge of her bed, staring at the dim morning light that gleamed like a pearl through the milky glass of her bedroom windows.

She'd sent Duncan and Lachlan away the night before. She wanted the company of neither. She asked Bonnie to help her bathe away the blood and the dust of battle, and just before she fell asleep, Cadell came into her room wearing his human skin and held her tightly as she wept.

She could feel her dragon overhead, curled in his natural form and waiting in the half-ready state he seemed to inhabit anytime she was near.

"Cadell, I need to go home."

Her time in the Shadowland had been two weeks, but it felt like two months.

I will take you to the fae gate, Nêrys. Tell me when and I will take you.

She blinked back tears. "But if I go home, you can't come with me, can you?"

Cadell was unusually silent.

"Cadell, I don't want to leave you."

You do not have to. His voice was resigned. *I will follow you into the Brightlands, my lady.*

Carys blinked. "Come here. I need to see your face."

Are you dressed? Humans feel shame in their natural form, and I don't want—

"I'm dressed. I have my nightdress on."

A moment later a knock sounded at her door. Carys went to open it and found Cadell on the other side.

She narrowed her eyes and looked down the hallway. "Where do you—"

"There is a balcony not far from here that is accessible by air only." He stepped through her door and stood at attention near the cold fireplace. "Robb had it added to the castle when Seren and Lachlan married."

Cadell bent down and added a piece of wood to the fire, then gripped his hand into a fist, and Carys saw a red glow coming from his palm. Moments later he opened it and lobbed a ball of fire into the hearth. The small fire sprang to life, and heat permeated the air.

"I didn't know you could do that." Carys sat on the edge of the bed, staring at the fire, wrapped in a heavy cloak.

"There is much you do not know." He stood and walked to her. "You have been gone from your world for two weeks. That is not enough time to learn anything."

"I've learned that I can talk to a dragon." *In my mind.* She tried out the new feature.

"Yes, very good." He cocked his head. "Have you studied languages? Cartography? History? Basic saber fighting? Hand-to-hand combat? Military history and wing formations? Magic incantations and basic spell—"

"Okay yes!" She raised a hand. "Obviously I'm not going to learn that much in two weeks. I didn't even get a training montage."

"I don't know what that means."

She rubbed her face. "You have a lot to learn too."

"You are nêrys ddraig. It is my responsibility as your dragon to see that you are prepared to fly into battle if necessary. That you are prepared for anything this world might confront you with."

"Why?" She crossed her legs and drew her cloak tighter. "I could go back to the Brightlands. The biggest danger I'd face there is a car accident or heart disease."

His eye twitched.

"You really don't like that idea, do you?"

"The gods do not grant magic to humans for no reason," Cadell said. "You have a purpose here."

"What?"

"That is not my place to say."

How convenient for him. "You're saying that I have some kind of… destiny?"

"You're not like the cross human. He is mundane."

She felt vaguely offended on Duncan's behalf. "I wouldn't say that. He forged a dragon-steel sword, didn't he?"

"Fine." Cadell cocked his head. "He has skills but no magic. You can speak to me. You hear the water horse. The ellyllon recognized you. The Crow Mother bargains with you."

"What are you saying? That I'm not human?"

"You *are* human," he insisted. "But not like the Brightkin we know. You are more."

"But if I go home, you'll come with me?"

"I must. You are my nêrys."

It was the first time that Cadell's friendship had felt like a burden. "But you'd lose your magic in the Brightlands."

"Yes."

Carys thought about it carefully. "If I stayed in Scotland—"

"You'd be closer, but it would not be your home. And I would still need to go with you."

"Wait a minute." She tore through her memory, shifting through the deluge of information that had been dumped on her in the past few weeks. "The fae took Lachlan."

"Allies of his father, yes. Robb does not travel to the Brightlands."

"Yeah, but they took him when he was out on a hike by my house." She looked up. "Cadell, there's a fae gate. Like, right by my house."

Cadell's eyes brightened. "Then I am definitely returning with you to the Brightlands. You'll smell of the Shadow now. You'll be marked. There will be creatures and beings from the Shadowlands who might seek you out."

"In Baywood?"

"Every place has a shadow, Nêrys."

"But Baywood?" A sleepy college town on the Northern California coast wasn't exactly a hotbed of myth and legend. Except...

Carys narrowed her eyes. "Oh my God, Bigfoot is real, isn't he?"

His chin jutted out and he narrowed his eyes. "I have no idea what that is. A creature with large feet? Do you mean giants?"

"Oh God, I didn't even think about the giants." Carys's mind was spinning. "Would you be able to go through the fae gate by my house if you moved to California?"

"The Shadowlands are my home." He took a breath and carefully nodded. "I should be able to cross any fae gate and return with your help since you are a native of the Brightlands."

"So you'll be able to dragon out when you need to." She released a breath and the knot in her chest loosened. "I mean, it's still not ideal, but at least you wouldn't be tied up in this human body all the time. If you come."

"That is not a question."

Carys stood up. "Cadell, I don't want you to lose your magic."

"Then I will take you to Cymru. You can attend the dragon academy there. You'll be the oldest student by far, but the children will be commanded to give you respect and the teasing should be minimal."

Not even Cadell believed the words that were coming out of his mouth.

Carys forced a smile. "Well, doesn't that sound like every child-hood nightmare come to life? Absolutely not."

Cadell crossed his arms over his chest. "Then you may stay in Alba.

I'm sure Lachlan has not changed his affections. His feelings are quite sincere, though recent events have brought his feelings for Seren to the forefront of his mind, and he might—"

"Nope." She shook her head. "Definitely not that option." She let out a breath and felt her chest tighten up again. "Not... yet anyway. How do we make this work?"

"I will follow you to Baywood," Cadell said softly. "You will return to your life. We will find the fae gate, and we can cross there. Dafydd will find some way to send you trainers even in that place. Dragon kingdoms have many diplomatic relations, and I know of at least two in the Americas."

"I'm not going to avoid the PE part of this whole thing, am I?"

"I don't know what that means."

She let out a long breath. "We can make this work."

Cadell's normally severe expression softened. "Of course we can, Nêrys."

"What about your children?"

"There are others who will care for my young. Dragon lives are long, and they are never alone."

"You'll be away from them. Maybe for a long time."

"That is the way of our kind. My children will understand that as they grow."

She stared at Cadell, but the stoic expression on his face didn't waver. "Okay." She took another deep breath. "Okay."

"Then it is agreed," Cadell said. "We will take our leave here and return to the Brightlands."

"You're going to need... documents. Identity things. Paperwork. You'll have to fly on a plane."

"Of course. King Dafydd has an associate who arranges those types of things. I will speak to Mared." His lip curled slightly. "And I'll... survive the plane."

She looked him up and down. "Maybe talk to Dafydd about that private jet, because I don't know how you'd fit on a commercial airline."

"These are details, Carys. We'll figure them out."

"Right." She took a deep breath. "I'm stalling, aren't I?"

"You need to speak to Lachlan."

"Right." She nodded and closed her eyes. "Yeah. I need to speak to Lachlan."

LACHLAN WAS in the North Hall, holding audience with his father. Robb sent the rest of the court from the room when Cadell and Carys walked in.

She looked at Robb and Lachlan. "I'll be returning to the Brightlands shortly."

"What?" Lachlan sat forward in his chair. "No."

Carys tried to read his expression, but he was carefully masking his feelings.

"I need to go home," she said. "I've been here over two weeks. I have a life there. If I don't return to it, people are going to start raising alarms."

"You're on sabbatical from teaching," Lachlan said.

"I have friends," Carys said firmly. "If I don't return, they won't just accept it and move on. They'll come to Scotland just like I came. They'll track my phone. They'll call the police. The fae gate could be compromised."

"Nothing in your world can compromise the gate," Robb said softly. "You don't think the magic will protect itself?" He smiled a little. "Your... modern police officers are hardly the greatest challenge the Shadowlands have faced."

Carys turned her attention to Robb. "So you're fine with keeping me captive here against my will?"

"I told you I wanted answers." Robb stared at her. "I don't have them."

"Father" —Lachlan interrupted— "you cannot keep Carys here if she wants to go."

"Why not?"

"King Dafydd for one." Cadell spoke in a firm voice. "He will not take lightly any attempt to confine his niece." Cadell seemed to grow bigger and wider in the throne room, and heat poured off his body. "And me. You will not keep my nêrys where she does not wish to be."

"Hold." Lachlan stood and ran an unsteady hand through his hair. "Everyone, please be calm."

Robb kept his eyes on Cadell. "Fine. I will let your nêrys return to Cymru."

"Okay, sure." Carys threw up her hands. "And then I'll just go through a fae gate there and cause even more questions in my world. You think that's better? You're not being logical."

Robb was clearly stumped, but he wasn't giving up. "So you found your sister's murderer, incited an international conflict, and now you are content to leave."

Carys opened her mouth, but nothing came out.

Robb narrowed his eyes. "The queen of Éire will want *answers*. Her daughter and granddaughter have been killed. She will want an explanation. War between Cymru and Éire could be on the horizon, and you want to leave?"

And she hadn't even told them about the maps yet.

"You could mention the part about her having a half-fae daughter and not telling anyone," Carys said softly. "I feel like she might want to keep that quiet."

"Rumors and innuendo are not international relations!" Robb rose to his feet. "You leave Briton teetering on the edge of war."

Well, fuck. When he put it that way, Carys definitely understood why Lachlan's dad was pissed off.

She looked at Cadell, but his face was as expressive as ever.

Fantastic.

"I..." She started slowly. "I have faith in my uncle's wisdom." Carys swallowed the lump in her throat. "And Queen Eamer's sway with her mother. Dafydd and Eamer know that breaking the Queens' Pact would have horrible consequences. And I'm sure Queen Orla does too."

Robb persisted. "There was mention made of maps that could cause a war. These were the reason Seren was killed."

Well, shit. How did he find out about those? Was that Duncan or Lachlan? One of them must have said something. Tattletales. She was trying to make a clean break with Robb and all this mess because she was more than done being a political football. She was clearly not Seren in so many ways, and this was one of them.

Her sister's murderers were dead. Or one was dead and one had been taken by the kelpie, so she was as good as dead. She knew where Lachlan was, and she knew the truth about their relationship. And Duncan was... Duncan.

Right now all Carys wanted was to go home.

She took a deep breath and looked at Robb. "I kind of think Seren was killed because Regan was a chaos monster who liked to torment Aisling, but yes, there might have also been some maps." She plowed on. "Before you ask, Cadell and I already gave them to Mared, who is going to deliver them to Dafydd. All of Seren's journals are with her father, so if you want to know what to tell Queen Orla, talk to him." She stepped away from the throne. "I am not a queen or a king. I'm not a diplomat. This isn't even my world." She raised her hands. "I'm *done*."

Carys saw from the frustrated expression on Robb's face that he was out of arguments.

She turned to leave with Cadell at her side.

"Carys."

Lachlan ran to her, grabbing her arm and spinning her around.

Cadell snarled and put a swift hand around Lachlan's neck.

"Wait!" Carys held up a hand. "Cadell, it's fine."

Lachlan's eyes drilled into her, and he spoke in a rush. "Don't go. Stay with me. Marry me. You could be a queen here. Go back to Baywood if you need to, then come back." His voice turned pleading. "And be with me."

Carys let out a harsh breath. "How could you ask me that?"

Lachlan frowned. "You know I love you."

"The woman who murdered Seren died *yesterday*." Carys closed her eyes and turned her face away. "You were grieving my sister *yesterday*. And you ask me this today?"

"I love you."

"You love... a version of me maybe?" Carys opened her eyes, and her heart broke looking at him. "And I loved a version of you." She put a hand on his cheek. "But neither of us knew the whole truth. I don't even know who I am anymore, Lachlan." She took his hand from her arm and knit their fingers together. "*Don't* ask me that question today."

"Not today does not mean never," he said softly.

"No." Her heart softened, and she gently kissed his cheek. "It doesn't mean never."

Lachlan opened his mouth, then closed it, pressing his lips together to hold in whatever he'd been about to say. He nodded, then let her hand go.

He was so beautiful he made her heart ache, and in the softness of his expression and the openness of his face, she saw everything she'd fallen in love with months before.

"I'll see you again." She looked at Robb, then over at Cadell. "I have a feeling this world isn't done with me yet."

"I'll see you again." His voice was firm. "And there will be no more secrets, Carys."

"We don't need them anymore." She turned and walked out the door.

"I'M TRYING to figure out how I'm going to explain a giant seven-foot Welshman moving into my house in Baywood when I left America to look for my missing Scottish boyfriend." Carys and Cadell were walking toward Duncan's cottage on the road that led down from Sgàin Castle.

Cadell shrugged. "Tell them we are family."

Carys looked down at herself. Barely over five feet. Dark hair. Blue eyes. Completely average figure.

And beside her was Cadell, nearly seven feet tall, golden-haired and golden-eyed, his arms as long as both of hers put together.

"Okay, sure." She nodded. "Everyone is going to buy that."

"Families come in many shapes, Nêrys."

They were passing through the village, Carys sending polite waves to the harried villagers who eyed her with suspicion.

"Not real fond of me anymore, I guess."

"The humans of the Shadowlands are suspicious by nature, and in their eyes, you caused a battle to nearly break out with the unicorns, the fae have been angered by Regan's destruction of the old fort, and Aisling—the healer who took care of the village—is dead."

"None of that is my fault though." She kept her voice low and kept her head down. The last thing she needed was a rotten apple thrown in her direction. Cadell would react and someone would get crispy.

"Things were less exciting before you arrived." He shrugged. "They will forget eventually."

"Right."

The baker and his wife eyed her with frowns before they walked back inside and shut the door soundly.

Carys tried not to whine. She really had loved their scones.

A trading cart with southern colors rumbled past them, the air behind it thick with the scent of spices and southern warmth. Behind the cart rode a couple mounted on horses who nodded as they passed.

"What is Anglia like?"

"We can visit on another trip," Cadell said. "It is lively and much more diverse than Alba. People from the continent brave the crossing with some regularity now since the Frisians have developed spells to repel the leviathan."

"Leviathans." She nodded. "Right."

"The creatures avoid the channel now" —he nodded at another tall man who passed them— "and generally keep to the northern seas."

Carys waited until they were out of the village before she asked, "Was that big guy you nodded at another dragon?"

"No, he was obviously a wolf." Cadell looked down and sighed. "You have much to learn."

She forced a smile. "Looking forward to it?"

Carys carried a small backpack with a few mementos of her time in the Shadowlands. Her gold dragon brooch from Dafydd, the gold mirror from Eamer, a beautiful bound journal from Lachlan, and a unicorn embroidery from Elanor.

She looked at Cadell walking beside her in his leather armor. He carried one single thing—a letter from Dafydd they were going to have to show his contact in Scotland when they crossed over.

"Can you wear normal clothes?"

"If you mean Brightlands clothing, I can if I have to."

"Are you sure this guy is going to come through with papers and stuff? I mean, I'm sure you can stay at Duncan's house, but I don't want to be stuck there for weeks if I can avoid it."

"It will be fine, Nêrys. You worry too much."

"You should try using my name more. My friends will think it's weird."

"Tell them it's an affectionate nickname." Cadell glared at her. "Nêrys."

"Right." She rolled her eyes. "So affectionate."

"Your uncle has already sent emissaries to the Chahta nation, who are the closest geographic dragon nation to your home. He will coordinate your education with their permission."

"Great." She shook her head. "Can't wait."

"I am hoping to see a thunderbird." The corner of his mouth inched up. "Mared has seen them, and the rumors of their power are intimidating."

"You're actually excited about this, aren't you?"

He looked down at Carys, then returned his eyes forward. "Briton is cold."

"Okay, so not a fan of cold weather." She grimaced. "I have unfortunate news about Northern California, my friend."

"I am adaptable." He veered to the left and paused. "You should wait here."

"Why?"

Cadell kept his eyes on something in the distance. "Have you spoken to Duncan?"

"Since we rummaged around the ruins of his house yesterday? No."

"But he knows you are returning to the Brightlands?"

"You said he was coming with us."

"Yes." Cadell looked up. "He said he'd be ready at midday."

She looked up at the sky, which told her... absolutely nothing. There was no sun. "What is going on?"

"I feel very strong magic." Cadell pushed Carys behind him and walked through the hedges that led to Duncan's cottage.

"Hey, at least there's not an evil mage making a giant hill that we have to climb, right?"

Cadell kept a hand on her, forcing her to stay at his back as he walked through the alley of trees that guarded the house. The lane was narrower than it had been, and Carys noticed there were thorns on either side of the path, mixed in with the flowering bulbs and wildflowers.

"I think Auld Mags has been at work," Cadell said.

They walked under the green archway and into the small meadow in front of Duncan's home.

"Yeah." Carys tried not to gape. "I think so."

The cottage that had been ruins two days before was nearly rebuilt. The thatch on the roof needed to be trimmed and the stone was fresh and bare of moss, but the garden around the cottage was as verdant as ever, the wattle-and-daub walls were freshly painted, and a pile of old house timbers was neatly stacked along the side of the garden shed to use as firewood.

"Oh my God." Carys blinked. "How did he—"

"Not Duncan. Auld Mags." He looked down. "I told you bwbach have strong magic."

"But..." Her head swung from right to left, taking in the house, which looked brand-new. "How?"

"Angus helped." Duncan stepped out the front door and leaned against the log holding up the front porch. "Hello, Carys Morgan."

"Duncan." She suddenly felt... shy. "Hi." She was unsure of herself. She'd said goodbye to Lachlan but had no idea how she was going to bid farewell to his brother. "Cadell said you're coming with us."

"Angus and Auld Mags are keen to get me out of their way." He hoisted a backpack over his arm. He was already dressed in his Bright-lands clothing. "I've your clothes in here if you want to change."

Carys looked down at her comfy wool leggings, long tunic, and cloak. She suddenly realized how much she was going to miss the clothes here. They were warm and comfortable.

"But not the shoes," she muttered.

"What's that?"

Carys walked over and sat on a stone bench. "Maybe just my hiking boots."

"Done." He took the pack from his shoulder and dug around. "I woke up in the shed this morning, walked out the door, and saw all this."

"In one night?" Cadell leaned against the cottage wall. "She's very powerful."

"She finished the bones of the cottage yesterday after you left. Said she'd been healing well enough and didn't want to 'let that hairy-eyeballed witch win.'" He glanced at Carys. "That's a quote."

"You'll need to bring her a cow for all this." Carys took the hiking boots Duncan held out. "A bowl of milk isn't going to cut it."

"She's already put in an order for a 'nice wee coo with ruddy hair' for the garden."

Carys couldn't stop her smile. "Am I ever going to meet Auld Mags?"

Duncan raised an eyebrow. "Do you want to spend a night or two? I'm sure Cadell could make himself scarce."

Carys felt her cheeks warm. Duncan wasn't acting like a cross human anymore. None of his rough edges had worn off, so maybe she was just getting used to him.

"I think we better get back to Scotland," she said. "I don't even want to think about my email inbox."

"The fae gate it is." Duncan hoisted his pack over his shoulder again and held his hand out. "Back to home."

"Whatever that means anymore," Carys whispered.

The corner of Duncan's mouth inched up. "You'll figure that out, Carys Morgan. I have faith."

They started walking down the path leading to the fae forest, and Carys didn't look back.

CHAPTER THIRTY-NINE

Carys stood in the shadow of the trees, staring at the dried hawthorn branch and its bright red berries. She reached into her pocket and grabbed an acorn, then knelt down and dug into the ground at the edge of the meadow and planted the acorn, marking the spot with the hawthorn branch.

"You never know." Cadell looked down at the stick. "It could grow."

She stood and brushed off her hands. "Why not?"

"Why not indeed." Cadell stared through the trees. "I love them."

"The trees?"

His head craned back as he looked up and up and up. "The redwoods."

Carys smiled and looked at the giant who had learned to wear flannel instead of leather armor. "There's finally a tree proportional to your height, dude."

He growled. "For the love of all fire gods, stop calling me that."

Carys grinned. "You're in California now. You must learn to speak dude."

"I do not." He turned and walked toward the shed, which he had taken over.

In the weeks since her return from Scotland, Cadell had managed to settle in well enough, though he was still searching the forest behind the house every day for the fae gate, which seemed to be hiding.

Cadell was standing in the middle of the meadow, his face turned to the sky as the sun broke through the clouds. "Have you talked to either of your suitors today?"

Carys sighed. "Please stop calling them that."

"There are two men vying for your romantic affections. What is the correct terminology in the Brightlands for this situation?"

"A pain in the ass."

"I don't think that is correct."

Duncan texted her every few days, mostly sending her pictures of truly adorable cows, things he was working on at the smithworks, or occasionally a very bad selfie. Once, he'd called, but he was so awkward on the phone she told him that texting was fine, and she could tell he was relieved.

She invited him to California for a visit. To see Cadell, of course. He was looking at his calendar.

Lachlan was more complicated. Somehow he managed to send her letters nearly every day, delivered to her door with no return address, no envelope, and no sign of how they were being delivered, sealed with wax and often including flowers.

They were gorgeous love letters that included poetry that made her toes curl, and she had no way of responding.

"I'm going to have to figure that whole thing out eventually, aren't I?"

"Not if you don't want to." Cadell stared at the trees. "You don't owe them anything."

"It's not that." She didn't know her own feelings, and it irritated her. "I don't want to ignore them, it's just..."

"You have time."

"And I'll have to go back to the Shadowlands eventually, right?"

Cadell cast her a dark look. "You owe the Crow Mother a favor, Carys. She's not going to forget it."

"Right."

"But as I said, you have time." He scanned the forest. "I'll find the fae gate soon, and then we'll be able to travel much more easily."

"I *am* going back to work, you know."

"We can get around that." He eyed her up and down. "We should start running in the mornings."

She winced. "Oh God. The training montage is coming."

"Perhaps your friends will want to train with us." He stretched his arms and cracked his knuckles. "It will be... fun."

Cadell hadn't met her friends yet, but Carys had warned them she'd found a cousin from Wales who was coming to stay for a while. She'd have to wait and see if Laura and Kiersten bought the fiction when they came over for dinner that night.

"You remember that they're coming over for dinner tonight, right?"

"Yes." He closed his eyes and turned his face back to the sunshine.

Sometimes she found him sitting in the middle of the meadow, lying on the ground and baking like a cat, and the only words she could find to describe his expression were "confused wonder."

Cadell loved the sun. He was currently figuring out how to use all of her father's power tools so he could build a roof deck on the barn. Probably so he could lay out naked and sunbathe.

"Hey, Cadell?"

He was silent, and Carys realized he was probably speaking with his mind even though she couldn't hear him anymore.

"Cadell?"

He blinked and looked at her. "Yes, Nêrys?"

"You need to come in the house." She held out her hand. "Come on. You can't keep lurking around every night while I'm sleeping without ever going inside. Even my very-not-nosy neighbors are going to start asking questions."

"I'm guarding you."

"It feels like lurking. And I should show you around before my friends come over. If you don't know where the bathroom is, they're going to look at you weird."

He frowned. "I don't care."

"I do."

Cadell hadn't been in her house once, and Carys still wasn't sure if the man was sleeping in the forest at night or in the shed. He said he was sleeping in the shed, and he'd taken the cot and sleeping bag she gave him, but she had no idea.

Could dragons sleep inside? Any interior space felt too small for him, but until they found the fae gate, Cadell was forced to adapt.

She'd offered to fly him back to the UK twice now, but he declined. He followed her everywhere but refused to learn to drive. Officially he had a passport, a green card, and a Social Security card, but he seemed to have no intention of using them.

If he didn't start working or hunting though, she was going to have to take out a loan to feed the man. He put away more barely charred meat than anyone she'd ever seen.

Cadell eyed the deck and the back door with trepidation. "How tall are your ceilings?"

"Are you claustrophobic?"

"I don't know what that is."

She took his hand and dragged him toward the steps leading up to the deck. "My ceilings are normal-sized. You're not going to hit your head, but you'll probably have to duck through the door. They're taller inside."

He halted in his tracks. "Oh."

She spun around. "Oh my God, did you think the height of the door was the height of the house? No wonder you haven't wanted to come inside."

"I don't know anything about Brightkin dwellings." He looked a little embarrassed.

"It's fine." She squeezed his hand. "I know everything is new. You can stay on the deck when they get here if you want."

It was going to start raining though. Kiersten and Laura might have questions.

"I will adapt." He set his face into a determined expression. "Let us go inside."

Carys suddenly realized something else. Kiersten was going to hit on him. He was exactly her type, and he was almost a foot taller than her. Her tall Scandinavian friend would be in raptures.

"Why are you smiling?" Cadell asked.

This was going to be hilarious. "Nothing. I'm just really looking forward to you meeting my friends."

"Very well." Cadell eyed her with suspicion, looked at the door, then took a deep breath. "I will go inside the human dwelling now."

Oh yeah. Laura and Kiersten were going to have a *lot* of questions.

"Great." Carys opened the door. "Okay?" She crossed the threshold. "Come on inside. It doesn't bite."

Cadell ducked his head and walked inside, looking around the kitchen with suspicion. "It is not as small as I imagined."

"It's cozy." She stepped to the side and leaned against the counter. "Go ahead. Look around. You can go anywhere you like."

"I don't want to violate your privacy, Nêrys." His words belied his curious staring. Cadell ran his hands along the fridge and pressed them to the side as the machine hummed. He walked to the sink and moved the lever around until the water came on, and then he moved it again until it shut off. "An indoor well."

"Wait until you see the toilet."

Cadell muttered, "So much metal."

"And this house is made of wood."

He frowned. "What else are houses made of?"

"Brick. Stucco."

"Brick I know. I don't know what stucco is."

"You'll find out."

She watched him wander through the house until he came to the wall of paintings her mother had finished. She'd just finished hanging them in a beautiful arrangement on the largest wall in the living room.

It was a mix of large landscapes, smaller portraits, and fantastical botanical studies.

Cadell froze when he spotted the wall of paintings. "Where did you get these?"

She walked over with a smile. "Those are my mother's work. They look like the Shadowlands, right? Duncan thinks maybe she dreamed—"

"This is Cair Goch." He pointed at a painting of a stone fortress high on a snowy mountain. "This is Gareth's Ring." He pointed to another painting of a stone circle.

"That's cool." She smiled. "Gareth was my dad's name."

Cadell turned to her with wide eyes. "These are places in Cymru. Specific places." He looked back at the wall. "These are cliffs in Kernow."

She frowned. "Kernow is Cornwall, right? Maybe the cliffs are the same in both—"

"How did she see these places?"

Cadell stared at the pictures of the castles and the dragons. The bright fae and the dark kelpies. They were all things that Carys had seen with her own eyes now, so seeing them through her mother's paintbrush was even more special.

Cadell seemed a little freaked out. "These things do not exist in your world."

Carys felt a twist in her gut. "I told you, Duncan said that sometimes Brightkin dream of the Shadowlands through the eyes of their twin."

He shook his head slowly. "Like this? Did you ever dream like *this*?"

"Well... no." Carys felt a chill creeping over her skin. "I don't know what you mean."

He stared at Carys. "We need to speak about your mother. You were born in the Brightlands, Carys."

"I know. I have a birth certificate from a hospital in Caernarfon and—"

"It's very possible" —he looked at the paintings, then back at Carys — "it's *probable* that your mother was not."

"No. She couldn't..." Could she?

Cadell raised one eyebrow. "It would explain some things."

"Like what?" Carys let out a harsh breath. "How would she even—"

There was a sharp rap at the door, and Kiersten's bright voice sang through the house a moment later. "Hello-o!"

"They're here," Carys hissed. "We'll talk about this later."

"Yes, we definitely will."

Kiersten walked into the living room, a giant smile on her face. "Oh my gosh, you have a cousin!" Her eyes went wide and her mouth fell open. "You have a *cousin*." She blinked. "Hi. I'm Kiersten."

Cadell stared. "Hello."

Laura was right behind Kiersten. "Hey! I brought Jim again so your cousin isn't the lone male in the estrogen soup—I hope you don't mind. He brought some fish he caught this morning so..." Laura froze when she saw Cadell, and her eyes went wide.

Cadell squared his shoulders and faced both Laura and Kiersten, straightening his posture in a way that made the giant man look even taller than he had before.

"Hello," he said awkwardly. "Dudes."

Kiersten blinked, then grinned. "I love the accent."

Laura didn't seem to be able to speak.

"Laura, Kiersten, this is my cousin Cadell. He's a cousin on my father's—"

"Mother's."

"My mother's side," she said. "Right. He's a cousin on my mother's side, and he decided to come to California for a visit."

Both her friends were still silent and gaping.

"Please don't be rude," Carys said through a tense smile. "He's still getting used to it here."

Laura looked at Carys, then back at Cadell. "Carys Morgan, why did you bring a dragon to Baywood?"

Kiersten frowned. "A what?"

Carys blinked. "What did you say?"

Cadell repeated, "What did you say?"

Laura opened her mouth, shut it. Looked at Carys, who was giving her "what the hell" eyebrows, then back at Cadell. "Right," she finally said. She looked back at Carys. "Okay, this is awkward."

"Yeah." Carys nodded, then turned to Kiersten, who was smiling uncomfortably.

"What's going on?" Kiersten asked.

Carys looked at Laura, then at Cadell, and back to Kiersten. She walked over to her friend. "So... do *you* believe in fairy tales?"

Book Two of the Shadowlands
The Shadow Path
is coming April 2025!

Please visit ElizabethHunter.com for more information and sign up for my newsletter to get the latest updates about upcoming projects.

THE SHADOW PATH

SHADOWLANDS BOOK II

COMING
APRIL 2025

DRU & NAIDA'S SONG

Sing me a place where sea becomes sky
Where stone swallows mountain
Where this world goes to die.

Write me a poem of heather and firth
Where forest touches night
And night becomes earth.

The shadows, they call you
When life becomes still.
They call you to taste them
They tempt you to thrill.

The darkness it holds you
Don't try to turn back.
Its wild weathered places
Are all that you lack.

The Shadowlands offer the life that you miss
And the ruddy wind whispers
A dark prince's kiss.

ACKNOWLEDGMENTS

I would first like to thank my family—the Jones, the Buells, and the Hazels—who instilled a love of fantasy in me from a very young age. Like Carys, I was raised reading MacDonald and Lewis, Tolkien, L'Engle, and Baum. Some of my favorite memories of childhood were paging through "Flower Fairies" books at my grandparents' house and reading the illustrated version of *The Hobbit* around the table after dinner. When I was ten, my Grandfather Bill showed me how to translate all the runes from the maps in *The Lord of the Rings*, and like Seren, I have been obsessed with maps ever since.

All that to say that as much as I have made a career of vampires, contemporary fantasy, and fallen angels, this book—my own portal into a greater fantasy world—has been in my heart and lurking around my brain for a very long time.

I'd also like to acknowledge three important creative companions during the writing of this book: Martin Shaw's book *Courting the Wild Twin*, Hozier's *Unreal Unearth* album, and Guillermo Del Toro's extraordinary film, *Pan's Labyrinth*.

I'd also like to thank my incredible agent, Kimberly Brower, along with all the staff at Brower Literary, for their support and encouragement. And many thanks to the public relations professionals at Valentine PR for all their work and advocacy.

Much love to my sister and assistant Gen for all of her tireless work making the Elizabeth Hunter Shop happen.

As always, the readers, the bloggers, and the reviewers are the ones who fill my cup and thrill my heart. Thank you for your endless encouragement and love for my work. I promise I'm working on the next book right now.

Finally, I would like to thank all of the creative professionals who contributed to the final publication of this book. My editors, Amy Cissell, Anne Victory, and my proofreader Linda. The incredible cover artists at Damonza.com, and the interior illustrations by ArtCreations-Design. Thanks also to Jen at Painted Wings Publishing who did the beautiful printed edge for the hardcover edition of FIRST LIGHT.

Finally, to my very own forever romance hero Dawit. I can write four hundred pages of fiction, but I don't have the words to tell you how much you mean to me. *Betam wedehelew, yene fiker.*

ABOUT THE AUTHOR

ELIZABETH HUNTER is an eleven-time *USA Today* and international best-selling author of romance, contemporary fantasy, and paranormal mystery. Based in Central California and Addis Ababa, she travels extensively to write fantasy fiction exploring world mythologies, history, and the universal bonds of love, friendship, and family. She has published over fifty works of fiction and sold over two million books worldwide. She is the author of the Elemental Mysteries series, the Irin Chronicles, and other works of fiction.

ELIZABETHHUNTER.COM

ALSO BY ELIZABETH HUNTER

<u>The Shadowlands</u>

First Light

The Shadow Path (April 2024)

<u>The Firebird & the Wolf</u>

Blood Mosaic (December 2024)

<u>The Irin Chronicles</u>

The Scribe

The Singer

The Secret

The Staff and the Blade

The Silent

The Storm

The Seeker

<u>The Elemental Mysteries</u>

A Hidden Fire

This Same Earth

The Force of Wind

A Fall of Water

The Stars Afire

Fangs, Frost, and Folios

<u>The Elemental World</u>

Building From Ashes

Waterlocked

Blood and Sand

The Bronze Blade

The Scarlet Deep

A Very Proper Monster

A Stone-Kissed Sea

Valley of the Shadow

THE ELEMENTAL LEGACY

Shadows and Gold

Imitation and Alchemy

Omens and Artifacts

Midnight Labyrinth

Blood Apprentice

The Devil and the Dancer

Night's Reckoning

Dawn Caravan

The Bone Scroll

Pearl Sky

Tin God

THE ELEMENTAL COVENANT

Saint's Passage

Martyr's Promise

Paladin's Kiss

Bishop's Flight

Tin God

THE SEBA SEGEL SERIES

The Thirteenth Month

Child of Ashes (Summer 2025)

www.ingramcontent.com/pod-product-compliance
Lightning Source LLC
Chambersburg PA
CBHW070402310726
48977CB00003B/531